Immaculate Resurrections

Book II
TEARS OF CONSTANTINE

RANDALL LOWE

outskirts
press
Denver, Colorado

Immaculate Resurrections
Book II Tears of Constantine
All Rights Reserved.
Copyright © 2012 Randall Lowe
v2.0

Outskirts Press, Inc.
http://www.outskirtspress.com

ISBN: 978-1-4327-8318-1

Outskirts Press and the "OP" logo are trademarks belonging to Outskirts Press, Inc.

PRINTED IN THE UNITED STATES OF AMERICA

Chapter 1

On the campus of Portland College, students started arriving early in the morning for the start of the second semester. By early afternoon, hundreds were busily unpacking their bags and catching up with friends they hadn't seen in nearly a month.

Caitlin and Allison were in their dorm room with Harper talking about the brand-new SUV Caitlin's parents bought her during the break. Caitlin was hoping for a cute little hybrid, but her parents didn't go for it—even after she tried to convince them that SUV drivers were nothing but heartless Republicans intent on destroying the ozone layer while dining on the flesh of endangered species. In the end, she decided an SUV was better than no car at all, and that she might be able to talk them into trading it in for something more environmentally friendly when she went home for the summer.

Lucas joined them after unpacking his suitcase. "Where's Felix?" Lucas asked as soon as he stepped into the room.

"It's nice to see you, too," Caitlin replied, frowning. "I guess you missed us a lot, huh?"

Lucas smiled and scooped Caitlin off the floor like a chivalrous knight rescuing a delicate damsel in distress. "Ah. I'm sorry, little Caitlin," Lucas said without even a hint of sincerity. "You know I missed you terribly these past four weeks. And I missed you guys, too," he said, looking up at Allison and Harper. "So don't feel left out. There's enough of the kid to go around."

"Put me down," Caitlin shouted, kicking her feet like a swimmer. "You're such a whack job. Why'd we start hanging out with you?"

"Because I'm awesome," Lucas replied, gently setting Caitlin back on her feet.

"So you don't know where Felix is?" Harper asked.

"Uh-huh," Lucas answered. "He's not in our room. I thought he'd be down here with you guys."

"We thought he was with you," Harper said. "I texted him when I got here, but he didn't reply."

"Figures," Lucas said, shrugging his muscular shoulders. "He won't return my texts. I texted him like a thousand times during break. I feel like maybe he dumped me or something." Lucas laughed, but nobody joined in.

"Is his stuff in your room?" Allison asked, looking concerned. "I never heard from him either."

"You didn't?" Lucas exclaimed. "The room's the same upstairs. It's like he never left. Even his toothbrush is there. Not even dudes leave their toothbrush behind, you know."

"So he stayed here the whole time?" Caitlin asked.

"Wait a sec!" Lucas shouted. "I thought he was going to your house for Christmas," he said, looking at Allison.

"He was," Allison replied. "He never showed up."

"He was supposed to have Christmas with your family?" Harper asked, arching an eyebrow.

"That was the plan," Allison answered, looking anxious. "I texted and called him like a million times. He never got back to me."

"Okay, that's kinda weird," Lucas said seriously. "Nobody goes any-where without their cell. Why'd he bail on Christmas?"

"I don't know," Allison said. "That's not like Felix at all. He'd defi-nitely let me know if he couldn't make it."

"He's probably just...I don't know," Lucas said weakly. "I hope he's all right. I don't think he was getting much sleep before we left for break."

"He wasn't?" Allison asked, looking pointedly at Lucas. "What do you mean? Was something going on?"

Lucas looked conflicted. "Oh, no, no. He was just…um…tossing and turning a lot during the night. Not a big deal. But hey!" he continued. "How psyched are you guys that you have your old room back?"

"Yeah," Caitlin said, smiling, "it was such a pain living so far away from you guys. You know, I'm sure Felix is around here somewhere. Maybe he's at the gym? It's almost time for dinner, anyway. He'll probably show up before then, right? He'd never miss a meal."

Chapter 2

Felix didn't return for dinner that night at the Downey cafeteria. Two days later, he was still absent. Allison and Harper stopped by the campus bookstore to see if Felix had picked up his textbooks for the new semester. In the back of the bookstore there were just three small stacks of books on the "freshman table." An index card was placed on top of each stack indicating the student's name. Attached to the card was the corresponding course schedule. On one of the cards, written in black Sharpie, was "Felix August." Felix's typewritten class schedule was stapled to the card.

On their way back to Downey, Allison's cell beeped. She snatched it from her pocket. The message said: *My office tonight 8PM—Bill.*

Harper watched Allison out of the corner of her eye. "Is that Felix?" she asked anxiously.

"No. It's just my mom; nothing important."

At dinner that night, Lucas and the girls had a heated discussion about whether it was time to contact the police and report that Felix was missing. Classes were already under way, and he hadn't been heard from in a month. Lucas, Caitlin, and Harper finally decided they'd call the police right after dinner.

"Ummm...I think...I think we should maybe wait one more day before we do that," Allison suggested.

"Why?" Harper asked.

"Because...because Bill asked me to come to his office tonight. I'm sure it has something to do with Felix."

"Bill?" Lucas asked skeptically. "Groundskeeper Bill, you mean? What would a groundskeeper have to do with this?"

Allison paused, struggling to find the right words. "I don't think he has anything to do with it. I just think...I think he might know something about where Felix is."

"Why would he know when we don't?" Caitlin asked sharply.

"I'm not exactly sure," Allison replied. "I just think we should wait before we call the police. Just until I meet with Bill. Okay?"

"That's not okay!" Harper shouted angrily. "He's been missing for at least two days. For all we know, he could have gone missing a month ago. He could be lying dead in a ditch somewhere. And the groundskeeper might know where he is? I think I'm missing something here."

Allison looked Harper straight in the eye. "Dead in a ditch? Seriously? I think we're all missing something! That's why I need to speak to Bill before you go off and call the police. I'm sure Felix wouldn't want the police notified if he's just holed up somewhere trying to work things out in his head." Her eyes suddenly grew wide. "If he's just holed up somewhere trying to work things out," she repeated in a whispery voice, as if to herself. "Look, I think I might know where he is, but I need to talk to Bill first. Just to find out what's going on. But for now, please don't call the police, okay?"

"So you know where he is?" Lucas asked anxiously.

"I've got a pretty good idea," Allison replied. "Caitlin, do you mind if I borrow your car? I know it's new, but I promise I'll take care of it."

"Sure," Caitlin said, shrugging. "I hate SUVs, but my parents wouldn't be happy if you totaled it. So try to be gentle with it and..."

"I'll be careful," Allison said, smiling.

"I wanna go too!" Harper shouted. "I think I should go!"

"Yeah, me too!" Lucas said.

"And it's my car, after all," Caitlin added. "I'm going."

Allison looked at them one by one. "Listen, I know you just want to help. But I don't even know for sure where he is. But if he's where I think he is, and he's been there for a month, he's probably in pretty bad shape. I don't know if...I mean...look, I've known Felix for a while. He's more complicated than you could ever…um…he's going through some shit right now. He may not want to talk about it. And if I'm going to convince him to come back to school, I think we'll have to have a long talk. And I'm not sure he'll do that if everyone's around. Please…please trust me on this."

They continued to protest, but by the time dinner was finished they all conceded that Allison's plan made the most sense. Finally, Caitlin gave Allison the keys to her new SUV, and Allison left the dorm for Bill's office.

Chapter 3

"Come in," Bill called out. "It's unlocked."

Allison opened the door and stepped into the office.

"Would you mind locking the door behind you?"

Allison did as she was asked and then took a chair across from the desk where Bill was sitting.

Bill looked extraordinarily tired. Stubble covered his face, and dark smudges were visible under unusually puffy eyes. A faded New England Patriots hat concealed unwashed hair. He wore a nondescript gray sweatshirt that had seen better days. He looked like he hadn't slept in a long time.

He closed his laptop. "Thanks for coming, Allison. I apologize for the short notice, but I understand that Felix hasn't returned yet. I was hopeful that he'd be back for the start of classes, but, well…"

"Did something happen?" she asked. "Did something happen to Felix?"

Bill looked around his office and sighed. "Yes. I'm afraid so. Have you heard from him at all? Has he called you?"

"No," she said, shaking her head rapidly. "Nobody's heard from him since the last day of finals. We've texted him a thousand times. What is it? What happened? Is he okay?" Her voice was rising with anxiety.

"It's difficult to explain. But if anyone can understand, it would be you. Were you aware that Felix was having nightmares?"

"No. But…but Lucas, his roommate, said something the other day about Felix sleeping badly. But he didn't say anything about nightmares."

Bill nodded and scratched his chin. "Felix was having a recurring nightmare that was becoming very disruptive. I agreed to help him."

"But how could you do that? You're..."

"What I am isn't important right now. I performed something similar to hypnosis on Felix, hoping that he'd be able to see the details of his nightmare. But when he reached a state of total relaxation, he and I were pulled into the dream."

Allison looked stunned. "*Pulled?*"

Bill sighed and rubbed his stubble. "Yes. The nightmare was actually a repressed memory."

"Wait," Allison said, her forehead creased in thought. "So the dream was actually a memory. But what did it do? It pulled you into..."

"Felix told you about the journal, right? And I assume he told you that it has special properties. Namely, the person who reads it feels what his aunt was feeling as she was writing. Did he talk to you about that?"

"Yeah, he told me about it I guess, but..."

"Now, in Felix's case, when he retrieved the memory from his subconscious, he and I were both pulled into the memory itself—just as a person who reads the journal gets pulled into the words. Do you understand?"

"Not really. I mean, I think so. I don't know. So what was the memory about?"

Bill paused. He scratched at his nose and rubbed his eyes. "You're obviously aware of what Felix did to your room. You were there and you witnessed it."

"Yes." She shifted in her chair and sat up straight as if bracing for an attack.

"I'm afraid that wasn't the first time."

Allison stared at Bill. And then her jaw dropped as the meaning of Bill's words worked its way into her consciousness.

"Oh my God! You don't mean the fire was...the fire at his home was..."

"I'm afraid so. While Felix slept, his body turned into an object of pure energy—an object of total destruction. I don't know how else to describe it for you. But you've seen it yourself."

Allison was stunned. She sat speechless for a moment. "You know, I ran to his house the morning of the fire. I saw it. There were pieces everywhere, all up and down the block. It didn't really even look like a fire. I mean, it did and it didn't. I thought there was something strange about it."

Bill just nodded.

"Oh my God! And his parents? What exactly happened to Felix's parents?"

"They were banging on the door to his bedroom. They thought it was just a fire. They were trying to get in, trying to wake him up. They couldn't get the door open. His bedroom, and then the entire house, exploded and burst into flames. His parents didn't stand a chance."

"And because...and because you and Felix were actually inside the memory, he saw all of this happen?"

Bill nodded. "Yes. He saw himself destroy his house. He saw himself kill his parents."

"Oh my God! Oh my God! Poor Felix! How much more can he take?" Allison started to cry. "I'm sorry. Just give me a minute. You didn't know them. They were such good people. And Felix is such a good guy. Hasn't he been through enough?" She sobbed into her hands.

Bill watched and said nothing.

"Do you know where he is?" she finally asked, wiping at her tears with the sleeve of her shirt.

"No. I have some contacts who are in the business of finding people, bounty hunters you could call them, and they've been searching every town from Vancouver to Tijuana. They haven't come up with anything. I was hoping you might be able to tell me where he might be. You've known Felix longer than anyone. Can you think of any place he might go? It would likely be somewhere he's been before—a place where he feels comfortable."

"I have an idea," she said, wiping at her eyes again. "When did this happen? The hypnosis?"

"The day after final exams."

"It's been an entire month?"

"Allison, I don't want to alarm you, but do you think there's any possibility that Felix may have…may have done something to harm himself…may have taken his own life?"

"What? There's no way! I don't think…I…um." She exhaled slowly and took a deep breath. "Before all this shit happened, I would have said no way. But now? After you've told him that he's the Second Coming. Then he actually watched himself killing his parents. I just don't know. I mean…"

"Okay, Allison. I'm sorry. For what it's worth, I don't believe he'd do something like that."

"I'd better be going." Allison jumped out of the chair and grabbed her coat.

"Where?"

"The coast."

"The coast? Would you like me to go with you?" Bill stood up behind his desk.

"No. I should go alone."

"Are you sure?"

"Yes," Allison said firmly.

"Okay. Be careful. Oh. Allison, there's just one more thing. I think there's something you ought to know before you leave. I don't believe you're aware of why Felix's birth mother died."

Chapter 4

In the best of conditions, the drive from the PC campus to the Oregon coast was about an hour. But at night, and in a steady downpour, it took Allison twice as long. When she reached the small coastal town of Lincoln Bay, it was nearing eleven o'clock. She then turned north and drove along the Pacific Coast Highway through a downpour. Forty-five minutes later she came to the town of Cove Rock, Oregon.

Cove Rock was located just inside the Oregon side of the border between Oregon and Washington. Originally a fishing village, over the years it gradually became less reliant on the unpredictable fishing industry and more reliant on its ability to attract tourists willing to spend money at the shops, restaurants, and hotels. Cove Rock's main attraction was its location along a particularly rugged section of Pacific Ocean coastline. And although there were fewer than 5,000 full-time residents, the town's population nearly doubled during the tourist season.

The cove, around which the town was built, provided a natural barrier against the rough seas that would have otherwise pounded the shore, protecting the salmon fleets for generations of fishermen who lived there for more than two centuries. On the south side of the cove, far away from the condos and beach houses of the well-to-do weekend and summer people, were three docks extending several hundred yards into the bay. Commercial fishing vessels and smaller charter boats were moored there year-round.

In the center of the cove, exactly one hundred feet from the shoreline during low tide, was the object featured on nearly every postcard sold in every store in town: a 250-foot-tall monolithic rock jutting out of the ocean like a giant finger. The huge basalt formation was called Cove Rock by the early settlers who fished there in the second half of the eighteenth century. Eventually the surrounding area itself assumed its name.

Allison slowed her speed to twenty miles per hour as she reached the town limits. All the shops and restaurants were closed. The tourist season had ended months ago, and most of the shops, if they were open at all, closed by six o'clock. The rain had been coming down in torrents since she passed through Lincoln Bay, and she drove through Cove Rock's abandoned streets with the wipers barely able to keep up, even on their fastest setting. The wind rocked Caitlin's SUV as Allison crept through town.

With only four traffic signals in all of Cove Rock, it didn't take Allison long to reach the end of town. She drove for another mile past the last traffic light, until finally coming to a weathered stop sign that said "STO." She turned left and proceeded slowly down a gravel road. The road was never used by tourists.

There were no streetlights, and the surface was heavily pocked by rain-filled potholes. As the SUV bounced along the uneven road, Allison strained to see her surroundings. There wasn't much to see other than the dark shapes of small houses set back from the gravel road behind low fences and hedges. No porch lights were on.

She came to a cul-de-sac where three small houses were spaced evenly along its perimeter. Parked in the driveway of the center house was a dark-colored, mid-sized American-made car bearing a rental car company's sticker on the bumper. She parked the SUV next to the car and got out, stepping into a deep puddle of cold water.

"Shit!" she said aloud. She didn't think to bring an umbrella in her rush to leave campus. The rain was coming down even harder than before. The wind was gusting. There was a loud clanking noise in the distance, the sound of a chain banging against something metallic in the wind.

The darkness was nearly impenetrable. The rain ran down Allison's forehead and into her eyes. She wiped it from her face and fought against the wind, struggling to walk up the short driveway. A narrow, vertical strip of lamplight, no more than a few inches wide, shone through a window alongside the front door. The light appeared to be escaping through a small gap between two curtain panels. Allison stepped off the cracked concrete walkway leading to the front door and sloshed over to the window through the muddy yard. She squinted her eyes, trying to see into the house. Her face was just a few inches from the rain-streaked glass. There was furniture; a chair, a small table, and...

"What do you want?" a gruff voice shouted from close behind her.

Allison screamed and wheeled around. She slipped on the rain-soaked grass and fell onto her back. The ground was muddy and slippery, and she scrambled to get back to her feet. She couldn't get any traction and fell again.

She looked up. A figure approached her. It was tall and wore a hood, obscuring its face. She lay on the ground, flailing and slipping as she tried in vain to get back to her feet. The figure drew closer. Allison screamed again, but the sound was drowned out by the wind and rain. It was nearly on top of her. It bent its hooded head down until it was nearly touching her face.

"Allison?" it said.

"Whu...what...who?"

"Allison?"

"Yes. Who...Felix? Is that you?"

"Allison, what are you doing here?"

"Oh my God! Felix! I swear to God you nearly scared me to death!"

"Come on," Felix said listlessly, helping her to her feet. "Let's go inside. You shouldn't be out here."

He led her around to the side of the house. He opened the door and held it for her. She walked into a dark room. Felix followed behind, closed the door against the elements, and turned on the light. Allison looked around the small room. A washing machine and dryer were up against one wall, and a coatrack was affixed on the opposite wall. She looked at Felix. He was wearing a yellow hooded rain slicker. He turned toward her and pulled the hood back.

Allison gasped. It was like looking at a stranger. Felix's face was covered in uneven patches of light-brown stubble. His hair was darker than she'd ever seen it before—oily and matted against his scalp. His pale blue eyes were bloodshot, and there were dark circles under them.

Allison stood there gawking, dripping water onto the floor. She was covered in mud. "Felix! What happened to you? You look terrible!"

He shrugged, took off his rain slicker, and hung it on a wall hook.

"Everyone's been worried about you. Classes started two days ago, and nobody knew where you were. Everyone's been texting you. You didn't even respond."

Felix shrugged again and handed her a dirty towel from a heap of laundry on top of the dryer.

"Here. You're wet."

Allison took the towel from him and dried her hair. "Is that all you can say?" she stammered with something approaching anger. "We've been worried sick about you! Nobody had any idea where you were. Something could've happened to you, and nobody would've known!"

Felix's expression remained placid. "How'd you find me?"

Allison took off her muddy shoes and placed them in front of the door. She pulled off her socks, putting them on the washing machine. "I figured, where else could you go? You weren't going back to Coos Bay Bridge. And I knew about your grandma's place up here. I've been here a few times before, you know. Remember?"

"Oh," Felix replied, without any emotion.

"Oh? Is that all you have to say? I've been driving all night in the goddamn rain to get here! I thought I was about to get killed by an axe murderer in the front yard. Felix, I've been worried about you! We all have."

"You should go back to school, Allison." Felix's eyes didn't meet hers. He looked over her head at the wall. "You don't want to be here. You shouldn't be around me."

"And what are you gonna do? You're just gonna drop out of school? You're all done after one semester? Is that it? You're just gonna throw it all away?"

"*School?*" Felix said mockingly. "You think school has anything to do with this?" And for the first time since she arrived, there was emotion in Felix's voice. "You don't know... you don't know what I've done."

"I do know. I spoke to Bill. I know what happened. I'm so sorry that..."

"So you know what I did!" Felix shouted, his eyes bulging. "You know that I... that I killed them! I'm a fucking murderer, Allison! I killed my own parents! I shouldn't even be here. I should be in prison. I should turn myself in..."

"You were asleep, Felix! It wasn't your fault!"

"Tell that to my parents!" His face was crimson and he looked desperate. He stormed out of the room.

Allison followed behind into the kitchen, dripping muddy rainwater onto the floor.

The sink was piled high with food-smattered plates, and cereal bowls and dirty glasses covered the counters. Half-eaten cans of baked beans and empty soup containers were strewn about. Pizza boxes were stacked haphazardly on the small card table in the corner. The floor was covered by a mound of overflowing plastic trash bags. Cases of empty beer bottles were littered along the counters and on top of the stove. The room smelled like rotten food and mold.

"Felix, I'm sure your parents were..."

"I blew my parents into a million fucking pieces!" Felix yelled. "I didn't just kill them. I disintegrated them. And all they were trying to do was wake me up! That's it."

"It wasn't your fault. You can't blame yourself for something that happened in your sleep."

"Why not? It could've been you too! That night in your room, if you didn't wake me up, what do you think would've happened? Are you getting this? I would've killed you!"

"But it's not your fault, Felix! It's just something that happens to you—something you can't control yet. Isn't that why Bill's trying to help you?"

"Bill? How can he help me? I'm a time bomb! Nobody's safe around me. I'm not...I'm not normal. I think I'm just like him, like Landry. Bill said I can't be. But what the hell does he know? I killed my parents! There's something wrong with me! I think maybe I'm the Antichrist!"

"That's ridiculous! You are not the Antichrist, Felix! And you are normal! I don't give a shit if you glow red and destroy things in your sleep. I've known you a long time, and I swear to you, you are the most normal person I know!"

Felix smiled an odd, humorless smile. "Normal? Do you think this is normal?" He raised his right hand toward the counter on the opposite side of the kitchen. He exhaled. One of the empty beer bottles shot off the counter and flew across the kitchen and into Felix's outstretched hand. He turned it over and examined the label. He smiled that strange, mirthless smile again and then extended his arm.

He let go of the bottle. It fell, but just before it struck the floor, it stopped. It remained suspended a foot above the floor. Allison stared at the hovering bottle in disbelief. Felix made a slight flicking motion with his index and middle fingers, and the bottle hurtled through the air toward the other side of the kitchen. It smashed against a cabinet and broke into shards.

"Do you call that *normal?*" Felix asked, stomping out of the room.

Allison followed Felix into the living room in the back of the house. Dark brown shag carpet covered the floors, and a brown plaid sofa was pushed up against one wall. Two matching chairs sat in the middle of the room across from an old TV placed on a badly chipped stand next to a tarnished brass floor lamp that was horribly bent near its base. On the wood-paneled walls were a series of four inexpensive seascape prints, one on each wall. The room smelled damp. Felix stood with his back to Allison and looked out the picture window at the blackness. Allison knew from prior visits that the window faced the Pacific. The only time the ocean was visible was during the winter when the trees were bare. But in the darkness of night, all that could be seen was Felix's reflection staring out the window and Allison approaching from behind.

"Felix," Allison said softly, "being normal isn't about what you just did in the kitchen. Normal is how you view the world and how you treat people. You're a good person. For as long as I've known you, you've never wanted to hurt anyone. You've always done the right thing. And I'll never believe that you could ever be responsible for hurting someone, let alone killing them. And I know it sounds cheesy, but you have a good soul. It doesn't matter if you're the reincarnation of some Druid or if you have special powers."

Felix continued staring out the window. Allison walked up next to him. And there they stood in the damp-smelling room filled with old worn-out furniture, staring at their reflections in the glass.

"You know, Felix," Allison said, looking at his reflection, "I don't really understand what's happening. The world is not what I thought it was. It's a scary place. But in a way, it's kind of cool, you know? It's like there's this whole other universe out there that nobody knows about. And you are in the center of this universe. I don't know how you're able to make a bottle fly across the room. I don't know why you turn into an energy bomb in your sleep. And you can tell me about Constantine, Myrddin, the journal, curses, and Templar Amulets all you want, but I'll never understand it. But what I do know is that none of this is your fault. You didn't ask for any of this to happen to you. It just did. And that's it. And you're gonna have to deal with it."

"That's easy for you to say," Felix said.

"Is it? Do you think this is easy for me? Knowing the truth about the world isn't easy. There's nothing easy about it. You know, Felix, Bill told me about your mother. Your birth mother I mean. Did he tell you about her?"

"I don't know. Maybe a little."

"Do you know how she died?"

"She died in a mental institution," Felix said flatly. "She was sick when Bill met her. And she just died."

"That's true, but did he tell you nothing was wrong with her? That she died of guilt. That she died because she could never forgive herself for killing her best friend—even though it wasn't her fault."

"Yeah, well…"

"Well nothing, Felix! Your mother died because she couldn't forgive herself. Is that what you want to do? Do you want to honor your parents' memory by slowly committing suicide? Because if you want to kill yourself, I'd have a lot more respect for you if you just walked down to the ocean and drowned yourself instead of drowning yourself in self-pity!"

"But I…but I killed them, Allison. I *killed* my parents!"

"And you're going to have to live with that for the rest of your life. I know it won't be easy for you. But what good does it do anyone if you isolate yourself from the world and stew in your own guilt? You didn't mean to kill your parents, Felix. It wasn't your fault. You're gonna have to forgive yourself. Because I swear to you, I will not leave you the hell alone until you do! And I can be pretty goddamn annoying and persistent when I want to be!"

Felix could see Allison's reflection smiling at his own. He smiled back. She took his hand in hers and held it. They stared at their reflections for several minutes before either spoke again.

"And besides, I need you," Allison said, finally breaking the silence.

"You need me? For what?"

"I found out something while I was home during the break. I remembered that my sister said something a long time ago about how my parents renovated a bunch of rooms in the house right before I was adopted. Well, I talked to my mom and I got her to tell me that they did get a lot of money for adopting me. She said the adoption agency paid it over to them, but that it was some kind of a donation made by someone anonymous. She said that wasn't the reason they adopted me, but they weren't going to refuse the money."

"Okay. So what?"

Allison let go of his hand. "Remember what you told me about the journal? And what Bill told us? Vessels are created as teenagers, right? But because older kids are harder to place, A.E.I. funnels money to families willing to adopt them. That's what you told me, right? Don't you see? That's exactly what happened to me and my family! That's the story of *my* life."

"You're not a Vessel! There's no possible way!"

"How do you know that? Even you have to admit there's a chance. Maybe even a pretty good chance. And that's why I need you. I can't spend my life wondering if I have a soul or not. Or whether another person's soul and consciousness will replace mine at any given moment. And I can't live my life thinking that I might die any minute because I'm not human and the Templar Amulet can't keep me alive for very long without a soul—or however it works." Allison wiped a tear from her face with the sleeve of her muddy shirt.

"Allison, I still don't think…"

"Felix, I just need you to destroy the goddamn Amulet! I need you to end this. Because when you do, then I'll know. One way or the other, I'll know. And that's all I want. I just want certainty."

"But I don't even know if I can destroy it."

"Of course you can! Didn't you tell me that the back of it says the Holder can either use its power or destroy it?"

"But I'm not the Holder! The Holder is Landry. I'm just…I don't even know what I am."

"Well, maybe you're just Felix. But I think that's enough. I believe in you."

He sighed heavily, shaking his head. "I just don't know. But you're right about one thing."

"What's that?"

"I didn't ask for any of this. I just want to be normal. I don't want to be the Second Coming. I don't want this gift. I don't want to have anything to do with this. I'm just hurting everyone around me. I don't want anyone else to get hurt. I can't take it!"

"I know, Felix. But you are who you are, and it doesn't do any good to wish you were somebody else. I know it sucks not to have a choice. But if it's any consolation, you're not alone. I'll be by your side just like I am now, staring at the reflection of a girl who looks like she just lost a mud-wrestling competition."

Felix laughed. "I'm sorry. I forgot you were slipping around in the mud out there. There's some old clothes in the back bedroom that you can change into. They used to be my mom's or my grandma's. I'm not sure whose. You can throw the ones you have on in the washer if you want."

"Okay. I'm gonna clean up real quick and change. It's way too late to head back to Portland tonight. I guess we'll have to stay here. But I'm gonna text Caitlin and Lucas and let them know you're all right. Can I also tell them you're coming back to school tomorrow?"

He looked at the tired face staring back at him in the window. He couldn't stay at his grandma's house forever, he thought. As bad as he felt about what he'd done, he knew it wouldn't help to stay in the house. And Allison needed him. He was responsible for making her think she was a Vessel. He was the only one who could do something about it. He had to at least try to help her. And he couldn't do that if he didn't go back to school. He had to try. He owed her that. He turned from the window and faced Allison.

"Yeah. I'll be back tomorrow. You can tell them." He turned back to the window and cleared his throat as Allison started to walk away.

"Hey, Allison!" he called out.

"Yes."

"Thanks for coming out here to get me. You're a good...you...it means a lot to me. Thanks."

"You don't ever have to thank me, Felix. But if you really want to, you might consider taking a shower and shaving before we leave tomorrow."

Felix laughed. "Okay. You can sleep in either of the two bedrooms back there. I'm gonna sleep on the pullout sofa in here. It's actually pretty comfortable, and I like being in this room for some reason."

"Okay," Allison shouted from the back of the house.

Felix pulled out the mattress from the worn-out sofa and grabbed a blanket and a pillow from the closet. He lay down on the bed and turned on his side to face the window. He heard Allison in the back bedroom. It was strange to hear the sounds of someone else in the house. He'd been alone for nearly a month. The sound of drawers being opened and closed made him remember vacations spent there with his family. He hadn't slept much in the past four weeks. The nightmares had gone away. But sleep was elusive.

He felt someone climb into bed behind him.

"Close your eyes and go to sleep, Felix," Allison whispered, pulling the blanket over her and wrapping her arms around him. "I've never seen anyone look so tired. Just close your eyes."

"I never asked for any of this, Allison," he whispered back to her in the darkness of the living room.

"I know you didn't. Close your eyes...close your eyes."

Felix closed his eyes and slept.

Chapter 5

The next day Allison got up early and put her clothes in the dryer. Felix was still sleeping soundly, and she let him sleep. She found a towel and a washcloth and showered. When she came out of the bathroom, Felix was starting to stir.

"Your turn," she said. "And don't forget to shave. You look like a reject from a nineties grunge band."

While Felix showered, Allison attempted to clean up the mess in the kitchen. She washed dishes, swept the kitchen, and tossed out uneaten pizza crusts, beer bottles, and several bags of garbage. By the time Felix emerged from the bathroom, he looked like his old self.

"You see!" she said, smiling. "You clean up nice. All it took was a little sleep and a shower."

Felix had to admit that he felt a little better. But that didn't mean he forgave himself for killing his parents. He never would. He knew in his heart that he'd never be able to forgive himself. What he did was beyond unforgivable. If there was a hell, Felix would definitely be going. But Allison was right. Isolating himself from the rest of the world in his grandma's house wouldn't solve anything. He couldn't hide from his pain and guilt—it would follow him everywhere, always. But he resolved to not let it destroy him the way it destroyed his mother.

He was grateful that Allison drove to Cove Rock to find him. And it was cathartic to tell her what he was feeling. But what he did to his parents was something he didn't want anyone else to know—ever. He asked Allison to keep everything between the two of them. It would be their secret forever.

Felix helped Allison finish cleaning the kitchen. Afterwards, they drove to a nearby diner for breakfast. He'd rented the sedan from an agency on First Street, not far from Downey. After breakfast, Felix drove the sedan to Portland with Allison following in Caitlin's SUV. It was a rainless day and they made good time. Felix pulled into the car rental agency just after noon. He finished the paperwork for the rental and then he and Allison took Caitlin's car back to campus.

Chapter 6

Felix spent the next several days trying to get caught up in his classes. He picked up his textbooks and class schedule at the bookstore and was relieved to see that he was in all the classes he registered for during the previous semester:

> Western Civilization Part II
> Introduction to Psychology Part II
> Business and Economics
> English Literature

Also waiting for him when he returned to campus were his first semester final grades. When he logged onto his school account, his heart was palpitating. He prayed that he passed all his classes. That was really all he could realistically hope for given his psychological state during final's week. When he saw three C's and one B on his transcript, he let out a little sigh of relief. He knew it was nothing to boast about, but at least he got passing grades. He just needed to do better this semester. His overall GPA was now hovering dangerously close to 2.0. Anything below that would automatically result in academic probation—and that would mean not being able to play football next year.

Lucas was happy to see Felix after such a long hiatus, and he was even happier that Felix was now free of his recurring nightmare. When Caitlin first saw him, she practically jumped up and down with excitement, gave him a big hug, and kissed him on the cheek. The only person who didn't seem very happy about his return was Harper.

Out of everyone, Felix thought Harper would be the most excited to see him. Because of what happened at the Caffeine Hut just before finals, he was hopeful they'd just pick up right where they left off. Didn't she imply that what made him happy was her? Didn't she give him a look that said "I'm really into you, and I want to hook up"? But Harper was back to her pre-Caffeine Hut meeting behavior—polite and casually friendly but without even a hint of flirtatiousness.

Felix couldn't help but wonder if he'd misconstrued everything that happened at the Caffeine Hut. Maybe she was just being a friend and held his hand to comfort him. Allison did the same thing at his grandma's house, and he didn't think anything of it. He was sure Allison didn't think anything of it either. It must be the same with Harper. She just took his hand. Big deal. That didn't mean anything. And he thought it did—which just meant he didn't understand girls. And that he was an idiot. He and Harper were just friends. And that was better anyway, because being close to him was dangerous. People literally died.

More confused than ever about his feelings for Harper, and her feelings for him, he consulted with Lucas. But Lucas was just as perplexed and had no idea why she was back to being cold and distant.

"Maybe something happened to her during the break?" Lucas finally suggested.

"Like what?"

"I don't know, dude," Lucas replied, shrugging.

On his way back to the dorm from his Western Civ class, he received a text from Bill: *Welcome back, Myrddin. Please come to my office at 4.*

Chapter 7

Felix went straight to Bill's office after his last class of the day. He rapped on the door and was surprised when Bill opened it while Felix's hand was still poised to knock once more. Bill was smiling, and for an instant, Felix thought Bill might hug him. He put his hand on Felix's shoulder, gave it a little squeeze, and ushered him into the room.

"Felix," he said, gesturing for him to take a seat at the table by the window, "I can't tell you how glad I am to see you! Take your coat off. You can toss it over there. When you ran out the last time you were here, I really thought...let's just say I was preparing myself for the worst."

Felix nodded and sat down. "I don't really even remember leaving. I think I went straight to the rental car place. I didn't even stop at the dorm to get my stuff."

"Where did you go? You were off the reservation for a month, you know."

"Yeah," Felix said. "It was kind of like time didn't matter. I was just there and I didn't think too much about the future." He frowned and scratched his nose.

"Would you like some tea?" Bill asked. "Maybe I can tempt you with a little Earl Grey? Hot tea on a cold day like this is a wonderful thing."

Felix rolled his eyes. "What is it with you and tea, anyway?"

Bill looked perplexed, apparently not understanding how anyone couldn't enjoy tea as much as he did. "So where did you take the car?"

"To my grandma's place in Cove Rock over on the coast. My parents inherited it when she died five years ago. We used to have little vacations there all the time. Sometimes I'd take friends, which is why Allison knew about it. She went up there with me and my parents two or three times, I guess. Anyway, my parents loved it. They were planning to fix it up after my dad retired and spend their summers there. I guess you could say that was their dream." Felix dropped his eyes and picked at a fingernail.

"That's a nice dream, Felix."

"Yeah," Felix said, still looking at his finger. "So, anyway, back in September my parents' attorney sent me the keys to the place and all the paperwork. So, I guess it's mine now—that kind of sounds strange. Me, a homeowner, and I'm still eighteen."

Bill smiled.

"Oh!" Felix exclaimed. "What's with the text? The 'welcome back, Myrddin' thing?"

"Isn't it obvious?"

Felix didn't think so. "We're not gonna have another semester of you asking me questions I can't possibly know the answers to, are we? I don't think I'm up for it."

Bill laughed. "And to think I'm the one who dislikes professors and their Socratic methods. I didn't mean for the text to be so cryptic. After being in your memory, and seeing what we both witnessed at your parents' house, I think it's obvious that you are no mere gift wielder."

Felix's eyes grew wide. "So you think that..."

"No. I don't think. I know. I suspected as much after what happened in Allison's dorm room. But now there is no doubt in my mind. You are without question the Second Coming of Jesus Christ. *You* are the reincarnation of Myrddin."

"Are you sure? Are you sure I can't be something else?"

"Like what?"

"I don't know," Felix replied, shrugging. "I mean, I killed my parents, and I'm no saint or anything. So I was thinking that maybe..."

"You are not anything like Landry, if that's what you're getting at!" Bill shouted. "You are his opposite! You were born without a father! You can't be like Landry. Even if you wanted to be, you couldn't. It's not in your DNA, Felix. That isn't your fate. It's his fate. You understand that, right?"

"Yeah, I guess," Felix said, noncommittally. "So if I am the reincarnation of Myrddin, what does that mean exactly? Am I Felix? Am I Jesus? Am I Liam? Am I a Tinshire? Or am I just Myrddin?"

"I suppose you're all of those things."

Felix's brow furrowed in thought. "So does that mean I'm like a Vessel? That Myrddin is gonna take over my body, or something like that?"

"No, no, no, no. You are already Myrddin. You have always been Myrddin. There's no separation between Felix and Myrddin—you're the same person. It's just that until recently you weren't manifesting your powers."

"But since I just started to use my powers, will I also start to have Myrddin's personality? You know, become more like him?"

"No, Felix," Bill said sternly. "I know this is hard to grasp, but you are not becoming anything. You are simply who you are."

How can he know these things? Felix wondered. *Does he really have the answers to everything or is he just talking out of his ass?* "Okay," he replied, trying to sound as though he was convinced.

"Now tell me about your nightmares," Bill said. "Have you had any more since you..."

"Nope. I haven't had the dream since."

"That's good. Because, and I know I'm stating the obvious here, your power is extraordinary. But it's also terrifying, and if you're sleeping and..."

"I'm not worried about that anymore," Felix interrupted.

"And why is that?"

"Well, the last few times we went to Devendon, I figured out that the skin on my entire body gets this strange tingling sensation whenever my gift is close to the surface. And now that I know that, whenever I feel it tingling, I can try to focus my gift or I can just shut it off. It happened a lot at my grandma's...at my house...in Cove Rock. I was so pissed off all the time, I would get this sudden weird feeling on my skin. I could feel it happening, so I just relaxed and sort of willed myself to turn it off. It also happened a couple of times while I was sleeping. It was like I could feel it in my sleep. I just woke myself up and kind of...I don't know...I just turned it off."

"That's great," Bill said, smiling. "That is such a *huge* step. You're finally learning to control it."

Felix shrugged. "Yeah, I just wish I figured it out a long time ago."

"I know you do. But there was no way you could have known..."

"I know that," Felix said. "I know that in my head, anyway. I'm just gonna have to try to get through this."

"And you will. You will. Just coming back to school after what happened shows that you may not be such a stupid teenager after all."

Felix laughed. "I wouldn't count on that. And you know, if it wasn't for Allison, I think I'd still be at the coast drinking beer and eating beans out of a can."

"Yes, she's really an extraordinary girl. You're lucky to have her as a friend."

Felix paused for a moment and looked thoughtful. "I'm still confused about what will happen when the Templar Amulet is destroyed. What exactly is gonna happen to the Vessels?"

Bill stood up and started fixing himself a cup of tea. "That's a good question, Felix. And to be honest, my answer is based to some degree on speculation. I believe that people who have transferred their souls to a Vessel, let's call them *Soulless Humans*, and the Vessels who have received a soul—we'll call them *Human Vessels*—will both survive the destruction of the First Templar Amulet.

"And that's because the Soulless Humans once possessed a human soul, and the Human Vessels have been touched by a soul. It's the soul which gives life, and sustains it even if the First Templar Amulet is destroyed. It's really all about the soul, Felix. The Vessels, on the other hand, are creations of the Amulet—which is why they all die within six years if they don't receive a soul. The Amulet creates the Vessel and gives them life. But it cannot sustain them indefinitely. And since the Vessels rely solely on the Amulet to sustain their life, once it's destroyed, the Vessels will die."

Felix ran his hands through his hair and looked troubled.

"I know what you're thinking," Bill said, sitting back down at the table with a cup of steaming tea in his hands. "We talked about this. If Allison isn't human, then she cannot be a Soulless Human, and she cannot be a Human Vessel. If she was, Landry would be aware of your existence and my role in helping you. Landry, as you'll recall, owns the minds of Soulless Humans and Human Vessels like they were his own. And as we discussed before, that would mean we'd both be dead. And because we're still alive, we know for certain that Allison is either human or she's a Vessel."

"So once the Amulet is destroyed, Allison will die," Felix said, staring out the window at the Courtyard.

"If she's a Vessel, then yes. But what's this about? Did you notice something in her behavior?"

"No. Well, yes, I guess. She found out that her parents got a bunch of money from an anonymous donor when she was adopted. She thinks that…"

"Yes, yes, of course. That's not the only explanation, but we can't be willfully stupid about this."

"How can I even try to destroy the Amulet if I know I could be killing Allison? I can't do that! You can't ask me to do that! Not after what happened with my parents and…"

"Let's not get carried away," Bill said in a calm voice. "We don't know for certain that she's a Vessel. We have to proceed as if she were not."

Felix stared out the window.

Bill took a sip of his tea and watched Felix.

"There's something else I wanted to talk to you about," he said.

Felix turned his head from the window and looked at him.

"I've already told you that I've been with A.E.I. for a very long time. And you know that the only reason I work there is to obtain information that will enable us to destroy the Antichrist."

"Landry, you mean?"

"He's one and the same, Felix."

"Right." *Wait a minute*, Felix thought, suddenly anxious. *Did he just say* destroy? *What did he mean by that?*

"But," Bill continued, "destroying the Antichrist isn't as simple as walking up to him with a gun and pulling the trigger——or detonating a bomb under his car."

"You're talking about *killing* him then, right? And a bomb wouldn't do it?"

"No. There's only one thing that can kill Landry, and he's sitting in my office right now."

"Oh," Felix said, feeling like he might pass out. *So there it is*, he thought. He was supposed to kill Landry. How could Bill say that so casually? Weren't they just going to stop Landry? Isn't that what Bill had told him? They would stop Landry. Or stand in his way. Or defeat Landry. And all along it was really all about killing Landry.

"So I'm supposed to kill him?" Felix asked.

"No one else can. It's you or nobody. That's your fate."

Felix felt sick to his stomach. "But you want me to kill him. Actually kill him. Like try to kill him, and then kill him. Like, not by accident or anything. But actually kill him."

"What did you think this was about, Felix!" Bill snapped irritably. "This isn't a children's story. Landry's not going to fail simply because he's the bad guy! This is the real world and the Antichrist doesn't fire warning shots. He'll rip your heart out and eat it. Then he'll swallow your soul. So when you get the chance to kill him, you better god-damn kill him!"

"Okay," Felix said quietly, not wanting to provoke Bill any further.

"But you have to remember that Landry isn't just the Antichrist," Bill continued. "He's the Holder of the Templar Amulets, with the ability to access their power. That makes him an even more formidable threat. And you, you are young and just learning to control your powers. Sending you up against Landry now would be suicide. My goal is to keep you away from him for as long as possible—until you've realized your full powers. But until then, we're going to engage in guerilla warfare."

Felix tried to sound calm. "What does that mean?"

"We're going to use speed and deception. We'll use hit-and-run tactics. We'll hit below the belt and we'll destroy his assets. We may not be able to destroy him just yet, but we can deprive him of those things that make him more powerful."

"You mean the Amulet, right?" Felix asked, regaining some of his composure. Destroying an object didn't sound quite as bad, he thought. At least it was better than killing someone.

"Yes. We'll destroy the First Templar Amulet."

"How are we gonna do that? Do you even know where it is?"

"For sixteen years I've been trying to figure out where he's creating the Vessels. Finally, I'm close."

"You are?"

Bill nodded and sipped his tea. "At first, I thought he was using Ashfield Manor, which is what he calls his mansion. It's an exact rec-reation of Ardsley Castle. Considering what happened there, I find it interesting that he'd want to live in a replica of his boyhood home.

"But let me back up and give you a short tutorial about what Landry is doing in your home state of Oregon. Not only does he own the land where his headquarters were built, he owns two hundred square miles of forest land surrounding it. It used to be owned by the state, but when he moved his headquarters to Portland, he required the State to sell it to him—apparently he wanted his own private forest."

"Why'd he want that?"

Bill smiled. "That's exactly what I asked myself. It's pretty simple, really. Landry wanted enough land so that he could use it for his own purposes without worrying about prying eyes. He has so much land, in fact, that the forest was renamed Ardsley Forest. If you check the local maps, you'll see that it's now officially renamed."

"*Ardsley Forest?*" Felix shouted. "You mean where those people were killed? Holy shit! That's gotta have something to do with Landry, right? It's his forest!"

"I actually don't think there's any connection at all," Bill replied calmly. "I've looked into it, and I honestly believe that it's the work of a sociopath. Or perhaps even two or three sociopaths who have teamed up and embarked on a killing spree."

"Like that Mormon Mephistopheles guy everyone's talking about?"

"Perhaps. His real name's Nick Blair. He's a polygamist from Utah. One night a few years ago he decided to use his collection of hunting knives on his four wives and their eight children. He massacred them all. He's a vile son of a bitch who deserves to die an excruciatingly painful death. Nick escaped from a federal penitentiary in Sacramento last April. So it's not inconceivable that he made his way up to Oregon. He could be hiding out in the forest and murdering hikers he comes across."

"But it's Landry's forest!" Felix protested. "Don't you think Landry's got something to do with this? It can't be a coincidence!"

"It is a coincidence, Felix. Trust me on that. I've been in those woods. I've seen evidence there's someone living there in tents and makeshift shelters. There may even be two or three people."

Felix was shocked. "You've been in the woods?"

"Yes. I'll get to that in a minute."

"But if you have evidence that someone's out there killing people, shouldn't you tell the police?"

"I would love to. But unfortunately, that would bring to light certain goings-on in Ardsley Forest that would jeopardize our mission."

"Really? But..."

Bill's face turned red and he slammed his hand down hard on the table. "What's more important, Felix—a few idiots who insist on hiking in the woods knowing that people have recently been slaughtered there, or the fate of the world?"

"Come on," Felix pleaded. "You can't look at it like that."

"No?" Bill replied, holding out his hands, palms facing up. "Five morons." He gestured at his left hand. "The fate of the world." He gestured at his right hand. "Pick one!"

Felix just shook his head.

"We all have to make sacrifices!" Bill shouted. "And that includes being prepared to sacrifice a few if it means saving the whole. That may suck and sound heartless, but that's life in our brave new world. Now, can I please get back to what I was trying to tell you?"

This guy is so intense sometimes, Felix thought. *As soon as he encounters a little resistance, he freaks out.* He recalled not long ago when Bill threatened to brain him with a baseball bat. He glanced around the office to see if Bill was still keeping it close by.

Felix just nodded.

"The public is obviously aware that A.E.I.'s headquarters are in Ardsley Forest, and that the office buildings are connected to the nearest public street by a four-lane road called Hermann Boulevard. The public also knows about Ashfield Manor. The mansion is roughly three miles northwest of A.E.I.'s offices and connected to the buildings by a paved road."

"He has his own private three-mile road?"

"Yes. And let's just say you wouldn't want to use it without permission. But there are things the public doesn't know. The reason Landry wanted his own forest was to construct an extensive network of underground buildings. Many of the structures are connected by tunnels. Based on information I've come across over the years, I believe there are literally miles of tunnels in Ardsley Forest and millions of square feet of usable space."

"What's he doing with all that?"

"You have to remember that A.E.I. is in most respects a perfectly legitimate business. It's involved in everything from aerospace technology to pharmaceuticals. So the majority of the space is used for ordinary business purposes. You should also keep in mind that the vast majority of A.E.I.'s employees are just regular folks who come to work, do their jobs, and go home to their lives and families."

Bill took another sip of tea before continuing. "But of course Landry is anything but your typical CEO. The facilities aren't all used for research and development."

"That's where he's creating the Vessels!" Felix exclaimed.

"Exactly. But I don't believe anyone working in a facility used to create Vessels would be human."

"You think they'd either be Soulless Humans or Human Vessels?"

"Yes."

"How'd you even find out about these places?"

"A.E.I. couldn't keep it a secret forever. The employees who work there are instructed to keep their work confidential. But people sometimes talk."

"Someone talked to you?"

"Several people, actually. I spend my time at A.E.I. counseling employees who are suffering from a variety of mental issues—primarily anxiety and stress-related disorders. When I talk with any employee, part of my job is to understand what their role is at the company. I tell them that anything they tell me is strictly confidential. I've talked to a number of individuals who have worked in the underground facilities. I've also talked with people who were involved in the actual construction of the facilities themselves.

"One man in particular has been very helpful. He supervised the installation of the massive backup power generators which provide auxiliary energy for the entire A.E.I. complex. He came to see me for stress-related issues. It was difficult for him to maintain a power source with the capacity to power a small city with just a skeleton staff to help him. Over the years, and through dozens of sessions with him, I learned that A.E.I. originally wanted this man to install enough backup generators to provide auxiliary power for every underground facility in Ardsley Forest.

"However, with only a small number of people on his team, it would have taken him decades to install enough equipment to provide power for the entire underground network. He was told that twelve buildings needed a guaranteed backup power supply. The five buildings that are used as the company's corporate headquarters and seven underground facilities."

"You think the Vessels are made in one of those seven?"

"I've actually narrowed it down to three. The construction supervisor was kind enough to provide me with a map of Ardsley Forest showing the locations of all the backup generators. I told him it would help me understand his problems better."

"You have the map?" Felix asked.

"Yes, I made a copy of it. I can't exaggerate how important it is. Without it, I would be searching for one building in two hundred square miles of dense woodlands."

"So how'd you narrow it down?"

Bill drained his teacup. "Process of elimination. Over the years I've counseled a lot of employees who work in the underground facilities. Once I'm satisfied that they're working on legitimate business operations, I determine which facility they work in and then I cross that particular building off the list of possible locations."

"That doesn't sound exactly foolproof."

"It's not—which is why I check on these things myself."

"So that's why you've been in the woods."

"Yes. I watch the facilities from a distance, obviously careful not to get spotted. And then I observe. I watch who comes in and who leaves. I pay attention to how many people use the facility and at what times they enter and leave the building. Is there garbage pick-up at the facility? I look for anything out of the ordinary. I'll watch a facility for weeks to determine if the activities there appear legitimate or not."

"Holy shit!" Felix shouted. "You're spending weeks out in the woods where people have just been killed? Where people have just disappeared?"

"Yes."

"Doesn't that scare the shit out of you? What if someone tried to kill you?"

"I don't go unprepared, Felix," Bill replied casually.

"What's that mean?"

"That's not important right now. What's important is that I've narrowed it down to three locations. And once I've eliminated two of them, we'll need to take action."

Felix suddenly felt very alert. "Take action? What does that mean? You mean, destroy the Amulet?"

"Yes," Bill answered. "Once I've identified the exact location."

"Okay," Felix replied, fidgeting with a pen he'd taken from the table. "You think you'll figure it out soon?"

"I understand you're feeling nervous about this," Bill replied, examining Felix closely. "But it's imperative we destroy it as soon as we know where it is. I'm hopeful I'll have the answer soon."

"Okay, but what do you mean by *soon*?" Felix asked anxiously. "Are you talking about a few days? Or a few years, or what?"

"We can't wait years. I'm confident I'll know in the next few months. With any luck, we'll be going over our plans to destroy the Amulet before the end of the semester."

"This semester," Felix whispered under his breath. He shook his head a little and looked at Bill. "What's the plan?"

"At this stage, the plan is for you to better control your gift. That will have to suffice for now. We'll go over the plan in detail when the time is right."

Chapter 8

Two weeks later, Felix had eased back into the comfortable rhythms of college life. He got caught up with his class assignments, spent his evenings in Dale's Room and his weekends playing basketball and working out with Lucas in the Bryant Center. Satler students threw two welcome back to school parties. One ended with Caitlin and Lucas having a few too many cocktails and getting into a shouting match.

Lucas told Caitlin he didn't think it was appropriate for someone so sanctimonious about her environmental consciousness to be driving a gas-guzzling SUV. Then he made the mistake of calling her "carbon footprint Caitlin." She responded by calling him "Piper's Boy Toy" and a "Reality Show Retard." The resulting argument ended with Caitlin crying her eyes out and Lucas feeling very bad about the whole thing. The next day, with Felix's help, Lucas brought her a bouquet of flowers and a card in which he apologized profusely and poetically. After reading the card, she hugged him and said all was forgiven.

Sometimes as Felix sat at the table in Dale's Room watching Lucas and the girls studying, or having coffee and catching up with campus gossip at the Caffeine Hut, he had to remind himself that he wasn't like them. He wasn't a normal college student. It was so easy to forget sometimes. When he reminded himself that he was the reincarnation of Myrddin, it seemed fake and made-up. He worried that he'd lost his mind and conjured up the whole story.

A few days before at the Caffeine Hut, while his friends were engrossed in a conversation about Dirk Johnston's latest movie, he was lost in his own internal struggle and came to the conclusion that he had to be crazy. Anyone who believed they were the Second Coming of Jesus Christ had to have lost their grip on reality and needed to check into a mental institution. Abruptly excusing himself from the table, he walked into the bathroom, turned out the lights, and waited in total darkness until he started glowing like a giant red candle. Satisfied that he wasn't crazy after all, he willed his gift off, turned on the lights, and returned to the table to finish his coffee.

After dinner that night, Felix, Lucas, and Caitlin grabbed their backpacks and left the dorm to get a cup of coffee. Winter had arrived in Portland. It was another damp and frigid night. They walked the footpaths wearing heavy winter jackets and gloves. Caitlin was wearing black earmuffs that matched her jacket and leather gloves. She wouldn't go out unless her wardrobe was perfectly coordinated, and Lucas never passed up an opportunity to make fun of her because of it.

Lucas was in rare form. He told a joke that involved ice fishing, golf, and three prostitutes. Each time one of them burst out laughing, a great cloud of vapor would shoot out into the air in front of them. Felix's laughter was cut short when something caught his attention.

They'd just turned a corner when Felix noticed two people walking with their arms linked about fifty yards ahead. The girl had blond hair and wore a white coat. There was something familiar about the way she walked. He tried to get a look at her profile, but they were all walking along the same footpath and he didn't have the right angle to see her face. He could only see her back. Felix looked at Lucas, but he was fidgeting with one of his gloves and didn't seem to be paying attention to anything around them. Caitlin had just started telling a story about lunch and someone spitting buffalo chicken across the table. Then she stopped in mid-sentence and walked along silently with her head down.

"Hey guys," Felix said, "does that girl look familiar? Do we know her?"

"Who?" Lucas asked, looking all around.

"The girl up there with that guy. Straight ahead. The one with the white coat. She looks familiar, doesn't she?"

Felix sped up. Lucas kept pace, but Caitlin fell back a step. Felix gradually closed the gap between them.

If only he could get a look at her face, Felix thought. Where'd he know her from?

The girl turned her head and smiled up at the guy next to her.

Felix stopped in his tracks. It was Harper.

"Dude, that's Harper, isn't it?" Lucas said, stopping next to him. "But who's the dude?"

Caitlin caught up with them in the middle of the footpath. "That's Dante Smithwick," she whispered. "He's a junior. He went to our high school. They used to date."

"Who? Who used to date?" Felix asked, still stunned at the sight of Harper smiling at another guy.

"Harper and Dante. Harper dated him her entire sophomore year of high school when Dante was a senior. He actually broke up with her when he came here. Harper was pretty heartbroken at the time. Said she'd never trust men again and all that crap."

"Oh," Felix replied weakly. "I haven't seen him around campus."

"That's because he spent last semester studying abroad in Italy," Caitlin said. "I think he was in Florence for the semester. Then he traveled all over Europe for a month. Pretty cool, huh?"

"Yeah, that's just splendid," Lucas said sarcastically. "I'm so happy that Dante was able to study in Italy and that he enjoyed himself on his European vacation. Maybe we can check out his pictures later on Facebook?"

"You're such an ass sometimes, Lucas," Caitlin said. "I was just explaining why you haven't seen him around campus."

Felix looked like he was in shock. "So…are they…are they like going out, or what?"

"I'm not really sure," Caitlin said uneasily. "I guess, maybe. She really liked him in high school. And now that he's back from Europe and they're going to the same school again, I guess I'm not surprised."

"But I thought you said earlier she was having dinner with a friend in the city!" Lucas exclaimed accusingly.

"Yeah, well, what Harper does is her business!" Caitlin said sharply. "If she wants to tell you guys that she's dating someone, she'll have to do it herself. I'm not doing it for her."

"All right," Lucas replied. "I was just saying."

"Look," Caitlin said, "I love Harper to death, but it's no secret she falls for guys who treat her like crap. I'm not a psychoanalyst, but she likes guys who screw with her. She might go for you, Lucas, because you're an ass. But Felix, you're way too nice for her."

They walked the rest of the way in silence. Felix was stunned. And he was angry. He was angry at Dante for sweeping in from Italy and taking Harper from him. He was angry at Harper for not giving him a chance. And how could he be too nice for Harper? Hadn't she told him she wanted a nice guy? And why did everyone think he was so nice, anyway? If only they knew what he'd done—they wouldn't think he was so nice then.

There were so many things he could say to Harper. So much that he wanted to tell her. But by the time they reached the Caffeine Hut, he decided he wouldn't say a word to her. He wouldn't give her the satisfaction of knowing she'd hurt him. Screw Harper. He didn't need her. If she wanted to date Dante, then she should date Dante. Screw her. And screw Dante. He wouldn't care. He wouldn't be bothered by it. He knew how to put on a game face. There were a lot of girls at PC who thought he was hot. He was a six-foot-three, blue-eyed football star. He could have any girl he wanted. Harper Dupont and Dante Smithwick could go fuck themselves silly for all he cared.

Chapter 9

The next week passed with glacial slowness. Felix tried not to dwell on the fact that Harper was dating her ex-boyfriend. It was impossible not to think about. He never saw Harper alone, and when she was with the group, the subject of Dante, and Harper's relationship with him, was never mentioned. It was like everyone tacitly agreed that it would be more awkward to discuss the topic than to pretend like the relationship didn't exist. Felix tried to stick to his game plan. He tried to appear like he didn't give a shit. But he couldn't even look at her, let alone talk to her. Whenever their eyes met, he felt the anger boiling away at his innards and his heart pounding in his temples like a Japanese taiko drum.

As he sneaked out of his room that night to meet Bill at Devendon, he was glad for the opportunity to focus on something other than the image of Harper walking arm in arm with Dante Smithwick. A few snowflakes were falling as he walked across campus. When he reached Devendon, he let himself in through the side door and made his way up to the old library, barely making a sound. Bill had already arrived and was busy lighting candles in the corners of the room.

"Hey, Bill," Felix said as he entered the room.

"Hello." Bill was wearing a pair of loose-fitting jeans and a heavy blue winter jacket over a dark-colored sweatshirt.

"Cold in here," Felix said, rubbing his hands together.

"Yeah. I think we'll be keeping our jackets on tonight."

"I don't think you need the candles," Felix said.

Bill was hunched over in the far corner of the room next to the fireplace. "Why's that?"

"It's like I told you last week, I sort of figured out when I'm using my gift. I don't need to check if I'm glowing or not."

"Oh. Okay. Then why don't you turn on the lights over there and I'll blow these things out."

Felix flipped on the wall switch next to one of the room's two entrances and started to make his way over to the table in the center of the room. He looked up at the chandeliers and counted five out of the twelve that were working. The stack of books on the table seemed like a fixture that had been there forever. When Bill finished blowing out the candles, he joined Felix on the opposite side of the table. Felix stared at the books as sinewy spirals of white smoke from the candles wafted to the ceiling.

"Okay, Felix. I know it's been a while since you've done this. I want you to think back to what you did before. Focus on your core. Focus on the feeling in your stomach when you locate your gift. Focus on the sensation of…"

The topmost book on the stack suddenly shot off of the table and flew across the room at chest level. Bill reflexively held out his hand. The book flew right into it with a resounding *whump*!

Felix smiled. Bill looked at the book in his hand and then looked back at Felix. And then he too smiled.

"Well, well, well! It seems you did some practicing while you were in Cove Rock."

"I did," Felix said, his crooked smile getting bigger. "The whole time I was there I was a total emotional mess. And my gift was coming to the surface constantly—I was glowing red at least half the time. And when it happened, I would concentrate on what I was feeling just before I started to glow. I eventually locked in on that feeling so I could make myself feel that way whenever I wanted. I don't even have to be all emotional to do it either, but it happens faster if I'm pissed off about something."

"I see." Bill scratched his chin. "How are you controlling it?"

Felix shrugged. "I spent so much time trying to turn it off…I was so angry about…well, you know, that I was afraid I'd go nuclear again and destroy my grandma's house. But it happened so much I kinda got the hang of not turning it off, and not going nuclear. It's hard to explain. It's just a feeling. Anyway, I spent a lot of time sitting in the living room trying to move shit around. I practiced on bottle caps. Then I moved up to beer bottles."

"Sounds like you were on a liquid diet," Bill said with a slight smile.

Felix laughed. "I know. I really treated myself like shit. But I got to the point where I could fly a bottle around the room pretty easily. Then I tried to do more than one bottle at the same time and heavier stuff, but I just ended up breaking a lot of shit. I'm getting better at it, but it's hard."

"Well, let's see if you can move the stack of books off the table. That's what we set out to do the first night we came here. Go ahead. Oh! Wait! I should put this book back." He held out the book Felix sent flying across the room to him. "I don't want you to feel like you were cheated out of an opportunity to move the entire stack." Bill put the book back onto the top of the pile, smiling wryly at Felix.

Felix smiled back at him and then took several deep breaths. He stared at the books and raised his right hand. A moment later the stack started to move. Slowly at first, it crept an inch across the table. It moved a few more inches and then it lurched forward several inches. Then it stopped. After another moment, the stack started to vibrate. It lurched forward three or four inches and then stopped again. And then it moved another inch, and another inch. Then it pitched forward a few more inches. And then suddenly the entire tower of books shot across the table and flew through the air several feet. When it finally hit the floor, it made a great crashing sound that reverberated throughout the room.

"Yes!" Felix shouted as he raised his arms into the air. He jumped up and down several times in an apparent imitation of Rocky. "What do you think about that?"

"That was very good," Bill said calmly.

Felix stopped his celebration. "Very good? I've been trying to move those goddamn books forever. I finally did it. C'mon, that was better than very good. Wasn't it?"

"I don't want to minimize what you just accomplished. But let's try to keep in mind that you are the reincarnation of Myrddin. Moving some books is just the beginning. And now that you've managed to pass the first test, we're going to move on to the next one."

"What's that?" Felix asked apprehensively.

"If you're going to destroy the First Templar Amulet, you'll need to work on some things."

Felix frowned. "What sort of things are you talking about?"

Bill walked past Felix toward the back of the room where several tables and chairs were scattered about. He picked up two chairs and carried them over next to the table.

"Have a seat," Bill said, sitting in one of the chairs. "I think I gave you some idea about what we're facing in Ardsley Forest."

Felix sat down. "You mean with the underground buildings and all that?"

"Yes," Bill said, nodding. "But it's more than that. The facility I'm still looking for won't be your typical building. It's not going to be like breaking into your neighbor's basement."

"So is it like a bomb shelter or something?"

"Something like that. It'll be designed to withstand a direct strike from a bomb. The walls and ceilings will be reinforced concrete and steel several feet thick. And there will be only one access point—one door, which will be solid steel, bulletproof, and practically impregnable. The only way to open the door will be by entering a security code and passing a thumb-print signature test. Oh, and I believe you'll also need to pass a retinal scan. And there are sure to be security cameras everywhere."

Felix's jaw dropped. "How the hell do you expect us to get through that?"

Bill paused before he answered. "Felix, unfortunately, *we* won't be going through the door together. As much as I would like to go with you, if we're spotted, or if my image is captured by a security camera, I'll no longer be of any value to you."

Felix frowned. He never considered the possibility that he might be doing something like this on his own. He always just assumed that Bill would be with him. Especially if he was gonna do something crazy like break into a building in Ardsley Forest. And why wasn't Bill going with him, anyway? Couldn't he just wear a hood or a mask if he was so worried about someone seeing him? That seemed like a seriously weak excuse.

Bill seemed to sense Felix's consternation. "Felix, my primary value to you lies in my ability to acquire information about Landry. Without that inside knowledge, we'd be lost. If Landry were to find out about what I've been up to, he'd have me killed. And as much as I'm willing to accept that risk, I'm not willing to unnecessarily give up my access to that information. Do you understand?"

"Yeah, I guess." Felix frowned. "I just didn't think I'd be operating solo, you know. It's not like I have any experience breaking into reinforced bomb-proof bunkers. I only broke into something once. And that was the door to the garage when I locked myself out of the house. We kept a key in the garage and I just kind of gave the door a little nudge with my shoulder. My dad wasn't very happy with me though. I had to mow a shitload of lawns to pay to get it fixed. And I don't think I'll be able to just give a steel door a little nudge and watch it fly open."

Bill laughed. "No, it'll take a little more than that."

"Right. It's bulletproof and there are a bunch of those scan things going on. It sounds impossible."

"That's exactly why I wasn't jumping up and down with you earlier."

"Huh?" Felix said, feeling confused. He paused for a moment and his brow was furrowed. And then his eyes grew wide as he understood

Bill's intentions. "You've gotta be kidding! You expect me to break through that door? I can't do that! I can barely move books!"

"But think about where you were just a short while ago," Bill replied. "It wasn't until recently that you've been able to bring your gift to the surface. And it was just during winter break that you realized you can channel it. So assuming you'll make the same leap in your development during the next several months, I believe you can do it."

"Seriously? I don't know. That doesn't sound possible. I mean, I can't even…"

"Which is why you're now going to shift your attention from moving objects to breaking objects. We'll leave that for next time. But I want you to start thinking about it."

"Okay," Felix said, taking a deep breath and trying to remain calm. "So why don't you tell me the rest of this great plan? After I do the impossible and get through the unbreakable door, then what? What am I supposed to do? What if there are people there?"

"I know that the First Templar Amulet will be in the room where the Vessels are created," Bill answered calmly. "In the journal it says that at Ardsley Castle the Amulet was placed against the wall at the front of the room where the Vessels were made. The journal also says that there was a blue light emanating from it to the Vessels, and that the Vessels were suspended in the air. When you disengage the door, you should proceed into the building and look for a room with a blue light. I can't really be any more specific than that, unfortunately."

"And when I find this blue room?" Felix asked, gesturing for Bill to provide more information.

"Destroy the Amulet. It's as simple as that."

"And how does that work? I know the journal says the Holder can either use the power of the Amulet or destroy it, so…"

"Exactly," Bill interrupted. "You're the Holder of the Templar Amulets just as Landry is the Holder. But whereas Landry uses the First Templar Amulet, you'll destroy it."

"And if I'm not the Holder, then obviously I won't be able to destroy it, right? I mean, if I'm not, it can't be destroyed by anything, right?"

"That's correct. But you're the reincarnation of Myrddin. I have no doubt that you are a Holder."

"Okay, so let's just say that I am the Holder and that I can destroy it. How do I go about doing it? Do I say 'hocus pocus' or wave a wand at it, or something like that?"

"I don't know," Bill said flatly. "But I wouldn't suggest waving a stick at it."

"But, if you don't know, then..."

"I believe you'll know once you're there. After you see it, I think you'll just know what to do."

"And what if I don't know what to do?" Felix asked.

"Then you'll be in trouble," Bill said, smiling. "I wouldn't worry about it."

He didn't just say that, did he? Felix thought. *Don't worry about it?* That was easy for Bill to say. He'd be all cozy in his warm house drinking some weird flavor of hot tea while Felix was breaking into a bomb shelter in Ardsley Forest.

"Okay, I guess," Felix said. "But what about people? What if there are guards there?"

"It's what we discussed in my office. I don't believe anyone involved in the creation of the Vessels will be human. They'll either be Soulless Humans or Human Vessels. In any event, I believe the facility used for making Vessels is only used when Landry himself is there. The First Templar Amulet is his most important asset, and his presence is needed to create the Vessels. Therefore, the facility will be unoccupied unless Landry is there."

Felix suddenly looked terrified. "But what if he's there? Wouldn't he just..."

"I have absolutely no intention of sending you into Ardsley Forest if there is even the remotest possibility that Landry will be there. If he were to find you, he'd kill you in an instant."

"That's good to know," Felix said, wide-eyed.

Bill smiled. "In fact, I won't send you there until I have confirmation that Landry is out of the area. Ashfield Manor is probably just a few miles from the facility. So if he's there or at his office and he becomes aware that you're attempting to destroy the First Templar Amulet, he could be at the facility very quickly. Probably in minutes."

"How will you know he's not around?"

"I'm working on that. I have reason to believe that Landry will be in Egypt during the last week of April. I haven't confirmed that yet, but when I do, we'll have to seize that opportunity. So between now and then I need to identify where the facility is. And you, Felix, you need to work on focusing your gift so that you're strong enough to break into the facility without alerting anyone of your presence."

Felix stiffened like he was suddenly overcome with rigor mortis. "What about that Nick guy? The Mormon Mephistopheles. Or those other serial killers hanging out in the woods? What if they show up?"

"I think Nick and the others, if there are any, have moved on. I haven't seen anything in the woods recently indicating anyone's still there."

"That's very reassuring," Felix said sarcastically.

"A lot can happen in just a few months," Bill said evenly. "I'm not terribly concerned about that particular risk."

How could he not be concerned about a serial killer, or a pack of serial killers, stalking around Ardsley Forest? Felix wondered.

"So that's the plan, huh?" he said, trying to sound casually brave, like they were making plans to go see a baseball game. "We wait until Landry is hanging out in Egypt. I sneak into Ardsley Forest, find the underground facility, break through the steel door, and destroy the Templar Amulet before anyone notices. I almost forgot. I'll be doing all this hero shit in April."

"That's the plan."

"That'll never work in a million frickin' years!" Felix exclaimed, laughing.

"You're probably right," Bill replied, sounding serious.

Felix laughed again, but he wasn't sure if Bill was joking.

Chapter 10

During the next two weeks, Felix struggled against the routines that defined his life when he tried, sometimes successfully, to be just an ordinary college student. Pretending he was no different than anyone else was like swimming against the current. He could do it for a while, but in the end, he had to let it carry him to a place entirely outside of his control. He just wished he knew where it was taking him. How could he even pretend that classroom lectures and campus gossip were important when he knew what was waiting for him in Ardsley Forest? Weren't those mundane things meaningless and insignificant compared to what Bill had planned for him? Bill's plan...

Felix thought Bill's plan bordered on sheer lunacy, and he couldn't escape the feeling that Bill was expecting way too much from him. And there was something else that bothered him. If he was right, and the plan really was insane, then wasn't Bill recklessly throwing him in harm's way? But why would he do that? Didn't Bill need him? Wasn't he the only one other than Landry who could be a Holder? So why couldn't he trust Bill completely? It wasn't in Bill's interests for him to fail, after all. And Bill had been patiently waiting and planning since Felix was just a baby. Did he have any justifiable reason not to trust Bill, or was he just being paranoid and stupid?

Lucas noticed that Felix was preoccupied with something and asked him frequently if everything was all right. Felix always replied that everything was fine and that his classes were stressing him out. He felt like an asshole for lying, but what choice did he have? Harper, on the other hand, seemed utterly oblivious to Felix's state of perpetual anxiousness. Their conversations were always shallow and strained, and he found it difficult to maintain the superficiality for long periods of time.

That Friday, a group of upperclassmen on the football team invited Felix to a party on the second floor of Cutler Hall. Cutler was a dorm for juniors and seniors adjacent to Ferguson Hall, where the team ate their pre-game meal. Felix and Lucas usually walked past it when they went to the Bryant Center, but they never had any reason to go inside.

When Felix, Lucas, Caitlin, and Allison reached the second floor, they saw a scene that was becoming very familiar—dorm parties all looked basically the same. It didn't matter if the party was at Satler, Cutler, or Downey. It took them almost thirty minutes to find a room with alcohol—working their way through the crush of bodies in the hallway was like being digested by a python. As Felix squeezed his way into the room, he saw that it was already packed with students drinking beer from cans and a hard alcohol mixture out of plastic cups. About half of the crowd was on the football team, including Larry, Jonas, Salty, Brant, Scott Adelman, and Aaron Rosenberg.

"Hey guys, what's going on?" Felix shouted, trying to be heard over the music.

"Felix, my man!" Larry's booming baritone greeted him.

"Hey, Larry, how's it going?" Felix asked. "Hey, you guys know my roommate Lucas, right?"

"Minnesota Meier!" Larry yelled from across the room. "Everyone knows Minnesota Meier! This guy's my fucking idol. Didn't you see what he did to that blond chick on TV?"

"Larry's had a few already," Brant whispered to Felix and Lucas.

"I heard that, Brant!" Larry shouted. "You might be the quarterback, but I will throw your skinny little Texas ass right out the goddamn window if you accuse me of public intoxication!"

"Brant may be the quarterback, but I'm the kicker," Aaron said. Aaron was short with brown hair and was stocky in the kind of way suggesting he'd probably struggle with his weight when he got older.

"So hey, Felix and Lucas, this is my brother Gabe's room," he continued. "We've got some beers and drinks and stuff here. You just need to give me a twenty and it's all yours."

Felix and Lucas paid Aaron and grabbed two cans of beer. An hour later Felix realized that Allison and Caitlin hadn't followed them into the room. They chugged the rest of their beers and stepped out into the hallway—it was still completely clogged with students.

Felix and Lucas fought their way through the crowd, searching for Caitlin and Allison. At about the halfway point, Felix caught a glimpse of Allison at the other end of the hall. Then he lost her behind a group of students coming out of a room. The far end of the corridor looked dark, darker than it should've been. Felix noticed that the ceiling bulbs were removed for the party. *Come on,* Felix thought, still threading his way through the crowd. *Just get out of the way so I can see what's going on down there.* Moving like a school of fish, the same group of students entered another room and Allison reappeared.

Allison, Caitlin, and Harper were all standing together at the end of the hall—and they were talking to Dante Smithwick. Felix and Lucas stopped simultaneously. Dante was in the center of the group. Harper was standing very close to Dante, so close that their arms seemed to be touching. Caitlin was casually leaning up against the wall, and Allison's back was to Felix and Lucas. Dante was talking animatedly about something, and gesturing a lot with his hands. The girls laughed uproariously as he apparently reached the punch line of his story.

It was the first time Felix saw Dante up close. He was of medium height and on the thin side, although his shoulders were broad. He had black hair, dark eyes, his skin was very tan, and he had a small dimple in the middle of his chin. His smile was wide and his teeth were extraordinarily white. He was impeccably dressed, especially for a Friday night dorm party. He wore designer jeans, sneakers, and a button-down shirt that hung out from his pants except for one corner in front, which was tucked slightly into his jeans.

The girls seemed positively enamored with him. They weren't only laughing, but laughing like he was the funniest standup comic on earth. Felix could hear their peals even above the noise of the crowd and the music blasting from rooms up and down the hall. Dante said something that caused everyone to laugh again, and Caitlin reached out and lightly touched his arm.

"Screw this!" Lucas shouted as he started walking toward them, pushing his way roughly through the crowd. "That's about enough. C'mon, Felix. Who does this guy think he is?"

As Lucas approached the group with Felix close behind him, Caitlin was the first to spot them. It looked like she was about to say something, but Lucas didn't give her a chance.

"Hey, everyone!" Lucas said, with his broadest reality star smile. "Caitlin, Allison, Harper. How are you guys doing? Oh! Hey!" he said, turning toward Dante. "We haven't met you. Shouldn't one of you girls introduce us?"

Allison looked at Felix, and Caitlin looked at Harper. Lucas's eyes were fixed on Dante. He stood at least two inches taller than Dante and was much more solidly built, but Dante didn't seem to be intimidated in the least by the approach of Felix and Lucas. Nobody said anything, and the awkwardness grew with each passing second.

"This is Dante," Allison finally said. "Dante, these are our friends Lucas and Felix."

"Ah, Lucas and Felix," Dante said smugly. "Have you been to Cutler before?"

Neither answered.

"I'll take your silence to mean no," Dante said coolly. "And am I safe in assuming that the two of you are freshmen? I'm sure you are, so don't bother answering. So tell me, Lucas and Felix, how does it feel to be drinking beer with people who are actually old enough to drink?" He laughed.

"I didn't realize you had an issue with freshmen," Lucas said, continuing to glare at him. "Because if I'm not incorrect, and I'm not, all the girls you're putting on a performance for here are freshmen. But don't worry, I'm sure they're as impressed by your date of birth as we are."

Dante burst out laughing. "That's funny. That's very funny. You know, Felix, or are you Lucas? I forget. Anyway, it doesn't matter. Whoever you are, that reminds me of this Italian expression I heard while I was on the Amalfi Coast recently that is quite apropos. It goes…"

"Does it translate into any other language? Like English?" Lucas interrupted. "Or is this Italian expression so wonderfully unique and quirky that it can't be translated into anything else?"

Dante looked at Lucas and smiled. "Nice meeting you, Felix. Harper, come on. I want to show you something in my room." Dante headed back down the hall, and Harper followed along obediently at his side. They disappeared into a room a few doors down.

Felix could feel himself getting hot.

"What a douche bag!" Lucas shouted.

"What the hell are you doing, Lucas!" Caitlin snapped, her face growing red. "We were just talking. We're having a perfectly nice conversation and then you have to come over and insult him. Nice job!"

Lucas looked surprised. "I insulted him? I just said hello. He insulted me. Yeah, like I'm so impressed to be having a beer with a junior. Big frickin' deal. The guy's a total douche bag! What the hell does Harper see in that guy?"

"Well, for one thing, he's pretty damn hot," Caitlin said matter-of-factly. "Maybe you didn't notice, but he's extremely good-looking. And he's been places. And he's rich and he's…"

"Oh! So it's all about money, is it?" Lucas shouted. He was becoming agitated. "It's not like he's ever made a dime, you know. Maybe his parents have money, but Dante didn't do shit. He just spends their money and walks around using words like *apropos*. Who the hell says apropos?"

Caitlin was visibly angry. "Just because you flunked the verbal section of your SAT doesn't mean that he's a douche bag."

Felix felt himself getting hotter. He didn't even like to hear someone say SAT. It reminded him of what he did just to get into college. It made him feel self-conscious and anxious. And after just seeing Harper follow Dante into his room, he wasn't feeling very well-equipped to deal with his anxieties at the moment.

"For one," Lucas yelled, "you can't flunk the SAT. And second, I know what the word means. And I know that non-douche bags don't use it!"

"Ah, Lucas," Caitlin said, with a hint of despair, "I don't know why I like you. You're such an idiot sometimes."

"You just realized that?" Lucas asked, smiling.

Caitlin giggled and Lucas started laughing. No one seemed to be able to stay mad at Lucas for very long. Not even Caitlin.

Felix concentrated on his breathing. *Just relax*, he told himself. *Concentrate on your breathing and relax. Slow your breathing. Just take it easy.*

"You know what," Allison said, glancing furtively at Felix with a worried expression, "if I had to go on record, I'd definitely agree with Lucas. Dante's a douche bag. Come on, Caitlin, be honest with yourself for a minute. The guy's an asshole."

Caitlin laughed again. "Yeah, maybe. But don't tell Harper that."

"Screw him," Lucas said with a dismissive gesture. "He's a douche. So anybody up for a drink?"

"Yes," Felix said immediately.

They found another room with alcohol where a group of students were playing an intense game of beer pong. Felix wasn't in the mood. The thought of Harper following Dante into his room to see something was causing him to lose his enthusiasm for the party.

After a couple of drinks, Caitlin suggested going down to the first floor to see Amanda, an upperclassman she knew from her Political Science class. Lucas volunteered to go with her.

The beer pong contest quickly consumed all of the available alcohol in the room. Everyone cleared out to search for another room with beer. Felix and Allison stayed behind. They'd already had enough to drink for one night, and the little altercation between Lucas and Dante had put a damper on the evening. They looked out the window. It faced two buildings used as classrooms and labs. It wasn't much of a view.

"Are you all right?" Allison asked.

"Sure, why wouldn't I be okay?" he answered a little too quickly.

"I can think of about twenty reasons off the top of my head."

Felix laughed. "I'm hanging in there, Allie."

"Allie?" She laughed. "You haven't called me Allie since we started college."

"Really? It feels like we started college a hundred years ago."

"It does, doesn't it? I can't believe everything that's happened. Life was so much simpler back in high school. Back then, you weren't levitating beer bottles across the kitchen, and I didn't know I was created by the Antichrist with the help of a Templar Amulet."

"You're not a Vess…"

"It's fine, Felix. That's just the beer talking. I had a few tonight, you know."

Felix looked closely at Allison. Her forehead was even more wrinkled than usual. He hated to see her like this. It was all his fault. It made him feel guilty. She brushed the hair away from her face and looked back at him. Her green eyes sparkled.

"Allie, I'm sorry this is happening to you…to us…but I promise I'll do everything in my power to take care of you. I don't know if I have it in me or not, but I promise that I'll try."

"I think that might be the beer talking in you, Felix," Allison said and smiled. "We should probably head down to the first floor to meet her friend. What was her name again?"

"Caitlin."

"Not Caitlin, you dummy." She punched Felix jokingly in the arm.

"Ow! That hurt! You're pretty strong, you know. I think her name is Amanda."

"Amanda! Damn, you have a good memory. I bet you're almost smart enough to use apropos in a sentence."

"Probably not," Felix replied. "All right, let's go get Lucas and Caitlin and meet this Amanda." They left the room and started walking down the hall. It had completely emptied out in the last hour.

"The party must have moved to the first floor," Allison said.

"I was just thinking that. Maybe Lucas and…" Something out of the corner of Felix's eye caught his attention. It looked like two people hooking up. There was something about it that seemed strange. He took a step back and looked into the room. Two people were standing in the center of the room making out. The girl was tall and blond and she wore leggings and a black shirt. The guy was a few inches taller than the girl. He had dark hair and wore designer jeans, and…and… Felix realized he was looking at Harper and Dante.

They were locked in a passionate embrace. And to make matters worse, Dante was running his hands all over her. Felix didn't want to watch, but it was like trying not to stare at the scene of a highway accident. There, standing not ten feet away from him, the girl he really liked was totally going at it with another guy. He was transfixed. He couldn't take his eyes off of them. They were so engrossed in each other they didn't notice or care that the door to the room was wide open.

They continued kissing, and Dante ran his hands over Harper's body. He wrapped his arms around her and grabbed her hair. He pulled her head back. She looked at him for a moment, and then she smiled. It was Harper's smile—the smile that made the dimples in her cheeks stand out. And then she started kissing him again even more passionately than before. He pulled her into his body. She reached down and did the same.

Allison stood slightly behind Felix, but she also had a front row view of Harper and Dante. Allison's first impulse was to move along and give them their privacy, but Felix was standing in the hallway as if he were rooted to the floor. She felt awkward and was sure that at any moment Harper or Dante would look up and see that she and Felix were engaging in a little late night voyeurism. She was trying to think of a way to get Felix to move down the hall without making too much noise.

And then Felix started to glow.

Felix and Allison were all alone near the end of the hall where the ceiling bulbs had been removed and the area was mostly dark. Felix's entire body was turning a deep shade of red. He clenched his fists and a strange look came over his face as he continued to stare into the room. Allison grabbed Felix by the shoulders and pushed him as hard as she could. Felix didn't budge.

He raised his right hand and began speaking in a whisper. "So this is what happens to nice guys. The nice guy doesn't get the girl. The nice guy watches the girl hooking up with someone else. Let's see how nice you think I am when I turn your fucking boyfriend inside out."

Allison looked into Felix's eyes. They were the same pale blue as always, but there was something different about them. It was like looking into the eyes of a person she didn't know.

Panicked, Allison pushed Felix with all her might, but he barely moved. It was as if his body was made of lead. Refusing to give up, Allison felt a surge of adrenaline course through her. She threw her arms around Felix's waist and, locking her hands together, used the strength in her legs to drive him backwards. She pushed and shoved until finally she pushed him well past Dante's room. Felix didn't seem to notice what was happening until he found himself halfway down the corridor with his back up against the wall. Someone was standing in front of him and screaming.

"Felix, what the hell do you think you're doing? You realize you're glowing? Look at yourself, goddammit! Are you listening to me? You don't have the option of getting angry! Don't you get that? Felix, can you hear me?"

Felix shook his head and tried to focus on the person who was yelling at him. She was saying something about how he couldn't get angry.

"Allison?" he asked.

"Yes, Felix. It's me. It's Allison. I'm right here."

"I'm sorry, Allie," Felix said dejectedly, hanging his head as the red glow surrounding his body gradually dimmed and then went out, as if he were an electric heating element whose power switched off. "I was just watching Harper and Dante…and…and I guess I was pissed off…"

"You've gotta pull yourself together! You can't let yourself lose control! You know what could happen! I don't care what you have to do. But you can't let this happen!"

"You're right. I know you're right. I just don't know what to…"

"And what the hell were you saying back there?"

"What do you mean?" Felix asked, perplexed. "What'd I say?"

"Never mind. Felix, listen to me. I know you have feelings for Harper. I'm not stupid. We all know that you like her. It's not a secret. And I know it hurts when you like someone and they don't like you back. Believe me, I know what that's like. I know how much it hurts. But Felix, you're different. You can't put yourself in a position where you could lose control. And I know this is harsh, and it's not what you want to hear, but I think you should just stay away from Harper. She's with another guy now and she looks happy. It's obviously tearing you up. So just leave it alone. Besides, you have enough going on in that head of yours."

Felix nodded and rubbed his eyes. "This really sucks, Allie. I don't know what I did. I don't know why it worked out like this."

"That's just kind of the way it is, right? Life just sucks sometimes. You know that better than anyone. Come on. Let's go downstairs and see what Lucas and Caitlin are up to. Whatever it is, I bet they're not having as much fun as we are." Allison smiled and put her hand lightly on Felix's shoulder.

"Yeah, right," Felix said. "This whole year's been a walk in the park."

"Well, at least you've still got your sense of humor."

"Sure. At least I've got that."

Chapter 11

Harper didn't show up for breakfast the following morning. On weekends, it was practically a tradition for the three girls to meet Felix and Lucas for breakfast in the Downey cafeteria at around eleven o'clock.

Allison and Caitlin had barely seated themselves at the table when Lucas started firing questions at them. "Where's Harper? Is she here? Wait, don't tell me. She liked Cutler Hall so much she couldn't bear to come back to Downey."

Caitlin frowned at Lucas and took a bite of her wheat toast.

"So," Lucas continued, undaunted, "has she made the walk of shame yet, or should we wait in the lobby and welcome her back to the fold when she gets here?"

"Lucas," Caitlin said, still nibbling on her toast, "the day just started and you're already being a jackass. Why do you care so much about who Harper hooks up with anyway? She didn't give you a hard time when you were hooking up with that ugly pale-faced girl with the bright red hair."

"Her name's Piper."

"Oh! That's right. Piper. The chick dating Gary, the psychotic Beta."

"Hey!" Lucas shouted. "Don't turn this around on me. Harper's the one hooking up with that toolbox!"

"He's not a toolbox," Caitlin replied, "he's just a little...a little... what's the word?"

"Pretentious?" Allison suggested as she sliced a banana into her bowl of granola. "Ostentatious? Pompous?"

"Exactly," Caitlin said, nodding. "All of those. He can be a little pretentious, but he wasn't really that way back in high school. Okay, well, maybe a little bit, but now it's probably gotten worse. But I don't know what to tell you. Harper likes him."

"I still think he's a douche bag," Lucas said.

"We know you do, Lucas," Allison said and laughed. "But listen, I'm being serious. Harper is actually up in her room right now, and the reason she didn't come down is because she didn't want to deal with all of this."

"All of what?" Felix asked, wiping his mouth and putting down his large glass of apple juice.

"You know, she doesn't want to talk about last night. She doesn't want to hear a bunch of questions about her and Dante. She definitely doesn't want to hear you guys calling him a douche bag."

"Well, that's too bad," Lucas said, swallowing a piece of bacon, "because those are the consequences when you hook up with douche bags!"

"Lucas," Caitlin said sternly, picking up the banana that was next to her plate, "I swear to you that you will not like what I'm gonna do with this banana if you don't at least try to act like an adult."

"Well, that might be interesting," Lucas deadpanned. "I never thought about doing anything like that before. But now that you brought it up, we are at the age where we're supposed to be experimenting with our sexuality and…"

"Lucas, come on," Allison said patiently as Caitlin elbowed Lucas in the arm. "Harper's our friend. We all love her and we want to spend time with her. But if you make her feel uncomfortable, she's going to avoid us. And you know what? I think we can all agree that Dante is in fact a bit of a douche bag. But sometimes it takes a while for the person involved with the douche bag to realize that they actually are a douche bag. I went out with Todd a few times before I realized he was a douche bag. But you guys knew it before I did. I just didn't see it until I spent some time with him. Let's just give her time to figure it out on her own. Okay?"

Felix still couldn't believe that he'd unwittingly used his gift the night before. And not at a book or at a beer bottle. But at a person. What would he have done to Dante if Allison wasn't there? His feelings for Harper were just making matters worse for him. He needed to focus on himself, get his head on straight. Maybe it really was better that Harper was with some other guy.

"Allison's right," he said, trying to sound like he was just being supportive. "Let's just let Harper figure this out for herself. Until she discovers that Dante is a pretentious douche bag, we'll just stay away from the subject. Agreed?"

"Absolutely," Caitlin said.

"All right," Lucas said grudgingly, picking at the bacon on his plate. "I suppose if I have to. I wouldn't want Caitlin to threaten me again with a banana."

Caitlin punched him on the shoulder and he laughed.

Lucas looked at Allison and Felix, who were sitting side by side across from him. "You know, I don't know what they put in the water in Coos Bay Bridge, but it sure makes you people sensible."

"They only seem sensible to you, Lucas," Caitlin said, "because the cold weather in Minnesota froze most of your brain cells when you were a child."

"Is that right? And this is coming from someone who lives right on top of the San Andreas Fault. It may be cold in Minnesota, but at least we're not in any danger of getting swallowed up by the Pacific."

"That's a fair point." Felix raised his glass of apple juice to Lucas.

"I thought so," Lucas replied, raising his own glass and toasting Felix.

Chapter 12

As February came to a close, Felix, Lucas, Allison, and Caitlin stuck to their plan, and Harper started coming around a few days after her semi-public display of affection in Dante's room. She never raised the subject of Dante on her own, and they all managed to steer clear of conversations that might result in someone accidentally bringing his name up. And with midterms just two weeks away, they had other things to worry about besides Harper's romance with Dante.

Felix had returned to Devendon on two more occasions. As planned, his focus shifted from moving books to breaking things. Bill brought an odd assortment of items to the old library. Most of them were scavenged from the building itself: rusted-out metal lockers from one of the bathrooms, filing cabinets of different sizes, and several heavy wooden doors he unscrewed from their hinges. He also brought a box full of cheap digital alarm clocks, bicycle locks, and a few lightweight padlocks.

Felix struggled with his new assignment. No matter how much he concentrated, he only managed to send objects flying across the room. During their last session, Bill asked him to tear a large hardcover book in half. But instead of tearing it, Felix sent it zooming across the room at such speed that when it hit a bookshelf, one corner of the book embedded itself into the thick, dark-stained wood. Bill walked over to the book and as he struggled to pull it out said, "I wouldn't want to get in the way of that."

That night, Felix hoped he'd be able to sneak out of his room without having to make up another ridiculous excuse for Lucas. But Lucas was listening to his iPod and didn't look like he'd be falling asleep any time soon. Finally, at ten minutes until midnight, Felix said that he felt like going out for a walk. Lucas agreed, saying that getting a little fresh air sounded like a good idea to him as well. Feeling backed into a corner, Felix played his "he just felt like being alone" card. Lucas shrugged and went back to listening to his music.

Felix walked out of Downey feeling like an asshole and thinking about how much he hated lying to his roommate. It seemed obvious that Lucas thought something strange was going on. But Felix didn't know what else to tell him. He had no choice but to lie, but he was a horrible liar. He always had been. He wished for the day when he could just be honest with everyone. But he knew that would never happen.

It was a clear, cold night, and the stars were visible for the first time in weeks. Felix had nothing against looking at stars, but more than anything, he was just glad not to be getting rained on. There were quite a few students hanging around the Courtyard and walking to and from the Woodrow Library, but as Felix approached the Old Campus, he was all alone. He slipped through the iron gates on the north side and proceeded as quickly as he could, walking past the front of Devendon and around to the side door. He let himself into the building and climbed up the creaky stairs to the old library. Bill was already there. The chandeliers were on, but it was still pretty dark. The furthest reaches of the dusty room were cloaked in shadows.

"Looks like we need some light bulbs," Felix said as he entered the room.

"Yeah. The damn things burn out as soon as I replace them," Bill replied without looking up. He was busily arranging objects on a long, narrow table he'd set up on one side of the room. On top of the table he'd placed several digital clocks and five locks—two small combination locks and three larger bicycle locks. The clocks were connected to extension cords plugged into an outlet on the nearby wall. They were all flashing 12:00, 12:00, 12:00. Behind the table, Bill wedged a wooden door between two metal filing cabinets. The door was about eight feet tall. The filing cabinets were roughly half its height.

"Are you ready to get started?" Bill asked. "You did okay last time, but you need to focus so that the object is impacted but doesn't move. You remember what you did to the book last time, right? That's an example of what not to do. I want you to break one of the alarm clocks. I don't care which one. You pick."

"Okay." *Looks like we won't be wasting any time tonight,* Felix thought.

On his first try, he only succeeded in causing the clock to smash against the wall and shatter onto the floor. But on his second attempt, the face of the clock cracked like a pane of glass trying to support too much weight. It also slid across the table a couple of feet, prompting Bill to yell at Felix, "Focus, dammit!"

On his third attempt, the clock exploded as if somebody had slipped an M-80 underneath it. Pieces of plastic flew in every direction. A large, jagged black hole was left on the table as the only reminder that it was ever there.

"Good. Good. That's good," Bill said without emotion. "Now let's try doing that on something with a little more substance than a plastic clock."

"What's the hurry?" Felix asked. "Come on. That was pretty cool, right? Did you see what I just did to that clock? I blew the shit out of it!"

Bill turned to face Felix. "Yes, you blew it up. You destroyed a little plastic alarm clock. That may be progress, but I'm not going to stage an awards ceremony for you!"

"I just thought…that it was pretty good that I…" Felix said defensively.

"You're not getting the big picture!" Bill shouted. "You can control matter, Felix. You're not one of these goddamn pussy characters in a children's story! You're not some kid who learns how to 'wax on' and 'wax off'! You don't need a utility belt! And you're not some ten-year-old brat waving a wand around and doing some *hocus pocus* bullshit! You're the reincarnation of Myrddin! The most powerful force the world has ever known! You're the Second Coming! When will you understand what you're capable of? You can control *matter*. You have the ability to do whatever the hell you want! Yes, you destroyed a goddamn clock! But you should be able to destroy this entire building!" Bill was gesturing wildly and screaming by the time he finished his diatribe.

Felix was stunned by the outburst. "Okay. What the hell? What'd I do? I'm trying to…"

"I'm sorry, Felix," Bill said, exhaling slowly and rubbing his temples. "That wasn't fair. I shouldn't expect so much from you. I would prefer not to put so much pressure on you. You've been through a lot. I know that. But the fact is you may only have a few months left to prepare.

"Once our window of opportunity opens, we need to take advantage before it slams shut on us. There are so many things outside our control, Felix. Landry could move the First Templar Amulet to a different location. He could decide to start wearing it around his neck. The only thing we can control is preparing you to destroy it. We need to make sure that you're ready."

Felix nodded. "Okay. I get it. I get it. I really do. I'll try harder. But why are you freaking out now?"

Bill sighed. "I know this isn't fair, but time is running short. And you have to be ready. Because if you're not, failure isn't the only risk."

Felix knew what he meant. He could die out in that forest. "I know," he said flatly as he looked at the objects on the table. "What do you want me to do next?"

"Destroy a lock. Just like you did with the clock."

Felix stared at one of the combination locks. It was a small, chrome-plated padlock exactly like the one on his locker at the Bryant Center. He concentrated. The lock vibrated on the table for a moment.

Then, suddenly, the lock burst into flames. The dark red flames sprung directly from the lock itself, shooting several feet into the air.

"Bill!" Felix yelled with panic in his voice.

Bill was already in motion. He grabbed one of the tattered moving blankets from the far corner of the room. He sprinted across the room, blanket in hand, jumped over a chair, and threw the blanket over the burning lock. With the roar of a hundred lions, the blanket ignited instantly as if it were doused in gasoline. The flames leapt higher into the air and raced across the top of the table. The flames were now taller than Felix. Half the table was ablaze, and smoke was billowing across the room in choking clouds.

"Felix!" Bill shouted. "There's nothing I can do to put this out!"

Felix stepped closer to the table and stopped next to Bill. "I have no idea!" he shouted and coughed, choking on smoke. "I don't know how I did this! How can I..."

"It came from you!" Bill yelled as the fire expanded before their eyes. "You can take it back. Do it now, Felix! This could get very ugly! Do it now! Do it now!"

The fire had spread across the entire tabletop, and smoke was beginning to fill the enormous old library. Felix lifted his hand toward the table and focused on putting out the fire. *Come on!* he thought. *Just go away. Go away!*

Suddenly, the flames jumped higher into the air, as if they were sentient and seeking to touch the ceiling. The heat from the flames was unbearable. Felix and Bill stumbled backwards, trying to shield themselves from the ferocious heat. The alarm clocks on the table were reduced to balls of melted plastic.

"Felix!" Bill shouted, shielding his eyes against the brightness of the flames. "The opposite! Do the opposite. Do it now!"

Felix reached out again with his hand. He focused on what he felt when he made the flames grow. He tried to imagine what it would feel like to make them shrink. He focused on that sensation and stared at the flames.

The flames began to diminish gradually at first, and then shrank more quickly. Within seconds the flames were reduced to no more than a few feet in height. They also receded from the edges of the table and were now centralized around the lock.

"That's it, Felix! Keep it going! Don't stop now!"

The flames grew smaller. Little by little they shrank until only the lock burned. And then, just as suddenly as it started, the fire winked out. Felix lowered his hand and took a deep breath. Sweat was pouring from his face even though it was freezing inside the old library. Smoke completely filled the room. Bill was coughing behind him.

"What the hell just happened?" Felix shouted, his body shaking.

"I can't believe it," Bill said, staring at the charred remains of the table.

"Can't believe what?" Felix asked with panic in his voice.

"I can't believe...I didn't expect...you just...you didn't just control matter. You changed it."

"What does that mean? Change matter? What does it mean?"

"It's nothing you should worry about," Bill said with a wave of his hand. "I'm just surprised. That's all. But that was really well done. Putting the fire out, that is. Not starting it. That part wasn't so great."

"Okay," Felix replied, his hands still shaking as he wiped the sweat from his face. "But how'd you know I could put it out?"

"I didn't. I just...I just hypothesized that anything that you can create, you can un-create."

Bill walked over to the table and held his hands just above the lock as though he were warming them at a campfire. He picked up the blackened, disfigured object and carried it over to Felix. "It's not even warm," he said reverently. "It's like it never caught fire. Here, touch it."

Felix touched it. "That's strange," he said, taking his hand off the lock. "It was shooting up flames ten feet high just a minute ago."

Bill nodded in agreement. "Well, if you're not too badly shaken up, I think we should continue. The other locks look to be charred but intact. Let's see if you can explode them without burning Devendon to the ground."

Chapter 13

Felix returned to his room at 2:30. He closed the door behind him as quietly as he could with a tiny clicking sound, trying not to wake Lucas. He changed out of his clothes, leaving them in a pile on the floor, put on a pair of boxers, and crawled into bed.

"Dude," Lucas whispered from across the room. "What the hell were you doing? You smell like a bonfire."

"Oh...I...I didn't notice."

"How can you not notice that? You smell like you were hanging out by a campfire."

"Oh. Sorry."

"No worries, dude. G'night."

"G'night."

Lucas lay in his bed, his hands laced behind his head, staring at the ceiling long after Felix fell asleep.

Chapter 14

"Do you have any idea what time it is, William?" the man on the other end of the phone said, sounding half asleep.

"Yeah, I know, Dad," Bill replied. "I'm familiar with the concept of time zones."

"So why the hell couldn't you wait until morning? It's five-thirty."

"Some people would consider that morning."

Bill was sitting at the large rectangular table in his kitchen nook overlooking the backyard. He stared out the windows but could only see his own reflection. He hadn't shaved in three days, and the scruff was unruly. Thick stubble covered his neck and cheeks, giving him the appearance of a lumberjack. His father coughed into the phone and then cleared his throat. Bill held the phone away from his ear until his father was finished.

"No, this couldn't wait," Bill finally said. "I was working with Felix in the old library and something happened. He...he was trying to explode a lock and it...it caught fire. The flames were twelve feet high."

"He what?" Bill's father exclaimed, suddenly sounding wide awake.

"It came out of nowhere," Bill continued. "One second the lock appeared to vibrate and then it just burst into flames."

"And then what happened?"

"He put it out. He extinguished it."

"In the same way that he set it on fire?"

"Yes. He just looked at it and focused. Then the flames just died out. Like they were never there. The melted lock wasn't even warm."

"I see," Bill's father said gravely. "Now we know for certain why there were fires in the girl's dorm room and his family's home. It was no coincidence. I had my doubts from the beginning about your theory."

"It wasn't a theory," Bill said irritably. "We had no reason to think that Felix was the originator of the fires."

"Of course not, son." His father paused and cleared his throat again. "But you do know what this means?"

"Actually, I don't. And neither do you. You can't draw any definitive conclusions from this. All we know is that Felix is not only able to control matter, he can create some kind of physical changes to matter."

"It's more than that, William! He didn't just melt an ice cube or freeze some water. What did he create the fire out of? The air?"

"No. No. It couldn't be that," Bill said thoughtfully. "Oxygen isn't combustible."

"Precisely," his father said, drawing out the word to emphasize it. "So how did he do it? Did he convert the oxygen into a more combustible gas? Like hydrogen?"

"Conversion? You think he's converting one type of matter into another? But that goes beyond the ability to control matter. Even beyond the ability to change matter. Myrddin himself couldn't do that."

"Then it appears he isn't the reincarnation of the old Druid," Bill's father said. "Forgive me for drawing such a definitive conclusion."

"But you're not considering that the only source we have on the subject of Myrddin, *The Druid,* is seventeen hundred years old. We can safely assume it's an incomplete source of information. Perhaps, well, I suppose we don't know for certain that Myrddin couldn't convert matter."

"You're grasping at straws, son. This is another sign. From the very beginning you've been observing the boy, looking for signs of what he'll become. Isn't this just another obvious indication that he is the Antichrist? So obvious that even the boy himself might recognize it for what it is?"

"I don't see it that way!" Bill said firmly. "And for what it's worth, I told Felix that he's not becoming anything. I told him that he is, and has always been, Myrddin. So there's no reason for him to be looking for signs."

"But how long will the boy believe your lies, William? Maybe you should give him more credit. I'm not so sure he believes everything you're telling him."

"How could you possibly know that?" Bill shouted. "Felix trusts me!"

"Whether he does or doesn't will soon be irrelevant. It's becoming clearer every day that the boy isn't the reincarnation of Myrddin!"

"It's way too premature to…"

"It's time for you to acknowledge that he is no less an abomination than Landry. All of the evidence is pointing to this conclusion. He looks like Landry. So much so that he could be his brother. He killed his parents. And now he's converting matter! Creating fire!"

"So what are you suggesting?" Bill shouted. "You want me to slit his throat in his sleep? Is that the answer?"

"Don't be so dramatic, William. Not until we use him to rid ourselves of Landry and the Templar Amulets. How many times must we discuss this? I doubt you're in the mood to talk again about your obligation to humanity at this hour. You know better than anyone that the beast must be killed before it can achieve its destiny."

"Beast? Felix isn't a beast! He's just a kid. And there's a lot of good in him. He's been through a lot. But he hasn't given up. He's trying to help. Can't you see that?"

"Maybe now," Bill father said dismissively. "But how much longer can you control him? What are you going to do when he becomes what he's destined to be? Look at the facts, son. He created fire out of the air! What are you going to do when he realizes his full powers?"

"It'll never come to that. I have faith in the kid. I refuse to believe he's like Landry. He can't be. The universe has got to have balance. For every Landry, for every Antichrist, there must be an opposite. Otherwise, there would be no order to any of this."

"Who says the universe has to be in balance?"

"I do," Bill said. "I've got to believe in something."

Chapter 15

A week after Felix nearly burned down the oldest building on the PC campus, Bill was at his desk in his small, drably furnished office in Building D at A.E.I. headquarters. He'd already completed two employee counseling sessions, and there was one remaining. The two executives were both suffering from work-related stress and anxiety. Their issues weren't unique. Bill had counseled hundreds like them over the years. Their stories were almost always the same.

They reported to bosses who expected them to be accessible at all times, day or night. As a result, they couldn't focus on their families even when they were home. Making matters worse, they were unable to focus on work while at the office because they felt like they weren't handling their responsibilities at home.

And while A.E.I. provided its employees with laptops, cell phones, and hand-held email devices, all ostensibly to offer employees the flexibility and convenience to work anywhere, most employees simply felt the devices were an invasion into their personal lives. The once-sacred barrier between work and home had been demolished by technological umbilical cords. As a result, most of the people Bill counseled were overwhelmed and dissatisfied with themselves, their work, and their family lives.

Bill's upcoming appointment was with Mary, a thirty-six-year-old mother of two who was experiencing similar issues. But it wasn't her psychological state that interested Bill. It was her position with the company. For the past three years, Mary had been employed as one of four assistants to Devory Portier. Devory was the personal assistant to the president of A.E.I., Landry Ashfield.

Bill checked his watch. It was 6:30. Mary was ten minutes late. In the two years she'd been meeting with Bill, she was never late. She was always on time. More importantly, her information was always reliable. He checked his email and waited.

There was a light knock at his door a few minutes later. He stepped to the door, opening it for Mary. She seemed rushed and apologized for her tardiness. Mary was short and slender, with long brown hair she pulled back into a knot at the nape of her neck. Her face was more lined than it should've been for a woman her age. She wasn't pretty, at least not by any conventional standards, but she did have nice eyes and full lips. She was dressed conservatively in black slacks, a matching blouse, low heels, a white cardigan, and a mid-calf black winter coat. She never wore makeup to accentuate her features. He asked her to sit down in the chair across from his desk.

"I'm sorry I'm late, William," she said apologetically, again. Her voice was surprisingly deep for someone so diminutive in size. "It's just been crazy these past few weeks. I got in at six-thirty this morning and I finally just finished. And I'm going to have to come in even earlier tomorrow."

"Devory has you burning the midnight oil again?"

"Doesn't he always?" she said and laughed. "It's just got to be so much easier for someone like Devory, who doesn't have a life outside of A.E.I., don't you think? Have I told you that in all the time I've worked for him, he hasn't asked me a single question about my family? Not one. If I miss a day of work because my son has the flu, don't you think it would be common courtesy to ask how he's doing?"

"Of course. Devory seems to have a single-mindedness of purpose that borders on..."

"Fanaticism," she interrupted.

Bill smiled. "I wasn't going to use that word, but that's certainly one way to characterize his devotion to the company."

"It's the only way. He doesn't have a life outside the company, and he can't seem to understand that the rest of us do. We have friends and families and outside interests, but he just doesn't care. I'm not sure how I'm supposed to work for someone like that. The money is pretty good, but sometimes I wonder if it's worth all the stress."

"Well, you're handling it in the right way, Mary. Just talking about it is a healthy coping mechanism."

"I know," Mary said, smiling. "Sometimes I feel like these are just venting sessions for me. But I feel much better after we talk. I don't feel like I'm going to explode by the time I get home. And the last thing my husband wants to hear is me venting all the time about Devory. He's heard so much about Devory already that he told me if I mention his name again I'll have to find another husband. That reminds me. Did I tell you what Devory did a few weeks back?"

Bill shook his head.

"No? Well, I was supposed to fax something to some bank in Switzerland, but I had to pick up my daughter early from day care. So I asked one of Devory's other assistants to cover for me. You wouldn't think that would be a big deal, right? The next day, I'm at my cube and Devory comes flying out of the double doors to Landry's wing. He gets right in my face and says, 'I am not in a position to tolerate mistakes, as my employer will not tolerate them from me.' For such a mousy little man, he can be a little terrifying."

"What was your mistake?"

"There wasn't one. Irene, the other assistant, faxed it to the right place. Devory just didn't like that I gave my work to her. Everything's so darn secretive up there. He doesn't even want his assistants to talk to each other. And there are four of us! And we all sit in a line of cubes! How are we supposed to not talk? Sometimes it's just too weird."

"Well, you know what they say; the higher you climb the less air there is to breathe."

Mary laughed.

"Well, we've talked about this before," Bill continued. "You could always walk away from your job. On the other hand, I realize your circumstances are somewhat unique here. It would be difficult to find work that pays anywhere near what you're making now."

Mary shook her head, looking discouraged. "It's a Catch Twenty-Two, isn't it? And that's why I come here and talk with you every two weeks. My job drives me crazy, but I can't afford to quit."

"There are a lot of other people in your situation, Mary. I know that offers little in the way of solace, but what you're experiencing is felt by millions of other workers all across the country."

"Yeah, I know. We're all working our fingers to the bone so the man at the top can make another billion dollars."

"Speaking of the man at the top," Bill said, "what is Landry's humble personal assistant having you do for Landry at all hours of the day and night?"

Mary shrugged. "Ah, nothing really out of the ordinary. I told you Landry's going to Egypt, right? He'll be there for six days. He's stopping off in London for two nights on his way back. I'm just making sure that everything goes smoothly."

"It would truly be a tragedy if Landry Ashfield's private jet had to wait on the tarmac for a few minutes, wouldn't it?" Bill said, smiling.

Mary laughed. "Yeah, wouldn't it be terrible if he had to suffer the indignity of being inconvenienced like everyone else in the world?"

"So, Landry is definitely off to Egypt, is he? What's the weather like in Egypt in March? I'd think it has to be hot, right?"

"Oh. I don't know. I haven't checked for March. Why would I? But I imagine it's warm. Isn't it always hot there?"

"Yes, I suppose. For some reason I thought you said he was going in March," Bill said off-handedly. "So I take it Landry's not going in March? I can't imagine that Devory wouldn't require you to provide him with the weather forecast."

"You know Devory far too well," she said and smiled. "He's going the last week of April. The stopover in London is May first and second and then he'll be back in Portland on the third."

Bill's expression didn't change. "But I thought he conducted the board meetings at the end of April for our biotechnology companies. I wouldn't want you to double-book Landry."

"Are you kidding? Devory would stuff and mount my head to a wall in Landry's wing. The board meetings start on May seventh. The last week of April was the only time we could schedule his trip to Egypt. Up until then he's booked solid doing some other things that I haven't been involved with. One of the other assistants is doing Devory's bidding for that."

"I hope good things happen while he's in Egypt," Bill said, smiling.

Chapter 16

Midterms descended on the campus like the dark clouds that had hovered over the city for the past two weeks. The residents of Portland were treated to periods of light rain followed by periods of heavy rain. Felix thought he was reasonably well prepared until his English Lit professor, Professor Marley, threw him a curveball. Instead of an exam, she assigned a fifteen-page paper, which was due on the first day of exams. The class had already been given three books to read. The professor's instructions required Felix and the rest of the class to identify a theme common to all three books and then analyze the theme's treatment by the authors. So thanks to Professor Marley, Felix was forced to work on a fifteen-page paper while he studied for three midterms. On the same day Felix learned about his English Lit paper, he received a text from Bill:

> *Felix, no time to go to Dev. until after exams. Come to my office on first Saturday after exams at 9 AM. Will be spending day outside; dress accordingly.*
>
> *Bill*

Felix wasn't disappointed. Last semester's finals didn't go very well. He needed to get his grades up this semester or he risked being put on academic probation. With an English Lit paper to write and three exams, he needed all the time he could find.

He spent the next two days struggling with the English Lit assignment without much to show for it other than a sour feeling in his stomach.

As he sat at the table in Dale's Room with Lucas and the girls, he was just trying to write anything that made sense. He'd already decided on the theme, but when he actually tried to compose something, the words just wouldn't come out. At one point he must have actually groaned, because everyone stopped what they were doing and looked up at him.

"All right, Felix," Caitlin said, pretending to be annoyed. "I know you've read the books and you have your theme. So what's the problem?"

Felix looked over the laptop screen he'd been staring at for the past hour. "I just don't know what to write," he said, discouraged. "I write a few words and then I read them. I don't like how they sound, so I delete them. Then I type a few more words and then I do the same thing all over again. So, after days of doing this shit, I literally have a blank screen in front of me. It's like the circle of stupidity."

"The circle of stupidity!" Lucas repeated and laughed. "I like that."

Caitlin glared at Lucas. "You know, Felix," she said, "my high school English teacher told me something that I'll never forget. She said the key to good writing is simple. All you have to do is stare at your computer and think. And then you have to think so hard that you form lines in your forehead. And once the lines in your forehead start to bleed, you'll know you're on the right path."

"That's what your high school English teacher told you?" Felix said in disbelief. "That's awesome advice! Let me just bleed all over my laptop until the paper writes itself."

"You're missing the point, Felix," Caitlin said, smiling at him. "The point she was making is that it's hard to write. Even exceptional writers struggle to articulate what they're trying to say in just the right way. You don't actually think the books you read for your class were written on the authors' first try, do you? There's a lot of editing and rewrites involved in the process."

"Okay," Lucas replied. "That's some interesting information and would be very helpful if we were all sitting around trying to write the next great American novel. But we're not. So let's say, for example, that you're just trying to write an English Lit paper, and you have a week to do it. How would you go about doing that if you didn't want to bleed on everything and you don't have an editor to help you write it?"

Caitlin looked very annoyed. "Lucas, if there's a bigger jackass at this school, I'd like to meet him."

"I can name seven off the top of my head," Lucas said, quickly counting off the imaginary jackasses on his fingers.

Caitlin shook her head in disgust at Lucas and then looked over at Felix. "Something else my high school English teacher taught me was how useful a good outline can be. If I were you, I'd just outline the concepts that you want to get into your paper. Once you've finished with that, you just sort of fill in the blanks. That's what I do. I think it works pretty well—especially if you have to write a long paper like yours."

"Yeah, that's pretty much what I'd do, too," Allison said, sitting back in her red leather chair. "I always use an outline when I write. I'd be lost without one."

Felix thought for a moment and looked back at his laptop. "Okay," he said, "I'll give that a try. I definitely like that option over the one that involves bleeding from my head."

Everyone but Caitlin laughed. She just rolled her eyes and said, "Why are guys such dummies? Do you attend some kind of secret school at night that teaches you how to be such idiots?"

"Shit!" Lucas shouted, slamming his hand onto the table so hard that his bottle of water nearly toppled over. "They're on to us, Felix! Dammit!"

Caitlin's tip proved to be helpful. Within two days Felix finished a rough draft of his paper. And having made progress on that front, he turned his attention to preparing for his midterms.

When he handed the paper to Professor Marley's teaching assistant, he had a fleeting moment where he wanted to snatch it away from the TA and read it again just to make sure it didn't suck. Instead, he let her keep it and walked out of the classroom, trying not to obsess about it. His Western Civ exam was on the same day, and he needed to change gears in a hurry. It wouldn't do any good to worry about the paper anyway, he thought. It was written and done—that ship had sailed. Besides, he thought it wasn't too bad. He just hoped the professor would agree with him. Or at the very least, not throw up on it.

Felix then took his Western Civ exam and followed that up with psychology the next day. Both exams went pretty well. Felix felt like maybe he was just getting the hang of it. This time around, he wasn't fooled by any of the questions, and he didn't run out of time. He also wasn't distracted by images of being burned alive as he lay in bed.

His last exam, Business and Economics, didn't go quite as smoothly. His professor, Professor Ishikawa, was painfully boring, and Felix didn't like the class to begin with. And even though he did his best to keep up with the class readings, he just couldn't force himself to be interested in the subject. There were four different sections on the exam. He struggled with two of them. He was slightly disgusted by his performance and swore he'd never take an econ class again.

He walked out of the Horace R. Manford Center of Economic Policy thinking he didn't really want to see his grade when Professor Ishikawa released it after spring break. But the sun was out for the first time in weeks. And even though it was a setting sun, it was still the sun. And the end of midterms marked the beginning of spring break. No more classes and no more studying for almost two weeks. Felix smiled. He stuck his small umbrella into his backpack and walked to Downey feeling as good as he had in a long while.

Chapter 17

When Felix got back to his room, Lucas was cracking open a Rainier and listening to a Hair Band song from the '80s blasting from a pair of speakers hooked up to his iPod. He gave Felix a little fist pump and handed him a beer. Caitlin and Allison knocked on the door a few minutes later. Lucas handed out more Rainiers from the apparently endless stash he kept in his closet. Caitlin took a quick gulp but was so excited to tell them about a huge party that everyone on campus was talking about that she forgot to swallow before speaking, and beer dribbled down her chin. She started to laugh at how ridiculous she must look, which caused the beer to go down the wrong pipe, resulting in a fit of coughing. Unable to get any information out of the gagging Caitlin, Felix resorted to texting Larry to find out if he'd heard anything about the party. Larry replied that he, Jonas, Salty, and the rest of the known universe would be at Astoria Hall within the hour.

They ordered pizza, drank Rainier, and listened to Lucas's iPod. Felix felt as if he were literally decompressing with each slice of pizza he ate and every tepid can of Rainier he drank. He knew that he should be worrying about more important things than school and exams, but he still felt enormously relieved to be done with his tests. He wasn't sure why he still cared so much about exams and grades, but he did. Maybe it was just ingrained, he wondered. He'd been taking exams for longer than he could remember. Or maybe it was because worrying about exams like everyone else just made him feel somewhat normal. And feeling normal was an increasingly elusive experience.

Celebrating the end of midterms was one of those times when

he could be just like everyone else. He didn't have to think about the horrible things he'd done. He didn't have to think about what it meant to be the Second Coming. Bill Stout and all of his apocalyptic ramblings could take a backseat. He didn't have to worry about killing the Antichrist or destroying Templar Amulets. He didn't have to worry about his fate. He was just Felix. He was a college freshman. And he was going to get drunk with his friends.

They inhaled pizza and chugged Rainier like they'd just been rescued from a deserted island and then left Downey for Astoria. Aside from Satler, Astoria was the closest dorm to Downey. It was also the largest of the six dorms on campus and housed every class year but freshman. As they approached Astoria's front steps, it looked more like the entrance to a nightclub than a dorm. This was obviously not going to be just another dorm room party.

Near the front doors were at least a dozen guys wearing red jackets with name tags pinned to their chests. Felix recognized three of them as Downey RAs. As soon as Felix and the others neared Astoria's entrance, one of them, Steve, according to his name tag, came over.

"Hey guys, can I see your student IDs?" he asked.

They pulled them out and Steve gave them a cursory look.

"I've seen you guys around Downey, but I have to check them anyway," he said.

"What's with the security and everything?" Lucas asked.

"The Student Union," Steve began, returning their IDs, "decided it'd be a good time to have a blowout party. The school's been doing this once a year since I've been here. With midterms over and the weather sucking ass for so long, Todd Siegrand thought it'd be a good time to have one. Anyway, basically, you're free to drink anywhere you want, hallways, living rooms, wherever.

"The kegs are in the cafeteria and a lot of rooms have drink stations if beer isn't your thing. There's hard liquor and stuff in there for mixed drinks or whatever. Only PC students are allowed. If you see any townies, let one of the RAs know. Before I forget, the school also wants us to tell you not to do anything stupid and to remember to drink responsibly."

"How awesome is this?" Lucas yelled as they made their way through the lobby and toward the cafeteria. The first-floor common area had been completely cleared of furniture and was transformed into a gigantic dance floor, complete with a deejay. There were dozens of students dancing around the deejay's equipment station, all with plastic cups in their hands. The cafeteria was also reconfigured; all of the tables and chairs were removed except for four long dining tables set up at one end of the room. On each of the four tables were four kegs. A giant banner stating the obvious announced KEG STATION in enormous, alternating green and orange letters on the wall behind the kegs. Plastic cups were stacked in teetering towers on each table, and RAs were filling them as fast as they could.

"I'm not good at math like Allison," Lucas said, "but I believe that four kegs multiplied by four tables equals sixteen kegs."

"You're underestimating your intelligence again," Caitlin said, smiling. "You're truly a mathematical genius."

Lucas laughed.

"I can't believe we didn't hear about this party until today," Felix shouted above the ear-splitting music blasting from the dance floor.

"I think it's because everyone will find out anyway. If they announced it earlier, it'd be more likely to get out of control," Allison yelled.

"I think it's already out of control," Caitlin shouted, laughing.

They waited in one of the beer lines for a few minutes and then took their foaming cups of beer to an unoccupied spot. They toasted the end of midterms, clicking their red cups together.

After getting their cups refilled, they bobbed and weaved their way through the throng of students until they found themselves again in the front lobby. By now it looked like the entire PC student body was packed into Astoria Hall.

They climbed up the main staircase to see what was happening on the upper floors.

The students were already getting out of control. They were chugging their drinks, dancing, and doing everything a little more frenetically than usual. Their festive mood was the result of a combination of factors. Exams had ended that day. They were also officially on spring break. But it was more than that. The school's loosening of its alcohol policy for the night had an interesting effect on their collective psyche. It was as if the students were prisoners and the warden had agreed to remove their shackles for just one night. The students were determined to take advantage of their newfound freedom.

Felix looked around and had the distinct impression that he was partying at someplace other than a PC dorm. It just didn't feel like a PC party. When they reached the second floor, Felix spotted Larry, Salty, Jonas, and Brant hanging out with a group of six girls dressed like they were out clubbing.

"Yo, Felix!" Larry yelled, even though Felix stood no more than three feet away. "And Lucas! Hey! What's going on, guys?"

"Hey, Larry," they replied in unison.

One of the club girls recognized Lucas from *Summer Slumming*. In an instant all the girls shifted their attention from Brant and the Sturgeons' offensive line to Lucas. Caitlin rolled her eyes after the girls insisted on getting their pictures taken with Lucas. Caitlin and Allison headed back to the first floor.

Several rounds of cheap vodka shots later, the girls decided they wanted to dance with Lucas and anyone who might be Lucas's friend. They inched their way down the crowded stairs until the lobby finally came into view. While Felix and Lucas were upstairs doing shots and flirting with girls infatuated with Lucas's celebrity, things had really gotten crazy. The dance floor had spilled over onto the lobby and into the hallways. Every square foot of space seemed to be occupied by at least four students. The music was pumping, and Felix's body vibrated with the pounding bass.

Lucas reached the lobby first, surrounded by his scantily clad posse, and yelled over his shoulder, "Dude, now this is a party!"

Felix was about to agree when Harper suddenly appeared. She was pushing her way through the crowded lobby and was coming right at him. She seemed to be crying. He didn't have time to get a good look—or even to react—before she turned and darted out the front door.

Without thinking, Felix spun around, pushed his way through the crowd, and ran out the door after her. He jumped down the stairs and sprinted ahead, looking in every direction. He found her standing under a large, leafless maple tree not far from the entrance to the dorm. She was wiping her eyes and trying to brush the hair out of her face.

"Hey there," Felix said, trying to sound casually cool, but to his ears not doing a very good job of it. "It's not actually raining tonight, you know? You don't need to stand under a tree." His attempt at humor seemed to fall flat. Harper didn't look up. She sobbed into her hands.

"Hey, I'm sorry," Felix said. "I saw you run out. I just wanted to make sure everything was okay. So…um…is everything okay?"

She wiped her eyes with her shirtsleeves and looked up at Felix. Her face was wet and streaked with tears. Felix felt an impossibly strong urge to reach out and comfort her. He wanted to take her in his arms and let her know everything was okay. Instead, he simply said, "What happened?"

"I don't know," she finally whimpered. "Maybe it's me. He does this every time. And I just let him do it."

"Who? Who are you talking about? Dante?" It was the first time Felix had said his name to Harper. It felt strange.

"Yes. He was…he was making out with some girl in the bathroom. I walked in with Caitlin, and he was like right there in front of me. I mean, what an asshole! Did he think nobody would notice a guy in the girls' bathroom? He's such an asshole. But he's always been an asshole. And you know what that makes me? It makes me an idiot for going back to him."

"You're not an idiot, Harper," Felix said gently. "You just trusted him. It's not your fault."

"I should've known," Harper said, shaking her head and sniffing. "He did this to me before, you know. He didn't just break up with me when he went away to college. He cheated on me a few times before he decided to end it. I only found out about it after the fact."

"He sounds like a douche bag."

"Felix, I don't..."

"No, listen to me, Harper. You could have any guy you want. You're smart and you're funny, and you're...you're...I mean, you're beautiful. You just are. That's a fact. I don't see how anyone could think...I mean. Look, I'll never understand how anyone could ever cheat on you. You deserve better."

"Felix...maybe...maybe you just don't know me. I always pick the wrong guy. I think I'm damaged goods or something. I always go for guys who treat me like shit. I'm so tired of that. I don't want that anymore."

"I know," Felix said, inching closer to her so that he could see her eyes.

They stood underneath the branches of the maple tree. He could hear voices behind them—the voices of students going in and out of Astoria Hall. But as he looked into Harper's amazing blue eyes, the voices seemed miles away. Felix felt like they were all alone.

"Felix...I...."

Felix put his hands on Harper's waist. It was small and tight. His heart was pounding, and he felt a little dizzy. He couldn't believe he was this close to her. Thank God he had those vodka shots. He felt like he could tell her almost anything. "Can I tell you something really cheesy?"

Harper nodded.

"There are times I look at you, and I think you're so beautiful I get tears in my eyes. And sometimes I have to literally catch my breath when I see you. I'm sorry. That probably sounded lame, didn't it? I'm not very good at telling people my feelings, or this romance stuff. I just…"

"Felix," Harper whispered, putting her finger on his lips. She looked into his eyes and then took a step closer to him. Felix couldn't quite feel her body next to his, but it was so close he could almost sense it in the darkness. Her eyes sparkled and he could smell her hair in the night air. She always smelled so good. He brushed a few strands of hair out of her eyes, and she smiled at him. She was so beautiful, he thought.

He reached his hands around her waist and pulled her body against his. His heart was pounding in his chest. Harper looked up at him, tilted her head, and they started to kiss. He gripped her body tightly against his—it was firm and her waist was small—and he felt her move against him. She began to moan softly.

"Felix! Felix! Felix!" a girl's voice screamed from somewhere behind them. "Felix! Felix!"

Harper jumped away from him, her eyes wide. "What was that? You hear that?"

Felix was lost in the moment. He stared back at Harper, not understanding what she was saying.

"Wha…" Felix started to say.

"Felix! Felix!" the girl continued to scream.

This time they both heard it.

"That's Caitlin!" Harper shouted.

"Come on!" Felix yelled. Taking Harper by the hand, he ran toward the entrance. Caitlin was on the top step. The students standing around the stoop talking and smoking cigarettes were staring at her, wondering why she was screaming "Felix" over and over.

"Felix, there you are!" she exclaimed, looking extremely frazzled.

"What's going on?" Felix asked, his head still spinning from what just happened under the tree.

"It's Allison—she needs your help!" Caitlin shouted, breathing heavily.

"What?" Felix shouted, confused.

"Just follow me! Come on!"

They fought through the crowd and pushed their way through the lobby and up the stairs to the second floor. When they reached the landing, they turned and ran down the hall until they were blocked by a wall of students standing in front of a doorway at the end of the corridor. Caitlin pushed her way through with Felix and Harper following close behind.

Finally managing to work their way through the doorway, they emerged into a large room that looked like a bigger version of Downey's common area. Several sofas, lounge chairs, and pool tables were all pushed against the walls, apparently in an effort to create as much open space as possible in the middle of the room.

It wasn't just the doorway that was crammed with students. They were everywhere. They had even climbed on top of the furniture and the pool tables to get a better view of whatever was happening in the center of the room.

Felix squeezed through a small opening in the crowd until he had a partial view of what everyone was watching. Although his view was partially obstructed, he could see Allison and Lucas standing shoulder to shoulder. And directly across from them was a cluster of people with a tall guy with long blond hair in its center. Allison was holding a red plastic cup and seemed to be yelling at someone. Felix couldn't see who she was yelling at.

Still holding Harper's hand, Felix roughly pushed aside the last few students standing between him and Allison and Lucas. With one last shove, he finally reached the center of the room.

Allison was yelling at Todd Siegrand. And standing next to Todd were Jimmy Clay and Gary Schimmel. Behind them were a group of Betas Felix had seen around but didn't know by name. They appeared to be very drunk and very angry. Todd was wearing a dark blue button-down shirt with a large stain directly in the center of his chest. He was now screaming at Allison, but Felix couldn't hear what he was saying through the din of the surrounding crowd. Jimmy Clay looked huge and imposing. Felix was struck by the size of his head, which, when combined with his lantern jaw and tight crew cut, gave him the look of a military commando.

"What's going on?" Felix shouted as he and Harper entered the fray.

Allison and Lucas turned around to see who was behind them. Allison was obviously infuriated. Her eyes were bulging and her jaw was clenched tightly. Lucas, on the other hand, didn't seem to be visibly upset by what was going on.

"Well, if it isn't the rest of the children," Todd said coolly. "It's funny how we keep meeting like this. I wonder if it's because you can't handle your alcohol or if it's simply because you're a bunch of fucking retards."

Allison turned back to face Todd. "Why don't you go take a flying fuck off the top of your stupid fucking…"

"And if you want to know what happened," Todd said, interrupting Allison, "your little girlfriend here decided to throw a cup of beer on me." He touched the wet area on the front of his shirt.

"Is that right?" Allison yelled at Todd. "Do you think that was maybe because you called me a *dirty fucking whore?*"

The crowd drew closer to the middle of the room as everyone tried to get a better look at the altercation brewing between the president of the Student Union and a group of freshmen. Most were drinking beer and harder alcoholic concoctions out of plastic cups.

"Is that what you said?" Lucas yelled. "Where do you get off calling my friend a dirty fucking whore?"

"Oh, I'm sorry," Todd said mockingly. "Did I hurt your feelings, too? Well, now it appears you have *two* boyfriends who want to protect you. That's really cute! It also proves that you really are a dirty fucking whore!"

"Is that right?" Allison said as she grabbed a plastic cup from a nearby student. "Then I guess I'll admit to throwing beer on you." She threw the contents of the nearly full cup at Todd. It was a perfect shot. It hit him directly in the face and splashed onto Jimmy and Gary and the Betas behind them.

Todd appeared momentarily shocked. He wiped the beer from his face, which was now a picture of disbelief and rage. "You fucking bitch!" he screamed as he moved toward Allison.

Felix let go of Harper's hand and stepped in front of Allison.

"What are you gonna do?" Felix said coldly, looking down at Todd, who was several inches shorter. "You gonna take a swing at a girl?"

"Get out of my way!" Todd snarled.

Lucas moved forward and stopped next to Felix, forming a shield in front of Allison. "Bring it on, asshole!" he yelled. "Give me an excuse to fuck you up!"

Jimmy pushed aside two students who got too close to the action as he, Gary, and the other Betas charged past Todd to get to Felix and Lucas. The two students hit the floor hard, spilling their drinks and rolling into the legs of other onlookers, causing them to tumble to the floor like dominos.

"That's enough!" someone yelled from near the door. "Okay everybody, break it up!" The crowd parted like Moses at the Red Sea as someone wearing a red jacket emerged through the crowd. Felix didn't know him. His name tag identified him as *Eric—Resident Director.*

"What's going on?" Eric shouted as he reached the center of the room.

"Hello, Eric," Todd said in a tightly controlled voice. "Nothing is going on. We were just having a conversation when a beer was inadvertently spilled on me."

When Eric realized that it was the president of the Student Union addressing him, he seemed to become nervous. "Oh. Hello, Todd. Yes…well, then. Okay. But I suggest that you and your friends should probably be on your way," he said, pointing at Allison. "And everybody else, please leave the room and go back downstairs! Thank you."

"We were just leaving anyway," Lucas said.

The large crowd grumbled in unison, apparently disappointed that the RD had thwarted what could have been an extremely entertaining fracas. With the excitement over, everyone quickly dispersed into the hallway.

As Felix and his friends turned to leave the room, Todd said, "I'm looking forward to our next meeting. I always have so much fun with these little encounters."

"And I look forward to the day you're not such a fucking douche bag," Felix yelled over his shoulder.

"I'd be very careful the next time you come out of the bathroom, little man," said a voice from behind. It was low and full of malice.

Felix recognized it. It was Jimmy Clay's.

Chapter 18

They left the dorm through a side door on the first floor. They walked at a fast clip and didn't say a word. Once they put a bit of distance between themselves and Astoria, they stopped on one of the footpaths leading to Downey.

Suddenly, and without warning, Allison lifted her face to the night sky and let out a loud shriek. Then she laughed and jumped up and down.

"I can't believe I just did that! I just threw two beers on the president of the Student Union! Oh my God! I can't believe I just did that! I should probably get my transcripts together, right? I'm definitely gonna need to transfer schools after that!"

Everyone started laughing. They were high on adrenaline. They were also pretty drunk.

Allison recapped what they missed: Todd went out of his way to bump into her. After she told him to watch where he was going, he made the "dirty fucking whore" comment. "I just reacted before I had time to think," she said excitedly. "I just threw my beer at him. I don't know why I did it."

"I know why," Lucas said, smiling from ear to ear. "He's an asshole, and he called you a dirty fucking whore. He deserved it!"

Allison laughed. "Yeah, he did, didn't he?" She then looked at Felix and her face was serious. "Felix, thank you. Thanks for doing what you did. For a minute there I thought Todd was going to…I guess, I don't know what he was going to do. But I was scared. Thanks for stepping in." She gave him a quick hug.

And then she turned to Lucas. "And you, Lucas. You were there the whole time. You had my back. I don't know what would've happened if you weren't there." She hugged him tightly.

"You're gonna make me blush, you know," Lucas said, laughing.

"I don't know about you guys, but I'm freaking out a little bit," Caitlin said, sounding nervous. "I've never done anything like that before. It was kind of exciting, though. But I think we should head back to the dorm, just in case Todd and his GI Joe look-alike cronies are out searching for us."

"That's probably a good idea," Allison said. They started walking again down the path to Downey.

Felix was standing next to Harper. As the group started to walk away, he leaned in toward her and whispered, "Hey, can I talk to you for a minute?"

"Okay," she said and turned toward him.

"I just wanted to...to tell you...to tell you that what happened earlier. You know. Under the tree. That I meant everything I said. I meant every wo..."

"Felix, I like you," Harper interrupted. "Believe me. I really like you. But this just isn't going to work."

Felix was stunned. What did she just say? Did he hear that right? He couldn't have just heard her say that. "What? Why not?" he croaked. "I don't understand. Why won't it..."

"Because you're split into too many pieces."

"Split into pieces?"

"It's complicated, Felix. I don't think even you know how...what's the right word...how fragmented you are."

"I don't know what you're talking about," Felix said, sounding desperate. "I'm not fragmented. I'm not split into pieces. It's just me and you. And I like you. Isn't it as simple as that?"

"It's never that simple. And it's not just me, Felix. I want to believe you, but I know there's someone else."

"Someone else?" Felix said, astonished. "Who? There's nobody else."

"Felix, don't you see it? It's Allison. Allison."

"*Allison?* What are you talking about? We're just friends."

"I know she spent the night with you," she said accusingly. "Right after the semester started and you didn't come back to school, remember? She went to go find you, and she didn't text Caitlin until three in the morning. And then you guys didn't come back to school until the next day."

"Harper, that's crazy! We're just friends. She stayed at my grandma's house with me, but we didn't do anything. We're just friends. We talked all night."

"And what did you tell her?"

"What did I tell her?" Felix asked, suddenly feeling like he was being interrogated.

"I assume you told her something. You talked all night, right? Isn't that what you just said? Besides, one day you're not coming back to school, and the next day after you talk to Allison you're on your way back, right? So whatever you said, it must have been pretty important. So what was it?"

"I don't know," Felix said tentatively. "Lots of things, I guess."

"Like what, Felix?" Harper said, her face getting red. "Did you share your private feelings with her? Did you tell her what was wrong? Why you didn't want to come back to school in the first place?"

"I...I guess...I don't know."

"Then why can't you share those things with me? I don't care if you guys stayed in the same place that night. I believe you that you're just friends. But she's the one you talk to when you're having a problem. Not me."

"But it's not like that. I didn't mean to..."

"That's what I meant when I said you're fragmented. It's like there are these pieces of you that you're hiding from the world, and the only girl you can share them with is Allison. I don't know what secrets you're hiding, but I'm not going to play second string for any guy. Not even you. Not anymore." Tears started to roll down her cheeks, and she wiped at them quickly with her hand.

"There's so much I want to tell you. I just don't know if…"

"If you can trust me? Is that it?" she said angrily.

"I do trust you! I swear!"

"Then let me into your life. Tell me the things you told Allison. What are you afraid of?"

"I want to tell you. I really do. It's just that I…"

"You can't? Is that it? You can't?"

Felix said nothing.

Harper's face was streaked with tears. "At least with a guy like Dante, I get everything—even if he is an asshole. But with you, all I'd ever get is a piece. And that just isn't enough." Harper turned her back and walked away.

Felix stood and watched her until she disappeared behind an old oak tree whose branches stretched across the footpath.

Chapter 19

When Felix's alarm clock went off the next morning, the events of the previous night flashed through his mind like a DVD on fast-forward. His head was pounding. He wanted to forget about everything and just drift back into a nice peaceful sleep. As he reached for the snooze button, he remembered why his alarm was making that god awful noise. He staggered out of bed, cursing at himself for agreeing to meet Bill at nine o'clock.

Lucas had to catch an early flight home to Minneapolis, and he was already awake, tossing wadded-up clothes into a duffel bag. Lucas looked as hungover as Felix felt. They had a quick breakfast in the cafeteria and then went up to the third floor to say goodbye to the girls. Caitlin and Allison were busily packing their bags. Caitlin was going to Mexico with Harper, where they'd be spending spring break with their families. Allison's mom was picking her up at ten. Allison didn't have enough money to spend spring break in Mexico. Exotic vacations weren't in her budget.

Caitlin promised to come back to school with a ridiculous tan. Lucas asked her about Harper. She shrugged and said she hadn't left her room. Felix thought about knocking on her door. But what would he say? Have a nice spring break? After she just dumped him after the shortest relationship in history?

They hugged, said their goodbyes, and then went their separate ways.

Felix left Downey dressed accordingly, whatever the hell that meant. If jeans, a sweatshirt, a light jacket, and a pair of old sneakers didn't fall within Bill's outdoor dress code, then he could take it up with the outdoor dress code authorities. It was a cold morning, but the sky was clear. Felix overheard someone at breakfast talking about how it was supposed to be a nice day. So far, they were right. He entered the Stamford Building and galloped up the stairs to the third floor with his head still throbbing. He should've taken some Advil, but he didn't, feeling like he deserved to be in pain after what happened last night. Bill's door was open. Felix stuck his head in and said hello.

"Come in. I'm just packing up a few things for our excursion."

Felix stepped into the office. Bill was zipping up a backpack.

"Should I have brought something?" Felix asked. "I didn't know we were..."

"You're fine. I'm just bringing some water and a few maps."

"Maps of what?" Felix asked, suddenly curious. "Where are we going?"

"I'll tell you everything in the car. Let's get going."

They walked across the Courtyard, eating up huge chunks of real estate with their long strides, and past the Woodrow Library to the school's main parking lot in the northeast corner of campus. They stopped when they came to a dark green Range Rover. After climbing into the car, Bill backed up and steered toward Bryant Street.

"This is a sweet car," Felix said, admiring the interior and the sound system. "Not bad for an assistant groundskeeper."

Bill laughed and took a right turn from the parking lot onto Bryant Street, heading south. "Thanks. I prefer sports cars, but we'll have to leave my M3 in the garage today. Where we're going, it wouldn't do us much good."

"I'm hungover and Harper dumped me last night after a thirty-second relationship. Could you please just tell me where we're going?"

"Sounds like a serious college romance," Bill said, laughing. "That brings back some fond memories. We're going to my house. It's on Willow Street just off of Eleventh. It's about a mile and a half from the main parking lot and not quite a mile from the football stadium."

They drove down Bryant Street past the Old Campus and Walter Stubbins Stadium, and then turned left on Eleventh. Three blocks later they took another left turn onto Willow Street. The neighborhood was entirely residential with comfortable homes set back behind wide sidewalks running parallel to the streets. Large oaks lined the sidewalks, their branches extending out over the street, blocking out much of the sunlight, but creating a quaint feeling that aspiring home-owners tended to fall in love with. The two-story colonials were very un-McMansion-like, having been built in the 1920s and 1930s. The homes blended in perfectly with their surroundings. Bill stopped the car on the corner of Eleventh and Willow.

"Felix, you see the house there?" he said, pointing at a white colonial-style home that looked to be one of the larger ones in the neighborhood. "That's mine. The address is one forty-six Willow Street. If you ever need to come here, go through the side gate to the left of the front door and go around back. The patio door's always open, and you can let yourself in, okay?"

"Okay. But why are we here?"

"Because there may be a time when you need to go somewhere other than your dorm. This house is close to campus and it's easy to find. But if you're directionally challenged, this will help." He reached into his pocket and pulled out a cell phone. "This is for you."

"I already have a cell."

Bill smiled. "Of course you do. Every kid over the age of three has their own cell. But this one contains certain information that yours doesn't."

"Like what?" Felix asked, curious again about what Bill was up to.

Bill pushed a few buttons on the phone, activating the touch screen. "First, it has a GPS application..."

"So does mine, and mine..."

"Felix, shut up for a second."

Felix sighed and crossed his arms.

"I had to play around with the app," Bill continued, "but I managed to input the location of the underground facility. The building where the First Templar Amulet is located."

Felix nearly jumped out of his seat. "What? You know where it is?"

"I'm still not one hundred percent certain," Bill said, cautioning with his hand for Felix to relax. "And I don't think I ever will be."

"Okay. So how sure are you?"

"If you're asking me for a percentage, I'd say I'm eighty percent certain."

Felix chewed on his finger nervously. "I assume we're gonna wait until you're more certain, right? Like one hundred percent certain?"

Bill shook his head, frowning. "I'll never be absolutely certain of the location. We won't really know until you're actually inside the building. But I am reasonably confident I know where it is."

"It sounds a little dicey." Felix chewed on a fingernail and watched a minivan full of kids drive by.

"I know. Once you gain access to the building, if the Amulet isn't there, all you can do is get the hell out as fast as you can."

"But if it's the wrong place," Felix said, trying to work through the implications in his head, "would I have time to get to the other places where it might be?"

"No," Bill replied, shaking his head. "The two other possibilities— the other underground facilities where it might be—are nearly ten miles from the one you're targeting. The logging roads have completely different access points. It just isn't feasible."

"It sounds like we've got one chance at this."

"Yes," Bill said.

"So when are we doing this?"

"The last week of April."

"The last week of April?" Felix shouted. "No way! That's just a month from now!"

Bill nodded. "We don't have much time to prepare."

He had to be joking, Felix thought. He wasn't ready for this. That was way too soon. Bill needed to take a step back and reevaluate the situation.

"Why so soon?" Felix asked. "Why can't we wait until I'm able to break locks and all that other shit you've dragged into the old library? Maybe by then you'll get some more information. You'll be more than reasonably confident about the location."

Bill sighed. "I haven't made this decision lightly. We need to strike as soon as the opportunity presents itself, right?"

"Sure," Felix answered, not feeling convinced at all by Bill's logic.

"I recently found out from someone at A.E.I. that Landry will be in Egypt the last week of April. I told you I wouldn't send you into Ardsley Forest unless Landry was far from here. His trip to Egypt is exactly what we needed. I know there isn't much time left, but sometimes circumstances dictate timetables. We either act now, or we run the risk of never having another opportunity."

Felix chewed on his thumbnail and looked nervously out the window as two robins fought over a worm, tearing it into pieces and gobbling it down. That's probably what Landry would do to him. He took a deep breath. "Okay, I guess. I definitely don't want to be anywhere near Ardsley Forest if Landry's around. It's just that…there's just so little time. I'm not ready."

"I'm asking a lot of you," Bill said gently. "I know that. But we still have time. Not much, but just enough to prepare you."

"Okay," Felix said, sounding braver than he actually felt. "If you say so. So what are we doing now? Are we going into your house?"

"No. Now we're going to have a look at the underground facility you'll be breaking into next month."

"We are?" Felix exclaimed. "Right now?"

"Yes," Bill said, grinning at Felix's reaction. "That's why I asked you to come prepared for a day in the outdoors."

"Do you know how to get there?"

"How else do you think I entered the location into the GPS?"

"I don't know." Felix felt very discombobulated. "I didn't think about it."

Bill shook his head disapprovingly. "I've been there on multiple occasions, and I've taken a few different routes—including one requiring a very long hike through the woods. It wasn't until my second trip there that I found the old logging roads I was looking for. The Forest Service maps are reliable, but some of the roads have simply disappeared. The forest has swallowed them up. The roads will take us to a spot within a short hike of the facility. There are some larger roads in the forest—former logging roads that have been expanded by A.E.I. to operate the facilities. They're used to shuttle employees, maintain the buildings, and the like. We'll obviously need to stay off those. We don't want to bump into anyone from A.E.I. And all of those roads are monitored."

"And the roads we're using aren't monitored?"

"No. They're basically abandoned. They haven't been kept up in decades, so they're in terrible condition. It makes for a pretty bumpy ride, which is why we're taking the Range Rover. But you'll see for yourself when we get there."

They sat in silence. Felix tried to collect his thoughts. He couldn't believe they were actually taking steps to break into some subterranean bunker in Ardsley Forest. Didn't they just discuss it for the first time like yesterday? And now he was sitting in Bill's swanky SUV about to drive into Ardsley Forest to scout the actual place where Landry was making Vessels. He thought it felt real when they first discussed the plan. Now it really felt real. Like there was no turning back.

"Okay," Felix finally said, trying to suppress his anxiety. "Let me get this straight. So we're going to use logging roads that aren't used by anyone. And the directions are in the GPS. All I have to do is follow the GPS. It will take me on the right roads, right? I don't wanna get lost in Ardsley Forest. There's a lot of weird shit going on out there, you know? Like people getting killed and having their heads removed."

"You'll be fine. And don't worry about that," Bill said dismissively. "I haven't seen anything suspicious in the woods lately."

Felix said nothing. He thought people getting slaughtered in the woods was a legitimate cause of concern. He didn't give a shit that Bill kept telling him not to worry about it.

"Keep in mind," Bill continued, "that the roads won't lead right up to the front of the facility. There's no parking lot, you know. It will take you to a secluded area roughly a quarter mile from the facility. From there, you'll have to hike through some pretty dense woods. But don't worry, once you know what landmarks to look for, it's easy enough to find. I'll show you how."

"Okay," Felix said, trying to get his heart rate to slow down.

"All right then. Let's get going." Bill put the car in drive and they began to move. "I don't imagine you've ever been to A.E.I.'s headquarters?"

"No. I just know it's way on the other side of town."

Bill nodded. "It's about a thirty-five-mile drive due east. The route we'll take is the same one I use to get to work. But rather than going in through the front gate, we'll drive several miles past it to the south. Then we'll circle back around to where we can access the logging roads."

"I've been downtown a hundred times," Felix said, chewing on a different fingernail. "But I haven't been anywhere near Ardsley Forest."

"You wouldn't have any reason to unless you worked for the company. There are still people who hike and camp in the woods and a few hunters, but maybe not so much anymore with the recent incidents there. It's private property, but that doesn't deter people who've been camping and hunting there for generations. Anyway, I'll leave the GPS off until we get closer. We're taking main roads. Try to remember the street names. We'll head north for several miles before we turn east.

We'll avoid downtown. Once we cross the Willamette River, we'll continue east until we hit Hermann Boulevard. Hermann runs north to south and parallels Ardsley Forest. The forest is shaped basically like a rectangle—it runs ten miles along Hermann and goes back twenty miles to the east."

Felix tried to commit to memory everything Bill was saying. He looked out the window as they drove away from campus, headed north past a residential neighborhood and into an area that was mainly industrial with a sprinkling of small mom-and-pop shops. Felix made mental notes of the street names and surrounding landmarks. He tried not to think about what it'd be like in a month, when he'd be making the trip alone. They drove in silence for several minutes and then headed east. Crossing the Willamette River, Felix could see downtown Portland in the distance, the tall buildings reflecting sunlight into the clear blue sky above.

Ten minutes later they came to the exit for Hermann Boulevard. Bill steered the car onto the exit and they headed south.

"Does the street name sound familiar?" Bill asked.

Felix thought for a moment. "No! It can't be. It's not named after Landry's grandfather, is it?"

"It is."

"But why would there be a road named after his grandfather? I mean, Landry kills the guy and then names a road after him?"

Bill rubbed his chin. "I'm only speculating, but perhaps he's grateful to his grandfather for bringing him into the world. Without Hermann, Landry wouldn't exist."

"That's still screwed up if you ask me."

"I agree," Bill said, nodding.

"Here's the entrance to A.E.I. headquarters off to our left," he said several minutes later, checking his rearview mirror for cars behind them and then slowing down.

Flanking the four-lane road were enormous signs carved into

granite supported by two thick columns. The signs said *Ashfield Enterprises Incorporated* in large letters. And towering above the tree line in the distance were five pyramids reflecting sunlight like enormous diamonds.

"Oh my God!" Felix exclaimed. "The buildings are shaped like pyramids?"

"Yes, Landry's very interested in Egypt. There's actually a pyramid on each of the five buildings. There are four buildings which form a square, and the fifth building sits in the square's center. The central building is taller than the other four, and the pyramid on top of it is also taller than the others. Landry's wing is on the top floor of the center building."

Felix craned his neck to see the buildings as they continued driving south on Hermann Boulevard. "Wow!" he exclaimed. "That's pretty impressive. The road we just passed with the huge signs, that's Ashfield Way, right?"

"Yes, that's the only way into or out of A.E.I. At least as far as everyone else is concerned."

Two miles later, Bill slowed the car and said, "Okay, here it is. This is Easton Street. Are you remembering all this?"

Felix nodded.

Bill turned the car left onto a narrow two-way street and then pulled it off to the side and stopped. He inserted the cell phone into a small plastic holder fastened to the windshield by a suction cup. He turned on the phone and scrolled down to the GPS application as Felix watched. He tapped the screen and waited for the application to download.

"Okay," Bill said a moment later. "There's only one address in the cell."

"Location A?" Felix said, reading from the screen.

"Yes." Bill tapped the screen. "I'm going to mute the volume. Now, I want you to check out your surroundings very carefully. You'll need

RANDALL LOWE

to rely on the GPS, but you should have a general idea of where you are."

They started to drive again. "This is mainly farmland out here," Bill said, gesturing with his hand. "There are still a few working dairy farms, but they're mainly grazing fields for cattle."

The road was paved but bumpy. There were vast fields of tall grass on either side, and Felix could see herds of cattle in the distance. Most were brown and white, but some were solid black. After several minutes they came to another road.

Bill slowed down. "This is the first subdivision off Easton Street. In the late eighties a rancher sold his land to a developer with aspirations of building subdivisions. If we turned left here you'd see a street that goes down for a half mile or so. At the end of it there'd be a cul-de-sac.

"The developer planned to build houses. But before he could even get started, the economy collapsed and he couldn't get the financing to start construction. There are four of these subdivisions on Easton. Not a single house was ever built. We'll be taking the third one."

Bill accelerated and continued down Easton. They passed another subdivision and then soon came to a third. There was a sign at the entrance which said Pine Street.

"Here it is," Bill said, turning the car into the subdivision. "Be sure to keep your eye on the GPS, but don't forget to look around, too."

They drove slowly down the deserted street. Felix looked out the window, but other than the pavement there wasn't much to see. The road itself was cracked in several places, and weeds had worked their way through fissures in the pavement. Rusty-looking steel stakes were driven into the ground in a few places. Some had fluttering orange ribbons attached to them, marking the lots for houses that would never be built.

If the land had ever been cleared of grass and weeds, it was no longer evident. What were once new home sites were now fields of thick, well-cultivated weeds and saplings. There was something strangely disconcerting about the empty subdivision. Felix was reminded of his first trip to the Old Campus.

They drove over a ridge and descended down a gradual hill. Ahead, Felix could see the cul-de-sac bordered by a grassy pasture. Beyond that, looming in the distance was Ardsley Forest. Bill drove toward the middle of the cul-de-sac and then suddenly accelerated, shifted into four-wheel drive, and jumped over the curb.

"Whoa!" Felix yelled in surprise as the Range Rover caught air and tore through the field. "You could've warned me, you know? I told you about my hangover, right?"

"That's the end of the paved roads," Bill replied, ignoring Felix's complaints. "Don't forget to keep your eye on the GPS. You'll need to be able do this alone. We're driving over what used to be a cattle pasture. Other than a few irrigation ditches, it's relatively smooth." The Range Rover bounced into the air. Felix nearly hit his head on the car's headliner.

"That must have been an irrigation ditch," Felix said sarcastically.

Bill smiled. "This field goes on for about a quarter of a mile. At the end we'll run right into the logging road. The GPS will lead us in the right direction. But to help guide you, I've tied a red ribbon three feet off the ground on a tree that lines up with the left side of the dirt road. It's only visible if you're out here in the field, and I wouldn't expect anyone else to be here."

They bumped along through the field and then Bill pointed. "There! See it?"

Felix looked in the direction Bill was pointing, but couldn't see any ribbon.

Bill slowed the car until it was nearly stopped.

"You're looking too high," Bill said. "It's only a few feet off the ground." Felix lowered his line of sight. "Ah!" he shouted. "Got it!"

"Good. Now look at the GPS to make sure you know which way it's directing us. Do you have it?"

"Yeah. I see it. I'm good."

"Now, the start of that tree line there is the very edge of Ardsley Forest. It marks the border between the forest and this field, which currently belongs to a bank that'll never be able to sell it. Once we enter the forest, we're on land that is owned by Landry. Laws and rules will cease to exist. If you're in danger, you'll need to protect yourself. There's no calling nine-one-one out here. If you see anyone in the forest, you should assume they'll try to kill you."

Chapter 20

Bill powered the Range Rover into the forest. Everything suddenly grew dark, as if they'd just entered a tunnel. Felix looked all around. Only a small penetration of sunlight filtered into the thick woods through the treetops. There seemed to be nothing but trees in every direction. Felix couldn't see the road. It seemed that Bill was just turning the car to avoid trees like a skier flying down the mountainside on an advanced slope.

Felix glanced at the GPS. He saw that Bill was doing the same. Eventually, Felix began to make out the shape of the road. It was packed earth, overgrown with vegetation and covered by fallen branches. Once he knew what to look for, it jumped out at him like one of those picture within a picture images he played with as a kid. The road seemed too narrow for the Range Rover, and Felix wondered how something as big as a logging truck could possibly navigate the road.

"It's so damn dark," he said, looking around.

"Not much light gets to the forest floor," Bill replied, concentrating on the road. "There are a dozen different varieties of trees, but most are Douglas firs. They're among the biggest trees in the world. Some are nearly four hundred feet tall and nine feet in diameter. You wouldn't want to wrap the car around one of those. This is by far the densest forest I've ever been in, and I've been everywhere. My father used to take me hiking in the Canadian Rockies, and that terrain has nothing on this. Are you keeping your eye on the GPS?"

"Yeah. It's pretty easy to follow, actually. But couldn't I just follow the road? It looks like it's the only bare spot out here."

"You could, but you'd get lost. This isn't the only logging road in the forest. There are literally hundreds of roads going in every direction. If you got on the wrong one, I don't know how you'd ever get back. I programmed the GPS for this one specific route. If you get off course you'll have to backtrack. Otherwise I don't know where you might end up. You could spend a week trying to get back to civilization. You wouldn't want that to happen."

"Got it. I'll stick with the GPS. So how far is it to the facility?"

"From where I tied that red ribbon to the tree it's about two and a half miles. Then we'll need to walk another quarter mile or so. I'm sure you've noticed that the road is anything but straight. We started out north and then went east. Then we circled around back to the west. We're now going to continue west for a bit and then it'll take us in a northwesterly direction. Then we'll take a sharp turn and go southwest. And then another sharp turn that'll take us northeast. Once we stop, we'll walk due north."

"Could that be any more confusing?" Felix said and sighed.

"Just follow the GPS. I couldn't tie ribbons to all these trees along the road without running the risk of somebody noticing."

Bill navigated the car expertly along the narrow dirt track. Felix bounced around in the passenger seat as they continued along the bumpy road. Tree branches blanketed the road, some as thick and as long as the smaller trees.

The road abruptly came to an end.

"This is the first sharp turn," Bill said, turning the steering wheel counterclockwise. "The GPS is telling us to turn to the left. You're following this, right?"

"Yeah, but there's also a road to the right."

"I told you there are logging roads crisscrossing the entire forest. That's one of them." Bill turned sharply to the left and continued down the road.

They came to another dead end a few minutes later. One moment there was a narrow but clear path between the tall trees, and the next, there was nothing but dense forest in front of them. Felix looked at the GPS. It was directing them to the right.

"And this is the second sharp turn," Bill said. "Once we turn here we'll head northeast for exactly six-tenths of a mile. At that mark we'll stop the car and get out. Keep your eye on the odometer if you need another reference point."

"Okay. Hey, Bill," Felix said, feeling anxious, "how far are we from A.E.I.'s headquarters?"

Bill thought for a moment. "In a direct line I'd estimate the facility is roughly three miles from company headquarters."

Felix groaned. "That's it? I could run that in less than twenty minutes."

"Not in these woods, you couldn't. But look, nobody's going to be running anywhere. If Landry and his Vessels want to get to the facility, they'd take the regular roads. I imagine they could be there in less than ten minutes."

"Shit! Is that all? It'd be nice if it took a little longer than…"

"Which is why," Bill interrupted, "you won't be coming here until Landry is on his way to Egypt."

"Right. But what about now?" Felix asked, feeling slightly panicked. "Where's the Antichrist now?"

Bill didn't respond.

"Bill! He's here, right?"

Bill sighed softly. "I believe he is. But you're not breaking into the facility this time. I'm just showing you where it is. We'll have a quick look. I'll show you how to find the door. Nobody uses these roads. If we see any activity at the facility, we'll turn around and get out before anybody's the wiser. It's a calculated risk, but we don't have a choice. I couldn't just give you the directions and expect you to find it."

The thought of Landry being only ten minutes away made Felix nervous. What could he possibly do if they were spotted at the facility? he wondered. There was nothing he could do. How could he defend himself? He couldn't. Landry would kill him and that would be the end of it. He'd die in Ardsley Forest and nobody would ever know what happened to him. Landry would simply make him disappear. Maybe his face would end up on a milk carton or he'd be on some TV show about missing teenagers.

Bill seemed to sense Felix's anxiety. "We'll be fine. We're not in any immediate danger. I've taken precautions."

Before Felix could respond, Bill braked the SUV to a stop.

"Okay, that's six-tenths of a mile from that last turn. Do you see that large rock between those two trees?" He pointed toward the front of the car. "That's our starting point for the hike. From that rock it's almost exactly a five-minute walk to the facility."

Felix followed Bill's finger and saw the moss-covered rock at once. It jutted out of the ground through the thick underbrush to a height of about five feet from the forest floor. Bill got out of the car, walked to the back, and opened the trunk. Felix got out and joined Bill at the back of the SUV just as Bill removed an enormous gun from a hidden compartment beneath the carpet.

"What the hell is that?" Felix asked, surprised.

"It's an Auto Assault AA-twelve twelve-gauge shotgun with a twenty-round drum," Bill replied like a military grunt. "Don't ask me how I got it and never tell anyone that I have it. It was developed for military use, and its possession is illegal for civilians. Don't worry. I'm a damn good shot with this thing. It's kind of hard to miss with it, actually."

"What do you need that for? Oh. It's Nick Blair, right? That's what it is! You think the Mormon Mephistopheles is here!"

"Nick Blair isn't here. And there are no other psychopaths in these woods, Felix," Bill replied, shaking his head. "They've moved on. I'm very, very confident of that. But I'd rather have it with me just in case we come across something."

"Like what? What the hell? You think maybe Vessels? But if there's Vessels, Landry would know 'cause everything they know he knows!"

"If we see anybody, we'll deal with it," Bill said matter-of-factly as he walked over to the rock in front of the car and stopped beside it.

"Are you going to elaborate on that or are you just gonna be an asshole?" Felix asked, not moving.

"Look, we won't see anyone out here. But if we do come across someone, I'd prefer to have this with me," he said, pointing at the immense shotgun cradled in his arms. "And if we come across Nick Blair or some other goddamn psychopath, I intend to blow him to pieces before he gets near us. It's just a precautionary measure. Don't worry."

"Yeah," Felix replied sarcastically as he shook his head. "Definitely nothing to worry about out here in Ardsley Forest. Lovely spot for a picnic, don't you think?"

Bill smiled. "Okay, from now on no talking unless it's in a whisper. And try not to break any branches. Just stay close and follow right behind me. At about the halfway point, there's another rock, similar in size to this one. That'll be the other marker. Pay close attention to everything and remember the path. Okay, let's go. Oh, if you see me raise the barrel of the gun, don't step in front of it unless you want to have a basketball-sized hole in your body."

Bill started walking. Felix followed close behind. The forest floor was uneven and covered in pine needles, rocks, and branches. Felix did his best to avoid stepping on the branches, but they completely covered the ground and were hidden under tree debris, pine needles, and moss. A few minutes into their hike, he stepped on a large, dry branch. The loud snapping sound it made seemed to echo throughout the forest. Felix cringed and shook his head, angry at himself. Bill turned to Felix with his index finger on his lips. Felix mouthed "sorry" and they continued on.

Felix could see that Bill was trying to walk in a straight line. But they were forced to walk around some of the larger Douglas firs and groups of trees that were so tightly packed together there was no way to walk between them. Felix had never seen trees like these. He'd gone on camping trips with his dad, but they never went places where the trees were so tall a person had to practically lie on their back to see the tops. A few minutes later, they came to another large rock. It must have been the one Bill was describing earlier, because he stopped.

"Okay," Bill whispered, once Felix caught up. He covered his mouth with his hand as he spoke. "We're at about the halfway point. We'll keep walking in the same direction for another two minutes or so. Then we'll stop, okay? Remember, it's a straight line from where we parked the car. It's due north, all right?"

Felix nodded. The trees were just as gargantuan here, but were less densely packed together. Oddly, hundreds of trees were knocked over. Most were lying on the forest floor, but several were propped up precariously by still-standing trees. Felix thought about what would happen if one toppled over while he was under it. He shuddered. They clambered over the fallen trees. Dirty strands of moss and bark got caught under Felix's fingernails.

Felix stopped and looked around the woods. If someone was hiding behind a tree, he'd have no way of knowing. A football team could practically conceal itself behind one of those things. He stopped and listened for sounds, but he heard nothing—not even birds or chipmunks.

He followed Bill around a clump of trees that required them to veer off from their straight-line course. Bill suddenly stopped, holding up his hand. Felix stopped in his tracks. He strained his eyes to see through the trees. What was Bill looking at? He couldn't hear anything. The forest was still eerily silent.

Bill turned toward Felix and motioned for him to move forward.

"I thought I saw something," Bill whispered. "I think it was just a deer. There are deer, elk, and even some bear in these woods. Don't be shocked if you encounter a large animal out here."

Bill started walking again, but less than a minute later he stopped behind a gigantic Douglas fir tree. Felix stopped beside him. There was a clearing before them about the size of a football field. Felix looked at it. A large portion of the clearing seemed to be raised, like an enormous mound of soil was spread across the ground. The mound was overgrown with weeds, grass, branches, and pine needles.

"Do you see it?" Bill whispered.

"You mean the big bump out there?"

"Yes. We're standing at about the midpoint of the underground facility. If you look closely you can see where it begins and ends."

"Where it slopes down on the edges, you mean?" Felix asked.

"Yes, those are the outside walls. It's difficult to tell what the width of it is from this vantage point, but I've walked around to the other side to get a better view. It's rectangular. The width is about half the length."

"I can't believe how big it is. It's gotta be huge."

"It is. Look at the far left side. Do you see where the mound slopes down there?"

"Yeah. Is that the..."

"That's the access point," Bill said.

"But I don't see how...where's the door exactly?"

"It's underground, remember? There must be stairs leading down to it. I think they're outside the building, but I didn't get close enough to see them. I couldn't risk being seen by anyone using the road on the north side—the side opposite of where we are now."

"You're sure the door is on that side?" Felix asked, pointing.

"As sure as I can be. The next time you're here, if the door isn't there, you'll need to circle around the building to find it. But we can't check it out now. We'd be spotted by anyone using the road."

Felix stared at the entire expanse of the clearing and the long mound of earth in front of him. He thought of what was below ground. And what Landry was doing there.

"That'll be the direction you'll go," Bill said, pointing to the side with the sharply sloped walls. "As much as you can, stay behind the tree line. I realize the trees thin out the closer you get to the perimeter of the clearing. But utilize what cover you have, okay?"

"Sure," Felix said, staring at the large trees in the distance. He was having a hard time believing he was actually getting instructions on how to breach an underground bomb shelter in the middle of a forest. He pictured himself walking around the perimeter of the clearing. He didn't like it. How could he not get caught?

"Maybe we should scope out the trees you'll use to..." Bill trailed off, suddenly looking very alert. He raised the shotgun waist high and began surveying the thick woods surrounding them, apparently searching for something.

What was he looking for? Felix wondered. And why was it so quiet? He never remembered the woods being so still.

"You see something?" he asked.

"No. No. Just another deer, I think."

"Okay. So let's say I find the door," Felix said tentatively. "How am I..."

"You'll disable the security system and open the door," Bill replied quickly.

Felix sighed, shook his head, and said with thick sarcasm, "Sounds so easy. Why don't you do it?"

"I have faith in you," Bill said, still surveying the woods. "I think we should find shelter."

"*Shelter?*" Felix asked, confused. There was no shelter out in the woods.

"The car," Bill replied. "We should get back to the car."

"I thought you wanted to check out some of the trees next to the clearing?"

"I changed my mind," Bill replied. "Let's get going. You lead this time."

"Me? But I...um...."

"You're going to be out here by yourself next time. Go ahead. I'll follow. Just retrace your steps. Hurry up."

Felix turned around and started walking the way they came. He climbed over an enormous Douglas fir tree that had flattened several smaller trees when it crashed to the forest floor. He continued in the direction of where he thought the nearest landmark rock should be. Everything looked the same in the woods. Every damn tree looked like the next damn tree. He walked over the uneven terrain, sure that the rock should be close.

He looked at Bill for guidance, but he gave nothing away. He just looked back at Felix without any expression. Felix looked around, searching the forest. He came that way and then he veered to the left at that group of trees, and then…yes! There it was. He strode confidently over to the rock with Bill right behind him.

From there he tried to walk in a straight line. But that was impossible given the enormous natural obstacles in his path. He walked lightly and carefully, trying to avoid stepping on fallen branches. In the distance he saw something shiny. He strained his eyes and made out a bit of sunlight reflecting off the hood of the car. He quickened his pace and reached the dirt-covered Range Rover a few minutes later.

"Very good!" Bill said, patting his shoulder and walking around to the back of the car. He opened the trunk and placed the shotgun back in its compartment.

"Thanks," Felix said, feeling proud of himself.

"Here are the keys," Bill said nonchalantly, handing them to Felix. "Now get us out of here."

"You want *me* to drive?" Felix asked in surprise, reluctantly taking the keys from Bill.

"Who do you think will be driving next time? A chauffeur? Once you destroy the Amulet, you'll be driving back to my house. Now get inside the car!" he said firmly, looking intensely into the woods they'd just emerged from. "Let's not loiter."

Felix got in the car and turned the ignition. Bill wasn't much taller than him, so he didn't need to adjust the seat or any of the controls. He backed the car up carefully and turned around.

"It's really as simple as going back the way we came. Just remember to use the GPS at all times. If you try to rely on your memory, you're going to get lost. All the logging roads look exactly the same, and there are far too many for you to remember which ones to take. It's impossible to get through this forest and out the other side without the GPS. Impossible."

Felix concentrated on the road in front of him, darting his eyes to the GPS every few seconds.

"You should keep your speed below twenty," Bill cautioned. "You go faster than that and you'll be off the road and wrapped around a tree. Also, there are two places where you practically have to come to a stop to make the turn. And if you're checking the clock, it should take you twenty minutes to get back to the cattle pasture."

Felix stared at the road ahead. He'd always been pretty good with directions, and he knew how to use a GPS—his parents had one in their car—but everything looked the same in the woods. There were trees and a dirt road and that was it. No distinguishing landmarks of any kind. He couldn't tell one tree from another. He gripped the steering wheel tightly and concentrated on keeping the car on the winding path.

"Just follow the GPS, and you'll do fine. Don't even look for landmarks. The forest will just play tricks on your eyes."

"You're not helping!" Felix snapped. "You sound just like Emma!"

"Who's Emma?" Bill asked bemusedly.

"My ex-girlfriend."

Bill laughed. "I'm six foot four. I can grow a full beard in three days, and you're comparing me to a teenage girl?"

Felix shrugged, trying to keep his focus on the road.

Bill kept silent for the next fifteen minutes, so Felix assumed he was on the right road. Either that or he really didn't like the Emma comparison. He steered the car gradually to the right for at least a minute. He recognized it as the half circle near the edge of the forest. Within a few minutes he could see bright sunlight on the other side of the trees in the distance.

"That's it!" Felix shouted excitedly. "That's the end!"

"Yes. Stick to the GPS. If you try to exit anywhere other than where we entered, you'll bottom out or hit a tree."

Keeping his eyes on the GPS, Felix drove out of the forest and into the cattle field. He breathed a heavy sigh of relief.

"Good work, Felix! Do you think you can get back to my house without using the GPS?"

"Yeah, I think so," Felix said as he sped through the field. He looked up. The sky was still blue. "Once we get out of here we'll be in the sub-division—Pine Street—and then I'll turn right on Easton. And then another right on Hermann Boulevard and from there it's pretty easy."

"Good." Bill took the cell phone from its holder on the windshield and tucked it into his pocket.

Felix drove through the field. When he reached the end, he jumped the curb and onto the cul-de-sac of the houseless subdivision.

"Did you notice how long that took?" Bill asked.

"I think it was about an hour to get there from your house. Then we walked around for…what? Twenty minutes or so?"

"It's a forty-minute drive from my house to the entrance point of Ardsley Forest. From there, it's another twenty minutes to get to the first rock where we parked the car. If you include the five-minute hike, it's just slightly over an hour."

"Okay," Felix replied as he turned out of the subdivision and onto Easton Street.

"Do you feel confident you could make the trip by yourself?" Bill asked, examining Felix. "That you could get from campus to the facility?"

Felix thought for a moment about the old logging roads that

wound their way through the forest. He frowned and then finally said, "Yeah, I can do it. As long as I have the GPS."

"Good," Bill said, and then he repeated himself. "Good. That's very good, Felix." He looked out the window and stroked his narrow chin.

"What's the problem?" Felix asked, shooting a glance at Bill.

Bill continued to rub his chin. "Felix, do you think you could find the facility at night?"

Felix was dumbfounded. He looked at Bill to see if he was joking. Bill wasn't smiling.

"*At night?*" Felix exclaimed. "You're kidding, right? I'm not even sure I can do it in the day!"

Bill turned to look at Felix. "I know how it sounds. But if you think about it, the GPS will lead you to the first landmark rock whether it's day or night. And once you get there, you just need to walk in a straight line until you find the second rock. Then if you stay on that straight line, you'll come to the clearing. It shouldn't be any harder than finding it during the middle of the day."

"Really? No! No! No! That's crazy! I don't wanna be anywhere near that frickin' forest at night! No way!"

"It may sound crazy," Bill conceded, stroking his chin, "but you need to do everything you can to ensure you'll get in and out of the facility without being seen. And you're much less likely to bump into someone at three in the morning than at three in the afternoon. Wouldn't you agree?"

Felix was feeling flustered. It was hard enough to imagine being in Ardsley Forest by himself during the day. But the thought of breaking into the facility at night was terrifying.

Bill didn't wait for Felix to respond. "The greatest risk to you is someone seeing you when you're there. If they see you, they'll try to kill you. We must minimize the likelihood of you being seen. The only way we can do that is for you to be in the forest in the middle of the night."

Felix just stared at the road as he navigated through traffic on Hermann Boulevard.

"Felix," Bill said, almost pleadingly, "I realize that it's…"

"Fine! I'll do whatever you say! But I'm not gonna lie. I don't like it. I don't know if I can do it."

They drove on, neither of them speaking for several minutes. Felix's mind was so cluttered he nearly missed the exit.

"Felix," Bill said gently, "I know you've got a lot on your mind right now. But there's one other thing we need to do this week."

"What's that?" Felix asked distractedly.

"With everyone away on spring break, we need to concentrate on your training. Now that you know how to find the facility, you need to be able to get into it once you're there."

"Yeah," Felix said flatly.

"So I think we should meet at Devendon every day this week. The times may vary because of my schedule at A.E.I., but I'll text you."

Felix didn't respond. He stared out the windshield as the Portland skyline became visible to the south.

Bill looked at Felix with concern. "I know this is a bit overwhelming, but we need to put everything we have into your training this coming week and…"

"I think I'm gonna spend some time in Cove Rock."

"Cove Rock? What about your training? You only have a month."

"I just need some time by myself," Felix said wearily. "I just need to think…to think things through. Everything's just happening so fast."

"I know. I know I'm asking a lot of you. But after seeing the facility for yourself, you must realize that you can't get inside unless you're prepared. And you're not prepared right now! We must continue your training!"

Felix ran his hand through his hair and frowned. "I hear what you're saying, Bill, but I just need to get away for a while. As soon as I get back, I promise I'll train. I'll train every day. Twice a day. I don't care. I'll train as much as you want."

"But Felix!" Bill shouted, exasperated. "We're running out of…"

"I also want to talk to Allison."

Bill rubbed his chin thoughtfully. "What are you going to tell her?"

"The truth. I mean, in a month, with a lot of luck, the Amulet will be destroyed. And you know she…you know she thinks she's a…a Vessel. I don't want to believe it. But…but if she is…well, I think she has a right to know she only has a month to live."

Bill said nothing for several minutes. "I think that's fair," he finally said. "But don't forget that if she is a Vessel, and she becomes a Human Vessel, Landry will know everything. I don't think we can take that chance. Perhaps you shouldn't…"

"I'm telling her!" Felix shouted. "I owe it to her. I don't believe she's a Vessel. But she'll never forgive me if I don't tell her that the Vessels could all be dead in a month."

Bill nodded, but didn't look pleased. "Let's just hope this turns out to be the right decision."

Felix drove the rest of the way in silence. He was exhausted from the stress of their trip, and he wasn't in the mood to debate with Bill about his training or whether he should tell Allison. He drove the SUV to First Street and got out of the car. He told Bill he'd see him after spring break.

Bill simply nodded.

Chapter 21

Felix arrived at his grandmother's house later that day. He rented a white Ford Taurus that smelled like his dad's Old Spice and made the trip in an hour and a half. By the time he reached Cove Rock, the weather had changed from sunny to overcast. Minutes after arriving at the house, a light rain started to fall. The house felt drafty and smelled like mildew. He looked in the refrigerator and the cupboards for something to eat, but the best he could find was a can of chicken noodle soup and some saltine crackers whose use-by date expired three years ago. He was tired of driving and didn't feel like shopping for groceries. He ate the soup and stale crackers and washed it down with a slightly skunky Rainier. He turned on the TV and tried not to think about Ardsley Forest.

He spent the rest of the day at the beach. It was a short walk to the ocean, but it wasn't for the faint of heart. The house sat at the end of a cul-de-sac and was perched near the top of a cliff. A path of sorts wound its way to the beach below, but it hadn't been maintained in years and was badly eroded by the rain that regularly pounded the shoreline. Felix went very slowly down the path, being careful not to lose his footing. If he were to slip and tumble down the cliffs, he'd be lucky to escape with just a broken leg.

It was a thirty-minute walk from the bottom of the cliffs to the enormous rock in the center of the harbor for which Cove Rock was named. The town wasn't a spring break destination. This time of year, it was generally cold and rainy, and the ocean was hypothermia-inducing. Felix walked slowly along the beach close to the lapping waves, stopping occasionally to pick up sand dollars, which he tossed back into the Pacific.

He wasn't the only one on the beach. Near the center of town, there were several families with young children and a few silver-haired couples, strolling along, holding hands, and laughing. Some of the kids were flying kites, laughing like only children can when their kites spun out of control and nosedived into the wet sand.

Felix found a rock the size of a picnic table not far from the tourist shops and clam chowder restaurants lining the beach. He sat on the rock and watched the tourists. The rain had stopped for the moment, but the wind was blowing hard, making it feel like winter hadn't yet yielded to spring. He zipped up the light jacket he was wearing over a hooded sweatshirt. It seemed so unbelievably strange to Felix that people could be outside on the beach actually enjoying themselves—laughing, flying kites, holding hands, sharing bags of saltwater taffy—when less than two hours away, the Antichrist was creating an army of soulless slaves.

His birth mother knew. She died locked up in an insane asylum knowing that her sister gave birth to the Antichrist. What good did it do her to know the truth? Bill knew. Bill kept Elissa's secrets for almost twenty years. He probably spent many days doing exactly what Felix was doing now: watching ordinary people living their lives as he pondered what it was like before he knew the truth about the world.

A part of Felix was envious of the people on the beach. Things would be very different for them if they knew what he knew. How would they react if he stood up on the rock and announced that he was the Second Coming of Jesus Christ? What if he told them that their Bible was really about a Druid who controlled matter? They'd think he was crazy, of course. It must be nice to believe that the world was a safe place. Even if they didn't know the truth, the lies they'd been told made them feel secure and happy. Was he envious, or did he feel sorry for them? Did he want to be like them, or did he think they were no more aware of their world than the cows grazing in their emerald pastures near Ardsley Forest?

What did it matter, anyway? Why did it even matter what he thought? Or what he wanted? He didn't have choices. Did he? Wasn't his fate determined thousands of years ago? He was the reincarnation of a Druid who died so long ago that Felix found it difficult to wrap his mind around the number. Wasn't he born for the sole purpose of killing the Antichrist? He was the only one who could do it. That was his destiny. His fate. And it didn't matter who got in the way of that fate. He'd killed his parents—blown them into so many pieces the funeral home padlocked their caskets to prevent an accidental viewing. They were the collateral damage of his destiny. The forces that had been at work for thousands of years weren't caring or sympathetic. They didn't care at all. They didn't give a shit. The battle between Myrddin and the Drestian was for everything. What did a couple of lives mean when compared to the fate of the world? Nothing. Their lives meant absolutely nothing. Isn't that what Bill believed?

What was even the point of trying to resist? Felix wondered. What was the point of believing he controlled his life? If his destiny was already determined, why fight it? Why not just do everything Bill asked of him? Before that day in Bill's office, he never even thought about free will. He never even considered the possibility that he didn't have complete control over his life. He was the one making the decisions. He was in control. But now he realized that was all just an illusion. He was never in control of his life. He wasn't even the person he thought he was. He wasn't Felix. He was the reincarnation of a two-thousand-year-old Druid. He glowed in the dark. He moved things with his mind and exploded plastic clocks.

He wasn't like the people on the beach. He'd never fly kites with his children or go on long, romantic walks with his wife. He was destined for other things. He'd destroy Templar Amulets. He'd battle the Antichrist for the future of the world.

He spent the next several days doing the same thing—walking along the beach, watching other people enjoying their lives, and wondering why it was his fate to save the world from the Antichrist. There was so much on his mind, he didn't dwell on what happened with Harper. It just wasn't meant to be. She was better off with someone who could give her things that he never could. He never asked her, but she probably wanted to have a family. She probably liked flying kites and strolling along the beach. Felix couldn't promise her those things. He could only promise death.

Felix made plans to see Allison the next day. He'd tell her in person that next month she could be dead.

Chapter 22

Felix hadn't returned to Coos Bay Bridge since last August when he left for Portland. After being released from the hospital, everyone from the minister at his parents' church to his high school football coach offered their homes to him. He decided to stay at a small motel on the outskirts of town. He appreciated the gestures, but he just wanted to be alone.

As he crossed the town limits, he had a sudden impulse to turn around and go back to Cove Rock. It occurred to him that he might see someone he knew. It was his hometown. He could very easily bump into someone, even his parents' friends. Oh God! He couldn't handle his parents' friends. They'd give him that *look*. They always gave him that look. It said, "Poor Felix. He lost his parents. He must be in such pain. Oprah and Dr. Phil say I should look him in the eye and squeeze his arm to let him know that I care. He'll like that. I'm such a good person for caring for this poor boy." If anyone gave him that look, they might have to look at his fist as it punched them in the face.

He took a few deep breaths and turned up the radio, singing off-key with the lyrics. He tried to remind himself that he wouldn't see anyone he knew besides Allison. He'd go to her house, talk to her, and then get back to Cove Rock as soon as he could. No one knew him in Cove Rock, and he could be alone there. Alone and far from the place where everyone gave him the same goddamn pitiful look.

He drove through town, wearing sunglasses and avoiding eye contact with other drivers. Ten minutes later, he arrived at Allison's neighborhood—a twelve-block grid of nondescript average-sized single-family homes built in the 1950s. All were set on lots no larger than a quarter of an acre.

He passed by Clements Street, Treeline Street, and then he pulled to the curb, shifted into park, and cut the engine. He looked up and read the reflective letters on the green sign. They spelled out Springfield Street—the street where he grew up. Without thinking, he restarted the car, turned, and drove slowly down Springfield. He seemed to be on autopilot, like someone else was steering the car. He was just a passenger, he thought—the perfect metaphor of his life.

At 121 Springfield Street the car stopped. There was nothing there. No house, no front porch, and no basketball hoop in the driveway. Everything was cleared away as if wiped clean by the hand of God. Only dirt remained—dirt and a For Sale sign. Just like the subdivisions near Ardsley Forest.

He shouldn't have been surprised. The proceeds from the insurance company were already deposited, along with his dad's life insurance policy, into an account in Felix's name. His parents had lived in the house for almost forty years and owned it free and clear. Before he left town for football practice, he met with his parents' attorney, a kind man in his sixties who had known Felix's dad since their high school days. He was one of the few people in town who didn't give Felix the look.

The attorney asked him what he wanted to do with the land—rebuild the house, or sell it? Felix told him to sell it. He knew it wasn't sold because he was still getting real estate tax statements every three months. But the sight of the barren land was surreal.

Felix got out of the car and crossed the street. He walked through the dirt and weeds that was once his home. In his mind he pictured himself inside the house. He stood in the living room, where he and his dad spent so many hours watching football. And around this corner was the kitchen, where his mom made sure he did his homework at the counter while she cooked dinner, bribing him with cupcakes. And this was the staircase up to his bedroom. The room where he...

He remembered what he saw with his own eyes when Bill hypnotized him. How he destroyed everything, sweeping through the house, glowing like the sun and unleashing the terrible power that literally blew the house apart. He thought of his parents pounding on his bedroom door, begging him to open it. He heard their screams. And then the door and the bedroom walls exploded through the other side of the house, tearing his parents apart. They never had a chance.

The wind began to blow, and a few stray leaves whipped around. The sky seemed to darken, and dust blew across the lot, forming eddies encircling Felix. He watched their graceful pirouettes and felt tears start to well up in his eyes.

He fought them back. He'd cried enough. Why cry over things he couldn't control? It was like crying over the weather. Why be such a baby about it? He wasn't going to shed any more tears.

He wanted to tell his parents he was sorry. He was asleep. He didn't know what he was doing. He wanted to tell them he loved them. But that was shallow and meaningless. Just words. Meaningless words. Nothing would bring them back. They'd never know how sorry he was.

He walked to what he thought was the center of the house, with the wind whipping around him, and said in a clear voice, "Mom, Dad. It's Felix. I know you can't hear me. I know I'm just doing this to make myself feel better. I know it's selfish. But I just wanted to say that I love you. And I miss you. I really miss you. And I'm sorry. I'm so sorry for everything."

Felix turned and slowly walked back to the car.

Chapter 23

A few minutes later he parked on the street in front of Allison's house. He took a few minutes to compose himself and then got out of the car. The house was a gray raised-ranch with a one-car garage fronting the street. It had a small porch in front and red window shutters that looked like they were in need of a fresh coat of paint. The driveway was cracked in a few places, and the flower beds were on the verge of being overrun by weeds.

He walked to the front door and rang the bell. The sign above the door said "Jasner Residence" in wood-burned script on varnished pine.

Felix heard footsteps behind the door and then it swung open. Allison was wearing a pair of dark jeans and a white tee shirt with "Portland College" across the front in bright orange Old English letters. Her long brown hair was tied back in a simple ponytail with a thick elastic band.

"Felix!" she said with a bright smile, stepping onto the porch and hugging him tightly. "How are you? Come in." Felix had been to Allison's house dozens of times over the years and knew his way around.

"Where are your sibs?" Felix asked.

"Angie's in Colorado. The evil stepsister is around here somewhere."

Angie was older than Allison by three years. When Allison moved to Coos Bay Bridge as a freshman, Angie was a senior. She treated Allison with a kind of benign indifference, like a stranger on an extended sleepover, and mostly just ignored her. Angie remained in Colorado after graduating college in Boulder and rarely visited.

The evil stepsister was Molly. Molly and Allison were the same age, but that was the only thing they had in common. From the very beginning, Molly went out of her way to make life difficult for Allison. On Allison's first day at Coos Bay Bridge High School, Molly and her friends circulated a rumor that Allison's former family got rid of her because she had a sexually transmitted disease. The rumor spread throughout the entire student body in a matter of days. Allison spent her entire freshman year hearing people whisper "herpes" behind her back.

That was just the beginning.

Molly was pretty, but in a superficial kind of way. After being told repeatedly that Molly was such an adorable baby that she should go into modeling, Mrs. Jasner started entering her in beauty pageants when Molly was four. Molly basked in the attention of being on center stage in front of an audience, beaming as the elaborate tiara was placed on her teased hair as she was crowned Little Miss Western Doll or Little Miss Glitz. When Molly was six, Mrs. Jasner stopped entering her in pageants. The cost of the entrance fees, frilly dresses, professionally applied makeup, plus all the singing and dancing lessons was a con- siderable drain on the family's finances. Mrs. Jasner tried to explain all of this to Molly, but Molly simply responded by throwing a violent temper tantrum that lasted for weeks. Molly's mother, fearing that Molly would never forgive her for the perceived betrayal, resorted to bribery to win back Molly's love. In celebration of Molly's seventh birthday, Mrs. Jasner staged the biggest birthday party the neighbor- hood had ever seen, complete with ponies for the guests to ride and entertainment provided by a clown named "MoMo."

In high school, Molly didn't really excel at anything that would im- press a college admissions office. Her grades were average, she didn't participate in any sports or play a musical instrument, and she didn't do any extracurricular activities to speak of.

The one thing Molly did excel at was spreading rumors about Allison, both at school and on the Internet. The list of things Allison supposedly did was long and impressive: she cheated on tests, killed the neighbor's kitten with a hammer, snorted cocaine, got arrested for shoplifting, cut herself with razor blades, was bulimic, had sex with her math teacher, was a lesbian, kept a flask of vodka in her school locker, and once punched her mother in the face for undercooking her chicken. The list went on and on.

Felix looked around the house. It was just as he remembered it. Allison's mother was extremely tidy, and there wasn't an object in the house that was out of place. The furniture was simple with clean lines, and Mrs. Jasner had decorated the walls entirely with pictures of flowers. In every room of the house there was at least one framed floral print on each wall.

"Hey!" Allison exclaimed, sounding excited. "Did you hear they found the bodies out in Ardsley Forest?"

"What bodies?"

"You know, the three campers who went missing last summer."

"Oh? Really? They finally found them, huh?"

"Yeah, it's all over the news. The police are now saying that the Mormon Mephistopheles is the main suspect. Somebody saw him outside of a bar in Portland, so they're searching for him all over the city. Crazy, huh? Oh, and they're saying that just partial remains were found."

"That means..."

"There wasn't much left. Probably like the other two, who were all dismembered. It's so messed up."

"Where in Ardsley Forest?" Felix asked. "Did they say?"

Allison shook her head. "I don't know. Just out in the woods somewhere. Why?"

"Shit," Felix said, like he was talking to himself. "I wonder if it's near the...um..."

"Near the what?"

"Nothing. I'm thirsty. Got anything to drink?"

"Sure." She turned and headed toward the kitchen. Felix followed.

"What do you got?" he asked.

"Your favorite."

"Nice. Thanks."

She poured him a large glass of apple juice and popped a can of Diet Coke for herself.

"So why the cryptic phone call?" Allison asked, getting straight to the point.

Felix took a long drink and wiped his mouth. "What was cryptic about it? I just said I wanted to talk to you in person."

"If you tell me you can't say something over the phone, I'd consider that cryptic." She placed a hand on her hip to show she was serious.

"It's not that I couldn't. It's just that I thought it'd be better to tell you in person."

Allison looked closely at Felix. "Is this about the…the…"

"I thought I heard someone in the kitchen," a girl said in a high-pitched saccharine voice as she sauntered into the room. She was medium height with long blond hair falling well past her shoulders. She had a round face, soft brown eyes, and a chin that came to a sharp point. She wore white leggings and a revealing, tight pink tee-shirt that didn't completely cover her stomach or her breasts.

"Felix!" she gushed. She smiled widely and hugged him. He could smell her perfume; it was overpowering. As usual, she was wearing too much makeup.

"Hey, Molly," Felix said, trying to sound enthusiastic.

Molly didn't acknowledge Allison as she walked past her and opened a cabinet above the counter. There was something extremely sexual about the way she moved, Felix thought. When she walked by Felix, he couldn't help himself. He looked her up and down. She had a tramp stamp tattoo on her lower back that he didn't notice before. It looked like a dragon or maybe a butterfly. Her face might be a bit overcooked, but there was absolutely nothing wrong with her body.

Allison slammed her can of Diet Coke down on the counter and narrowed her eyes at Felix in a glare.

Molly apparently couldn't find what she was looking for. She closed the cabinet door empty-handed, turning to face Felix and Allison.

"So, Felix," Molly said, standing cross-legged and twirling a strand of hair around a finger. "How's school? Do you like it? Is it just so much fun?"

Felix looked at Allison and then back at Molly. "It's all right. It's a lot of work, but we still have fun. Right, Allison?"

"Huh?" Allison said distractedly. "Yeah, sure. It's just one huge party. That's all we do. It's a lot like Cancun, only a little rainier."

Molly looked at her sister and scowled. "Wow!" she said sarcastically. "That's exactly how I pictured it, Allison. But you wanna know something cool? I'm doing so well at school, I'm thinking about transferring from Coos Bay Bridge Community College to PC next year. Wouldn't that be great? You know, living at home isn't all it's cracked up to be. Allison, we could spend so much time together at PC and go to all those awesome parties. We could even be roommates. Just like at home."

There was an awkward silence. Allison and Molly stared at each other from across the kitchen. Felix drank his apple juice and looked at the wall.

"So, Felix," Molly said conspiratorially, "I heard the craziest rumor the other day. I heard that the fire...the gas explosion...whatever it was at your house that burned it to the ground and killed your mom and dad? Well, I heard that *you* caused it."

Felix nearly dropped his glass. His mouth hung open. Allison looked just as surprised. How could Molly know that? Allison would never in a million years tell her what really happened. Would she?

Molly smiled and played with her hair, appearing to revel in Felix's reaction.

"You what?" Felix finally asked, trying to stay calm.

"I heard you caused the fire," Molly said, still smiling. "You fell asleep smoking a cigarette. The fire department and the police know all about it. But because you're a juvie, the police records are sealed."

"What the hell is wrong with you!" Allison yelled at Molly. "Felix doesn't smoke! And there aren't any secret police records! There was a gas leak at the house that caused the fire and the explosion. How could you even say that?"

"Hey," Molly said to Allison sweetly, "don't shoot the messenger. I'm just telling you what I heard."

"The only time you heard that was when you were talking to yourself in the mirror," Allison said, glaring at her sister.

Molly smiled and shrugged.

"Come on, Felix," Allison said. "Let's go up to my room."

Allison walked quickly out of the kitchen and toward the foyer. Felix followed behind. As he walked past Molly, she winked at him and smiled. He ignored her and followed Allison up the stairs to the second floor.

Allison's room was at the end of the hall. She opened the door and walked up three small stairs inside the room. He'd been there before a few times, but he couldn't remember why. Maybe they studied together or listened to music, something like that. Her bedroom was originally the attic, but her parents converted it just before her adoption. The ceilings were pitched and so low in places that Allison couldn't stand up straight. A twin-sized bed was pushed up against the wall on one side. On the opposite wall was a small white-painted desk and a matching chair with a red and blue striped cushion placed on its seat.

The room was so narrow that the bed frame nearly touched the desk. The only window was a small dormer directly above the desk that looked out onto a neighboring house. Other than a few posters and a full-length mirror attached to the closet door, the walls were bare. Next to the bed was a large dresser. On the chest sat a digital alarm clock, some books, and a picture in a gold-colored frame.

Felix recognized the picture. He picked it up and looked at it more closely. It was a picture of Felix and Allison at their high school's Sadie Hawkins dance when they were freshmen. They were seated on a bale of hay with Felix facing the camera and Allison sitting next to him with her body turned toward him. Allison was looking straight at the photographer, but her legs were draped over Felix's lap. She held a cowboy hat high in the air with her left hand. Her right hand was wrapped loosely around Felix's shoulders. They wore matching cowboy boots, plaid shirts, and jeans. Felix clutched a long piece of straw in his teeth. They were both smiling.

"I like this picture," Felix said, grinning. "We look so young. Like kids."

"We were kids. I love it though. It's also the only picture I have from high school where I'm not with some guy I don't like anymore."

"That's the advantage of going to a school dance with a friend." He returned the picture to its place on the dresser.

"I'm sorry about my sister, Felix. She's a..."

"She's a bitch. I've actually known her a lot longer than you, you know. I've known her since the first grade. She's crazy."

"You don't think she was being serious about going to PC, do you?" Allison looked like she had indigestion. "Of all the schools out there, she couldn't pick ours, right?"

"I don't know," Felix replied, shaking his head. "She sounded pretty serious. I guess she could just be screwing with you."

"Yeah, who the hell knows what's going on in that head of hers? I wonder if she'll grow out of this evil stepsister thing?"

Felix shrugged. "You can't really call it a phase anymore. If anything, it's getting worse."

Allison groaned and sat down on the bed. "Okay, now that we have that behind us, can you tell me what's going on?"

"Oh. Right." Felix sat down next to her.

Over the next thirty minutes, Allison sat mesmerized as Felix told her about the plan to destroy the Templar Amulet. He told her that Bill was reasonably confident about its location and about their scouting trip into Ardsley Forest. He concluded by telling her that he was going back to the forest to destroy the Amulet while Landry was in Egypt during the last week of April.

Allison didn't interrupt. When he finally stopped, she asked, "So you're going into Ardsley Forest by yourself in the middle of the night? And you're doing this a month from now?"

"Yes."

"No you're not!"

"What do you mean? I don't have a choice. Landry will be in Egypt, and I have to destroy it then, before…"

"No. No. No. I meant you're not going by yourself. I'm going with you." She spoke in a flat, commanding tone, the way she did when she really wanted something and there was no convincing her otherwise.

Felix was shocked. He didn't expect her to volunteer to go with him. He definitely didn't think this through. Dammit! He didn't know what to say. Allison just stared at him with a look of resolve in her large green eyes.

"Allison," he finally said, after finding his voice, "look, I'm not sure you understand what it's like out there. This underground bunker thing is in the middle of this horrible forest. There's nothing there but the biggest trees you can imagine. They don't even look like they're from this planet. And don't forget about all those people killed out there. Right? Weren't the bodies of the last three just found? And you know they were all totally hacked up. Bill says there are serial killers out in the woods. You don't wanna have any part of that, right? When I went before, Bill had this gun with him. I mean this thing was a cannon. It was frickin' huge. So something's going on out there even if he's not saying. And didn't I tell you about the logging roads? They're barely wide enough for bikes. You can't even see 'em. And I'm going at night. I can't even imagine how scary that place will be at night. And

I've been there. Did I mention that if anybody sees me, I'm a dead man? This isn't a game."

"How can you tell me it's not a game?" Her cheeks were flushed and her eyes were full of intensity. "You don't think I know what this is all about? Once the Templar Amulet is destroyed, I'm going to die, Felix. I have more to lose than anyone. But I want you to destroy this goddamn thing! I'm not gonna live the rest of my life wondering if I have a soul or not! Or if I'm gonna drop dead in a year, or a month from now, or…"

"You're not a Vessel!" Felix shouted. "I keep telling you that!"

"There's only one way to be sure, right? You'll destroy it. Then we'll see what happens. But I want to be there, Felix! I deserve to be there. When you destroy it, I want to be standing right next to you. If that's how I'm going to die, then I want to go out with my eyes wide open. I'm not going to bed that night wondering if I'll wake up in the morning."

"But Allison, it's going to be dangerous…"

"Of course! I know that. But I have the right to go with you!"

"But I don't even know if I can do it," Felix said, shaking his head bitterly. "It's not like we're breaking into your neighbor's house."

"That's why I should be there!" She was pleading with him now. "I can help you. Bill might be telling you to do this by yourself, but is that what you want? Don't you think you could use a little help?"

Felix thought for a moment. He studied Allison. He knew he wouldn't be able to convince her not to go. Maybe later he'd try to talk her out of it. "Yeah, I suppose I could use a little help."

"Good!" Allison smiled and sighed with relief. "Then it's settled."

"There's one other thing," Felix said in his most serious voice.

"What?" Allison said, concerned. "What is it?"

"I'm starving."

"You're very funny. I can get you some more apple juice, you know."

"I was thinking of something I could chew. And someplace where Molly doesn't live. How about a burger?"

"Fine," Allison said, smiling. "But you have to drive. My piece of crap car is rusting out in the garage. My parents won't insure it during the school year."

Chapter 24

They drove to the nearest burger joint, a local place called West's. As soon as they got in line to order, the couple in front of them started whispering a little too loudly about the "kid whose parents died in the fire." Felix gritted his teeth and ordered their food.

They sat at a table in the far corner, but the restaurant wasn't big enough to escape the muttering and gawking of some of the customers. A morbidly obese woman whose ass was hanging off both sides of her plastic chair seemed to spin her head completely around on her bulging neck like an owl, never taking her eyes off Felix.

Two bites into his double cheeseburger, Felix whispered across the table at Allison, "I can't eat with these animals staring at me. Let's go."

They grabbed their food and ate what was left of it in the car, but it seemed to have lost its taste. Allison said she was sorry. Felix told her not to worry about it—it wasn't her fault.

He dropped Allison off at her house. She asked if he wanted to come inside. He told her he'd had enough of Molly for one day. She laughed and gave him a long hug. He told her he'd see her back at school and asked her not to worry about "things."

She promised to do her best. Felix drove away thinking he didn't like the look in her eyes.

Chapter 25

Spring break came to an abrupt conclusion like a horn signaling the end of a football game—just like that, it was over. Felix returned the Taurus to the rental car agency and arrived on campus ahead of Lucas and the girls. When Allison showed up a few hours later, he was already bored and suggested they get some coffee.

Allison was in good spirits, but she'd spent her remaining days in Coos Bay Bridge worrying about everything that could possibly go wrong in Ardsley Forest. When Allison latched onto a problem, her analytical brain tended to vivisect it into its component parts. Three large mugs of house blend later, Felix thought he'd convinced her that their mission into Ardsley Forest wasn't a problem that could be quantified and solved like a mathematical equation.

Practically buzzing on caffeine, they decided to make their way back to Downey to see if Lucas and the girls were back on campus. The sun had set hours before, and as they emerged from the warmth of the well-lit bistro and into the darkness of a cool, starless spring night, a primal fear was triggered in Allison.

Suddenly, she was terrified they wouldn't be able to find the underground facility at night. It would be too dark to see anything. What if they went right past it? And even worse—what if they got lost in the woods? Felix did what he could to allay her concerns. He had the same fears, but he kept them from her, not wanting to exacerbate her anxiety.

They walked back to Downey speaking in hushed tones. Allison told a story about a camping trip she took with her family in high school. One overcast night she wandered away from the campsite in search of a sharp marshmallow-roasting stick for making s'mores. When she finally found the perfect stick, she bent down to pick it up. When she looked up she couldn't see anything—she completely lost sight of the campsite. She was all alone out in the woods. She'd wandered too far into the forest and couldn't hear anyone's voices. She panicked for a moment before realizing that a large tree was blocking her view of the campfire. Once she saw the fire, she practically sprinted back to the campsite. She tripped over a protruding tree root, just like in a bad horror movie. And then she...

"Hey guys! What's going on? We were looking for you!"

Lucas was standing in the lobby with Harper and Caitlin. Felix was so focused on Allison's story, he didn't realize they were back at the dorm. Allison must have been thinking the same thing, because she just stood there with her mouth open.

"We didn't mean to scare you or anything," Lucas said, appearing amused at their reaction. "What were you guys talking about—national security? Looked like something important."

"No. We were...uh...campfire with...um...just..." Felix stammered.

"Okay," Caitlin said, looking very tan and much blonder than usual. "That didn't make any sense at all. Why don't you try that again?"

"Ah...you know, we were just talking about some things going on at Allison's house," Felix said, desperately trying to recover from his earlier blathering. "You wouldn't believe her sister Molly. She says the craziest shit. I was talking to her for about a minute, and she says..."

"Where were you talking to her?" Harper interrupted.

Felix tried to avoid looking directly at Harper. But now he didn't have a choice. He glanced at her. She didn't look very happy.

"Where was I...?"

"Yes," Harper replied. "Where were you talking to Allison's sister?"

"Oh. Well...I was...I was actually in Coos Bay Bridge during the break. I saw Molly at...Allison's house."

Harper arched an eyebrow. "I see. So you guys spent some time together over the break?"

Felix was completely perplexed. "Well, no…I mean, not really…I was just…"

"Felix came down for one day during the break," Allison said cool-ly, staring at Harper. "He spent the week at his grandmother's house in Cove Rock and then decided to drive down the coast. He ended up at my house for a few hours. We went out and grabbed a burger. We didn't go to Vegas and get hitched or anything."

Lucas laughed. "Good to know. All right then. Harper, if you're done with your line of questioning, can we go get some coffee? I'm going through good coffee withdrawals after drinking a bunch of mo-tor oil-tasting shit in Minnesota all week." He looked at Felix and Allison. "You're coming, right?"

Felix and Allison both laughed.

"What's so funny?" Lucas asked.

"That's where we came from," Felix said. "I already had three cups. If I have any more I'll be awake for the rest of the month."

"Don't be such a girl," Lucas said, smiling. "You can never have too much coffee."

"All right," Allison said. "I'll go. But I might have to go with the decaf even though I'm aware that's sacrilegious."

"I'm in too," Felix said. "But you can't abuse me in public when I order decaf. All right?"

"We'll give you guys a pass this time, but never again," Caitlin said.

"I don't think I'm gonna go," Harper said.

"What's wrong?" Caitlin asked.

"Nothing," Harper said. "I just think I'm a little tired. Too much fun in Mexico, I guess." She smiled weakly and shrugged. "Maybe I'll just catch up on my sleep."

"It's eight-thirty," Lucas said. "Seriously? It's your bedtime now?"

"It feels later than eight-thirty," Harper said, glaring at Lucas.

"Sorry guys. I'm just not feeling up to it. I'll see you tomorrow." She turned around and walked up the stairs that led to the upper floors.

"Hmmmm. She didn't seem tired before," Caitlin said, shrugging.

"Anyway!" Lucas said cheerfully. "How was Cove Rock? That place sounds like loads of fun! Did you collect some nice seashells and enjoy long, romantic walks with yourself?"

Felix laughed. "That's exactly what I did. I spent a lot of quality time with myself. You wouldn't believe what an interesting person I am."

Allison smiled.

Chapter 26

A week later, Felix met with Bill at the old library. When he arrived, Bill was already there. As he stepped into the room, Felix thought he could smell just a hint of smoke. A reminder of the fire that almost became a conflagration. He was wearing a light jacket and an orange PC baseball cap to shield him from another rainy Oregon night. He also brought a backpack that made clanking sounds whenever he took a step. Winter may have officially concluded on the calendar, but Devendon felt as chilly as ever. Felix put the backpack on a chair and kept his jacket on.

"Hello, Felix," Bill said warmly. "You look like you're in a good mood. I hope the time away was what you needed."

"It was pretty good. It was good to get away from school—away from all of this for a while."

Bill nodded. "Good. I know you needed to clear your head. But I also hope you realize just how little time we have left. I need you to be absolutely committed to your training this month, okay? After tonight, we'll meet again in five days. And after that, we'll meet every night until you're ready."

"Okay. I can do that."

"Then let's get started. I want to start with the locks again. And this time, I don't want you to burn down the building, so try to…"

"I want to show you something first."

Felix unzipped his backpack and carried it over to the table that was so badly charred during their last session. He pulled out six empty Diet Coke cans and placed them side by side in a row across the table, spacing them evenly apart. Then he turned and walked toward the center of the room, stopping some twenty feet from the table.

"I hope this is good," Bill shouted from beside the table.

"Don't get your hopes up. I'm a little wild."

Felix held up his right hand and stared at the table. He began to glow softly red in the pale light of the room. The far left can started to vibrate. It shook and wobbled for a moment. Then with a loud, crunching crackle, it was reduced to a small object shaped roughly like a ball. It was like an invisible hand with supernatural strength crushed the can in its grip.

Bill picked up the aluminum ball and appeared to study it closely.

"Do you mind if I keep this?" he asked.

Felix shrugged. "I'm not done with the other cans though."

Bill slipped the aluminum object into the pocket of his well-worn jeans and stepped away from the blackened table.

Felix raised his right hand once again and began to glow softly. The far right can started to quiver. And then with a loud screech, the top half of it ripped away from the bottom and went spinning across the room, where it thwacked against the wall and fell onto the floor, making a tiny puff of dust.

Bill approached the table and examined what remained of the can. He ran his index finger along the top of the sheared-off aluminum. "It's sharp!" he shouted. "You could cut your finger on this." He stepped back from the table.

Felix raised his right hand for the third time. He gritted his teeth and focused all his attention on the four remaining cans. This time, the four remaining cans began to vibrate. The two cans in the center floated off the table and hovered a few feet above it. A moment later they were joined by the two outside cans. The four cans levitated motionless for several seconds and then, in a sudden burst of movement, collided into each other with a loud, tinny clang. The cans made a crumpling sound as they bent and twisted into amorphous shapes until finally merging together to form one seamless mass.

But Felix wasn't finished. The aluminum object remained perfectly still, hovering a few feet above the table like a large, disfigured, flying egg. And then a small sliver detached itself from the object, as if it were sliced off with a knife. It hit the charred tabletop with a light *thump*. Then another sliver came off and landed on the table. And then another. Again and again small slivers separated from the levitating aluminum blob until all that remained of it were the sheared-off slivers of aluminum spread out across the table.

Bill picked up one of the pieces. He examined it closely, holding it up to his face. It was very thin and the sides were smooth.

"It's almost like the pieces were sliced off by a surgical instrument or a laser," he said. "The sides are completely smooth. You should really have a look at this."

Felix joined Bill at the table. "I know. I spent a week practicing that at my grandma's house. I was hoping you'd be impressed."

Bill frowned. "I'm glad you worked on something during the break. I really am. I was worried you'd be sitting on your ass drinking beer and doing little else. And look, what you did to these cans is a nice trick. You're definitely controlling matter more artistically than before. But I need you to be less Rembrandt and more wrecking ball! You're going to be breaking into a bunker. Not playing spin the bottle with empty soda cans."

That wasn't the reaction Felix expected. He was sure that Bill would be impressed. It took him days to learn how to do that. At the very least, he thought that Bill would clap him on the back and tell him he did a good job. "I should've known," Felix said dejectedly, unable to conceal his disappointment. "I don't know why you're so hard on me! I'm the one who's gotta break into that bunker, you know? Not you! It's not easy to practice blowing shit up when you're in a house. What am I supposed to do? Just completely trash the place?"

Bill smiled. "I see you didn't leave your temper in Cove Rock. I think what you've taught yourself to do with the cans may have some practical applications. But from now on, just do what I tell you, all right?"

Felix fumed. Would it kill Bill to tell him he did something well? He'd practiced that goddamn can thing for days. What the hell! He tried to relax. He concentrated on slowing his breathing. It wouldn't do any good to fight Bill, anyway. Didn't he decide that the other day? Just go with it—it didn't matter. None of it mattered, anyway.

"Fine," he said, emotionless.

"Before we start, how did it go with your friend?" Bill asked. "You said you were telling her about the plan. How'd she react?"

"She listened to what I had to say. And then...and then she told me she wanted to help. She wants to go with me into Ardsley Forest."

Bill didn't look surprised. "I suspected she might."

"Really? I had no idea she'd do that. I always thought people tried to avoid danger."

"She wants to meet her fate head-on, right? Isn't that it?"

"Yeah. That's pretty much what she said. She wants to be next to me when I destroy the Templar Amulet."

"She's a brave girl."

Felix's brow creased. "But we can't let her go, can we? It's not a camping trip. I don't really think she's a Vessel. And she could die out there. I don't think I can put her in that kind of danger."

Bill looked thoughtful. "Allison feels she is just as much a part of this as you. She may be right. Who are we to say she has no right to go?"

"I didn't expect you to say that. What the hell? I have no idea what anyone is thinking anymore! So you think I should let her go?"

"No," Bill said, shaking his head. "I think you need to make that decision. I can't make it for you."

"I just don't want things to go bad. If something happened to her out there, I don't know what I'd do. I've already hurt enough people. My parents…"

"You're not making Allison do anything," Bill interrupted. "If she decides to go, she has to take responsibility for the consequences."

"But if something happens to her, it's my responsibility!"

"I disagree," Bill said authoritatively. "But I don't think you even have a choice here. Do you really think you can convince her not to go at this point?"

"Probably not."

"Then why are you wasting my time? Let's get back to work."

Felix spent the next ninety minutes attempting to break steel locks. He managed to put some spiderweb cracks in two of them, but he couldn't replicate what he'd done to the aluminum cans. The discussion over Allison had screwed up his concentration, and he couldn't seem to regain his focus. Finally giving up in frustration, Felix slumped down on a table and told Bill he'd had enough. He didn't have anything left.

Bill took the ball of aluminum out of his pocket. He threw it against a wall and told Felix that Landry had nothing to worry about. He then walked out, leaving Felix alone in the old library.

Chapter 27

In the days that followed, Felix came to an important decision. He couldn't determine his fate. He knew that now. He'd spent several days contemplating that apparently immutable fact while on the beach in Cove Rock and had resolved to accept it. He was the reincarnation of Myrddin. It was his destiny to kill the Antichrist. Or at least attempt to kill the Antichrist. And as bizarre as that seemed, there was no cheating fate. He decided not to deny it or fight it any longer. But as he saw things, he still had a decision to make. Just because his fate was predetermined didn't mean he couldn't make any choices at all, right? Maybe he could decide how he wanted to live his life while fate carried him along to its final destination like a giant star-crossed conveyor belt.

After all, the full-on assault against the Antichrist wouldn't be launched any time soon. Felix wasn't ready for that. Learning to control his gift was a maddeningly slow process, and the thought of Landry turning him inside out made him want to throw up. The final battle with the Drestian that was foretold over two thousand years ago might not happen for years. Of course there was still the matter of destroying the Templar Amulets and engaging in guerilla warfare. But those were also long-term projects.

So what was he supposed to do with his life in the meantime?

One path led to a place where he'd be forced to acknowledge that his life as a college student was a meaningless exercise in play-acting. What was the point in going to class, studying, taking tests, and worrying about grades? Would it really matter in the universal scheme of things if he was placed on academic probation and couldn't play football next fall? Would he really be striking a blow against the Antichrist if he led the PNFL in touchdowns?

For all he knew, he might not even be alive next fall. Getting killed in Ardsley Forest seemed as real a possibility as not maintaining a 2.0 GPA. And even though there were times when he found it comforting to sit in class listening to lectures on Charlemagne and Jung, he couldn't help but feel that the theories and histories passed off by his professors as knowledge were all built on a reality that didn't exist. The entire intellectual, philosophical, and religious foundation of the world was one great big lie. He wasn't a genius, but he knew that much.

The other path would allow him to at least pretend he was normal. He could still hold on to the familiar routines of college life: classes, studying in Dale's Room, the Caffeine Hut, dorm parties, playing football, and being with his friends. And maybe football, friends, and dorm parties didn't mean very much when compared to the fate of mankind. But even so, he liked those things. They made him happy. They kept him sane. He didn't want to isolate himself anymore, obsessing over the steaming piles of shit that fate had left for him along the road to his final destiny, especially when the rest of the world knew nothing about it. Why should he be the only one who had to sacrifice everything while everyone else enjoyed their Hallmark moments on the beach?

So what was he supposed to do? Was his happiness completely irrelevant? Did being the Second Coming mean that he had to drop out of school to fixate on fulfilling his destiny? Screw that. He'd lose his mind. The boredom might literally kill him. He needed school and he needed his friends. He wouldn't give that up, even if it was all meaningless. Maybe his logic wasn't flawless, and maybe it was self-serving. But so what? He made his decision. He'd continue to care about the unimportant things that made him happy. The things that made him feel normal.

Allison seemed to be experiencing her own internal conflict, although the roots of her malaise were different from Felix's. And while the roots weren't visible, her symptoms were plainly obvious. She was perpetually distracted, unable to focus, and often fell into near trance-like reveries. She had trouble holding conversations and would often stare off into space. Two different times during the past week, Lucas had snapped his fingers in front of her face when she fell into one of her stupors. And when questioned by Harper one night in Dale's Room about her odd behavior, Allison replied that she was just a little stressed and wasn't sleeping well. Then she muttered something about all the rain causing her seasonal affective disorder.

Felix approached Allison one morning at breakfast when they were alone and asked her how she was holding up. She told him she was fine, and he shouldn't worry about her. He had enough things to be concerned about, after all. Of course he knew why she was acting so strange. With each passing day, the night of their trip to Ardsley Forest grew closer, and she believed that her life grew one day shorter. He tried to convince her she couldn't be a Vessel. She told him there was no way to know for sure until the Templar Amulet was destroyed. She didn't need Felix's assurances; she needed him to destroy the Amulet. Until then, she wouldn't talk about it. With only a few weeks to live, she told him he should consider that her final wish.

Chapter 28

With the month of April nearing its midpoint, and taxpayers across the country scrambling to file their tax returns with the IRS before the deadline, Bill informed Felix he'd be training at Devendon every night until he was prepared.

The night before, Bill instructed him to explode six alarm clocks he'd lined up in a neat row on a table, one after the other. Felix had blown up an alarm clock before. So he thought Bill was just warming him up, like stretching before a football game. He destroyed the six clocks one at a time, just as he was asked. It wasn't very hard. The last clock exploded with such force that pieces of plastic became stuck in the ceiling. Bill had wisely overturned a long reading table and used it to shield himself from flying shrapnel.

Felix was also able to break open a combination lock for the first time. When he accomplished the feat, he felt like letting out a primal roar in celebration. He restrained himself at the last possible moment. He knew that Bill would probably just tell him that the multi-ton steel access door to the underground facility wasn't barred by a combination lock purchased from Walmart. Felix didn't want a repeat of what happened the last time they were in the old library. As much as Bill pissed him off sometimes, he still didn't want to disappoint him.

That night they met again. Bill brought more alarm clocks and a box of sturdy-looking padlocks, which were an apparent upgrade over the smaller and less weighty combination locks. Bill had also pushed the charred table out of the way to the other side of the room, and in its place there were now four metal gym lockers. Each locker was as tall as a person. Bill secured the locker doors with the heavy padlocks.

On top of each locker sat an alarm clock. Dismissing Felix's greeting and commentary about the damn rain with an impatient wave of his hand, he instructed him to break the padlocks, the alarm clocks, and the locker doors—and to do it all at the same time.

Felix spent the next two hours blowing things up. It didn't take him long to simultaneously explode an alarm clock and the locker doors, but he had difficulty breaking open the large padlocks.

Bill gave Felix instructions and said nothing else. He would simply place an object in front of Felix, tell him to destroy it, and then Felix would blow it to pieces. Bill never took a break and was absolutely relentless. Felix was determined to keep pace. When Felix ran out of things to explode, Bill would hurry to the other side of the library and return with a fresh supply of locks, alarm clocks, and gym lockers. There seemed to be an endless supply of objects for Felix to destroy. Bill was indefatigable.

Felix was tired and ready to quit, but he refused to stop until Bill called it a night. Finally, Bill told him he could leave once he simultaneously exploded an alarm clock, a padlock, and the locker doors. With the extra incentive, Felix had no problem exploding all three in an instant. The explosion left a large divot in the oak floors and one twisted locker door embedded in a bookshelf ten feet away. Felix allowed himself a slight smile, but he was careful to control any display of self-satisfaction that might be too obvious.

By then, they'd been in the old library for over three hours. Felix surveyed the fruits of his labor. One side of the room looked like a scrap heap at a recycling center. Dozens of twisted and contorted metal lockers were lying on their sides. Pieces of metal, plastic, and wiring from the alarm clocks were strewn all across the floor. Metal and plastic shards were embedded in every surface of the room. Some of the metal lockers were so twisted as to be unrecognizable.

"This is a huge mess," Felix said. He was exhausted and wanted to go to bed.

"It's definitely that. We'll move it into the other rooms when we have time. For now, we'll continue to focus on increasing the size of the pile."

Felix laughed tiredly. "You know, it's actually kind of fun to blow all this shit up. It's like when I was a kid and I'd spend hours making these skyscrapers and towns and things out of building blocks. Then I'd just stomp the hell out of them."

Bill smiled.

"Are we done?" Felix asked. "I'm beat."

Bill nodded and told Felix to meet him there the following night. They left Devendon together and then went their separate ways.

Chapter 29

The next day Felix left Downey for his three o'clock Western Civ class. On his way out he bumped into Lucas in the lobby. They made plans to meet in the cafeteria for dinner at 6:30. Lucas went up to their room and plopped his book-heavy backpack onto his desk. He sat down and checked the time on his cell phone. He appeared nervous. He tapped his fingers on the desk and checked the time again.

There was a light tapping at the door.

He jumped out of his chair and opened it. Caitlin and Harper stood in the hallway.

"Get in—quick!" Lucas said, ushering them into the room. "Felix is out until dinner, but I don't know about Allison. Where is she?"

"Down in our room," Caitlin whispered. "I told her I had to meet with my teaching assistant. What's going on?"

Harper looked around the room for a moment before sitting in Felix's desk chair. "So what's all this about?" she asked.

"Like you don't know," Lucas said, frowning. "It's about Felix."

"What do you mean?" Harper asked, looking confused. "What is this? Some kind of intervention? There's nothing going on with Felix. I…"

"Not that," Lucas said impatiently. "It's about Felix—not about you and Felix. He's up to something. And I think Allison is, too."

"Up to something?" Caitlin asked, sitting on Lucas's bed after flicking away some imaginary dust from the comforter. "I think they're just friends."

"They are just friends," Lucas exclaimed. "What the hell is wrong with you two? I'm not talking about anyone having sex! Jesus Christ!

I'm trying to tell you that Felix and Allison are up to something, and it has nothing to do with them having sex with each other or anyone else."

Caitlin's brow creased. "Okay. Well, now that you mention it, Allison's definitely been acting strange lately. It's hard to even have a conversation with her anymore. It's like she's lost in her own world. I feel kind of uncomfortable asking her about it though. I mean, I want to…but…I don't know. The one time I did say something, she just brought up that thing about seasonal affective disorder and how much it rains here."

"I think she's lost some weight," Harper added. "And she doesn't look very good. You know, kind of pale and tired all the time. But what does that have to do with Felix?"

"It has everything to do with Felix," Lucas answered. "I think Allison knows about whatever it is that Felix is doing, and it's making her have a nervous breakdown. She's totally loopy."

"That's a nice theory, but what exactly is it that Felix is doing?" Harper asked, suddenly looking worried. "You don't think he's doing anything weird or illegal, do you? I mean, he's not doing drugs or anything like that, right?"

"I don't think it's that," Lucas said, shaking his head. "I guess you can never be sure, but I don't think he'd do anything illegal. I mean, why would he? He hasn't talked about it much, but I don't think he has money issues. He inherited all of his parents' stuff. There had to be life insurance policies and shit like that."

"I'm not following you," Caitlin said. "Then what makes you think he's involved in something?"

Lucas took a deep breath. "I'm only telling you this because I feel like I have to. I promised Felix I wouldn't say anything. But I think under the circumstances, I don't have a choice. Do you remember just before winter break how Felix was acting kind of strange? And then he missed the first couple days of class?"

"Of course," Harper said. "And then Allison borrowed Caitlin's car and brought him back to school the next day. We were all ready to call the police. How could we forget?"

Lucas nodded. "Well, what you don't know is that during the last month or so before the break, Felix was having these really bad nightmares! I mean shit right out of a Freddy Krueger movie! You know, the leather-faced dude with the claws? Anyway, he'd wake up in the middle of the night screaming his frickin' lungs out—like somebody was trying to kill him in his sleep."

"That is pretty weird," Caitlin said.

"But that's not the half of it," Lucas said. "After he woke up he'd look around the room all crazy like. Sort of like he was checking to make sure everything was still there. And he had this look in his eyes that freaked the hell out of me."

"He did that every night?" Harper asked.

"Yeah. Every single night. I thought I was gonna lose my mind. I felt bad for him, but I felt bad for me too. I was having some serious sleep deprivation issues, you know."

"What were the dreams about?" Caitlin asked. "Did he tell you?"

"I asked him a few times, but he always said the same thing," Lucas answered. "He couldn't remember."

"Wait a sec—is he still having them?" Caitlin asked.

"No. After Allison brought him back, it never happened again. He didn't really say anything about it. I didn't want to bring it up. I'm not gonna make him talk about something if he doesn't want to."

No one spoke.

Finally, Harper broke the silence. "But that doesn't prove anything! We all know Felix lost his parents in a fire last summer. He's had a hard time with it. And the only person he ever opens up to is Allison."

"First," Lucas replied, looking directly at Harper, "Allison and Felix are from the same town—she knew his parents. It's only natural he'd talk to her about it. And second..."

"So what's the big conspiracy then?" Caitlin asked. "Felix is having some issues dealing with his parents dying, and Allison is helping him. So what? Seems pretty normal to me."

"Maybe if you let me finish," Lucas said, annoyed, "you might reach a different conclusion."

"Okay, okay," Caitlin said. "Don't get all heated up, Minnesota. We'll let you finish."

"Thank you. You might find it interesting that starting last semester, Felix leaves the room just before midnight and comes back two or three hours later."

"What?" Harper exclaimed. "He does?"

"Yeah. At first, it was just every few weeks or so. He's been going out more often lately. He went out once last week, and he's been out the last two nights. And he always leaves at eleven forty-five and comes back a few hours later."

"Where's he going?" Harper asked. "Have you asked him?"

"He always says he's going out for a walk. A couple of times I've asked him if he wanted me to go with him. But he just said he wanted to be alone. Oh! And then one time he came back to the room smelling like smoke…like from a fire."

"Do you think maybe he is just going out for a walk?" Caitlin asked.

"At midnight? In the middle of the winter? When it's raining out? Last night he came back at three in the morning. Who goes for a walk at that time when it's raining and freezing out?"

"That is odd," Harper said, nodding and looking at Caitlin, apparently for confirmation.

"Yeah," Caitlin agreed. "I wonder where he's been going?"

"I've been wondering the same thing," Lucas said. "And I think there's only one way to find out."

"How?" Harper asked. "You already asked him and he didn't tell you."

"We're not going to ask him," Lucas replied. "We're going to follow him."

Caitlin and Harper looked at each other with stunned expressions.

"No way!" Harper shouted. "Really? You wanna follow him?"

"It's the only way to find out what he's doing. It'll be simple. I've already worked out the plan in my head."

"Great," Caitlin said sarcastically. "I can't wait to hear about this."

Lucas rolled his eyes. "I apologize for not enlisting your magnificent intellect when I was in the planning stages. But with such a simple plan, I didn't think it'd be necessary. So here's the plan—we follow him after he leaves the dorm."

"You came up with that all on your own?" Caitlin said. "I'm impressed."

Lucas bit his tongue.

"But if he only goes out every few weeks," Harper said, "how are we gonna know when to follow him?"

"Okay," Lucas said excitedly. "First things first—he's been out the last two nights, so whatever he's doing, I think it's escalating. I think he might be going out again tonight. And we already know when he's going to leave. It's like clockwork every time—eleven forty-five. So here's what we're gonna do—tonight at eleven-thirty, I want you guys to leave the dorm and go out just past the old pine tree on the other side of the Freshman Courtyard. When Felix leaves the room, I'll text you that it's a go. When you get the text, just stay where you are. From behind that tree you'll be able to see the entrance to Downey, but Felix won't be able to see you. I'll follow Felix just a few minutes after he leaves the dorm. You'll need to watch him to see which direction he goes. Okay so far?"

"Sure," they said in unison, but they both looked skeptical.

"When you see me come out of Downey, once Felix is out of sight, flag me down. Then we'll follow him at a safe distance."

"Okay," Caitlin said. "That doesn't sound too stupid. But what if Felix doesn't go out tonight?"

"Then I'll go to the bathroom and send you a text at midnight to let you know. The worst thing that can happen is you'll have to hide behind a tree for thirty minutes."

Nobody said anything. Caitlin and Harper appeared to be deep in thought.

"Do you really think Felix will go out tonight?" Harper asked.

"Yeah. I don't know for sure, but I have a hunch he'll make it three nights in a row."

Caitlin appeared anxious. "What should I wear?"

"Something that accentuates the blond highlights in your hair!" Lucas shouted. "Are you being serious? Just wear dark clothes and don't wear heels. We don't want him to see us or hear us."

Caitlin pouted. "Geez. Take it easy. I've never followed anyone before, you know."

Harper looked a little nervous and exhaled loudly. "All right. I'm in. Maybe it's just my curiosity getting the better of me, but I'd really like to know what he's doing."

"Sure," Caitlin said. "Why the hell not? We'll probably just find out that Felix is an insomniac and a closet smoker who likes to take long walks at night."

"Good!" Lucas said. "Now, all we have to do is get through the rest of the day without acting suspicious. We don't want Felix or Allison to think we're up to something, okay? Everyone just act natural—business as usual, all right?"

"Okay," Harper and Caitlin said, nodding in unison.

Lucas clapped his hands together loudly. "So that's the plan! Now it's all about execution. If one of you screws this up, I can't even tell you how pissed I'll be. We're all gonna meet for dinner at six-thirty, right? Business as usual, okay? I'll see you then."

Caitlin and Harper left the room, leaving Lucas sitting in his chair tapping nervously on his desk.

Chapter 30

Felix sat on his bed pretending to read the notes he scribbled in his last psychology class. He checked the time on his cell phone: 11:40. He yawned. He was out late the previous night at Devendon and had to get up early that morning for class. He was desperately in need of a good night's sleep, but he was supposed to meet Bill in twenty minutes. He considered texting Bill with some excuse about why he couldn't make it. He knew Bill would be absolutely irate. The image of Bill breaking into his room with a baseball bat in hand didn't seem all that outlandish. He checked the time again: 11:45. He glanced up at Lucas. He was slouching in his desk chair with his feet propped up on the bed listening to his iPod. He looked half-asleep.

Felix groaned and stood up. "Lucas. I think I'm gonna take a walk to clear my head. I'll see you in the morning."

Lucas pulled out one earplug and looked up at Felix. "All right, dude," he said groggily. "I'm going to bed. See you tomorrow."

As soon as Felix closed the door behind him, Lucas texted Caitlin and Harper: *It's a go.*

Caitlin and Harper had been standing behind the large pine tree on the Satler side of the Freshman Courtyard for the last fifteen minutes. It was another overcast night, but at least for the moment, they were staying dry. They felt a little foolish lurking behind the tree, but the few students who went in and out of Satler didn't pay any attention to them.

"What time do you have?" Caitlin asked.

Harper looked at her cell phone. "Eleven forty-seven. Lucas better not be screwing with us! Can you imagine if he's just doing this to mess with us! What if Felix is in on this, too? What if it's like a bet or something? You know, I bet I can make the girls hide behind a tree for thirty minutes."

"I'd kill them," Caitlin deadpanned.

"I'd do worse than that. I'd cut off their..."

Their cell phones buzzed at the same time. They'd set them to vibrate before leaving their rooms. They looked at Lucas's text: *It's a go.*

"Oh my God!" Caitlin exclaimed. "What do we do now? What do we do? What do we do?"

"Don't panic. Just wait for Felix to come out. Once he does, we need to keep an eye on him until we see Lucas."

Caitlin took a deep breath as the taller Harper peered over her shoulder, their bodies mostly hidden behind the tree.

"There," Harper whispered. "Is that...I think that's...it is. That's Felix!"

They watched as Felix exited Downey, turned, and started walking in the direction of the Courtyard. He was wearing a gray sweatshirt and a green PC baseball cap. He was staring straight ahead, appearing oblivious to anything around him.

Caitlin and Harper moved cautiously away from the protection of the tree to get a better view. If Felix happened to look back toward Satler, they'd be completely exposed.

"Okay," Harper said, crouching low as they moved slowly across the Freshman Courtyard. "Keep your eye on him. As soon as Lucas comes out, we'll need to make up some ground. Felix is walking pretty fast. Those damn long legs of his. Come on, Lucas. Get your ass out here! He's heading toward the Courtyard. Lucas better get out here quick or we're gonna lose him."

They crept toward Downey, watching Felix as he grew smaller and then finally disappeared from sight. They glanced anxiously at Downey every few seconds to see if Lucas was coming out. Anyone looking at them would have thought they were watching a tennis match by the way their heads were moving in unison from side to side.

Lucas emerged from Downey at a half run, his head on a swivel, obviously searching for something in the distance. They all saw each other at the same time.

"Lucas!" Caitlin hissed. "This way. Come on. We have to hurry."

Caitlin and Harper started jogging toward the Courtyard, with Lucas running to catch up.

"Where'd he go?" he whispered as he ran past them, taking the lead.

"He went this way," Harper said under her breath, "but then we lost him waiting for you."

"Damn!" Lucas said. "What was he wearing when…"

"There he is!" Caitlin exclaimed in a whisper-shout, apparently excited at being the one to spot Felix.

Felix was walking quickly along one of the cobblestone footpaths that ran parallel to the Courtyard. He was still staring straight ahead, apparently very focused on where he was going. There were several students out that night walking along the paths, but with finals approaching, that was to be expected.

"Nice!" Lucas said as they slowed their pace to a brisk walk. "Now we just have to keep a little distance between us in case he turns around."

"What if he does?" Caitlin asked, panicked.

"Stop, drop, and roll," Lucas replied.

"That's for fires, you asshole," Caitlin said. "God, I hate reality stars."

Felix walked past the Courtyard and Cutler Hall before turning toward the Bryant Center.

"Maybe he's going to work out?" Caitlin offered.

"The gym closes at ten," Lucas said, shaking his head in disgust.

"I know that," Caitlin snapped. "I was joking! Does everybody from Minnesota not get sarcasm, I…"

"Would you guys shut up!" Harper said sternly. "Geez! Now where's he going?"

Felix continued past the Bryant Center and then turned down a different path.

"Looks like he's headed toward the football stadium," Lucas said.

"But that's all locked up at night, isn't it?" Harper asked.

"Yeah," Lucas said. "I don't know where..."

"I know where he's going," Caitlin said in a stage whisper.

"Where?" Lucas and Harper asked in unison.

"The Old Campus."

As if on cue, when Felix reached the ancient iron gates on the north side of the Old Campus, he slipped through them without even slowing down.

They quickened their pace to close the gap, but Felix was walking fast and had the advantage of knowing where he was going.

"Why the hell's he going in there?" Lucas asked. "The Old Campus hasn't been used in years. It should get the award for the creepiest place on campus. C'mon, hurry up, guys. He's gonna lose us."

They reached the north gates and sidestepped through the narrow opening, trying not to disturb the swinging gate and its rusty hinges. Based on their appearance the hinges hadn't been lubricated in a hundred years. As they entered the Old Campus, it became noticeably darker, as if somebody hit the dimmer on the lights. Most of the bulbs in the lamp posts were burned out, and the grounds appeared to have fallen into disrepair during the winter months. Weeds overgrew the mulched flower beds, and the lawns were patchy and cluttered with leaves.

They could see Felix in the distance. He walked past one of the buildings and appeared to be increasing his pace.

"This place is freaking me out," Caitlin whispered. "Why'd he have to come here?"

"Did you think he was going out for a nice ice cream cone?" Lucas asked.

"Stop talking to me," Caitlin replied.

"Shhhhh," Harper said, glowering at Lucas.

Felix walked by another building, this one in the center of the Old Campus, and then turned the corner. Caitlin, Harper, and Lucas followed not more than fifty feet behind. When they reached the end of the building, Felix was nowhere in sight. They stopped and looked all around.

"Where'd he go?" Caitlin asked. "He was just here. He turned right here and then he just disappeared. So he must have…"

"He must've gone into that building," Harper said, pointing behind Lucas and Caitlin at the side entrance to Devendon Hall.

"I think you're right," Caitlin whispered. "What would he be doing in there? And how'd he get in?"

Lucas walked up the steps and examined the door like it was a foreign object. He reached out and turned the doorknob. It was locked. "He must have a key," he whispered over his shoulder.

"What do we do now?" Caitlin asked, looking very uncomfortable.

"Well," Harper said, looking around her. "We can either go back to Downey and wait for Felix to return—and when he does, we can ask him where he's been, or…"

"We'll never get anything out of him!" Lucas said, shaking his head.

"I was about to say," Harper continued, "or, we can confront Allison. She knows what he's up to. And she's more likely to talk than Felix. But we still need to know what Felix is doing in there. We need to use it as leverage when we talk to Allison."

"So what are you saying?" Caitlin asked.

"She's saying," Lucas interjected, "we're not going back to the dorm yet. We're gonna wait for Felix to come out, right?"

"Exactly," Harper said.

"Great!" Caitlin said dejectedly. "I was really hoping we'd just hang out all night in this weird place."

"Well, it looks like you're gonna get your wish," Lucas said, smiling. "I guess we can assume that if Felix went in through this door, then he'll be coming out the same way, right? So we just need to find a place where we can watch the door without being seen. You guys are pretty good at this—didn't you just spend some quality time together hiding behind a tree?"

"We did," Caitlin said, giving Lucas a face. "And you're welcome to go find your own tree."

"Actually," Harper said, ignoring their banter, "there are some overgrown shrubs next to that building over there." She pointed to the building diagonally across from Devendon. "We should be able to hide behind those. Let's go check it out."

The building offered an unobstructed view of the side door to Devendon, and the shrubs provided just enough cover so that anyone coming out wouldn't be able to see them. Crouched down behind the shrubs, Caitlin looked around with her arms crossed, like she was trying to hug herself. "I didn't think it could get any worse, but this is definitely worse. So now what do we do? Sit here and wait?"

"Yes," Lucas replied. "Now we sit here and wait."

Bill was dragging a wrecked metal file cabinet across the oak floors of the old library as Felix walked in.

"Hey, Bill. What's going on?"

Bill straightened up and wiped perspiration from his forehead. His clothes were filthy, and his hair was even more disheveled than usual. "I was going to move this into another room, but that can wait. How are you?"

"I'm good—a little tired from last night. Other than that, I'm all right."

"I'm not planning to keep you here as late tonight, but that's really up to you. I've been setting up for a while."

Felix looked around the room. It didn't appear any different than the night before.

"What are you talking about? Looks like the same mess to me."

"It is." Bill smiled. "We're not staying here tonight."

"Where are we going?"

"Follow me." Bill walked out of the old library and into the hall. Felix paused for a moment, wondering what Bill was up to, and then followed behind. The hallway was illuminated just enough for Felix to see the walls and Bill's back as he walked down the hall.

"I've been here for a few hours," Bill said over his shoulder. "Many of the inner offices have multiple entrances and multiple doors—that works well for what you're going to do. The doors that are closed are braced with file cabinets, desks, and just about any heavy object I could scrounge up. Okay, here we are."

They stopped in front of a closed door.

"Even in this light you can see that the door is still attached to the hinges," Bill said. "The doors in this building are actually very well constructed. The wood is solid and the hinges are bolted into the frames. Behind this particular door I've placed two large metal file cabinets, a desk, and two chairs. I want you to blow the door off its hinges. And do it with enough power so that the door and everything behind it gets pushed to the back of the room."

Felix appraised the door in front of him. "So this is supposed to be practice for when I have to get through the steel door in Ardsley Forest, huh?"

"It's the best we can do. Aside from having you break into a bank vault, there isn't a way to replicate what you'll be facing in Ardsley Forest. This is the first of eight doors you'll practice on tonight. There are three more on this floor and four on the third. Let's get started. Unless you want to stay up all night again, that is."

Bill stepped away from the door as Felix shook his head in an emphatic "no."

Felix looked at the door and raised his hand. The door began to shake and then, with a great booming sound, it exploded inward and moved several feet inside the room. He lowered his hand and stepped into the room to assess the damage. The door remained mostly intact but was splintered along one side where it ripped away from the hinges. The metal file cabinets, desk, and chairs were also pushed back into the room, but only six or seven feet. The door was still standing, but was leaning at a forty-five-degree angle against one of the file cabinets.

Bill stepped into the room and stopped next to Felix. He surveyed the room, shaking his head. Felix could sense that Bill wasn't pleased. "You're just not exerting enough energy to force open a steel door," he said firmly. "These wooden doors should be obliterated. The furniture should be crashing into the far wall. The door shouldn't be upright like that. If that were a steel door, nothing would've happened. You would have accomplished absolutely nothing."

Felix sighed. He thought he did pretty good. That was the most power he'd ever generated. And Bill was ripping him a new asshole. "Okay," he said. "I'll go at it harder next time."

"Good. The next one is across the hall."

Felix walked out of the room and into the hall. He studied the door for a moment—it looked exactly like the last one—and then raised his hand. Within seconds the door exploded off its hinges and flew to the back of the room, where it slammed against the wall with a loud *ka-thunk*. The office furniture also smashed against the wall; a desk shattered into pieces, and the metal file cabinet partially broke through the drywall, getting lodged in the rotting plaster. The echo of the explosion reverberated throughout the building.

"There!" Lucas said. "You must've heard it that time."

"I heard it," Harper said. "It's definitely coming from the building Felix went into."

"What the hell's he doing in there?" Caitlin asked.

"I have no idea," Lucas replied. "But that last one sounded like a bomb went off."

Felix had just destroyed his seventh door. After finishing with the doors on the top floor, he and Bill walked down one flight and went from office to office on the west side of the building directly below the old library. After the difficulty with the first door and the ensuing tongue-lashing from Bill, Felix had no trouble with the rest. As he demolished one door and moved on to the next, he couldn't believe how hard it was, and how much time he spent, trying to manipulate tiny little objects like bottle caps, books, and beer bottles. Just to move a little stack of books forced him to concentrate so hard he was surprised he hadn't induced a brain aneurism.

And now, it just seemed so easy. He felt like he could twitch his finger and effortlessly send that same stack of books flying from here to Cove Rock. He felt the power inside him. And he knew how to use it. It was so simple! All he had to do was think. It was all in his mind. Controlling matter was as simple as just wanting to control matter. He felt good. He felt powerful. He felt like Myrddin—or at least what he imagined Myrddin must have felt like.

They went to the end of the hall and stopped at the last door.

"This is the final one," Bill said. "This time, splinter the door as much as possible. That way, if you use too much power, it shouldn't go flying through the back wall."

"Sure." Felix raised his right hand and smiled. He thought about blowing the absolute shit out of the door.

Instantly the door was ripped away from its hinges and splintered into thousands of pieces. It flew into the room along with two steel lockers and a desk stacked up behind it. What was left of the door hit the wall and fell harmlessly to the floor, looking like someone had left behind an enormous collection of toothpicks. The steel lockers, however, zoomed through the air with such velocity that the wall couldn't bear the force of their impact. Both lockers crashed through the wall like it was made of paper and continued into the adjacent room, finally coming to rest after colliding against the inside of the exterior wall, just missing a large window overlooking the football stadium.

He turned to Bill and shrugged.

Bill grinned. "Well, at least they went through the inside walls. I'm not sure I'd want to explain how two gym lockers ended up out on the lawn."

Felix laughed. "Yeah. That'd be a tough one."

"Less Rembrandt and more wrecking ball. You're finally listening to me."

Felix nodded. "It was all in my head. Can we call it a night? I could use some sleep."

"Oh my God!" Lucas said. "The whole frickin' building just shook! What the hell's going on in there?"

"Is he blowing things up?" Caitlin asked, looking perplexed. "Why would he be doing that? And why here?"

Harper shook her head. "I don't know what's happening in there, but this has gone way beyond really weird. I mean really, really weird!"

"Where would he get explosives?" Lucas asked, scratching his head. "He smelled like smoke once before when he came back to the room. But I didn't think..."

"Lucas! Quiet!" Caitlin whispered. "He's coming out! Look!"

They looked toward Devendon. Felix was exiting the building, but he didn't close the door behind him. Rather, he held it open, and a second person followed. The man looked about the same height as Felix. He wore a black jacket and dark pants. His hair was dark, but it was difficult to make out any facial features from their hiding spot. The man started to walk away. Felix seemed to say something, and then he too turned and walked toward campus.

"I know who that is!" Harper said. "That's Bill! The groundskeeper guy Felix told us about. Remember? The guy who came to the football game. I'd swear that's him."

"*Bill?*" Caitlin said, surprised. "Didn't Allison meet with him before she went looking for Felix last winter? It was Bill, right? What would he be doing in there with Felix? You don't suppose they're part of some right-wing militia, do you? Maybe they're domestic terrorists or something like that."

"Too frickin' weird!" Lucas whispered. "I don't know what they're up to, but we're gonna find out tomorrow. We'll corner Allison and then we'll grill her until she spills her guts. Now we've gotta beat Felix back to the dorm."

"We do?" Caitlin asked, surprised.

"Yes," Lucas answered. "Felix is moving pretty fast, but if we run up the campus toward the library, we can cut across the Courtyard and beat him to Downey. But we're gonna have to go now! C'mon."

They took off at a sprint. By the time they reached the library, they were out of breath. But when Lucas quickened his pace, Harper and Caitlin kept up without complaint. Reaching Downey, they ran up the stairs two and three at a time. Before they separated at the third-floor landing, Lucas said, "Not a word to Allison or Felix until we talk tomorrow."

And with that he bounded up one more flight. He entered his room and quickly changed out of his clothes. He was breathing heavily and sweating profusely. He climbed into bed and tried to slow his breathing.

Felix made his way across campus at a leisurely pace. Maybe being Myrddin wasn't all bad, he thought. After all, he could do all kinds of amazingly cool things just by thinking about it. He checked his cell phone. It was just after 1:30. At least he'd be able to get a little sleep tonight. Once he reached the dorm, he took the stairs up to the fourth floor, not wanting to wait for the elevator. He unlocked the door to his room and closed it behind him without making a sound. He could hear Lucas snoring on the other side of the room. He changed into a pair of boxers and crawled into bed. He was exhausted. He fell asleep in seconds.

Chapter 31

Felix slept in late. He didn't have class until eleven, and he took advantage of the opportunity to catch up on some much-needed sleep. When he finally got out of bed, he still felt the effects of the adrenaline high from the previous night. Destroying those doors at Devendon was such a rush.

But as powerful as he felt the night before, he knew that Landry wouldn't be using wooden doors to bar access to the subterranean bunker. He had a hard time even imagining what the actual door would look like. Even though Bill had described it for him, Felix could only envision it as one of those giant mechanical bank vaults he'd seen on TV. And if it was anything like one of those, what was he supposed to do? Sure, he could practically disintegrate a hundred-year-old wooden door. But what would happen when he tried to break down a solid-steel door that weighed tons?

What if he couldn't do it? He imagined having to tell Bill he couldn't even get into the bunker. "Gee, sorry, Bill, I just couldn't get the door to open, so I got back in the car and drove back to campus. Aren't you gonna offer me a cup of tea?" Bill would probably kill him.

After his last class ended at three, he walked over to the Student Center to see if he had any mail. He hadn't checked his mailbox in nearly a week, and after going through the pile of junk mail, he decided that was probably too often. He tossed the solicitations into the recycling bin and noticed a group of twenty or so unusually well-mannered young people standing near the entrance of the student bookstore.

The group formed a semicircle around Todd Siegrand, who was talking and gesticulating with the polish of a seasoned politician. It appeared that Todd was conducting a campus tour for a group of high school students. Probably trying to get a jump on recruiting a new crop of assholes for his posse, Felix thought.

He didn't want Todd to see him. The few times he'd bumped into him since the incident at Astoria, Todd tried earnestly to cast menacing looks at him. Felix thought he looked more theatrical than intimidating.

Turning away from his mailbox to leave the Student Center, Felix was stopped in his tracks by a large object standing in his path. Slightly dazed, he looked up to see Larry—and standing on either side of him, Jonas and Salty. They were all having a good laugh at the look of consternation on Felix's face.

"Shit, Larry," Felix said, rubbing his shoulder, "it's like running into a wall. You've gotta be pushing two-fifty, right?"

"Actually, two-seventy," Larry said, smiling. "But that only seems big to you because you're a skinny-ass receiver."

Felix laughed. "I'm only skinny compared to you fat-asses. If you don't cut down on the food, you're gonna be shopping for clothes at the tent store. "

"It's solid muscle, jackass," Salty said, flexing his tattooed biceps.

"Salty, when are you gonna stop wearing your sister's tee shirts?" Felix asked, laughing.

"Never," Larry replied, elbowing Salty hard enough to knock over a normal-sized person. "You should see him try to do his Hulk Hogan thing. He stands there flexing so hard he nearly shits himself. He's such a pussy he can't even shred his little girl's tee shirt."

"Fuck you," Salty said.

"Fuck both of you," Jonas said. "Hey Felix, we just picked up the DVD of last season's games from Coach's office. We're heading over to our room to watch the good parts. Wanna come?"

"Yeah, sure," Felix replied, checking the time on his cell phone. "As long as you don't show the last play against Milford. I've already seen it on YouTube like a hundred times."

"Are you kidding?" Salty said, laughing. "We're putting that on a loop! Just one more inch—one more frickin' inch. But you couldn't do it, huh?"

They watched the DVD in Salty and Jonas's room for the next three hours. Just as Salty promised, he replayed the infamous "one-more-inch play" several times. And each time, Jonas did the play-by-play in his best announcer's voice. "And the ball is caught by Felix August. He's streaking down the sideline—he's heading towards the end zone—if he scores, the Sturgeons will win the game—they'll play for the Rain Cup—he's at the twenty, the ten, the five. He's going to score! He's going to score! It's a touch... no, wait...he's out...he's out of bounds...he's out at the one-inch line...the one-inch line! The Sturgeons lose the game. They will not be playing for the Rain Cup because Felix August couldn't make it just one more inch! Oh, the human tragedy of it all! The tragedy! The tragedy!"

Each time, they'd all laugh hysterically.

Felix left Satler just before 6:30 to meet Lucas and the girls for dinner. He went up to his room expecting Lucas to be there, but the room was empty. He hadn't seen Lucas all day. He also hadn't seen Allison, Harper, or Caitlin. He couldn't remember if there was ever a day when he didn't see at least one of his friends before dinner. He went down to the third floor to see if they were hanging out in one of the girls' rooms. As he neared their rooms he could hear voices from inside Allison and Caitlin's room.

"I don't know what the hell you're talking about!" a girl's voice said loudly.

Felix stopped just outside the door. Who was that? Was that Allison? She sounded angry. Was she having an argument with Caitlin?

"Come on," a guy's voice said, "we know that isn't true. There's something going on, and we just wanna know what it is. We're all friends here, right? Why don't you just tell us what you guys are doing?"

That sounded like Lucas, Felix thought. He turned his head so that his ear was almost touching the door.

"I'm telling you, I don't know anything, and that's the truth," the same girl's voice said.

That was definitely Allison, Felix thought. *But why is Lucas in her room? And what the hell are they talking about?*

"Allison," a girl's voice said, "we didn't want to do it like this. But unless you talk to us, we'll have to notify the school. We're genuinely concerned that you guys might be doing something illegal. We don't know if it's a terrorist thing or if you're planning to blow up the school or something like that. But we can't just sit around after what happened at Columbine and Virginia Tech, and..."

That was Caitlin, Felix thought. He was sure of it.

"For the last goddamn time," Allison screamed, "I don't know what you're talking about! And if you don't believe me, then ask Felix!"

Felix nearly jumped back from the door when he heard his name. What the hell? Why were they asking Allison about him? And what did Caitlin just say about terrorists and blowing up the school?

He pounded on the door with his fist. "Hey!" he called out. "It's Felix. Let me in."

There was silence in the room for several moments and then the door slowly opened.

Lucas was standing in the doorway. Allison was leaning against a desk in the back of the room. Her face was red and her green eyes were spitting out sparks of anger. Harper was sitting alongside Caitlin on her bed. They were looking at the floor and appeared to be embarrassed.

"Hey Felix," Lucas said, sheepishly.

"What the hell's going on in here?" Felix demanded. "I could hear you out in the hall!"

"Oh," Lucas said, "then you know we were just asking Allison about what's going on."

"What do you mean what's going on?"

"Felix, maybe you should come in and close the door," Lucas said calmly.

Felix stepped into the room. He looked at Harper and Caitlin, but they didn't make eye contact with him.

"Look," Lucas said, "I know how this looks, but we were just trying to find out if there was something going on with you."

"With me..."

"A lot's happened this year, right? And there were some things that were pretty weird and..."

"What things?" Felix shouted.

"C'mon, dude. Your midnight walks, for one. You've been going on these three-hour walks in the middle of the night—and whenever I'd ask you what you were doing, you'd tell me you were just going for a walk. But c'mon, Felix, I'm not a retard, and..."

"I like to walk at night! I...I have a hard time sleeping and I just like to walk. It clears my head. What the fuck's wrong with that?"

"We followed you last night," Harper said, looking up at Felix for the first time. "We know you went to the Old Campus. And that you were there with Bill the groundskeeper guy. And we know you were in one of the buildings blowing things up with explosives."

"You...you what? You followed me?"

Harper nodded.

Felix was speechless. He looked back at Harper, not knowing what to say. She stared back at him for a moment and then she looked away. He looked at Allison. Her cheeks were no longer quite as red as before, but she was still pissed off. She frowned and looked down at the floor.

A hundred thoughts swirled around in Felix's head all at once. They followed him to Devendon last night. It must have sounded like he was detonating bombs in there. How could he explain that? What the hell should he do? Should he just tell them? Tell them everything? Or should he just deny everything, no matter how irrational that would make him look? But they'd know he was lying. They weren't idiots. If he lied to them, he might as well just tell them to fuck off. That he didn't want to be friends. But if he told them the truth, their lives would change forever. He'd be responsible for that. What right did he have to do that? And why would anyone even want to know the truth about the world? It always seemed that people made the truth out to be such a great thing—everyone was always talking about getting to the truth of a matter. But the truth was that people were happier living in a world where the New Testament wasn't about a Druid named Myrddin and the Antichrist wasn't living on the other side of town. Why the hell would anyone want to know about that?

Allison suddenly grabbed Felix by the arm, shaking him out of his reverie, and whispered into his ear, "Felix, you can tell them whatever you want—that's up to you. But do not tell them I'm a Vessel. They can't know. Promise me."

She pulled away from Felix and looked at his face intently; her green eyes were full of intensity.

Felix nodded.

He walked across the room to the window and looked outside. It was still light out and the sky was clear. A pair of robins flew past the window, and a squirrel darted across the Freshman Courtyard and scurried up a tree. Bill was always lecturing him about unintended consequences, but what was the point? If he told them who he really was, what would the consequences of that be? If he were to open their eyes to the real world, they wouldn't like what they saw—he knew that much. They couldn't possibly imagine what the real world was like.

He'd spent so much time inside his own head trying to understand what it meant to live his life when his destiny was preordained thousands of years ago. But he didn't really consider that his destiny might involve others—even his friends. He'd decided that he wanted to live an ordinary life; he needed school and his friends. But did that mean he had to bring his friends into his life—his real life? Was there no other way? If he told them the truth, was he just doing it to satisfy his own selfish needs? How could he possibly know the answers to all these questions? Wasn't that why they were called unintended consequences—because they were unintended? He couldn't possibly know the consequences of his decision. But he did know that he needed his friends. And didn't he have to make decisions based on what he knew? Wasn't that the only way he could live an ordinary life?

His decision made, he turned around and said, "Meet me in Dale's Room in fifteen minutes. I'll tell you everything."

He walked out without looking at any of them.

Chapter 32

Felix walked toward the Courtyard. He needed to be outside, to feel the cool dusk breeze on his skin. He'd made his decision. He hoped it was the right one. He didn't know if he made it for the right reasons, or even if there were any right reasons. It wasn't like anybody was ever in his position before. There was no roadmap to lead him in the right direction. He couldn't just go online and read some blog about how people in similar situations handled their problems. He wasn't looking for advice on something pedestrian, like which running back to select in a fantasy football draft.

He couldn't predict the consequences of his decision, but the one thing he knew was that the people who learned the truth about Landry tended to die. And most of them died horrible deaths. Landry murdered his entire family. Felix's own mother died locked up in a mental institution.

That only left three people who knew that Landry was the Antichrist: Felix, Bill, and Allison. And the only reason Allison knew was because of him. But Allison's situation was completely different from his. He was Myrddin. He was supposed to go to Ardsley Forest and destroy the First Templar Amulet. Allison was only involved because she talked him into it. When he told her about Bill's plan, he never anticipated that she'd insist on going to Ardsley Forest with him. Now he literally felt sick to his stomach when he thought about Allison getting hurt in the woods. He could never forgive himself if something happened to her, especially after what he did to his parents.

And if he told Lucas and the girls, as he was planning to do, how would they react? What unanticipated actions would they take? Felix walked around aimlessly. When he finally checked the time on his cell phone, he realized that nearly thirty minutes had passed since he left Downey. He quickened his pace and walked toward the library.

Chapter 33

By the time Felix arrived at Dale's Room, Lucas and the girls were already seated at the big circular table. The room was silent. All eyes were fixed on him as he stepped into the room. Lucas and Harper had brought a few textbooks, which were laid out on the table. Apparently they were planning to do some studying later. Felix laughed to himself. They definitely wouldn't be in the mood to study when he was done. He sat down in the red leather chair between Allison and Caitlin.

"Hey Felix," Lucas said, breaking the silence, "we all just wanted to let you know that we feel really bad about ganging up on Allison. We should've just talked to you and left her out of it. It was very uncool. We feel bad."

"They haven't stopped apologizing since we left the dorm," Allison said. "I already told them it's okay."

Felix thought Allison looked tired, like she'd been drained of her passion. It was hard to see her like this.

"You're right, you know," Felix said, looking at Lucas. "You should've just come to me. But I'm really the one who should be apologizing to Allison. It's my fault this happened. I'm sorry for that."

Allison smiled. "It's not your fault at all, Felix. I would never blame you for any of this. You know that."

Felix looked around the table.

Everyone looked back at him expectantly. He looked up at the ceiling, took a deep breath, and then rested his hands on the table.

"Well...?" Caitlin said. "I don't want to seem pushy, but..."

Felix exhaled and scratched his head. "Okay. I said I would tell you everything, and that's what I'm gonna do. But before I start, you should know it's a long story. And it's pretty strange. And you're probably gonna think I'm pretty crazy. And I'm not going to keep saying 'I know that this sounds crazy' or 'you're not going to believe this,' because if I do, we're gonna be here all night. Okay?"

Everyone at the table nodded.

Felix took another deep breath. "Okay, then. Where do I begin? How should I do this?"

He looked at Allison for guidance but only got a noncommittal shrug in response.

"I'll just give you the punch line and work backwards."

The room was silent. All eyes were glued to Felix.

He cleared his throat and then blurted out, "Landry Ashfield, the president of A.E.I., is the Antichrist."

Felix let the words sink in before he continued.

"And I, Felix August, am the Second Coming. You are looking at the reincarnation of Jesus Christ."

Felix knew he was deliberately provoking his friends. Maybe it was because he didn't like how they'd badgered Allison. Or maybe he just felt like it. In either case, it was having the desired effect. Caitlin looked like she'd just swallowed a bug. Harper appeared to be in shock, and Lucas was laughing so hard tears were streaming down his face.

"I knew it!" he shouted, slapping his hand on the table. "Dude, I knew you were screwing with us! I tried to tell them. But no, nobody would believe me. That's awesome. Too frickin' funny! The Second Coming!" He trailed off, laughing hysterically.

"So that's it?" Caitlin asked, looking around the table. "That's what we came here for? I don't think that's very funny at all."

Felix did his best to affect a little gravitas. "I didn't intend for it to be funny. What I just told you is the absolute truth. I would swear on a stack of Bibles."

Lucas stopped laughing.

Harper looked at Lucas as if she were seeking permission from him to speak. "Felix, the joke's over, right? I guess it was kind of funny. Not as funny as Lucas seems to think it is. But I guess I can appreciate the humor. But you're done, right? Can we move on now and study or go get a slice of pizza or something?"

"This isn't a joke," Felix said seriously. "I swear to you on my soul that I'm telling you the truth."

"Felix," Caitlin snapped. "I think that's enough."

"But don't you want to know why I'm the reincarnation of Jesus? Or why Landry Ashfield is the Antichrist?"

"Landry Ashfield?" Caitlin exclaimed, a look of utter disbelief on her face. "Are you out of your mind? *The* Landry Ashfield? Do you realize who he is? And you're telling us he's the Antichrist? And you! You're the reincarnation of Jesus? You can't be serious, right? You're joking with us! Why do I feel like you're filming this? You're just screwing with us, aren't you?"

Felix smiled. "What if I told you that a big part of the New Testament is a total lie? That there are parts in it that have nothing at all to do with Jesus. In fact, most of the interesting stuff, like Jesus being born without a father and his Second Coming, are really about a Druid priest named Myrddin. And that the Antichrist is really about something called a Drestian. What do you think about that?"

Caitlin's face was so red it looked like she'd spent one too many cycles in a tanning bed. "I may not be the most perfect Catholic in the world," she spat out, "but I still find this really offensive, Felix. I think the joke's officially over. You've already taken it too far. And I'm surprised that Allison was in on this. You and Lucas act like retards half the time, but Allison, I mean, come on."

"Felix," Lucas finally said, after a long pause, "I know you're just screwing with us, but you have a weird look in your eyes. Kind of like the look crazy people get before they do something extra crazy."

Caitlin nodded vigorously.

"But," he continued, "the thing is, I know you're not really crazy.

And even though you're in some strange 'let's screw with my friends' kind of mood, I don't think Allison is willing to go as far as you. So Allison, please tell us why Felix is fucking with us."

All eyes turned to Allison. She looked at Lucas and deadpanned, "He's not fucking with you. It's all true—every word of it."

Caitlin sighed loudly and shook her head. "I'm getting out of here. This is ridiculous! Harper, you coming?"

"Hold on a second, guys," Lucas said, smiling broadly. "Don't leave yet. I've got an idea. Maybe Felix can show us some proof or something. Come on, Felix. Let's see something! If you're the Second Coming, you should be able to turn water into wine or something like that, right?"

Felix thought for a moment and then looked at Allison.

She nodded almost imperceptibly.

"All right," Felix said, "I'll give you a demonstration."

"Really?" Lucas said, surprised. "I was expecting you to say no 'cause that's what always happens on TV. You know, the guy asks for proof and the other guy is always like 'sorry, no, you're just gonna have to trust me.'" Lucas seemed to realize he was rambling. "Oh! Sorry. So what are you gonna do?"

Felix thought for a moment and said, "I've got it."

"Okay," Lucas said eagerly. "What is it?"

Lucas was sitting directly across from Felix. An art history book was placed on the table in front of him. It was a heavy, hard-bound, illustrated text at least three inches thick, more like a coffee table book than a textbook.

Felix raised his hand. The book slid across the table. When it reached the center, it levitated into the air and flew toward him and into his outstretched hand. Felix held the book for a moment and then let it go, dropping it onto the table with a loud *thump*.

Lucas's jaw dropped, as did Caitlin's and Harper's. Caitlin's eyes bulged so much that Felix feared they might come shooting out of her head. Only Allison remained calm, a slight smile on her face as she looked at her friends around the table. Caitlin mumbled something unintelligible. Felix thought she might have said something like "nofrickinwhatwashuh." Harper still couldn't figure out how to close her mouth.

Lucas jumped up from his chair, his eyes wild with disbelief. "How'd you do that?" he demanded. He ran his hands on the table along the same route the book traveled. He looked up at the ceiling and waved his arms around in front of him, apparently trying to find a wire dangling from the ceiling. "How'd you do that?" he asked again. "Let me see that book!"

Felix raised his hand a few inches above the table. The art history book suddenly jumped up off the table like a Harrier jet and hovered a foot or so above Felix's head. It then traveled smoothly through the air to the other side of the table. Lucas held his hands out in front of him like he was carrying a basket. The textbook glided through the air and came to rest gently in his arms.

Lucas held the book up to his face and examined it closely. He looked at the front cover and then turned it over and examined the back. He opened it and quickly flipped through the pages. There was something frantic about Lucas's movements. Felix couldn't suppress a tiny smile. Harper and Caitlin were watching Lucas closely, apparently waiting for him to discover how Felix had done it.

"Lucas!" Felix shouted from across the table. "Hold onto the book tightly!"

"Huh?" Lucas said, confused.

"Hold onto the book! Put one hand on each side and grip it as tight as you can. And don't let go!"

Lucas did as he was instructed.

The book suddenly lurched toward the table, pulling Lucas's arms out in front of him until they were perfectly straight. "Whoa!" he shouted. He was then pulled forward so that his upper body was almost entirely on top of the table, while his legs were still firmly planted on the floor. Then he was pushed abruptly backward so that he was standing straight up again with his arms still extended out in front of his body. Three times he did this; first he was pulled down and then pushed back up as if he were a marionette controlled by a puppeteer using giant invisible strings. Lucas appeared to be engaged in a fierce battle. His eyes were wide with amazement, and he grunted loudly each time the book pulled him in a different direction.

"Don't let go!" Felix shouted.

Lucas's arms suddenly shot above his head with the book still gripped tightly in his hands. It looked like he was trying to show his art history book to someone who was watching far off in the distance. And then the book climbed toward the ceiling a few inches at a time. Lucas stood on the tips of his toes as he strained to hold onto the book.

"Don't let go, Lucas!" Felix shouted.

Lucas's feet came off the floor. He kicked as if he were in the deep end of a pool trying to find the bottom. The book continued to pull him upward. Higher and higher the book climbed until Lucas's feet were above the circular table where everyone sat watching, enraptured by what they were witnessing.

"Felix!" Lucas screamed. "What the hell are you doing? Let me down! This isn't fun!"

Felix ignored him. Lucas's body was pulled steadily through the air and across to the other side of the room. His feet struck the back of one of the lounge chairs that faced the coffee table. Lucas kicked out with his foot, trying desperately to find solid ground. But before his foot could reconnect with a solid surface, he flew past the chairs and hovered above the coffee table.

The seventeen portraits of President Woodrow hanging from the walls looked on serenely.

"Felix! C'mon, man! Can you put me down?"

"Not yet!" Felix shouted. "Hang on tight!"

Lucas's body began to turn in a circle—slowly at first, but gathering speed with each successive revolution. Faster and faster he spun until his legs were no longer perpendicular to the floor.

Lucas screamed.

With each revolution, his legs moved further and further away from the floor until they were nearly horizontal with the ceiling. Lucas was a blur as he spun around only a few feet from the ceiling, like he was tethered to a ceiling fan turned to high speed. All the while he was screaming for Felix to let him down.

Then gradually his body began to slow as each rotation took slightly longer than the one before. His legs descended to a forty-five-degree angle and then continued to drop until they were once again directly below his torso. He twirled in a circle a few more times like a figure skater doing a triple salchow and then came to a stop.

Lucas was still screaming. His hair was disheveled, his eyes were wide, and he looked absolutely terrified. It took him a moment to realize that he was no longer spinning. When he did, he stopped screaming. He was pulled through the air until he was just next to the coffee table. The book fell from its height, and it, and Lucas, continued their descent until Lucas's feet were touching the floor.

He collapsed in a heap, tossing the book aside as if it were burning his fingers. "Shit! I'm never touching that book again!" he moaned.

Caitlin ran over to Lucas and put her hands lightly on his shoulders. "Are you okay?" she asked, her eyes wide.

"I don't know. Am I still in one piece?"

"I think so," Caitlin said, looking him over.

"Then I guess I'm okay. I'm just a little dizzy."

Caitlin helped him to his feet.

"Dude," Lucas said, taking his seat at the table, "that was amazing! You've got like superpowers!"

Felix shrugged.

"You just turned me into a human helicopter. That was intense!"

"Wow!" Harper said softly, her eyes sparkling. "I always thought there was something different about you. I never thought it was something like...I mean...wow!"

Caitlin's eyes managed to remain in her head, but she still looked out of sorts. "I don't know what to say about any of this, but I'm not sure it proves anything you said before. I mean, about you being the Second Coming of Christ and all."

"I know," Felix replied, feeling much more relaxed than before. "So now I'm going to tell you everything."

Ninety minutes later, Felix finished telling the major parts of the story: Constantine, Myrddin, his adoption, the Tinshires, the McGaughey curse, the cycle, Eve's journal, Landry Ashfield, the First Templar Amulet, the Vessels, and the Lost Souls. As soon as he was finished, his friends started asking questions.

"Landry doesn't know about your father, or lack of a father, right?" Harper asked.

"Right," Felix answered. "Even if Landry knew about me, he'd just think my father was some random dude. He doesn't know about the cycle, so he wouldn't know—couldn't know—that I don't have a father."

"Okay," Lucas said, looking thoughtful. "So what are you supposed to do now? Kill Landry Ashfield?"

"Yes. But not now. I'm not ready for that yet."

"Holy shit!" Lucas replied. "You're really gonna kill him?"

"How are you supposed to do that?" Caitlin asked, looking sick to her stomach. "That's wrong, you know."

"He's not a person, Caitlin," Felix said. "He's the Antichrist, remember? The reason I was born is to kill the Antichrist. He's not a man. I already explained that."

"I know," she said. "I mean...okay. I guess it's just hard to grasp all this."

"I know," Felix replied, gently. "But I'm not trying to kill him. I can't. Not yet, anyway. I'm just gonna destroy the First Templar Amulet. Or at least I'll try to destroy it."

"And how are you supposed to do that?" Harper asked.

"Landry's keeping it in an underground facility in Ardsley Forest. The only way to get there is by taking logging roads that haven't been used in like forever. Bill and I went out there a few weeks back."

"You went out there?" Lucas asked in amazement.

"Yeah. Bill's sort of a counselor at A.E.I., but he's really just there to get information about Landry. He's the one who figured out where the Amulet is. Or, as he puts it, he's reasonably confident that he knows where it is."

"But, dude, isn't that the forest where all of those people were killed?" Lucas asked. "Where those three bodies were just found last month? It is, right? Isn't that where that Nick dude, the Mormon Mephistopheles freak, is supposed to be hiding out?"

"Yeah, that's the one."

"Did you see anything out there?" Lucas asked a little nervously.

"No," Felix answered. "But there's definitely something wrong with those woods. Bill thinks that Nick Blair was maybe there before. But not now. But I don't know."

"And that's where you're going?" Lucas shouted. "That's messed up."

Harper nodded. "So what are you planning to do? Break into this place?"

"Pretty much." Felix nodded. "It's actually like a bomb shelter. It's made of something strong enough to withstand a bomb. And the only way to get inside is to break through the strongest steel door ever made."

"And how are you supposed to do that?" Lucas asked.

"That's a good question. You saw me leave Devendon at the Old Campus last night with Bill, right?"

Lucas nodded.

"We were practicing. I'm working on busting down a steel door and destroying the security system before anyone knows I'm there."

A look of understanding suddenly washed over Lucas's face. "Oh? So you were in there blowing shit up. That explains all the loud noises we heard. And why you smelled like smoke that one night. But how do you know how to use explosives?"

"I don't," Felix said flatly. He took a long drink of soda.

Lucas looked confused. "Huh? Anyway, so Landry, this Antichrist dude, is taking over the world through these zombie things he controls?"

"Lucas, I told you they're called Vessels. And they're not at all like zombies in the movies. They're just like you and me. You would never know if someone was a Vessel or not. That's why this whole thing is so scary. Landry's been making these things for something like twenty years. He must have thousands of them already. Not to mention all the Lost Souls living inside him."

"This guy has to be stopped!" Lucas shouted.

"He does," Felix said. "And that's why I'm going to destroy the Amulet. It's the center of the whole thing. Without it, he can't create Vessels."

"What happens to the Vessels when you destroy it?" Harper asked.

"Bill thinks they'll die. But the Human Vessels and the Soulless Humans will still live. Bill also thinks Landry will still control the Lost Souls."

"But if it isn't destroyed, he'll just continue to create all these Vessel things, right?" Lucas asked.

"Exactly. That's why I'm gonna try to destroy it in the next two weeks."

Allison, who was sitting quietly, suddenly became alert. "You mean *we're* going to destroy it in the next two weeks."

Felix looked around the room, suddenly feeling apprehensive. "That's right," he said, warily.

"Wait a minute!" Lucas shouted. "Allison's going? She's going with you? If she's going, then I'm going!"

"I'm going, too," Caitlin said, looking at Felix. "I'm still not sure what's going on. And I don't know if I believe what you were saying about the New Testament and Jesus. But I've decided that you're not crazy. And I'm not going to be left out."

"Hold on a second!" Felix shouted. "None of you have any idea what you're saying. I'm talking about breaking into an underground building in the middle of Ardsley Forest. And I'm going in the middle of the night. And if anyone sees me, they'll try to kill me! I'm talking about life and death here. This isn't a football game with winners and losers. This is real life. There are no second chances. If you get caught, you'll die! On top of that, Nick…that Mormon Mephistopheles psychopath…he could still be prowling around the forest killing people and cutting off their heads. Five people were killed and mutilated. And that's why none of you are going!"

"Except for me," Allison said.

"Yes," Felix said quietly. "Except for Allison."

"What the hell?" Lucas shouted. "Why does she get to go?"

Felix looked at Allison, and her eyes dropped to the table. What could he tell them? He had to come up with something quick. And it had to be good. "Because she…um…because she can…because she can help me." That wasn't good, at all. He was such a terrible liar.

"And we can't?" Harper shouted. "If Allison can help you, then so can we! I'm going!"

Felix was flabbergasted. "I'm not looking for help! If you only knew what you were asking me…fuck…believe me…you don't want anything to do with this!"

"Why don't you let us make that decision?" Caitlin said. "We're all adults here."

"But it's not your goddamn decision to make! I have to do this. Don't you get it? I don't have a choice! I'm the only person who can destroy the Amulet! And I'm not gonna be responsible for all of you! And this isn't your fight, anyway!"

"But it's Allison's fight?" Harper said. "How can it not be our fight, but still be Allison's fight? Explain that to me."

Felix couldn't believe the situation he was in. He'd had to tell Allison everything because she saw him destroy her room. He didn't have a choice about that. Then he agreed to let her go with him into Ardsley Forest because she thought she was a Vessel. She wanted to face her own death. How could he have said no to her? He'd decided to tell Lucas, Caitlin, and Harper the truth because they followed him to Devendon. He didn't want to lie and lose their friendship. And now he'd painted himself into another corner. He'd promised Allison he wouldn't tell anyone she might be a Vessel. Now he either had to break that promise or allow Lucas, Caitlin, and Harper to go with him into Ardsley Forest. He glanced over at Allison. Her bright green eyes seemed to flash a warning at him.

What the hell? How could this have happened again? As much as he tried to control things, they just never worked out how he planned. Everything seemed to have a mind of its own. Once again he felt like he was a passenger on a train, and the conductor was controlling not only where it was going, but how it was going to get there. Why did he even try? Things just seemed to happen of their own accord, anyway. Felix groaned, and the words "unintended consequences" ran through his mind.

"Okay, guys. I really hope I don't regret this. You can go with Allison and me into Ardsley Forest. But you'll do exactly as I say. This isn't a democracy. I'll tell you what to do and when to do it. We'll have one shot to destroy the Amulet. If we do it the right way, we'll get in and out of there during the night without anyone knowing we're there. I'll destroy it and then we'll get the hell out! Okay?"

They all nodded in agreement. Felix thought he saw Allison give him a small smile.

"One question," Lucas said, raising his hand like a schoolchild. "What are you gonna do about Landry if he shows up? The Antichrist doesn't sound like someone you want to encounter at night in some haunted forest."

Felix looked at each of them individually, trying to underscore the importance of what he was about to say. "If we see Landry in Ardsley Forest, he'll kill us all. It's as simple as that. But…and this is the good news. We don't have to worry about it. Bill found out that Landry will be in Egypt at the end of April. That's why we have to do it then, while he's away."

Lucas looked visibly relieved.

"But, Felix," Harper said, "won't you be able to do something about him? Like whatever it was you were doing to Lucas with that book?"

"I've just started to figure out how to control matter. I've been practicing with Bill. It's why I've been sneaking out at night and going to the Old Campus. But I can only control small stuff, break down doors and shit like that. I wouldn't be able to protect any of you from Landry. You need to understand that. Eve said in the journal that Landry has the power to destroy the world. Think about that for a minute and then let me know if you still want to go. You can always change your mind."

They looked at each other nervously, but nobody spoke.

"So, I guess for now, we'll all just continue to do our thing," Felix continued. "We have finals soon, so that should keep our minds off what we'll be doing in a few weeks. And obviously, don't tell anybody about this. I'm sure you can all think of a lot of reasons why you shouldn't. Besides, everyone would think you're insane, anyway. But there could be students or professors at this school who are under Landry's control."

"It's pretty scary when you think about it that way," Caitlin said thoughtfully.

"But you know what's even scarier?" Felix asked, looking at Caitlin.

"If you tell any of this to somebody who's under Landry's control, Landry will kill you, me, Lucas, Allison, Harper, and Bill. You wouldn't live to see tomorrow. How's that for scary?"

Everyone stared at Felix. Lucas seemed to be having a hard time swallowing.

"Like I said before, this isn't a game. Landry is the Antichrist. He wants to rule the entire world and enslave all of us. And the only thing standing between him and his objective is us. Think about that when you try to sleep tonight."

Chapter 34

The concept of time is a strange thing. The clock on the wall marks the passage of time minute after minute, hour after hour, and day after day, unbroken and inexorable, oblivious to the significance of events, whether they be joyous or horrific. Time plays no favorites and it grants no favors. But the perception of time is a different matter altogether. For Felix, the next ten days seemed to last a lifetime.

He exchanged a few texts with Bill, and was told to be ready at a moment's notice. As soon as Bill received confirmation that Landry was in Egypt, Felix would return to Ardsley Forest—but this time, without Bill at his side.

With each passing day, it became harder to think of anything other than Ardsley Forest and what might be waiting for him in Landry's underground building. Not even the upcoming final exams proved to be a distraction. As much as Felix and his friends tried to talk about other things, the subject of Ardsley Forest kept coming up like the grotesque head of a mythological creature whose head kept growing back each time it was hacked off.

But to Felix's surprise, some things got better. He felt a great sense of relief after the meeting in Dale's Room. He no longer had to sneak around campus or lie to his friends about what was on his mind. He didn't realize how liberating honesty could be. And Harper started treating Felix differently. Just the way it was before winter break. The way it was before she started seeing Dante Smithwick.

Allison, on the other hand, grew more quiet and morose by the day. She ate very little and spent most of her time by herself. Felix tried to cheer her up, but to no avail. A few days earlier he'd gone to her room to see if she was okay. He'd asked her why she'd want to be alone if she really only had a few days left to live. Why didn't she want to be with her friends?

She looked out the window and stared at a group of students playing Frisbee in the Freshman Courtyard for a long while before she finally said, "Trying to understand what it means to be dead is a hard thing, Felix. Will my consciousness just end? Will my existence go blank like a TV when you hit the off button? It hasn't been easy. But I've made my choice. I'm going with you into that forest. And we'll put an end to all of it."

And though the hands on the clock seemed to be moving in slow motion, the minutes, the hours, and the days passed.

Chapter 35

Finals began on a Wednesday. Felix completed two exams that first week. During the tests, he tried to stay motivated. He reminded himself that he'd decided to live his life like an ordinary college student—that's what he thought he wanted more than anything. But knowing that Bill might contact him at any moment destroyed his concentration, and he wasn't able to convince himself that the exams were actually important. And even though his focus was completely blown, he recalled Bill's advice from their first meeting. He did what he could to regurgitate the professors' lectures.

He felt like he faked his way through the exams, but that was the best he could do under the circumstances. After finishing his second final on Friday, he walked out of the building determined to study in earnest over the weekend for his next two exams.

Of course Bill might contact him. And if that happened, he'd be spending the night in Ardsley Forest. Not exactly the ideal environment to prepare for finals. Felix shuddered at the thought of being in the woods at night as he unfurled his umbrella and walked to Downey in the rain.

Chapter 36

On the day of Felix's first final exam, Bill had sent Mary an email, ostensibly to inquire about how she was doing. She'd missed her scheduled appointment earlier in the week. And that was very unlike Mary.

Bill sat at his kitchen table sipping a cup of Darjeeling tea, leafing through the Saturday edition of the *Oregonian,* and glancing at his cell phone every few minutes. The cell phone next to his teacup beeped. He snatched the phone off the table and clicked on the message. It was from Mary.

> *William, I'm so sorry about missing our last appointment. Devory had me working around the clock on Landry's travel plans and I completely forgot about our meeting. I'm so sorry!!! But now that he's in Egypt—he flew out this morning—hopefully he'll get off my back for a few days. Again, I'm so sorry. Making travel arrangements for Landry is such a nightmare— everything changes 100 times!!! You wouldn't believe everything that goes into it. I promise I won't skip my next appointment!*
>
> *Mary*

Bill replied quickly to Mary that missing the appointment wasn't a problem, and he looked forward to seeing her at their next session.

He looked at his watch. It was 3:08.

Chapter 37

Felix was the last to arrive at the library. As he stepped into Dale's Room, he knew immediately that something was wrong. Lucas was sitting in his usual chair at the table with his laptop open in front of him. Harper, Caitlin, and Allison were huddled behind Lucas and bent over so that they could see his monitor. There was something about their expressions that gave Felix pause; it was a mixture of horror and revulsion. Caitlin looked pale and was holding her stomach like she was having severe cramps.

"What's going on?" Felix asked as he walked around the table to see what they were looking at.

Only Lucas glanced up from the computer, the others apparently mesmerized by what they were viewing. "It's a...another...they said it's two more people. They were out hiking and were killed...um... butchered out in Ardsley Forest. Another hiker came across the bodies, and the sick fucking dude uploaded a video on the net. It's like a minute long, and it's horrible—worst thing I've ever seen."

"I think I'm gonna be sick," Caitlin moaned, walking over to the sofa, where she sat down cradling herself.

Felix looked at the computer, but the images on the monitor didn't seem to be of anything discernible. "What is that?" he asked. "What am I looking at? I don't understand what..."

"Go back to the beginning," Harper said, choking back tears. Felix noticed for the first time that both Harper and Allison were crying.

"Okay." Lucas clicked on an arrow underneath the video window.

The images on the monitor bounced around, the amateur-quality video obviously taken by someone using a cell phone. Two objects lying close together on the ground suddenly came into view. They appeared to be about ten yards removed from the person taking the video. Even at that distance it was obvious that the two objects were human—they wore jeans and brown hiking boots. The area where they were lying was covered with thick underbrush, tree refuse, and moss-covered rocks. Beyond the bodies in the distance could be seen clusters of enormous old-growth trees. Just like what Felix saw when he was in the woods with Bill. The video was slightly dark, as if it was taken in a densely shaded area, or perhaps at dusk.

As the person taking the video moved closer to the bodies, their features gradually came into view. It became apparent that something unnatural had happened to them. At first it appeared that they were both wearing red masks and matching red jackets. But as their faces and torsos grew larger on the monitor, Felix realized what he was actually looking at. He fought the urge to throw up.

"Holy shit!" Felix exclaimed. "Is that what I think it is?"

"Yeah," Lucas answered. "Something tore out their throats. And the one there, the one on the left, he or she, I'm not sure, is missing everything from the nose down. Something ate most of her face off."

Felix stared at the monitor. Both people were lying on their backs with their arms and legs jutting out from their bodies at physiologically impossible angles. What was left of their faces was completely covered in dark red blood. Their throats were shredded. All that remained of their throats were thin strips of bloody flesh.

"There's so much blood," Lucas said in a hushed tone. "I've never seen so much blood."

The images of their mutilated and barely recognizable features played out on the monitor for several more seconds and then stopped as the video came to an end.

"That's it," Harper said, wiping the tears from her face. "I can't watch that again."

Felix pulled his eyes away from the monitor and sat in the chair next to Lucas. "How'd you get this?"

"My brother called. My mom's got him all freaked out because of all the murders out here. He gets alerts whenever anything's posted on the net about Nick Blair or the Mormon Mephistopheles. Once he saw the video he called."

"Who took the video?"

"It's just rumors now, but they're saying it was just another hiker. He uploaded the video and then took it to the police. It'll be shut down soon. You watch."

"It should be," Caitlin called over from the sofa. "It's disgusting!"

"He turned himself in?" Felix asked, perplexed. "They think he did it?"

"Haven't heard anything about that," Lucas answered, "but what idiot would kill two people, take a video of it, and then turn all the evidence over to the cops? Besides, how could a person do that?"

"Yeah, it's impossible," Felix said. "Nick Blair couldn't have done that. It looks like an animal got to them. Like a bear, maybe."

"Then that's the seventh person who's been killed by a bear since last summer," Allison said. "Seems pretty unlikely, doesn't it?"

"Yeah, I guess," Felix conceded.

His cell phone began to ring. He pulled it from his pocket. Everyone in the room instantly froze, staring at him as he held the phone to his ear and said, "Hey, Bill." The conversation lasted less than thirty seconds. Felix didn't say anything else. He put the phone back in his pocket and looked at his friends. They all seemed to sense that something was about to happen. They stared back at him. There was complete silence in the room.

"It's tonight, isn't it?" Allison said softly, breaking the calm.

"Yeah."

"Holy shit!" Lucas exclaimed, the color seeming to drain from his face. "We're going into that forest tonight?" He pointed at his monitor, which just moments ago had showed the images of two people muti-lated beyond recognition.

Caitlin exhaled loudly and got up from the sofa.

"What'd Bill say?" Harper asked.

Felix shook his head. "He just said it's tonight and to go to his house ASAP. I'm going over there now. I'll call you when we're done."

"Do you need a ride?" Caitlin asked, brushing strands of hair from her face.

"No, I'll walk. It's not very far. Oh! Hey, Caitlin, do you mind if we use your SUV tonight?"

Caitlin looked surprised. "No. But I thought Bill was going to rent a car."

"That was the plan. But I haven't actually told him yet that all of you are going with me. When I tell him that, I'll let him know we're taking your car. He'll like being even further disconnected from the whole thing. It'll protect his access to the info he gets at A.E.I."

"Good for him," Allison said disapprovingly.

"No shit," Felix replied. "We're going into that fucking forest while he stays home drinking tea. Anyway, I better get going. I'll call you."

He walked out of the room.

Caitlin, Allison, Harper, and Lucas looked at each other in silence. It was a long while before anything was said.

Chapter 38

Bill stood in his kitchen holding a cell phone to his ear as he looked out the window at a light mist that was moving across the backyard like an army of ghosts.

"Hello, William," said the man on the other end, with a thick New England accent.

"Felix is going tonight."

There was silence.

"Dad, what is it?" Bill asked.

"I'm sure you've heard about what just happened in Ardsley Forest. There have been two more."

"I just finished watching the video."

"As did I," Bill's father replied. "There's no doubt now. If ever there was any. Landry has the Second Templar Amulet in his possession. And he's released the Draganaks."

"I know."

"You realize the boy doesn't stand a chance against those things. If the manuscripts are true, and we have no reason to doubt them now, the Draganaks are monsters. They are ferocious beasts. And their appetites are insatiable!"

"There isn't any time to train Felix for this. We just have to hope that..."

"William! The Draganaks are the origin of vampire mythology! When the Templars called upon them to do their bidding, they left behind an ocean of blood. An ocean! It was those rampaging beasts that forced Pope Clement to eradicate the entire Templar Order."

"I'm aware of what happened," Bill said. "Don't forget that I'm the one who found the manuscripts in the Vatican Secret Archives."

"But these things, son, they're not sophisticated romantics who court pretty high school girls. If you encounter a Draganak, it'll rip out your throat and drink your blood. And if it's still hungry, it'll tear off your head, eat your face and organs and even your..."

"I know what they are!" Bill shouted.

"And you're still sending the boy into the forest?"

Bill didn't respond.

"What other choice do you have?" his father asked rhetorically. "Wait for another opportunity when Landry is out of the country? When will that be? Of course I would understand if you decide to send the boy even knowing that Landry has unleashed the Draganaks. The destruction of the First Templar Amulet cannot wait, after all."

"I already told you he's going into the forest tonight. I have no choice."

"Of course you don't," his father replied prosaically. "Perhaps the boy will survive. Who knows? Perhaps he's further along than we think. But in any case, you're doing the right thing, son."

"That's very reassuring, Dad. I guess I'll know by morning."

"You don't have the luxury of sparing the innocent or opting for the path of least resistance. You have an obligation to humanity. Don't forget that."

"How could I possibly forget? Felix will be here any minute. Goodbye."

Bill ended the call. He continued looking out the window as a light rain began to fall on the field of ghosts.

Chapter 39

Felix half jogged to Bill's house through a misty rain. Fifteen minutes after leaving the Woodrow Library, he was knocking on the front door.

"Felix, come in," Bill said as he opened the door. He was wearing a faded pair of jeans and a navy blue sweatshirt. His dark hair was slightly disheveled, and he hadn't shaved in at least a few days. Felix stepped into the foyer and closed the door behind him as Bill disappeared into another room.

"I'm in the kitchen," Bill shouted. "Come in and sit down. I'll get you a cup of tea."

Felix paused on his way to the kitchen to look around. He didn't know much about interior design, but everything looked like an antique. The place seemed a bit over-furnished. There was hardly any floor space not occupied by something.

"Felix, I've got your tea!" Bill shouted impatiently. "Get in here. We have a lot to discuss."

"Again with the goddamn tea," Felix muttered to himself as he followed Bill's voice into the kitchen.

Bill was sitting at a rectangular table in the eating nook. His laptop was opened in front of him. Papers and maps were spread out all across the table. Behind the table were two windows that looked out onto a nicely manicured back lawn that was slightly obscured by a milky-white mist that seemed to be settling in. Bill gestured for him to take a seat.

"Yeah, we do have a lot to discuss!" Felix said angrily. "Did you know that two more people were killed in Ardsley Forest? There's a video of the bodies on the Internet. They're mangled! Something ate their faces! There's blood everywhere!"

"I just heard. I watched the video myself. It's terrible. It's really terrible."

"I'm glad you agree! Are you still gonna tell me this has nothing to do with Landry? I mean, come on! I'm not a complete moron, you know!"

Bill sighed. "I think it's highly probable that the seven killings in Ardsley Forest are somehow related to Landry. I don't know how they're related. But I do know it doesn't pose any additional risk to you or your mission tonight. All seven people were killed on the eastern edge of the forest. That's far away from A.E.I.'s offices and the facility. There will be no police presence where you're going."

"Really?"

"Really."

"So you're telling me straight up that you don't know what's happening?" Felix asked. "You don't know what's killing all these people?"

"That's exactly what I'm telling you, Felix," Bill answered unwaveringly. "I have no idea what it is that killed those people. At first I thought it was Nick Blair, or even two or three serial killers working in tandem. But I may have been wrong about that."

He's holding something back, Felix thought. *He knows something about what's going on in that forest—why isn't he telling me?*

Bill quickly changed the topic. "How are you feeling?"

Felix tried to clear the image of the two mangled bodies in the forest. It seemed to be branded into his mind. "A little nervous, I guess."

"That's good," Bill replied, typing something on his computer. "Nervousness can be a good thing. An ally. Just try to keep it in check for now. You won't be leaving for several hours yet."

"So. What's going on? Did you get confirmation about Landry?"

"I'm sorry," Bill said, pulling his eyes away from the laptop. "Yes. Landry left for Egypt this morning."

"How long will he be there?" Felix asked, trying to keep his breathing steady and calm.

"One week. Then he's stopping off in London for two nights on his return to Portland."

"Is there any way to check with the airline to make sure he was on the plane?" Felix asked, looking at one of the maps on the table.

Bill shook his head. "Landry doesn't fly coach, Felix. He has his own private plane. And his own private runway not far from Ashfield Manor—there's no airline to call."

"Oh."

"But don't worry about that. I'm one hundred percent confident that Landry left for Egypt this morning. And even if his plans suddenly change, he won't be back for at least another day or two."

"Okay. I just don't want anybody running into Landry or whatever the hell else is out in that forest tonight."

Bill raised an eyebrow. "Anybody? You mean Allison, of course."

Felix looked out the window to the backyard. "Actually, I mean Allison, Harper, Caitlin, and Lucas."

"What?" Bill exclaimed. "How can you let…"

"Lucas, Caitlin, and Harper followed me to Devendon the last night we were there. They saw us coming out together."

"How did you let that happen?" Bill asked accusingly.

"Lucas is my roommate," Felix replied defensively. "He was getting suspicious about all my late night walks. He and the girls followed me to see what I was doing. What the hell was I supposed to do about that?"

"Goddammit, Felix!" Bill shouted. "You didn't have to tell them about this! And you sure as hell didn't have to invite them to participate!"

Felix took a step back, his face contorting with anger. "I didn't wanna tell them! But I wasn't going to lose all my friends by making up some bullshit story! If you're so smart, why don't you tell me how

I could've explained why we were coming out of Devendon together at two in the morning? And what about the explosions? How would you explain that?"

Bill took a deep breath and sipped his tea. "I'm sorry. It's just that…it's dangerous in that forest. And while you are prepared to handle those dangers, your friends are not. Look, I understand the predicament you were in, but it isn't just their lives that are in jeopardy, you know. I hope that you impressed upon them the importance of not uttering a word to anyone about what we're doing."

"They understand," Felix answered as his anger began to fade. "I told them that if they tell anyone, we'll all die. They got the point."

Bill nodded. "But why did you agree to let them go? I understand why you would allow Allison, but…"

"It's sort of because of Allison. When they heard she was going with me, they couldn't understand why they couldn't go, too. Allison made me promise that I wouldn't tell them she thinks she's a Vessel. All I could say was that Allison could help me."

"Ah," Bill said knowingly. "And if Allison can help you, then why can't the rest of your friends?"

Felix nodded. "Unintended consequences, right?"

"Indeed. Keep them close to you and try to keep an eye on them. I don't know what's out in that forest, but whatever it is, it's dangerous. If you see something, assume it's trying to kill you."

"I was already assuming that, but thanks for the warning. Oh. I won't be needing whatever car you rented for me tonight."

"Oh?"

"Caitlin has an SUV. It's a brand-new four-wheel drive. Her parents just bought it for her during winter break."

Bill appeared to think for a moment and then nodded. "Don't forget to fill it with gas before you leave tonight." He turned back to his computer and frowned slightly.

"What is it?" Felix asked.

"I was just checking the weather forecast. It looks like we're going to have light rain with some fog. The fog isn't going to help your visibility at all, so you'll need to completely rely on the GPS, okay?"

Felix imagined what Ardsley Forest would be like in the fog at night, and the hair on his arms stood up. "I can't say I like the sound of that," he said warily. "I've been in some fogs where you can't see ten feet in front of you."

"It's only supposed to be a light fog," Bill said, looking up from the computer. "It may actually be a bit of a blessing in disguise. You'll need the GPS to find the facility anyway. In the fog, it'll be practically impossible for anyone to know you're there. You can imagine the difficulty of trying to find something at night in the fog."

"Like an underground building in the middle of a forest?"

Bill smiled. "Which is why you'll need this," he said, handing Felix the cell phone they used when they went into the forest together. "I already showed you how to use the GPS app. I've also saved one phone number in the contacts list. Call that number and you'll reach this cell." He pulled a phone from his pocket. "This is a prepaid cell that can't be traced back to me. Call that number when you're on your way back to campus. And, Felix, I'm sure you and your friends won't be bringing your cell phones with you. Or anything else that might go beep in the night?"

Felix's brow creased. "I'll talk to everyone before we go."

"Felix, is there something wrong?"

Felix sighed deeply. "I don't know. I was just thinking about the Amulet. I still have no idea how to destroy it. I mean, I know we talked about it in Devendon a while back, but the more I think about it, the more worried I get that I won't know what to do."

Bill looked at Felix thoughtfully and scratched his chin. "I've spent a lot of time thinking about that over the years. More than you would believe. And at the end of the day, I think you'll just know what to do."

"So when I find the Amulet, it'll just know that I'm a Holder? It'll sense that I wanna destroy it?"

"Yes. I certainly hope so, that is."

"You hope so?" Felix exclaimed.

"Felix, there are no certainties here. But I'm confident you'll know what to do."

"But how can you be confident that I'll know what to do, when I have no idea what I'm gonna do?"

Bill smiled. "Because I'm not the Holder—you are. When you find the Amulet, you'll just know. I've told you that before, and I still believe it. Now I just need for you to believe it."

"That's not very reassuring."

"That's the best I've got."

They spent the next several hours going over every aspect of the plan in excruciating detail. They only stopped to eat some barely palatable Chinese food Bill ordered in from a nearby restaurant. By the time Bill was satisfied that Felix was prepared, it was just past eight o'clock.

When they were finished, Bill walked Felix to the front door.

The finality of what Felix was about to embark on seemed to hover over them as they stood in the foyer. There was an awkward silence and then Bill finally said, "Just stick to the plan and you'll be fine."

"Okay," Felix said distractedly.

"And Felix, if you see something out there—even if it's something that seems unreal, like it shouldn't exist? Don't stop to think. Don't wait to find out what it is. Just destroy it. And when I say destroy it, I mean blow it to fucking pieces and worry about the consequences later."

"You mean..."

"Just protect yourself and your friends. Good luck to you, Felix."

Chapter 40

As Felix walked along Eleventh Street, he texted his friends to meet him at the Caffeine Hut in five minutes. He looked up at the sky and couldn't see any stars. Another overcast night, but the rain had stopped. The fog seemed slightly worse than before. Despite Bill's assertion that it would help to conceal their presence in Ardsley Forest, it worried him.

He checked the wall clock behind the bar as he entered the Caffeine Hut. It was 8:30. His palms were sweaty, and he wiped them on his jeans. He went straight to the back of the bistro to look for his friends. They'd already arrived and were sitting in a vividly contrasting assortment of brightly colored chairs and couches arranged in the shape of a semicircle, which was apparently intended to afford them more privacy.

Felix made a quick note of who else was there. Saturday nights were typically slow for the Caffeine Hut. Tonight was no different. Besides Felix and his friends, only three other students were there, and all were sitting at the small bistro-style tables near the bar. Lucas waved to get Felix's attention. Everyone watched Felix closely as he approached.

He took a seat next to Harper on a small purple sofa.

"We already got you a cup of coffee," Harper said, smiling nervously.

"Thanks." Felix took a sip and carefully placed the heavy mug down on the table in front of him. He looked at each of them. Their anxiety was almost palpable. Felix didn't want to prolong their agony any longer than necessary.

"We're going into Ardsley Forest tonight," he said in a whisper.

"We'll meet in my room at twelve forty-five. Then we'll walk across campus to the parking lot. We need to be in Caitlin's car by one. It takes an hour to get to the underground facility. That means we'll be there at two. We'll break in, and I'll destroy the Amulet. I don't know how long that will take. It really just depends on how long it takes to find it. But it can't take any longer than say thirty minutes. Any longer than that, and we risk somebody coming along to check on the facility—and once they see that we've broken in, we could have some issues. So let's say we're in and out in thirty minutes—that would put us back in the car by around two-thirty. We make the return trip in an hour. We're back on campus at three-thirty. With any luck, we're back in our beds before four o'clock."

Everyone stared at Felix with rapt attention, but nobody spoke. Felix drank from his coffee mug again before continuing.

"I'll be driving Caitlin's car. Bill gave me the cell phone with the location of the facility. I know how to get to the entrance point of Ardsley Forest. But once we get into the woods, the only thing I can do is follow the GPS. The logging roads go all over the place in every direction. We're dead in the water without the GPS."

"Felix," Caitlin said in a whisper. "I'm kind of getting nervous. Those people were just killed out there. I can't stop thinking about that video. I mean, we're really going into that place where all those people were killed. I just can't believe it. What if it is Nick Blair? What if he's really out there waiting to kill us?"

"It's okay to be nervous," Felix said. "I'm nervous too. We all are. But if you think you can't handle it, just let me know. You don't have to do this. You don't have to go."

"No!" Caitlin said loudly and then looked around to make sure nobody heard her. "It's not that. I wanna go. I'm just saying I'm a little anxious. That's all."

"But what about the cops?" Harper asked. "Won't they be investigating the killings and all that?"

Felix shook his head. "It's on the other side of the forest—twenty miles from where we're going."

"Felix," Lucas said, "all of us were talking about what we should be wearing out in the woods and…"

"Dark clothes," Felix interrupted. "Don't wear anything white or anything that reflects light—no white sneakers or running shoes with the reflectors on the back, okay? Also, nobody bring a cell phone or anything else that might make a noise. The only cell we'll bring is Bill's."

They looked at each other and drank coffee. Felix finally broke the silence. "Do you guys have any questions?"

"Should we bring flashlights?" Harper asked.

"No," Felix replied. "They'd be too easy for someone to spot. We'll have to do everything in the dark."

She frowned. "But we were watching the weather report earlier. They were saying it's going to be foggy tonight."

"That's actually a good thing," Felix said, much more cheerfully than he really felt. "It will help conceal our movements in the forest. It'll be practically impossible for anyone to see us at night in the fog, right?"

Nobody protested, but Felix noted the concern on their faces. He was about to stand up when he remembered something. "Caitlin, could you please go and fill the car up with gas? We don't wanna run out in the middle of the woods."

Caitlin smiled nervously. "No, we don't want that." She started rummaging through her brown leather bag.

"I'll go with you," Lucas said to her.

"Yeah?" she said, somewhat surprised. "Okay. Thanks. I could use the company—I'm feeling a little shaky."

Allison hadn't said a word since Felix arrived.

"Hey, Allison," Felix said. "What are you doing between now and twelve forty-five?"

She was spacing out again. It took a moment before she realized that Felix had asked her a question. "Huh? Oh…you know, I'm just gonna spend some time alone. I just want to think through things by myself."

Felix knew there was nothing he could say to lift her spirits. "Okay. Are you sure you want to be alone?"

"Yeah," she replied in a whisper. "Don't worry about me. I'm fine. I'll see everyone at twelve forty-five." She got up from her green lounge chair and walked out of the bistro.

Lucas finished the rest of his coffee and slammed the mug on the table. "All right then," he said. "Caitlin, do you want to take a little trip to the gas station? Maybe we should pick up some snacks while we're out. We are going on a little road trip, after all. And what's a road trip without snacks? Any requests?"

"Yes," Caitlin answered. "I request that you not act like an idiot for the rest of the night."

"No promises," Lucas replied and laughed. They got up and left, leaving Felix and Harper sitting together on the small purple sofa.

"Well, it looks like it's just the two of us," Harper said in a low voice as she nudged Felix playfully with her elbow.

"Yeah, I guess it does," Felix said, smiling shyly. He was suddenly nervous, and it had nothing to do with Ardsley Forest. He couldn't remember the last time he was alone with Harper. He almost forgot how she had a way of making him feel like a thirteen-year-old with a crush on his teacher.

"Do you wanna go for a walk?" she asked.

"Um…sure. Where do you wanna go?"

"Oh, I don't know. I just thought we might start walking and see where we end up."

"All right. I'm too wired to sit around anyway. The coffee probably didn't help."

Harper got up from the sofa and walked toward the entrance, but then stopped to look at the old photographs covering the walls.

Felix stopped next to her. She was looking at a framed black-and-white photograph of ten students—six guys and four girls. They were standing on a lawn in front of a large stone and brick building. Three of the guys were holding lacrosse sticks. One guy and a girl appeared to be having a playful game of tug-of-war with another lacrosse stick. The girl holding the stick was laughing, her head held back so that she appeared to be looking up at the sky. The girls wore long skirts that fell nearly to the tops of their dark high-top shoes. The guys wore long trousers and sweaters. Two of the guys wore turtlenecks with "Portland College" spelled out in large block letters across their chests.

"Felix, do you ever look at these photos and wonder who these people were? They're so young. They're the same age as we are now, you know—in the photos anyway. But look at the year written in the corner of this one. Can you see it? This picture was taken over sixty years ago. If these people are still alive, they'd be nearly eighty years old. Don't you think that's strange?"

"Yeah, I guess it is."

"When this photo was taken, do you think any of them could have imagined that the two of us would be standing here sixty years later looking at it?"

"I don't know—probably not."

"But in this picture, these ten people will forever be college students. I'm sure they've lived full lives, you know. They must've met someone they fell in love with, had beautiful weddings and romantic honeymoons, bought homes, had lots of children and grandchildren. But to us, and to everyone who looks at this photo, they'll always be ten college kids playing with lacrosse sticks out on the Courtyard. And that's how they'll always be remembered." Harper spoke as if she were reminiscing about her own life.

Felix tried to come up with something to say, but he was struggling for words.

"Felix, how do you think we will be remembered? Years from

now, will people remember us as we are now or for the people we'll become?"

He shrugged. "I guess it depends on who's doing the remembering. The people we go to school with will remember us the way we are now, I suppose."

Harper ran her fingers over the photo of the ten students as she stared at it. "How do you want to be remembered, Felix?"

"Um…I guess I…I've never really thought about it. I guess it never occurred to me that anybody would be remembering me."

"But we all leave a legacy—especially you. You're different than everybody else, you know."

"Oh. I suppose. Um…I don't know. I honestly never thought about the future like that. I mean, I worry about the future all the time… my future…but I never thought about what other people might think about me. I never looked at it like that. Whenever I think about the future now, it's kind of…kind of depressing—like it doesn't even belong to me. That it was stolen by some guy who died a long time ago."

"I don't understand."

"That's okay. Neither do I. How do you want to be remembered?"

"I think I want to be like the people in this photo," Harper said. "They're young and full of life. It's almost like you can see it in their eyes. If you look closely enough, you can see their dreams and aspirations—it's written on their faces. I want to be remembered like them."

She turned to Felix and smiled. "Are you ready to go for that walk now?"

Chapter 41

Felix and Harper left the Caffeine Hut and ambled slowly in the direction of the Bryant Center. The night was cold and a light fog drifted across campus. Felix stuck his hands into the pockets of his jeans, trying to keep them warm. Harper walked alongside him, so close that their arms touched. They passed the Bryant Center and continued toward the Old Campus.

"It's cold, isn't it?" Harper asked with a shudder that was a bit too deliberate. "Aren't your hands cold?"

"Yeah, it's a little chilly." Felix kept his hands stuffed deep in his pockets.

Harper laughed. "Felix, you are so funny sometimes. You might be the last shy guy in the entire world."

"Huh?"

"I was trying to get you to hold my hand," she said and laughed again.

"Oh!" Felix said, feeling stupid. Why didn't he pick up on that? He knew he was distracted, but that was just really dense. He took a hand from his pocket and reached out. She took it in hers and squeezed it gently. Her hand was soft, just how he remembered it. He smiled. She smiled back.

They walked past the practice fields in front of the football stadium and then turned around, heading back toward the main part of the campus.

"You seem to be taking me somewhere," Harper said after a while.

"I am. There's something I want to show you—something I want to tell you."

"Okay. What is it?"

"Just something I wanna get off my chest," Felix said.

"So go ahead."

"Not here."

They passed by Cutler Hall and several other darkened buildings. Felix led Harper off the footpath and onto the grass. A short distance later, they came to a large Douglas fir tree.

"This is it," Felix said.

"What? Here? But this is just…"

"I know. It's just a tree. Turn around and face the other direction."

Harper gave Felix a quizzical look and slowly turned around. From their vantage point by the tree, they could see the fog drifting across the Courtyard through a large gap between two buildings.

"Okay," Harper said noncommittally. "I guess that's kind of cool."

"Well, the cool part is that you can see all the way to the Courtyard and nobody would even really know you were here. Nobody ever leaves the footpaths."

"Okay. I suppose that is cool."

"Maybe it's a little lame," Felix said, laughing. "But I didn't bring you here just to show you the view. I wanted to tell you something. Something I've never told anybody before."

"Really? You've never told anyone? Not even…um…so what is it?"

Felix took a deep breath and exhaled loudly. "My first day here at school—football started two weeks before all you guys got here—I finished practice and went back to the dorm. The sun had just set and I was feeling pretty crappy. I was thinking a lot about my parents. I wasn't really trying to make friends on the team or anything like that.

"Anyway, that first night I was just walking around campus and thinking about stuff. And then I found this place. It seemed out of the way, like I was alone. But I could still see a few people walking across the Courtyard and just hanging out. So I stood right here in this spot and just thought about everything. And more than anything, I felt scared. I was so scared I wouldn't be able to cut it here. I was afraid I wasn't smart enough to handle my classes. I was afraid people would think I was stupid—just another stupid football player, you know. And um…I was…I was also thinking…I was thinking about what I did on my SAT." He gritted his teeth and ran his hand over his face.

Harper looked at him curiously. "What did you do on your…"

"I cheated!" Felix shouted. "I cheated on my SAT! I paid some guy named Peter eight hundred dollars to take the test for me. I couldn't do it on my own. I took the test twice. Both times I got in the fifteen hundreds. I was desperate! I wanted to come here so badly. The only thing standing between me and this school was that goddamn test! So I did it! I paid him. He took the test. And now here I am! The only reason I'm here is because I'm a cheater."

Harper said nothing. He couldn't read her expression in the dim light.

"The night I came here was before everything happened," Felix continued. "Before Bill told me about who I am. Before I knew what I…before…before everything happened. That night I was just a fraud and a cheater, and I was afraid I couldn't make it in college. I thought about quitting school. I'd just quit. I'd just go back to the dorm, pack my bags, and head back to Coos Bay Bridge. I figured I could just get a job at the mill or somewhere. Then I wouldn't have to worry about whether I was smart enough to be here. You probably think I'm a total idiot now, don't you? I'm the dumbest person on the entire campus. I know that. I'm the only one not smart enough to pass the SAT. I wouldn't blame you for thinking I'm a loser."

"Felix, I can't say that I'm not surprised about what you did on the SAT. But I understand what it's like to want something that's just out of your reach. But seriously, how could I possibly think you're a loser? Does it really matter that you cheated on some stupid test? Of all the people at this school, you're the last person who should worry about whether they could cut it here. But that's part of what makes you such an awesome guy. You're special, Felix. But it's not because you can make books fly around the room—you're special because you don't realize what you have inside you. You're better than you think. You're not giving yourself enough credit."

Felix smiled. "It's strange to hear you say that—that I'm better than I think. Because I've spent the whole year thinking something's wrong with me. That I'm a cheater. That I've…I've done things…and that I'm so messed up I have to hide who I really am from everyone. That nobody knows the true me. Because the true me is not…not a good person. Not someone you should get close to."

She took both of Felix's hands in hers and looked into his eyes. "You are a good person, Felix. You need to stop beating yourself up. But you know, it's kind of sexy that someone like you isn't so full of himself. There are so many douche bag guys out there who think they're so awesome. Those guys are nothing compared to you. And I really, really like you."

"You do?" Felix asked, staring back into her eyes.

"I do," she said, and standing on her tiptoes she kissed him softly on the mouth.

"Felix, do you want to come back to my room with me?" she asked demurely.

Felix hadn't been with a girl since Emma, and she broke up with him last summer. Emma was the first girl Felix really liked, and getting dumped hurt—more than he wanted to admit. His ego was fractured, but instead of trying to screw every girl on campus to get back at her, he did just the opposite. He avoided girls. Why open himself up to more girl trauma if he didn't have to? He had enough problems to deal with anyway. But Harper wasn't just another girl. Felix knew that Harper's roommate had transferred to her boyfriend's college before the start of the second semester. Harper was living alone.

"Sure," he said.

"I was hoping you'd say that."

Chapter 42

For the first time in Felix's life, he experienced magic. For thousands of years, across every culture and every continent, poets and those skilled with the pen have tried to capture in words the uniqueness and intensity of the physical connection formed between lovers before the eve of battle—a connection often described as transcendental. But long before the advent of the written word, lovers have cradled each other in the dark of night, praying that the sun wouldn't rise, for the dawn would bring with it the certainty of war and the possibility of death—because life, like magic, is a fleeting thing.

For Felix and Harper, their journey into Ardsley Forest felt very much like an impending battle. They knew these moments could be their last. That every second was meaningful. Felix's senses were heightened beyond anything he thought possible. He lost himself in the moment. Nothing mattered except the beautiful girl in his arms. Ardsley Forest, the Amulet, the Antichrist, the end of the world; none of it meant anything to him. Those things could be sorted out later. It was just him and Harper, and nothing else. He was at peace. Everything in the world was right and perfect. The world finally made sense.

She smiled at him. He touched her dimples. He'd always wanted to do that. He held her tightly. He wished he could stop time. He breathed in the smell of her long blond hair and kissed the top of her head.

She ran her fingers up and down his arm. The room was quiet and still.

"Felix?" Harper whispered in the dark.

"Yes," he whispered back.

"We have to go soon, don't we?"

Felix craned his neck to see the alarm clock on the desk. "Yes."

"Are we going to be okay tonight?"

"Of course."

"I guess...I guess I thought at first that it'd be an adventure, you know? But now...now that it's here...I'm scared."

Felix stroked her hair. "We'll be fine. We'll break into the building and destroy the Amulet. We'll be back before breakfast."

Harper lifted her head and put her lips close to his ear. "You'll protect me?"

"Yes."

She kissed his ear softly. "You promise?"

"I promise."

She hugged him tightly and draped one of her legs across his waist.

"Felix, I think I...I think I...well, let's just say I really like you. I've always liked you. More than anyone I've ever known. I think my feelings scared me a little. I know I did some things that were kind of stupid. But I know this is right. We can talk about that later. We have all the time in the world."

Felix kissed her and then reluctantly crawled out of bed and got dressed.

"I'll see you in my room in fifteen minutes, okay?"

"Okay." Harper smiled. "I'll be there."

Chapter 43

"Where were you, dude?" Lucas asked as soon as Felix returned to his room.

"I was, um…I was…"

"No way! Did you and Harper finally hook up?"

Felix couldn't help but grin.

"I knew it! Well, it's about fucking time! I don't know what took you guys so long."

"Neither do I," Felix replied as he changed out of his clothes. "So what have you been doing?"

"Pacing around the room like a madman. I can't focus on anything. I can't even listen to music. I've never been this amped before. You think these clothes are all right?"

Felix looked him over. Lucas was wearing black jeans, a black hooded sweatshirt, and a pair of black cross-trainers.

"I don't think I'll be able to see you in the dark," Felix said with a crooked smile. "You might literally disappear into the woods."

"Dude, don't even joke about that!" Lucas said seriously. "You better not leave me in that forest. My mom would never forgive you."

Felix laughed. "Okay, I don't want to upset Mrs. Meier."

"But hey, seriously, are we gonna be okay? I thought I was cool with everything, but now I'm freaking out a little. It didn't help that two more people were killed out there today."

"We're gonna be fine. We'll be in and out. It'll be quick. If anything goes wrong—if we see anybody—we'll just put the car in reverse and get back to campus."

Lucas nodded as he paced back and forth across the room.

"Did you guys put gas in the car?" Felix asked, tying his shoelaces.
"Yeah."

"Did you get some chips? You know how much I like barbeque."
Lucas laughed.

"Hey, Lucas," Felix said, standing up and laying his black jacket across his bed, "before the girls get here, I just wanted to tell you that I need you to stay loose. Harper is pretty worked up. Caitlin could lose it at any minute. And I don't even know what to say about Allison— she's sort of comatose. So just stay loose. And one other thing—keep an eye on everybody when we're out in the woods. It's gonna be dark and the fog isn't gonna help. It'll be very spooky out there. I need you to be cool and in control."

Lucas stopped pacing and looked at Felix directly in the eye. "Got it. Don't worry about me. Think of me as the Rock of fucking Gibraltar."

Felix nodded.

There was a soft knocking at the door. Lucas opened it quickly and ushered Harper, Caitlin, and Allison into the room. They were wearing black from head to toe. Felix caught Harper's eye and she smiled.

"Damn!" Lucas exclaimed. "That's a lot of black! We'll be lucky to get to the parking lot without campus security arresting us."

"Arresting us for what?" Caitlin asked.

"I don't know," Lucas replied, shrugging. "Dressing suspiciously, maybe."

Everyone laughed. It may have been nervous laughter, but Felix thought it was better than everybody throwing up because they couldn't handle the pressure.

"Okay, guys," he said, as calmly as he could, "Lucas has a point. We look like we're going to a Goth party. We should avoid being seen. Let's go out the side door, and instead of cutting across campus, we'll use the sidewalk along First. We'll circle back to the parking lot when we get to Bryant, okay?"

He checked the time. "It's twelve-forty. Let's go."

Chapter 44

"Yes, Devory, I trust that you are calling with good news," Landry Ashfield said into the cell phone. Landry's speech was superbly controlled—utterly emotionless, any hidden meaning impossible to discern. He glanced down at a weathered, antique-looking map spread across the desk in front of him.

"Yes. That is very good, Devory. Once you have found the indicator, I will know the location of the Fourth Amulet. Once it is in my possession, you will focus your energies on locating the Fifth Templar Amulet and a certain Druid's cup whose whereabouts have eluded me for far too long.

"Devory, as you are aware, there are great rewards that come with loyal service. Your dedication to me has not gone unnoticed. Contact me when you have the indicator's location. I have matters to attend to here."

Landry tucked the cell phone into his pocket and walked across the room. He looked out through the floor-to-ceiling windows. Ardsley Forest was concealed in darkness. The brilliant white lights from two pyramid-shaped structures shone brightly into the sky, illuminating the heavy night fog like a radiant aurora.

Chapter 45

Twenty minutes later, Felix was driving Caitlin's SUV out of the campus parking lot. He'd already suction-cupped the cell phone receptacle to the windshield and slid Bill's cell phone into it. He kept to the side streets, taking the same route as the day he was a passenger in Bill's Range Rover.

Harper sat next to him. Caitlin, Lucas, and Allison were squeezed into the backseat like overgrown children. The roads were practically deserted, but the fog was noticeably denser than it was during his stroll through campus with Harper. He was no stranger to bad weather, having grown up on the Oregon coast. He knew that people underestimated how badly the fog impacted visibility. He drove cautiously. The last thing he wanted was to get side-swiped by another car before they even reached Ardsley Forest.

They crossed over the towering suspension bridge spanning the Willamette River. The thick mist concealed the dark waters below, creating the illusion that the car was floating on clouds. The lights of downtown Portland in the distance were fuzzily distorted by the fog blanketing the city, blurry and muted.

Not much was said. Lucas made a few half-hearted attempts at humor, trying to break the tension, which was as thick as the fog. No one seemed in the mood to laugh. They gazed out the windows, apparently lost in their own thoughts.

Thirty minutes after leaving campus, Felix turned the car south onto Hermann Boulevard just as the light, drizzly rain resumed after a short hiatus. When they passed by Ashfield Way, everyone crowded to one side of the car, attempting to get a better look at the enormous monolithic signs on either side of the entrance to A.E.I.'s headquarters. They continued on in silence for several minutes and then Felix slowed the car to a crawl before turning onto Easton Street.

"We're getting close," he said. There were no streetlights. The headlights only illuminated a few feet of the road. Felix tried to remember what it looked like during the day. He pictured a narrow country road bordered by farms on each side and cattle grazing in the fields nearby.

"That's the first subdivision," he said, gesturing toward his window with his thumb. "We'll take a left at the third one."

A few minutes later he turned the car onto Pine Street, the street sign barely visible in the mist. He drove slowly through the desolate subdivision. During daylight, Felix thought the uninhabited neighborhood was strange and a little surreal. But at night, it was positively eerie. He kept his face placid, but swallowed hard enough that Harper must have heard him from the passenger seat. She gave no indication that she did.

"What is this place?" Caitlin asked nervously.

"Some developer wanted to build houses here in the eighties, but he ran out of money," Felix answered. "Nobody wants to live this far from town, I guess."

"I sure as hell wouldn't wanna live out here," Lucas said. "This place is creepy!"

"We're coming to the end in just a second," Felix said, hoping that he sounded calm. "Then we'll go through a cattle pasture—it's a little bumpy—and then into the woods."

Felix touched the monitor on the cell phone to activate the GPS. The screen said *acquiring satellite*. Felix inched the car along, nearing the end of the cul-de-sac. The monitor continued to read *acquiring satellite*. Felix stopped the car and frowned at the monitor.

"What's wrong?" Harper asked, sounding worried.

"Nothing," Felix said. "Just waiting for the GPS to come up. It's still trying to find the satellite. Maybe the fog's screwing with it." He tapped his fingers impatiently on the steering wheel.

"Why don't you just use my GPS?" Caitlin asked. "It's built right into the dashboard. And it's new. I'm sure it works."

"Do you have the address for an underground zombie-making facility in your GPS?" Lucas asked.

"Oh," she replied, sounding embarrassed. "Yeah. I guess not. Sorry."

"Okay, here we go!" Felix said with relief a moment later, as the cell phone acquired the satellite and their route was illuminated on the tiny monitor. "Now we're going to drive through the cow pasture. Be on the look-out for a red ribbon Bill tied to a tree at the end of the field. That's the road we're looking for. The ribbon's just a few feet off the ground."

Felix jumped the car over the curb and engaged the four-wheel drive. They made their way across the field with Felix doing his best to avoid the irrigation ditches. Halfway across the pasture, he could just begin to see the tree line ahead. The trees grew so closely together, it was impossible to see into the forest. The tops of the taller trees were completely concealed by the fog shrouding the night sky.

"There's the ribbon," he said, pointing ahead. "The road's not much smoother than the field, so hang on. And let me know if you see anything funny."

"Funny like what?" Caitlin asked with trepidation. "Like genetically engineered killer bears that eat people? Or a serial killer wearing a hockey mask and carrying a chainsaw and…"

"Headlights," Felix said, cutting her off. "If we see any cars, we're getting the hell out."

Felix drove onto the narrow logging road, and they entered Ardsley Forest. The trees were so close on either side that small branches scraped against the car. One of the larger limbs whacked against Felix's side-view mirror as he angled the car to the left. Caitlin gasped, but didn't say anything.

"Why do I feel like I'm in some kind of weird tree tunnel?" Lucas asked nobody in particular.

It was raining steadily now, and the fog seemed to have thoroughly entrenched itself into the landscape. Felix thought back to Bill telling him that the fog could work to his advantage. He shook his head in disgust, thinking that Bill was full of shit. He couldn't imagine worse conditions. No matter how hard he strained his eyes, he couldn't see beyond the car's headlights, which reflected back at him in the white fog. There was only blackness and a thick mist swirling along in the SUV's wake. Every few seconds he darted his eyes at the GPS. If something went wrong with it, they'd be completely screwed.

"How long do we stay on this road?" Harper asked.

"About twenty minutes." Felix glanced at her. Even on a night like this, dressed only in black jeans and a black leather jacket, she looked beautiful. And she smelled so nice. She always smelled wonderful. He let his mind wander for a moment, recalling the time they spent in her room just a few hours before.

Whack!

"Felix!" Lucas shouted as a tree limb smacked against the side of the car.

Felix snapped the car back onto the middle of the path. He'd veered slightly off the road and come within seconds of crashing into a tree the size of a building. No more thinking about Harper, he chastised himself. For Christ's sake! Concentrate!

They drove in silence for several minutes as Felix maneuvered the car along the narrow dirt track. He tried to find something he recognized, but the roads looked completely different at night and in the fog. It was like he'd never been there before. Nothing looked familiar. Maybe they were already lost. He gripped the steering wheel, his knuckles white. His palms were sweaty.

He stared at the GPS a moment too long. Suddenly the path

appeared to run straight into the woods. Harper gasped and braced herself against the dashboard. Felix slammed on the brakes.

"What the hell happened to the road?" Lucas exclaimed as the car came to a complete stop.

Felix finally recognized something. "It's okay. I remember this. I know where we are now." He breathed a silent sigh of relief and turned the car without looking at the GPS.

"And you didn't before?" Lucas asked.

"Not really. But there's another dead end just like that up ahead." Felix tried to sound confident. Like he knew what he was doing. But he'd only been there once before, and the circumstances then were completely different. How the hell was he supposed to know how to get around on dirt paths in the middle of the wilderness? He tried to stay calm and to focus on the road. But the GPS wasn't giving him enough time to prepare for the sharp turns. If he crashed into the woods, the car would be totaled; there'd be no way to reverse it back onto the road. Just focus, he told himself. Concentrate on the road.

A few minutes later the road appeared to vanish again. Felix was better prepared this time and didn't need to slam on the brakes. He slowed the car to a crawl and turned sharply until the road reappeared.

"We'll be there in just a few minutes, guys," he said, accelerating the car down the rutted logging road. "It's six-tenths of a mile from that last turn. We're looking for a large rock that's wedged between two trees. That's where we'll stop."

He checked the odometer. At four-tenths of a mile he slowed his speed and peered into the fog, searching for the landmark. At exactly the six-tenths mark he found what he was looking for. He stopped the car with the front grille nearly touching the rock. He shut off the engine and turned off the headlights. The only sound was the raindrops on the roof. The darkness seemed impenetrable.

"I can't see a thing," Harper said, sounding worried. "Maybe we should've brought flashlights. I can't even see Felix, and he's like a foot away from me."

"Give it a few minutes," Felix said in a calm voice. Not bringing flashlights was a mistake, he thought. How could he find anything out there? "Your eyes should adjust to the darkness. We should be good to get to the facility—it's not hard to find. Now everybody listen up. I know we talked about it back at school, but let's go over it one last time. I can see the top of the rock in front of the car. Can you see it?"

Felix sensed that they were nodding, so he continued.

"That's our starting point. It's only a five-minute walk from here. Halfway to the building there's another rock just like this one. That's our second marker. Once we get there, we'll know we're going in the right direction. Then we'll go in a straight line for about two minutes. There are tons of fallen trees and other shit all over that part of the forest. Some of the trees are really big. But we'll just have to climb over 'em. It's not hard. Just be careful. When I stop, that means the building is in front of us. We'll circle around the edge of the clearing and approach the building from the west side. That's where Bill thinks the door is. Once we find the door, well…I guess that's up to me. Is everybody clear? Everyone okay? You can see a little better now, right?"

They nodded again. This time Felix could actually see their heads bobbing up and down.

"Okay. Everybody stay close. You can't see more than a few feet in any direction. So don't lose sight of the person in front of you. If you do, stop where you are and call my name. If anyone says 'Felix,' then we'll all stop, okay? That'll be the signal, okay? Nobody's gonna get lost in these woods. Nobody's getting left behind. If anybody wants to stay in the car, now's the time to say so. Anybody?"

There was utter silence.

Felix spoke rapidly. "Okay. Hold hands, grab a coat or whatever. Just make sure you're always in contact with someone. Okay? Okay, then. Try not to make any loud noises. Try not to talk unless you have to. Watch out for branches on the ground. The ground is wet, and that'll soften the sound, but a breaking branch makes a shitload of noise. Let's get out of the car. Be quiet when you close the doors. Ready? Everybody ready?"

"Motherfucker," Lucas whispered under his breath.

Caitlin started coughing.

Harper was breathing quickly, almost like she was hyperventilating.

"Are you okay?" Felix asked her.

She nodded. "Remember what you promised?" she whispered.

"Yes."

She smiled and opened the door.

They climbed out of the car, quietly closed the doors, and gathered alongside the rock. The night was cold and Felix thought it felt more like November than late April. The rain was pattering lightly on the ground. The fog engulfed them. A hint of moonlight haloed through the overcast skies, giving off just enough light to see the nearest trees and the ground below.

They were actually in the woods, Felix thought. Bill definitely wouldn't be doing this without carrying that cannon he kept in his trunk. Why didn't he give it to him? he wondered for the first time.

"Okay," he said, trying not to think about whether he'd feel more confident if he had Bill's military shotgun in his hands. "I can see everybody. Everyone okay? Can you see me? Harper, you take my hand. Harper, take Allison's. Allison, take Caitlin's. Lucas, you'll bring up the rear. Don't forget—always stay in contact with the person in front of you."

They took each other's hands and began their awkward march through Ardsley Forest.

The ground was soggy and their footsteps made almost no sound. Even the branches only made muted little crunching noises when stepped on. The forest was dense with some of the largest trees in the world. No matter how hard Felix tried to take a straight path, there were times when he was forced to deviate from his course.

He heard a thud behind him and someone said, "Ouch!"

Felix stopped and turned his head.

"Sorry," Lucas said. "I stubbed my big toe on something. I can't even see the ground. Sorry."

Felix strained his eyes, trying to see anything resembling a large rock. He stumbled through an area of thick underbrush. Then he saw it. He'd overshot the rock by several feet. He cursed under his breath as he led them to the second marker. Reaching the rock, they unclasped hands and gathered around him.

He looked at each of them one by one. They were scared. It was written across their faces. But why wouldn't they be? He was scared. They were stomping around in total darkness in what had to be the scariest place on the planet. He'd told them it would be just like this. But they refused to listen. They shouldn't be here. But what was he supposed to do? Turn around? Go home? Maybe send them back to the car? But what if something happened to them in the car? At least he could try to protect them if they were with him. Dammit! He should've never agreed to this.

Felix lifted his hand, signaling for everyone to be quiet. He cocked his head.

"What is it?" Caitlin asked. "Did you hear something?"

He did hear something. It sounded like a branch breaking in the distance. But there was something else—a *whooshing* sound. Like the sound of air escaping from a tire. He listened for it again, but heard nothing. Maybe he imagined it. Maybe it was just the wind.

"Felix?" Harper said, sounding very afraid.

"It's nothing," he said, trying to sound confident. "I thought I heard a branch breaking. There's lots of deer and raccoons and other cuddly forest creatures out here, you know. Let's move on. Remember what I said about all the trees on the ground. Stay close."

They gripped each other's hands again and resumed their slow, clumsy walk through the forest. Felix reached the first fallen tree in their path and clambered over it without letting go of Harper's hand. Harper had more trouble and was forced to let go of Allison's hand as she climbed. Felix stopped and waited until everyone was safely over the tree before continuing on.

He tried to walk in a straight line due north. But between climbing over downed trees and being forced to walk around clusters of tightly packed Douglas firs, he knew he'd strayed off course. He turned around frequently to make sure everyone was still behind him while trying to avoid tripping over moss-covered rocks and exposed roots.

Finally reaching the clearing, he realized he was some distance away from where he and Bill had emerged from the woods. He signaled for everyone to stop as he tried to figure out exactly where they were. He couldn't see the sloped earth in front of him—he knew it was fifty yards or more away. How the hell was he supposed to see that far at night? And in the fog? He knew it was there, just in front of him, but he was practically blind. Why'd he agree to do this at night? Bill told him to circle around to the west side of the building using the tree line as cover. But he couldn't see the facility from the perimeter of the clearing. Bill must not have thought of that. *Think, dammit! Stay calm and think.* He stared into the darkness and considered his options.

"We're at the clearing," Felix finally whispered, turning to face his friends. "The building's up ahead. We're just gonna have to walk until we see it. Once we do, we'll turn to our left and go all the way to the end of the building. Then we'll start looking for the door. I think we have a problem, though."

"What?" Lucas whispered, wiping the rain from his face.

"We need to find this exact spot after we get out of the building. The car is due south from here. But these goddamn trees all look the same—we can't use them as landmarks."

"I've got it," Lucas said. He untied one of his black sneakers and pulled a long white athletic sock from his foot. He put the shoe back on and tied it quickly. "We can just tie my sock to a branch. It's a good thing I'm wearing these lame-ass socks my mom got me. We should be able to see this, right?"

"Good idea," Felix said in a muffled voice. "We can just follow the tree line along the clearing until we see it." He took the sock from Lucas and tied it tightly around a thin branch that was four or five feet above the forest floor.

"All right," he whispered. "Everybody hold hands. We're gonna walk straight ahead until we see the building."

Felix started leading them across the clearing. The ground was wet. Felix's feet sunk into the soggy turf as he sloshed his way across the vast open space. He knew they were completely exposed. If there were night-vision security cameras scanning the outside of the building, they'd be sitting ducks unless the fog actually was concealing their presence. Maybe Bill was right about something after all. Felix stared straight ahead. It should be here, he thought. Didn't they walk far enough? He couldn't have missed it, could he?

He saw the faintest outline of a bulge in the earth that gradually came into focus as it drew closer. He stopped. Allison apparently wasn't paying attention. She bumped into Harper, causing her to collide into Felix. Felix wasn't expecting to get pushed from behind and was forced to put a hand on the ground to keep from toppling over; it sunk into the sodden turf up to his wrist. Regaining his balance and wiping the muck off on his pant leg, he motioned for everyone to gather around.

"This is it," he whispered, pointing over his shoulder. The mound protruding up from the earth was roughly at eye level. It went in both directions as far as their eyes could see, which wasn't very far, considering the lack of visibility.

"I'm not sure where the center of the building is, but it doesn't really matter," Felix continued in a whisper. "We're just gonna walk next to it until we reach the end. Once we get there, we need to find the door. Everybody stay close."

They slogged along through the clearing, keeping the facility within reach. Within a few minutes they came to the end of the building. Felix took a few cautious steps beyond it and peered around the corner. If there was anyone waiting for them there, they'd be helpless. But the space was completely empty; there were no people, no cars, no anything. It looked like everything else in the forest.

Felix turned to face the others. "The door's supposed to be on this side," he whispered. "Let me know if you see anything."

Harper stood next to him. Her face was streaked with rain. She looked scared.

"You okay?" he asked softly.

She smiled and nodded.

Felix forced a smile in return.

He searched for something that might be a door. His friends walked closely behind him. So close that he could hear their breathing.

"Felix!" Lucas suddenly whispered urgently. "Wait! What is that?" He shot past Felix, crouched over like a hermit crab searching for its shell. Lucas stopped and pointed at something on the ground. He gestured for everyone to follow.

When Felix reached Lucas, he could see immediately what Lucas was pointing at. There was a square-cut hole in the earth next to the mound. It appeared to be about ten feet across.

"Be careful!" Lucas whispered. "The ground's slippery. I don't think you'd wanna fall down there. It looks bottomless."

"I think I see a light down there," Harper said, walking around the hole to the other side, giving it a wide berth as she did so. "See," she said, pointing into the hole. "There's a light. But it's so fuzzy. I wonder what…"

"Those are stairs!" Caitlin exclaimed, a little too loudly. "Look!"

Sure enough, once Caitlin pointed them out, Felix could see steeply angled stairs leading down toward the blurry light.

"I think we found the door, Felix," Lucas whispered.

"Yeah," Felix replied, wiping the rain from his face. "This has gotta be it."

He tried looking down into the hole, but he could only see the first seven or eight steps and then they disappeared into darkness.

"Okay," Felix said, looking around at everyone, "let's go down one at a time. The stairs look like they're concrete, and probably slippery, so everyone pay attention to your footing. If you fall, try not to take everyone down with you."

Felix started down the stairs first, moving carefully and making sure that each foot was firmly planted before he took his next step. He was reminded of walking down the cliffs to the beach at his grandma's house in Cove Rock. Harper put a hand on his shoulder as she followed behind him. Felix strained his eyes, trying to see what was at the bottom. What were they walking into? What if it was the door and it was being guarded? What if there were people waiting for them down there? People with guns? And if the door was actually there, what would he do? Would he really be able to break down a steel door that weighed tons? Maybe he wouldn't have to worry about it. Maybe there was no door and they just couldn't get into the building. Bill really couldn't blame him for not breaking into it if there wasn't a door, right?

The light that Harper first spotted from ground level was growing brighter. As Felix continued his descent, he realized there were actually lots of lights. They were flashing like tiny Christmas bulbs; there were six or seven red lights, a green one, and several white ones that all seemed to be twinkling in the darkness. Two of the red lights were flashing on and off in what seemed like a regular sequence. The white lights pulsated almost randomly. The green light was continuous and didn't flash at all.

With one last careful step Felix reached the bottom. It was solid underfoot and seemed to be made of concrete, just like the stairs. He helped Harper with the final step and then went over to get a better look at the lights.

"That must be the security system," Harper said, coming up behind him. "It looks like some kind of control panel."

"I think she's right," Lucas said quietly, joining them with Allison right behind. "Do you think there are any cameras down here?"

Felix shook his head and frowned. "I don't know. I can't see anything."

"You're not going to like this, Felix," Caitlin said from behind.

Felix turned his head and searched for her. Caitlin was at the opposite end of the landing, near the stairs. She appeared to be staring at the wall. He walked over and stopped next to her.

"What is it?" he asked, but before Caitlin could even answer, he realized what she was looking at. They were standing in front of the door. He'd walked right past it a moment earlier and didn't even notice it, and for good reason. It looked just like the building's façade.

He stepped closer to the building until his face was only a few inches from the door. He ran his fingers across the surface; it was smooth and cold.

"I can't really tell where it begins and ends," Caitlin whispered beside him. "It's seamless."

Felix continued to inspect it. "I think this is the edge," he said, tracing his fingers along it. "At least on this side, anyway. It's smooth here and this part next to it is a little rougher. I wish it wasn't so damn dark down here. I think the door ends at this point. This rough part is the concrete the building's made out of."

Lucas, Allison, and Harper gathered behind.

"Damn! So that's the door, huh?" Lucas said.

"Yeah," Felix replied. He stared at it. So he was supposed to break this down? It was like asking him to break down a mountain. It just couldn't be done.

"Shouldn't we do something about the security system first?" Caitlin asked. "I feel like we're gonna set it off. It's freaking me out."

Good point, Felix thought. And that way he could start with

something smaller than a door the size of a Sherman tank. He walked back to the control panel on the wall. Everyone followed closely behind, apparently afraid that something very bad might happen to them if they didn't stay close to Felix.

"Guys," Felix said in a whisper. "Go stand over by the stairs. I'm gonna take care of this. I don't want you to get hit with any pieces or anything."

"What do you mean take care of it?" Harper asked.

"I'm gonna blow it up. You should stand over by the stairs. Maybe you should go up a few steps, just to be safe."

Felix waited until they climbed several steps. They were no more than fifteen feet away, but even at that distance it was difficult to make out anything more than their general shapes. He turned to face the control panel. He hadn't used his gift since he destroyed all those doors and a lot of other school property inside Devendon on the night his friends followed him. Felix raised his right hand and thought about doing serious damage to the blinking lights. Within seconds, he could see his extended arm glowing red in the darkness.

The control panel and a large section of the surrounding wall exploded with a loud, booming roar that shook the wall it was attached to, leaving a deep crater. A few shattered pieces of plastic and concrete were scattered around Felix's feet. He looked up at the stairs. Harper was already coming toward him at a trot. She was smiling. Felix smiled back.

"You were *glowing!*" Harper said in amazement. "You were shining and all red!"

"Oh," Felix said, somewhat shyly. "Yeah. What can I say? I glow. But you can really only tell in the dark."

"Do you think that killed the alarm?" Caitlin asked.

"Are you kidding?" Lucas replied. "Look at it. It's in a million pieces. Dude, that was awesome!"

Felix shrugged, somewhat embarrassed.

"Now we just need to get the door open," Harper said, pointing at the wall.

Felix walked over to the door and appraised it. He knew he'd have to focus an enormous amount of energy to break it down. He wondered if Bill had underestimated its size. It was huge. Felix wasn't sure if anything on earth could put a dent in it, let alone break it open. It looked completely impregnable.

"You want us to go back up the stairs?" Lucas whispered to Felix.

"No, that's okay. I'm gonna try to explode it into the building. Just stand behind me."

"Dude, that thing is frickin' mammoth," Lucas said over Felix's shoulder. "Are you sure you can do this?"

"Nope."

Felix raised his right hand and gazed at the door as his friends huddled behind him. His body began to glow a deep reddish color that bathed everything around him in its unnatural light.

Ka-boom. The noise seemed to echo all around them and into the night sky above. The door shifted within its frame, moving several inches inside the facility. A vertical indentation formed in the center of the door, beginning at the concrete floor and ending four or five feet above Felix's head. The concrete surrounding the door developed fissures. The wall crumbled as pieces of concrete dropped from the façade and fell to the floor with a clatter. But the door remained in place. Felix lowered his arm and shook his head discouragingly. The door had to be at least twelve feet tall and half that in width.

"That was really loud," Lucas whispered. "Is there any way you can do that a little more quietly?"

"I think you've almost got it," Harper said. "It's caved in the middle pretty good. And it's pulling away from where it's connected to the walls. I think another one of those—whatever you're doing—should do it."

"Okay," Felix said as he concentrated on the enormous door in front of him. "Everyone get behind me again. This time cover your ears." He raised his right hand, and once again, he imbued everything around him in a soft reddish glow.

The door vibrated and then started to shake as if there were an earthquake. The concrete around the door cracked and splintered, and golf-ball-sized pieces of cement fell to the floor. The door groaned loudly, making a terrible wrenching sound. Then a louder noise, like the roar of a jet engine, erupted all around them. The huge door suddenly imploded back and into the darkness of the building, jaggedly ripping away large chunks of the wall with it. Felix lowered his hand, and as the red glow faded, total darkness returned.

"Holy shit!" Lucas yelled, not bothering to whisper. "That was the loudest goddamn thing I've ever heard! I think you blew out my eardrums! Look at the size of that hole."

"You're right," Felix said gravely, surveying the uneven opening in front of them. "That was loud—too loud. We've gotta move fast before someone shows up."

Felix stepped over chunks of concrete rubble that had been uprooted from the floor and ripped violently from the walls. The room he entered was large, about the size of the Downey common area. The ceiling appeared to be at least twenty-five feet high. Large yellow-tinted lights encircled the room where the walls met the ceiling. The floor, walls, and roof were all constructed of concrete. Thick steel support beams ran across the ceiling and down the walls every four feet. The room was dry and considerably warmer than outside. Other than the massive steel door that came to rest in the center of the room like an unusual display of abstract art, the room was completely empty.

Felix quickly took stock of his surroundings. There were two identical-looking doors in the room, smaller versions of the goliath he'd just toppled. One faced the gaping hole in the wall that used to be the access door. The other was to the right of the entrance at the far end of the room.

"Are those emergency lights?" Caitlin asked, pointing at the ceiling.

Felix shrugged. "Whatever they are, at least we can see now."

Lucas stopped alongside Felix and pointed at the two doors. "Which one are you busting down first?"

"We just need to find a room with a bright blue light. I guess I'll start with that one," he said, pointing at the far wall. "We have to hurry! Come on!"

He streaked past the door opposite the truck-sized hole in the exterior wall and stopped in front of the door at the end of the room. On the wall next to it was a flat control panel. Felix wondered if it was some kind of high-tech thumbprint or retinal scan device. He hadn't seen one like that outside. Did he miss it?

His heart was racing. The First Templar Amulet could be just behind the door, just a few feet from where he was standing. He held up his hand. The door exploded into the room, ripping out the twelve-inch bolts connecting it to the steel frame. He peered inside. A white mist billowed out of the room, and a cold chill swept over him.

"What is this shit?" Lucas shouted, swatting at the mist like it was a swarm of bugs. "I can't see."

"Can't you feel the temperature drop?" Felix asked. "It's some kind of refrigeration room."

"I don't like the sound of that," Harper whispered.

Felix waved at the mist as he entered the room. It was cold. As the vapor started to clear, he could see that the room was large and ringed with the same yellow-tinted lights as the entry room. Several panels of blinking lights were set into the opposite wall. It appeared to be some kind of a storage room. Rows of shelves supported by stainless steel columns bolted into the concrete floor filled the room. On each shelf there was a large, thick bag formed of clear plastic. Felix walked over to the nearest row of shelves. He gripped one of the bags and tried to see what was inside, but it was frosted over. Lucas and the girls gathered behind him.

"Maybe we'll find the Ark of the Covenant in here," Lucas said. "There's gotta be hundreds of bags in here, right?"

"What's in them?" Caitlin asked.

Felix tugged on the plastic bag. It was stuck to the shelf. He pulled harder, finally freeing it—it slid from the shelf and hit the concrete floor with a loud thud. Felix looked it over. It was five or six feet long and half that in width. The plastic was too thick to tear with his hands. He groped in his pocket for Caitlin's car keys and jammed the ignition key into the plastic. As he used his fingers to expand the hole made by the key, he lost his balance and stumbled backwards, falling against a shelf.

Caitlin screamed.

Felix jumped at the sound, turning in circles as he searched the room.

Harper screamed.

What the hell was going on? Felix thought. Was someone in the building? He didn't see anyone.

"It's okay," Lucas said calmly, "it can't hurt you. It's dead."

Felix looked down at the bag. Unseeing eyes stared back at him through the hole he'd just made. The head in the bag was nearly hairless. Its eyes and the flesh on one side of its face were missing. Its lipless mouth smiled hideously at him.

"Damn!" he exclaimed. "That's really gross."

He looked around the room, and its purpose suddenly dawned on him. "This is it!" he shouted excitedly. "We're in the right building! This is the place! All these bags have bodies in them. There's hundreds, right? This is how Landry makes Vessels. He stores the bodies here and then takes them to the Amulet room to turn them into Vessels! The Amulet must be here!" He turned and sprinted out of the room.

Felix stopped at the only door remaining in the entry room—the only one he hadn't destroyed. He waited until the others clustered behind him. He raised his hand. His heart was beating fast. He could feel sweat trickling down his forehead and into his eyes. Almost instantly, the door crumpled in on itself and exploded into the room with a tremendous crashing noise.

And there it was. The bright blue he was searching for. It shone through the opening, illuminating them in its otherworldly glow. Felix took a few tentative steps inside the room with his friends following closely behind. The room was enormous—larger than the combined size of the two rooms they'd just left behind. The entire ceiling was flooded with a bright blue light. Every ten feet, a narrow beam of the same blue light shot down from the ceiling until it intersected with a body suspended horizontally above the floor.

Row upon row of bodies filled the room from one end to the other. There had to be hundreds. Some of the bodies appeared to be fully formed. Others were missing flesh and limbs. Some were little more than skeletons. In some cases, the blue beam shone down onto only one limb, or one limb connected to a torso. Felix approached a body that consisted of a half-formed skull, a torso, and one leg. Next to that strange sight was a girl. She appeared to be sleeping comfortably and looked to be fifteen or sixteen. She was tall and slender, with long brown hair, fine features, and skin that was smooth and white. He bent over to look more closely at her face. He put his ear close to her mouth and listened.

"Is she breathing?" Harper asked, standing beside him.

"No."

"She looks like Allison."

"Yeah, she kinda does."

Harper touched Felix's arm lightly. "It almost looks like she's smiling. She's alive, isn't she? Won't she die when you destroy the Amulet?"

The Amulet, Felix thought. That's why he was here, to destroy the Amulet. He was so entranced by the Vessels he forgot all about it. What the hell was he doing? They had to get moving!

"Felix!" Lucas shouted from across the room. "Get over here! I think we found it!"

Felix stepped around a row of Vessels to get a better view. Lucas, Caitlin, and Allison were all looking at something on the wall at one end of the room. Felix took Harper's hand and ran down an aisle formed by two rows of Vessels suspended above the floor by the blue lights from above.

When Felix saw it, he knew instantly that he was looking at the Amulet. He stopped in front of the wall and examined the object closely. It was a round disk made of gold and roughly the size of a dinner plate. In its center was a small circular hole, and within it was a small sapphire-colored sphere that wasn't connected to any part of the Amulet—it was perfectly centered and suspended within it.

A blue light streaked out from the top of the Amulet and to the ceiling. *That's where all the blue light is coming from*, Felix thought. The Amulet was at eye level, but it wasn't actually connected to the wall behind it; it was somehow suspended in the air a few inches away from the wall. The sapphire-colored sphere was spinning, but it spun so rapidly that its movement was almost imperceptible. Felix listened closely. He thought he could hear a faint humming sound. There was a Latin inscription across the top.

"What does it say?" Lucas asked.

"The front is supposed to say the Holder can control Vessels who receive souls willingly given," Felix said distractedly.

Why didn't anything happen? Felix wondered. He'd hoped it would just sort of explode once he entered the room. Wasn't it supposed to sense that he was the Holder? Didn't Bill tell him he'd know what to do when the time came? Well, the time was now, and he had no clue what he should be doing. Maybe he wasn't the Holder, after all. Maybe only Landry could control...

"Maybe you have to hold it in your hands, Felix," Allison said softly. It was the first time she'd spoken since they left campus.

Felix looked at her. Her green eyes were moist. Her brow was creased, even more than it normally was. Why were there always lines on her forehead? he wondered. Even when she was happy she found something to worry about. He loved that about her.

"Allison, I...."

"It's okay," she said, wiping at her eyes. "It's okay. If this is how it's going to end, then it'll end. That can't be changed now. I told you I wanted to be here with you. I'm glad I'm here."

"What's going on?" Harper demanded. "Allison, what are you talking about?"

Allison looked at Harper, and tears streamed down her face. "I'm a...I'm a Vessel."

"You're a what?" Lucas shouted. "What are you talking about? You can't be! Felix, tell Allison she's not a Vessel."

Felix didn't reply.

"Felix?" Caitlin said weakly.

Felix shook his head and looked at Allison. "I don't know. I really don't know. I'm sorry, Allison."

"Then you can't destroy it!" Harper shouted. "Allison will die, right? There's gotta be another way!"

Allison turned to Harper, putting her hand on her arm. "It's the only way. This is...this is bigger than me. Look around you. Look at what Landry's doing! This has to end."

"But Allison..." Caitlin said, tears welling up in her eyes.

"It's okay," Allison interrupted. "It's okay. Felix, please destroy it. And Felix, remember that I always believed in you. And one more thing—you should know that...I...I... Please. Just destroy it."

With every face turned toward him, Felix reached for the Amulet. As his fingers got close, it suddenly propelled itself into his hands. He jumped back in amazement. He held it up to his face and gazed at the sapphire ball spinning within its center. The Amulet felt cold and solid and heavy in his hands. He turned it over. There was a Latin inscription across the top. He couldn't read it, but he knew what it said, or what Bill told him it said, anyway.

He was just supposed to know what to do, but nothing was coming to mind. Should he try slicing it into pieces? Like the trick he performed for Bill with the empty soda cans? He knew that wouldn't work. He didn't know why, he just did. What did he want more than anything right now? That was easy. He wanted to destroy the Amulet. And how could he do that? Was it something like…was it all in his mind? Was it just like using his gift? Did he just have to think about it? Felix looked down at the Amulet and focused solely on how much he wanted to see it destroyed.

And for just a moment, he had a vision. The sapphire ball in the center of the Amulet slowed to a stop. The blue light extinguished itself. The Vessels fell to the floor as the blue light that sustained them faded into nothingness. The image grew blurry and then disappeared. Felix blinked his eyes several times and shook his head. Everyone's eyes were still focused on him. He smiled. He thought of the images and said loudly, "I am a Holder. And this Holder chooses to destroy this fucking Amulet!"

The room suddenly grew dark. The sound of hundreds of objects hitting the floor all at once reverberated off the walls of the cavernous room. Felix glanced at the Amulet. It looked dark and ordinary in his hands. The blue light had vanished. The ceiling was no longer cast in a cold blue light. The beams descending from the ceiling to the Vessels disappeared. Now the only light in the room came from the pale yellow bulbs ringing the ceiling.

The floor was literally covered with Vessels. The bodies were lying in awkward positions, scattered throughout the room. Felix looked again at the Amulet in his hands. The sapphire ball in its center was spinning more slowly than before. And then the ball came to a complete stop and fell from the hole, hitting the concrete floor with a loud crack! It broke into three pieces, and sand trickled out of it.

He watched the sand spilling in thin streams onto the floor and smiled to himself. He did it! He actually did it! He was the Holder. He actually destroyed the Amulet! And then he remembered Allison. *Oh my God! Where's Allison?* He spun around. She was standing directly in front of him with the biggest smile he'd ever seen. There were no lines creasing her forehead.

"You're alive!" Felix shouted as he embraced her and lifted her off the floor. He squeezed her tightly.

"You can let me go now," Allison said, smiling. "Felix, you're crushing me. Felix. I can't breathe."

He set her down on the floor and examined her. There were tears of joy streaming down her tired face. But she was fine. She was alive.

"I knew you weren't a Vessel!" he shouted.

"Dude, you could've told us about this, you know," Lucas said to Felix as Harper and Caitlin swarmed Allison, hugging her. "It kind of explains a lot, you know?"

Felix laughed. He was elated. Allison was alive. And he'd destroyed the Amulet. He could explain to Lucas later why he didn't tell him about Allison.

"Nice work with the Amulet though," Lucas said, laughing. "You definitely killed it."

Allison screamed up at the ceiling, "Thank you God! Thank you! I'm alive! I'm alive!"

The sound of something very heavy sliding across the concrete floor abruptly ended their celebration. They became silent in an instant. Felix lifted his hand to signal for everyone to stay quiet.

Lucas mouthed the words, "What was that?"

Caitlin pointed toward the room where they'd entered the building. Her eyes were wide and her hand was shaking.

Felix nodded and looked around frantically. He didn't notice it before, but there was a narrow doorway directly across from where they'd entered the room. He put his finger to his lips, pointed at it, and gestured for his friends to follow him.

He quickly led them through the doorway. The room they came

to was as long as the Amulet room, but narrower. Felix began searching for a door. If he could just find a door he could break it down, and they could escape from the building. They could make a run through the woods and get to the car. They'd be hard to find in the darkness and fog. He just had to find a way out.

Desks, tables, chairs, and office workstations filled the room. It looked like a small company was running a business there. Felix walked between two rows of desks and came upon what appeared to be a photograph station, like the ones he'd seen at the DMV. And next to it were dozens of racks filled with clothes and hundreds of shoeboxes stacked neatly against a wall.

There was nothing resembling an exit. But there had to be a way out, Felix thought. Just think! Think! Maybe he could make a hole through one of the concrete walls. But how would he get them to the surface? They were at least twenty feet below ground level. Damn! They were trapped. The only way out was the same way they came in.

Felix huddled his friends near the center of the room.

Allison whispered, "Maybe that noise was just...I don't know... maybe a rack in the refrigerator room collapsed or something."

Harper nodded in agreement. "Yeah, maybe that's all it was."

"That's not what it sounded like," Lucas whispered, shaking his head. "And I don't see any way out of here."

"Neither do I," Felix agreed.

"Just the main door in front, right?" Allison asked.

Felix nodded.

"Here's what we should do," Lucas said. "Let's wait by that door and jump whoever comes through. There's gotta be something here we can use. Anything heavy will work. Just aim for the head."

"That's crazy!" Caitlin hissed. "We should just sit tight. Maybe it was nothing."

"You're not getting it," Lucas persisted. "We won't be arrested for breaking and entering. They'll kill us. Right, Felix?"

Something exploded in the Amulet room. And then the sound of a man's voice could be heard.

Harper grabbed Felix's arm. "What do we do?" she asked. There was terror in her eyes.

Felix was about to respond that everything was going to be okay when he was suddenly lifted off his feet and thrown onto his back, knocking the wind out of him. A loud noise erupted from somewhere in the building. He clawed at the rough floor, trying to get to his feet. His ears were ringing. He looked to his left and saw Allison lying face-down on the floor. Lucas was trying to balance himself. He waved his arms like a tightrope walker fighting for balance, finally tripping over an overturned desk and landing on the floor hard on his side.

A piece of concrete fell from the ceiling, narrowly missing Felix's face. He looked up. Enormous cracks formed in the ceiling, and the ceiling was beginning to split apart. Pebble-sized chunks of concrete were falling like hail all around him. He covered his face. The ground shook and the building roared. And then the ceiling appeared to peel away from the building. Felix was now looking at the night sky. It was clouded in a thick white mist. But how could he be looking at the sky? How was that possible? What happened to the roof?

Then the floor heaved and shook, and Felix bounced around like a small child on a trampoline. The sound of concrete and steel tearing apart from their foundations filled his ears. An enormous wall of concrete passed overhead like a spacecraft, temporarily blocking out his view of the night sky before disappearing behind him. *Where the hell did that come from?* And then he heard what sounded like a building collapsing behind him.

Smoke and dust filled the room, blocking out much of the weak illumination afforded by the yellow lights. He heard another explosion behind him. He rolled onto his side to see what was happening, but was forced to cover his head as sections of concrete and chunks of earth came crashing down from above. He rolled onto his back. He'd never been so disoriented—not even when he read the journal. He didn't even know which way was up. The entire world seemed to have been turned upside down. He gagged on the dust and smoke that filled his lungs. Where was Harper? And Allison? Where were his friends? He had to get to them. He had to find them.

After what seemed like an eternity, the room stopped shaking. Felix braced himself against an overturned piece of furniture and stood up. The Amulet was still tightly clutched in his hand—he'd forgotten all about it. He searched for his friends through the haze. Allison and Lucas were to his right. Allison was helping Lucas up from the floor. Felix shouted Allison's name, but she didn't hear him.

Caitlin was leaning against the back wall behind Felix. She was brushing something from her leg, but didn't appear to be injured. Where was Harper? Where was she?

"Harper!" Felix shouted over and over as he searched in the hazy darkness.

"Felix!" someone called from up ahead. He spun around and saw Harper. She was crouched on the ground and holding her ankle. She grimaced in pain and coughed. Thank God! Felix thought. *She's alive.* She gave Felix a little wave and coughed again.

What the hell was happening? What happened to the building? Felix looked around the room. The twenty-five-foot-high concrete wall separating the Amulet room from the room where they just sought refuge no longer existed. It had somehow been wrenched out of the floor. Now there was nothing dividing the two rooms. And the ceiling was no longer there. Most of the roof was ripped completely from the building like the flimsy sheet-metal top of a trailer caught in a tornado. What could have done that?

Without the dividing wall, what remained of the roof hung precariously overhead, slanting downward at a steep angle like a ski jump. There were enormous gashes and crevices along the wall behind Felix, and piles of concrete heaped along its edge. In one corner, Felix noticed a gaping fracture that was much larger than the others—at least four feet across. He strained his eyes, and through the crevice, he thought he could see the earth and the misty sky above it. So they were at the far end of the building, he thought. If they could just get to that corner, they could climb out. He needed everyone to get there fast.

He shouted at Harper and started pointing at the corner of the room. She seemed to understand what he was trying to tell her, but then a very strange thing happened. The smoke and dust filling the room seemed to evaporate before Felix's eyes. One moment he could barely see Harper crouched down on the floor, and the next, she was as clearly visible as the yellow lights would allow. It was like an enormous vacuum cleaner had instantly sucked all of the dust, smoke, and mist right out of the room. Felix spun around to shout at Caitlin. As soon as he saw her, he knew something was wrong. Her mouth was hanging open, and she was pointing at something behind him. Felix wheeled around.

A man was standing in the rubble facing Felix, no more than ten feet away. He wore a dark blue suit with a white shirt and a neatly knotted blue and white striped tie. His dark brown hair was perfectly parted at the side, and he appeared to be in his forties. Felix was stunned. The man looked like a corporate lawyer. He expected to see men in camouflaged army fatigues carrying machine guns and grenade launchers, not some accountant-looking guy. Should he say something? Should he attack him? Didn't Bill tell him to attack first and worry about the consequences later?

Before Felix could formulate a coherent plan, he heard a piercing scream. Another man had entered the building, and he was advancing toward Harper. He had short, neatly trimmed reddish hair and was wearing khaki-colored slacks, a navy blue jacket, a white shirt, and a green tie. In his left hand he was holding a long piece of steel rebar. He halted, stood motionless, and stared at Harper. She was trying to move backwards, but was struggling on her injured ankle.

The man facing Felix turned his head and raised his hand. Felix turned to see what he was looking at. Lucas and Allison joined Caitlin, and they were huddled together with their backs against the wall. Not more than ten feet in front of them, a long, rusty, reinforced steel bar was protruding from a large chunk of concrete, which was clinging to one end of it. The steel bar suddenly lifted itself off the floor and hung suspended in the air. It then slammed itself against the concrete floor several times with tremendous force until the piece of concrete on the end of it shattered into small pieces. Then the steel bar sailed across the room at blinding speed, stopping a few inches from the brown-haired man, who wrapped the fingers of his outstretched hand around it.

So this was Landry Ashfield, Felix thought. He wasn't sure why, but he didn't picture him like this. He probably should've Googled his photo at some point. Why didn't he do that? And why was he having these random thoughts when he and his friends were all about to die? The man gripped the steel bar as if he were holding a baseball bat and stepped toward Felix, drawing it back into a swinging position. Out of the corner of his eye, Felix could see the man in the green tie stepping closer to Harper. She screamed.

"Wait!" a commanding voice said from behind the two men. They lowered their steel bars obediently and stepped back.

Where did that voice come from? Felix thought. He looked up. Three men were moving slowly through the wreckage from the far side of the Amulet room. The man in the center was taller than the other two. He seemed to walk without expending any effort, as if he were gliding across the floor. He wore dark gray slacks and a crisp white long-sleeved button-down dress shirt. He seemed to be casually surveying the room, as if he were out for a late night stroll.

There was something different about the man in the center. Felix could sense his power. It was like an emotion, like fear itself; it couldn't be seen or touched, but it was as real as the floor beneath Felix's feet.

He was looking at Landry Ashfield. He knew that for a fact. And for the first time that night, Felix was afraid.

"I see that you have something of mine," Landry said, his eyes boring directly into Felix's. His voice was clear and controlled.

Felix was startled. Did he just ask him a question? He was disoriented and struggling to comprehend what was happening. What'd he have of his?

Suddenly, he was lifted off the ground and pulled across the room. He tried to move his arms and kick his legs, but he was powerless. He was flying across the room toward Landry, and he couldn't do anything about it. He came to a sudden standstill directly in front of Landry. If Felix were able to overcome the paralysis in his arms, he could have reached out and touched the Antichrist.

It was strange being so near to Landry. He didn't look like the Antichrist, Felix thought. Nothing was horrible or demonic about his appearance—he didn't have fangs or horns. He didn't have a tail. He was probably considered quite handsome by most standards. He had thick, light brown hair and a narrow face with a thin nose and a strong jaw. His face was smooth and unlined, and there was an ageless quality about it. His skin was pale, but not overly so, and his eyes were light blue and cold. He appeared to be placidly calm and completely in control. But under the unassuming façade, something terrible was lurking. Felix could feel it—could sense it. Like a black hole devouring a galaxy in its vortex. It couldn't be seen, but it was there, just below the surface—and nothing could escape it, not even light. The two men flanking Landry wore dark suits, white shirts, and matching yellow ties. They were as expressionless as Landry.

"The First Templar Amulet, of course," Landry said. "The object of mine that you possess is the Amulet that you're holding in your hand."

Felix felt an icy chill whisper down his spine and he shuddered. Against his will, his right arm suddenly extended out from his body. His hand still gripped the Amulet tightly, but then his fingers loosened and it glided out of his hand and into Landry's. Landry looked at it for a moment, and Felix thought he saw a small frown cross his face.

Landry casually tossed the Amulet on the littered concrete floor as if he were disposing of rubbish.

"Why?" Felix asked, not quite sure why he asked the question.

Landry seemed to appraise Felix for a moment before he spoke. "Why? Why this, you mean?" gesturing with his long white fingers at the lifeless Vessels lying on the floor all around them. "This is merely a means to an end."

"You have no right!" Felix shouted.

Landry looked slightly surprised at Felix's outburst. "No right, you say? I am simply giving people a choice. I have never forced anyone to become someone else. It is only through the exercise of one's own free will that this is possible. I simply grant wishes."

"Looks like you won't be granting any more wishes!"

Landry looked at the Amulet lying on the floor next to him. "My numbers are already legion. The First Templar Amulet has already achieved its purpose. That which I have touched remains mine forever. The Vessels are merely the point of my spear."

His glacial blue eyes suddenly narrowed as he examined every feature of Felix's face. "But how is it that the ball in the center of my Amulet no longer turns? Why is it cracked and as dry as the desert? What is your name?"

"What do you care?"

"Don't test me! I'll ask you once more. What is your name?"

Felix struggled, trying in vain to touch the floor with his feet. He thought about not answering, but remembered that his driver's license and school ID were in his back pocket. Landry only needed to check his wallet.

"Felix," he finally answered.

"Felix. And what is your surname, Felix?"

"August. My name's Felix August."

"Felix August," Landry repeated softly. "Are you sure that's your name? Perhaps you were once known by a different name? Perhaps you were once called *Liam*."

"I don't know what you're talking…"

"I know exactly what you are," Landry said coldly as he took a step backward. "So it is true. My dear mother Eve did have a sister. And it seems that she bore a son." He paused for a moment, and his eyes appeared to have been set ablaze, burning with pure energy. "There's something else that I know."

Felix wanted to say something, something to challenge Landry, but he couldn't find the words.

"Curses never die. Only people die."

"Wha…what?"

Landry smiled and lifted his index finger ever so slightly. Felix was propelled backward like a circus performer shot from the barrel of a cannon. He slammed into the back wall and collapsed against a pile of finely crushed concrete. His entire body felt like it was on fire. He couldn't breathe. His head was spinning. *Curses never die?* Bill said that curses die once they're broken. What did that mean? Why would Landry tell him that? Felix struggled to think clearly, blinded by the pain that coursed through his body.

The force of the collision knocked the wind out of Felix. He struggled to find his breath. His eyes watered and he felt a sharp pain in his shoulder. He tried to move, but he couldn't force any life back into his limbs. He fought to hold his head off the floor, to see what was happening in front of him. He heard a scream—a girl's scream. Lucas, Caitlin, and Allison were grouped together off to his right. Lucas and Allison were brandishing something—pieces of wood from the remains of a splintered table. They were being stalked by the man in the striped blue tie. The man was wielding a long steel bar and preparing to swing it. His friends needed his help. He had to get up.

Felix got to his feet. He still couldn't breathe. The world seemed to be undulating. He saw Harper in the distance. She was trying to maneuver away from the man in the green tie, but struggled to get through the wreckage in her path. She screamed and limped backwards on her injured ankle. The man moved menacingly toward her, calm and deliberate, holding the steel bar in his hands like a sword.

Harper stumbled and nearly fell, catching herself with her hands. She scrambled to her feet and turned her back to the man, trying desperately to get away from him. She looked up and Felix could see the sheer terror on her face. And in that moment, her panic-filled eyes met his. She lifted her arm toward him, as if pleading for him to save her. The man behind her closed the distance between them in an instant. He held the steel bar menacingly at his side, and with one smooth motion, he drew it back and then drove it forward with unnatural strength into the center of her back.

Harper was wearing a black jacket made of thick leather. The steel bar pierced her between the shoulder blades. It was driven into her body with such ferocity that it came out the front of her chest, where it became lodged, unable to pierce the heavy leather. The violent force of the man's thrust lifted Harper completely off the floor. He held her up in the air as she screamed. Her feet kicked helplessly as they dangled high above the floor. Her arms flailed for a moment, searching desperately for something to grasp onto. Then they collapsed limply and lifelessly at her sides, her fingers pointing at the floor.

Felix couldn't believe what he just saw. That didn't happen. That couldn't have happened. It had to be a dream. A terrible nightmare. That wasn't possible. Harper? Harper? No! No! No! No!

The man in the green tie smiled and swung the steel bar like a baseball bat. Harper's body slipped off the end of the bar and bounced across the room, finally coming to rest against the back wall next to the crevice in the corner.

"Nooooooooooooooooo!" Felix screamed, glowing brightly in the dim light of the building as he ran toward the two men. His face was filled with fury and pain. He saw red. All around him he saw nothing but red. Like the world was drowning in blood. He stopped in front of Caitlin, Allison, and Lucas and reached toward the mist-covered sky with his hand. The man in the green tie and the man in the striped blue tie retreated backwards several steps and waited, gripping their long steel bars out in front of them. The man who had just murdered Harper, impaling her with his bloodstained weapon, continued to smile as he motioned smugly with his hand for Felix to come closer.

Hundreds of tons of concrete and steel suddenly crashed down on top of the two men like a force of nature. The roof was constructed of concrete ten feet thick and reinforced with steel beams. Felix ma-nipulated the roof like a hammer to obliterate the men like two insects hitting the windshield of a car at a hundred miles an hour. The im-pact sounded like a volcanic eruption. The concussion knocked Felix's friends off their feet.

There was now an enormous barrier between Felix and Landry— the roof formed a perfect wall between them. It spanned the width of the room and soared high above the building where it disappeared into the darkness and fog of the night sky.

Felix sprinted to Harper's lifeless form where it lay on the concrete floor near the back wall. Her body was twisted into an unnatural shape. Blood pooled around her. Her eyes were still open. Felix thought he could see the terror of her final moments written clearly on her face. He heard something behind him and turned to see Caitlin, Lucas, and Allison running toward him. He bent down and closed Harper's life-less eyes.

He'd vowed to protect her. And now she was dead, lying in her own blood on a pile of crushed concrete in some bunker in the middle of a godforsaken forest. Why'd he let her come with him? Why? He heard crying behind him. Someone gagged and then threw up on the floor. He heard Lucas trying to comfort Caitlin.

Everything seemed wrong—disconnected and surreal. How could

this be happening? Wasn't there a rewind button he could push? Couldn't he just make this go away somehow? Harper couldn't really be dead. He felt a hand on his shoulder. He looked up and saw Allison. Tears were streaming down her face. Felix scooped Harper's body up off the floor and held her. He held her tightly and closed his eyes. How could she be dead? How? Maybe it would all just go away if he wished it to. He'd hold her until she came back to him. He wouldn't let her go.

"Felix!" Lucas suddenly shouted. "Felix! Felix! Something's happening to the wall! Felix!"

Felix rested Harper's body gently on the floor and stood up, turning to face the only thing that separated them from Landry. He walked toward it. The enormous concrete structure Felix had brought down just moments before appeared to be vibrating. Dust swirled around its surface, and a sand-like substance was falling from it, collecting on the floor.

Something was terribly wrong. Felix reversed course and starting walking backwards, trying to distance himself from the wall without tripping on the piles of concrete, office furniture, and chunks of earth and debris scattered across the floor. The wall shook violently. Then it began to melt. He couldn't see the top of the wall because it was obscured by the night sky, but the highest point he could see appeared to be dissolving like candle wax. Felix stared in amazement. Then he realized that the wall wasn't melting; it was being reduced to sand. Within seconds, the entire structure was nothing more than a gigantic pile of concrete and steel powder stretching from one end of the building to the other. Dust plumes billowed high into the air. Felix strained to see through it. He knew that Landry was on the other side. They had to get out of the bunker. Everyone needed to get to the corner. He'd carry Harper out of there. He shouted at Lucas, trying to get his attention.

There was an explosion. An instant later, Felix was lifted off the ground and sent crashing into the back wall. He slid down the rough surface and fell onto the floor. The room was suddenly cast in total darkness. He tried to take a breath before realizing he was completely buried under tons of finely pulverized concrete powder. He choked on the dust. He couldn't breathe. He started to panic. He clawed furiously at the sand until he finally saw light. He pulled himself away from the avalanche, coughing and spitting up concrete particles. There was dust in his eyes, and it clogged his nostrils. He wiped at his face, feeling like he was rubbing it with sandpaper.

Finally regaining his vision, he searched frantically along the back wall for Lucas and the girls. Where were they? He looked across the room and saw Landry and the two men in yellow ties; they hadn't moved. And then he saw his friends. Lucas, Caitlin, and Allison had already managed to extricate themselves from the sand. They were huddled together in a tight cluster thirty feet in front of him. How'd they get up there? he wondered as he tried to wipe the dust from his eyes.

Landry casually pointed at the wall nearest him. Large chunks of steel and concrete peeled away from it and flew across the room, stopping next to him and hovering like a great constellation. Hundreds of jagged-looking steel and concrete fragments, some the size of a kitchen table and others no larger than a baseball, hovered beside him like a flock of obedient birds. Landry waved his hand. The deadly assemblage of debris, covering an area ten feet across and just as high, catapulted across the cavernous room toward his friends.

Felix sprinted ahead with his hand raised.

Lucas closed his eyes and stepped in front of Caitlin and Allison, trying to shield them with his body. Just as it appeared they'd be shredded by the barrage, something happened. As each object came within a foot of where they stood, it stopped and fell to the floor as if it had collided with an invisible and impenetrable wall.

Lucas opened his eyes and stared with a look of wonder at the huge pile of debris lying on the floor in front of him.

"Lucas!" Felix shouted. "Get behind me. Allison! Caitlin! Move!"

Lucas turned to see Felix approaching. He shouted at Caitlin just as Allison saw Felix coming up from behind. They raced over to Felix and huddled behind him.

In the distance, Felix could see Landry holding out his hands as if he were a supplicant. A white shadowy figure emerged from his body, and then another, and another, and another. An otherworldly sound filled the air—a terrible high-pitched screech unlike anything Felix had ever heard before.

Lucas covered his ears and screamed.

Hundreds of the white shadows flew across the room toward them.

What the hell are those things? Felix wondered.

"Ghosts!" Caitlin shouted. "Oh my God! Ghosts!"

"No," Felix said, realizing what they were. "Lost Souls."

At first, it looked like they were being attacked by an army of flying skeletons. The creatures looked skeletal, but the bones were nearly translucent. Their short, squatty torsos were connected to disproportionately elongated arms and legs, which ended with serrated claws as long as steak knives. Their heads were enormous, their faces flat and simian, and their gaping mouths were filled with rows of long, triangular, shark-like teeth.

They screeched their horrible cry and Caitlin screamed.

"What the hell?" Lucas shouted. "What are those things? Felix?"

Felix concentrated on stopping them at the same spot in the room where he had prevented the flying cloud of building scrap from mutilating his friends.

He held out his hand and focused. Just stop them, he thought. Just stop!

It didn't work. The Lost Souls flew through the invisible boundary as if it were merely a speed bump. Their shrieks echoed throughout the room as they hurtled across the ruined building with their mouths wide open, baring their terrible teeth.

A chorus of screams sounded behind him. The Lost Souls were close enough to touch.

And then they stopped. The creatures gnashed their teeth and flailed at the air with their clawed hands and taloned feet. But with each attempt, they were stopped just inches from Felix and his friends.

Felix focused with everything he had, but he was already losing control. It was like trying to grasp a shadow. It wasn't something he could feel. He focused on keeping them away, but he couldn't feel them. If the sun passed over a tree, how could he prevent the tree from casting a shadow? How could he push back a shadow? His control was slipping.

A clawed hand missed Felix's face by inches. He snapped his head back and fought to keep them away. The Lost Souls seemed to recognize there was a weakness in the unseen boundary and began to double their efforts. They scratched and clawed at Felix like dogs digging for a bone. A clawed foot slashed downward, narrowly missing Felix's shoulder. A Lost Soul pushed its terrible ape-like head closer and closer to Felix's face, its mouth agape, gnashing its rows of shark teeth.

"Felix!" Lucas shouted from behind. "You better do something!"

"Run!" Felix shouted back. "Get out through that opening in the corner!"

He felt a hand on his shoulder and heard Allison say, "We're not leaving without you!"

Felix saw red. These were his friends. He'd brought them here. They just wanted to help. And now Harper was dead. Dead! He'd promised to protect her. But he failed. Nobody else was going to die that day. Maybe the Lost Souls were already dead. But who says you can't die twice?

"Die, you fucking things!" Felix screamed.

The Lost Souls jumped back as if they'd been electrocuted. Dark red flames exploded from the floor like geysers and shot high into the air. The Lost Souls screeched and flew higher, trying to get away as the flames whipped around the room like burning tornadoes, chasing the Lost Souls high into the sky and driving them backwards.

"Holy shit!" someone said, sounding awestruck.

The flaming tornadoes spread quickly across the floor, merging and becoming a single tremendous inferno, driving the Lost Souls further and further back. As the Lost Souls drew close to Landry, he opened his mouth and swallowed them like a snake gorging on rodents. When the flames reached Landry, they parted like a rising tide with Landry standing on a circular-shaped area of higher ground. The two men wearing yellow ties moved even closer to Landry as the flames reached the opposite wall and encircled them. Only a few Lost Souls remained—they flew around Landry within the center of the circle, apparently waiting for an opportunity to escape the inferno surrounding them. The Vessels scattered across the floor caught fire and burned. The stench of their burning flesh permeated the air.

"We should get out of here!" Allison yelled. "He's turning red! Let's go!"

Peering through the smoke and flames, Felix could see that Landry was indeed beginning to glow—a brilliant, dark shade of red that stood out even through the flames surrounding him.

Somebody from behind pulled at him. "We need to get out of here!" Allison shouted.

Felix nodded.

They ran toward the opening in the corner of the room. Suddenly Felix stopped. Harper was no longer there. The entire area was now covered with sand, piled several feet thick in every direction. He fell to his knees and started digging desperately. He wasn't going to leave Harper in this place. Somebody clutched at him from behind, but he ignored it. He dug at the sand, frantically searching for Harper's body. He had to find her.

"Felix!" Lucas yelled and tried to pull him off the ground. Felix pushed him away and plunged his hands back into the sand.

"Felix," a gentle voice whispered into his ear. "Felix. We have to go. We can't get out without you, Felix. We need you. Please."

He looked up. Allison knelt down beside him. There were tears in her eyes.

She was right. They'd all die if they didn't get out now. He turned around. The flames were still burning high into the night sky. He glanced down at the sand where he knew Harper was entombed. How had it come to this? How?

"Okay," he finally said. "Let's go."

The crevice in the wall was wide enough for two people to pass through together, but several feet of coarse concrete sand slowed their progress. Getting down on all fours, they crawled through it until they came to a makeshift concrete ladder. A section of the roof Landry tore from the building had landed there, forming a steeply angled ramp that appeared to extend high above ground level.

"Hurry!" Felix shouted. Caitlin started climbing, followed by Allison and then Lucas. Felix went last. The concrete was slippery. He felt raindrops.

"Faster!" Felix shouted as he climbed. "Move! Move!"

He continued to clamber up the incline, exhorting his friends to move faster. There was earth all around him. They must be close to the surface, he thought. He looked up and saw Caitlin jumping off the concrete slab and onto solid ground. When Felix reached the top, his friends were there waiting for him.

"We've gotta get to the car!" Felix shouted.

"Where's the sock?" Allison asked.

Felix felt disoriented. He spun in circles, looking in every direction. It was still dark—he had no idea how long they were down there. And the fog hadn't cleared. Damn! He couldn't get his bearings. He couldn't remember where they'd tied Lucas's sock to the tree. Where the hell were they? What side of the building did they just climb out of?

"I think it's over there," Allison said, pointing into the mist.

An explosion erupted from inside the building, causing the ground to shake.

"What was that?" Lucas yelled, trying to steady himself.

"Landry!" Felix shouted. "Let's get the hell out of here. I hope you're right, Allison. Let's go that way! Everybody hold hands!" They ran across the rain-saturated ground and stopped moments later when they came to a row of trees.

"Nice job, Allison!" Felix shouted. "Now we need to find the sock! Lucas, you and Caitlin look to the left. Allison and I will look to the right. If you find it yell 'sock'! Don't go far! And hurry!"

They separated into pairs. At any other time, looking for Lucas's sock in the forest might have been considered comical. But now, finding the sock was literally a matter of life and death.

"Sock!" Lucas yelled in the distance.

"Where'd that come from?" Allison whispered. "It sounded far away. The woods are echoing. And I can't see a damn thing."

"Me either," Felix said. "Stay calm. Let's just follow the tree line. Lucas! Lucas! Where are you?"

"Here!" Lucas said from somewhere ahead in the darkness. "You sound close. Just keep coming this way. Follow the sound of my voice."

"Okay," Felix replied. "Just keep talking."

Seconds later Felix could see the fuzzy shapes of Lucas and Caitlin through the fog.

"It's good to see you guys," Lucas said. "Here's the sock." He pointed. It was tied around the tree just as they left it. It seemed like a year had passed since he tied it there. Harper was with him. And now she was buried in a pile of dirt in some fucking bunker and…

"Felix…" Allison said.

Felix shook his head, trying to clear his thoughts. "Sorry. We need to go in a straight line back that way," he said, pointing. "Don't lose sight of each other. Be careful climbing over the trees."

Another booming explosion erupted behind them, again sounding like it was from inside the facility. Small pieces of concrete, steel, and other debris rained down on them from above.

"Let's hurry the fuck up!" Felix shouted. "Stay tight."

They moved as quickly as the thick forest would allow, clambering over trees, with Felix trying to keep them moving in a straight line. Stopping to search through the mist for the rock that marked the halfway point, Felix was knocked off his feet by a tremendous explosion that rocked the ground. He covered his head as objects the size of small cars crashed to the ground like a shower of meteorites. What the hell was that? An enormous chunk of concrete missed him by less than ten feet. Was that what was left of the roof? What was Landry doing? Trashing the building?

"That was close!" Caitlin said, sounding relieved. She pulled herself off the ground, just as a tree came crashing down not more than a few feet from where she stood. Caitlin screamed and collapsed to the ground, cradling her head. Felix ran over and helped her off the forest floor, trying to keep her calm. If she lost her composure he'd have to carry her out of there. That would definitely slow them down. Finally she seemed to collect herself enough to move without Felix's help. He grabbed Caitlin's hand and led her and the rest of his friends as quickly as he could in what he hoped was the right direction. He breathed a sigh of relief when he saw the first marker.

"There's the first rock!" he shouted. "We can go faster now. Everybody hurry!"

They quickened their pace. There was another explosion. They crouched and covered their heads, waiting for the expected barrage from the heavens to descend. A moment later they were showered by a hailstorm of debris. The forest quaked. Huge trees snapped like kindling and crashed to the ground behind them. When at last quiet returned to the woods, they sprang back to their feet and continued through the forest with Felix in the lead.

They moved quickly, running at times, tripping over rocks, roots, and tree branches. Allison caught her foot on a large root concealed by underbrush and nearly fell onto a jagged-looking stump. Felix heard the noise behind him and turned his head just as she went sprawling onto the forest floor.

"Are you okay?" he asked, breathing heavily.

"It's my ankle," she said, grimacing in pain.

He helped her off the ground and half carried her as she limped along beside him. Felix spotted something reflecting the tiny bit of moonlight filtering through the trees. "That's gotta be the car!" he shouted. "Follow me!"

"I see it!" Caitlin exclaimed. Lucas and Caitlin ran passed Felix, who was struggling to help Allison on her injured ankle.

"We're almost there," he whispered to her under his breath. When they reached the car, Caitlin and Lucas were already in the backseat. Felix helped Allison into the passenger seat and then he ran around the back of the car.

He heard something. He stopped behind the trunk and listened.

Tha-whoomp.

There it was again. It sounded like air being released under pressure. What the hell was that? he wondered. That couldn't have been the wind, right? He turned around and scanned the woods bordering the edge of the dirt road. If there was something out there, he wouldn't be able to see it until it was almost on top of him. He only had to walk ten feet to get inside the car. But if there was something behind him, he might not make it in time. He thought about the images on Lucas's computer—two people mutilated with their faces chewed off.

"Come and get me, motherfuckers!" Felix screamed into the woods. He was burning with absolute fury. Harper was dead. He let her die. The guilt was already starting to consume him. He'd felt that kind of guilt before. After seeing himself murder his parents. He hated it. He hated that feeling so much. It was like acid burning away at his insides. What was there to live for now? His body turned a deep shade of red. It illuminated Caitlin's car and the area surrounding it.

His friends looked out the windows, their eyes wide.

"You wanna piece of me? I swear to God I will fuck you up!" he screamed as he started backpedaling toward the driver's side door. He kept his eyes focused on the trees. If anything came at him, he'd be ready. Just before he reached the door, Allison opened it for him. He climbed in and shut the door quickly.

"What the hell happened?" Lucas shouted.

"I thought I heard something."

"What was it?" Lucas asked.

"I'm not sure. It sounded like air or…I don't know."

"Can you flame off?" Allison asked, shielding her eyes. "You're lit up pretty bright."

"Sorry. Give me a minute. I'm kinda jacked up."

Felix turned the ignition, and the car started up immediately. He touched the monitor on the cell phone and selected the GPS application.

The monitor read *acquiring satellite*. Felix stared at it, waiting for the route to the Pine Street subdivision to pop up.

"What's wrong?" Caitlin asked.

Felix ignored her. "Come on, goddammit! Work!"

"It's the GPS, isn't it?" Caitlin asked, panic in her voice.

"Maybe it's the fog," Felix said to himself. "Fuck! Not now! Not now! Not now!"

An explosion jolted the car. It rocked back and forth on its tires as debris rained down, making a deafening racket on the metal roof.

"We have to get out of here!" Allison shouted.

Felix stared at the monitor; it still read *acquiring satellite*.

"Felix!" Caitlin screamed.

"I can't without the GPS! I can't see a thing!"

Another blast, this one even louder and sounding closer, rocked the car.

"We don't have a choice, Felix!" Allison shouted. "Get us the hell out of here! Now!"

Felix backed up the car and headed in the direction they came. Rocks, dirt, and trees fell out of the sky all around them. Allison instinctively covered her head as Caitlin screamed.

"That's not helping!" Felix shouted. "I'm trying to focus here."

"Sorry," Caitlin whispered.

"Okay. Six-tenths of a mile," Felix said to himself as he checked the odometer. He stared out the windshield. He didn't think it was possible, but the visibility was even worse than before. He gripped the steering wheel tightly and fought the impulse to stomp the accelerator to the floor. At six-tenths of a mile the road came to an abrupt stop. He turned left, wiping perspiration from his face.

His shoulder ached. He ignored the pain and focused on the rutted road ahead. Even in the best of conditions, the disused logging roads were more like winding, randomly crisscrossing footpaths than roads suitable for twenty-first century automobiles. On a night like this, they were nightmarish. A few minutes later the road seemed to disappear into the forest. Felix slammed on the brakes, barely avoiding a collision with several enormous Douglas fir trees bordering the road. Lucas gasped. Caitlin sobbed softly in the backseat.

Felix looked both ways, squinting his eyes and frowning deeply, as if he could make the road visible by sheer concentration. He thought he could just barely see the faint outline of a dirt road leading to the left and the right. He closed his eyes tightly for a moment and tried to visualize the way they came.

"Felix, not to pressure you, but we need to get moving," Allison implored.

Felix turned the car to the right and accelerated. "I think it's this way," he muttered to himself. "And then we'll need to go in kind of a half-circle up ahead somewhere. Fuck! This goddamn fucking fog! I can't see."

Allison put her hand on Felix's shoulder. "It's okay, Felix. You can do this."

The dirt road veered to the left, and they passed by another road that cut across from the right. Felix slowed the car, but continued on, not making any turns. Another dirt road intersected theirs, and again it went off to the right.

Felix stopped the car.

He shifted into reverse and backed up until the car was perpendicular with the dirt road he'd just passed. He peered out the passenger side window. He couldn't even see where the road ended. They needed to turn right, but he wasn't sure where. What road was he supposed to take?

Caitlin stopped sobbing. The only sound was the smooth humming of the engine. The windshield wipers went back and forth, but the rain had stopped.

"Felix..." Allison said gently.

He slipped the gearshift into drive and continued on, deciding not to turn. He could feel the tension in the car. He couldn't afford to make a mistake. Everyone knew what would happen if they got lost in the forest. It was a certain death sentence—he had to get them out of there.

"I think this is the right way," he said tentatively as the road gradually began to curve to the right. A moment later the road abruptly stopped as a row of monstrous trees seemed to jump right out of the road, blocking their path. Felix slammed on the brakes and turned left. At least he didn't roll the car, he thought as he accelerated slightly and glanced at the cell phone monitor. It still read *acquiring satellite*.

"I think we're getting close," he said. "Look for an opening in the trees."

They stared straight ahead in silence.

"I can't see anything," Caitlin sobbed.

The forest ended before Felix had time to react. They barreled out of the forest and into the field of uncut grass. Felix slammed on the brakes, and the car slid to a stop, fishtailing and leaving behind muddy ruts.

There was a moment of silence and then everybody erupted.

"Yes!" Lucas shouted. "We're out of the fucking forest! We're in that farmer's field, right? Right? Now you know where we are, don't you, Felix? Felix?"

Felix took his hands off the steering wheel and exhaled. He put the car in drive and sped through the field. The car went airborne as it jumped the curb at the end of the cul-de-sac. They flew through the abandoned subdivision in a matter of seconds. Felix turned right on Easton Street, barely looking to see if there was any oncoming traffic. He accelerated the car to sixty miles per hour, straining his eyes to see the faded yellow lines on the unlit street.

"Felix," Allison said softly. "We should slow down. I don't know what we'd say if a cop pulled us over."

She was right. He was driving a dented, mud-spattered car with three other people who were covered in dirt, sand, and who knows what else. They'd definitely be taken to the police station. And what about Harper? How would they explain that?

Harper... The image of the man in the green tie spearing her through the back and holding her off the floor in a sickening parody of a trophy fish as she writhed and screamed in pain came back to him in an overpowering rush. He'd promised to take care of her; he'd promised. And she'd looked at him. She'd looked at him. Counting on him to save her. But he couldn't. He wasn't strong enough. He let her die.

The realization of Harper's death must have also dawned on Caitlin. She began wailing in the backseat. It was a terrible sound, and Felix felt tears forming in his eyes. He fought them off. He wasn't going to cry anymore.

"We're not driving by the main A.E.I. gate, are we?" Allison asked, sounding frightened.

Felix looked over at her. Her eyes were moist, but she was trying to remain calm.

"No," he replied. He'd studied the maps at Bill's house and knew several routes that would get them back to campus. "We'll take a left at Hermann and head south."

Nobody spoke. Caitlin continued to sob, and Allison wiped at her eyes with her filthy sweatshirt.

"We should call Bill," Felix finally said. He glanced at the clock on the console in front of him. It was 3:25. Time didn't mean anything. It may as well have been the year 2020. Why did it matter? He touched the monitor on the cell phone and put it on speaker.

Bill answered the phone on the second ring. "Hello!" he said anxiously. "Felix?"

"Yeah, it's me."

Caitlin's sobbing grew louder. And Allison, despite her attempts to stay calm, couldn't hold back her tears any longer.

"What's wrong?" Bill asked. "Is that crying? Is everything..."

"Everything isn't all right!" Felix shouted.

"Did you destroy the Amulet?"

"The *Amulet*? Yeah. Yeah, I destroyed the goddamn Amulet!"

"So what happened? Was it Allison? Did she..."

"Allison's fine," Felix shouted into the phone. "It's Harper. She... she... she didn't make it."

Caitlin's cries from the backseat grew louder. Allison covered her face with the sleeves of her sweatshirt and sobbed.

"*Harper?*" Bill said in a shocked voice. "But what happ..."

"He was there!" Felix shouted. "Landry was there! And there were these men with him. And one of them... one of them killed her!"

Caitlin's cries reached a crescendo. Bill said something, but his words were drowned out by the sounds in the car.

"Felix!" Bill shouted. "Listen to me! Come directly to my house. Go to the side gate and come in through the back."

"Okay," Felix said lifelessly.

"Felix!" Bill shouted again. "Did you hear me? Don't stop anywhere. Come straight to my house. And do not get pulled over by the police. Understood?"

"Okay." Felix tapped the monitor to end the call.

They drove the rest of the way without speaking, the silence only broken by the sounds of sorrow that filled the car.

Chapter 46

Felix parked on Eleventh Street near the corner of Willow just after four o'clock. The fog still shrouded the area. They got out of the car and walked slowly to the elegant white colonial with the black shutters. As the adrenaline subsided during the drive, Felix's entire body began to ache. He could barely move his right shoulder, and a piercing pain somewhere on his upper back screamed at him every time it bumped against the car seat.

Felix opened the side gate that led into the backyard and closed it after them. Allison was limping badly. Lucas was practically carrying Caitlin, who appeared semi-catatonic. Walking around to the back of the house, they came to a patio with an outdoor table, several chairs, and a barbeque grill illuminated by lights shining through two windows on the first floor. Felix saw Bill standing at one of the windows. As soon as Bill saw them, he opened the door and came out to the patio, ushering them into the house. He hadn't changed his clothes from earlier that night. It dawned on Felix that he left Bill's house just eight hours before. It seemed like a lifetime ago.

In the light of the kitchen, Felix saw for the first time what had become of his friends in Ardsley Forest. They were completely covered in mud, dirt, and a grayish powdery sand. Their clothes were shredded. Their faces were barely recognizable—caked with dirt and concrete powder smeared by rain and tears. Caitlin was too weak to support herself. Bill helped her into a chair at the kitchen table.

"Please, everyone," he said. "Have a seat." He filled four cups with hot water and brought them over to the table. "I made some hot tea."

They sat at the table and stared at the cups without touching them.

Caitlin rested her head on her arms and cried loudly. Lucas's eyes were red and puffy, and Allison sobbed into her hands. Only Felix's eyes were dry.

Bill sat at one end of the rectangular table. "Felix, can you tell me what happened? I know this must be hard."

Felix took a sip of tea. It was too hot, but he drank it anyway. He deserved to feel pain. He began to talk. He told Bill everything. Or almost everything. There was one small item he omitted.

Landry told him that curses never die. Someone was lying to him—either Bill or Landry. And until he knew who it was, and why they were lying, he'd trust no one.

Bill asked several questions during Felix's narrative. He felt strange as he recited the story, almost as if he were talking about a dream, something too bizarre to have actually happened. When he told Bill about the men in neckties, and how they were able to move objects without touching them, Bill looked shocked. He asked Felix twice if he was sure about what he witnessed. The second time he asked, Felix gave him a look that said, "Ask me again, and I might punch you." When Felix finished, he simply said, "That's all."

Bill sat in silence for several minutes, as if allowing the story to completely sink in. Finally, he rubbed his eyes and began to speak. "I'm truly sorry about your friend. I know it's not going to make any of you feel better knowing that she died for the worthiest cause—the fight for the very survival of the human race. You've seen what we're up against—you've seen these things with your own eyes. You know better than anyone what's at stake. I know none of that matters right now. You just want your friend back. You want her to be alive. You will spend the rest of your lives struggling to understand the finality of death. But know this: your friend was lucky to have died in the company of people like you."

Allison cleared her throat and wiped the tears from her dirt-streaked face. "We saw...what we saw back there," she said weakly, before trailing off and becoming too choked up to continue. She wiped her eyes, leaving more dark smudges behind. "We saw Landry and his...his men. And they killed Harper. They killed her, and the man who did it smiled. He smiled."

Caitlin started to wail even louder. Lucas put his arm around her, trying to comfort her.

"I know how that must have..." Bill began.

"But won't they just come here and kill us?" Allison interrupted. "Landry saw us there. He knows what we look like. His men murdered Harper. Why wouldn't he just kill the rest of us?"

Lucas nodded in agreement, looking scared.

Caitlin managed to stop sobbing. She lifted her head from the table to look at Bill.

Felix drank the rest of his tea and looked beyond the window and into the backyard, half expecting to see Landry standing on the patio.

Bill rubbed his pointy chin. "Landry certainly knows who you are, but you're of no interest to him. You shouldn't be offended by that— it's a good thing. His only interest is Felix. He now knows that Felix is a Tinshire. Therefore only Felix is a threat to him. He'll almost certainly try to kill Felix, but I don't believe he'll go out of his way to kill anyone else."

"But he killed Harper, didn't he?" Lucas said. "If he killed her, why wouldn't he..."

"Landry won't go out of his way to kill you," Bill said with emphasis. "If you give him an opportunity, he most likely wouldn't hesitate to end your lives. I wouldn't recommend going back to Ardsley Forest, for example. Remember, he operates in secrecy and doesn't want to draw attention to himself. Killing you would just generate publicity and investigations."

"Really?" Allison exclaimed. "Weren't you listening to Felix? You just heard what he said, right? If it wasn't for Felix, we'd all be dead! Landry already tried to kill us. He'd have obliterated us with all the shit from the building he threw at us. And then those Lost Souls or whatever the hell you call them were trying to…I don't know…maybe they'd have eaten us or torn us to pieces, but we'd definitely be dead."

"Yes, but…"

"And we know the truth," Allison persisted. "And he knows that we know the truth. We saw him spitting out these ghoulish skeleton monster things and swallowing them up. He's the Antichrist. And we know it. We saw him! Wouldn't he want to kill us so we don't tell anyone?"

"Who would believe you?" Bill asked. "And if you start blogging and tweeting about Landry Ashfield being the Antichrist, his lawyers will get an injunction and you'll be sued for every penny you have. He's not just the Antichrist. He's the president of A.E.I. and one of the wealthiest men in the world. But listen to me—I truly believe that you are completely safe from Landry as long as you don't go out of your way to be near him or his interests. Okay? Please trust me on that."

Allison nodded, but didn't appear to be completely convinced.

"But what about Felix?" Lucas asked. "Landry wants to kill him, right? What's he supposed to do about that?"

Bill nodded. "Felix is quite capable of taking care of himself. I think you witnessed that. Landry knows that killing him isn't something that can be done easily and quietly."

Felix continued looking out the window, feeling strangely unaffected by the conversation. He should probably be more worried that the Antichrist knew who he was and wanted him dead. But he didn't care about anything at the moment. He felt numb. Even the prospect of his own death at the hands of Landry didn't have any effect. He was too exhausted to care.

"Now, unfortunately," Bill said as he looked around the table, "we're going to have to deal with one of the cold realities of life in this country—people cannot simply disappear without someone asking questions."

Lucas wiped his bloodshot eyes. "Right. How can we explain what happened to Harper? Nobody will believe us, right? And they'll think we killed—oh God—I can't even say it."

Bill nodded his head sympathetically. "I don't think it will come to that. I believe Landry will take steps so you're not put in a position where you have to decide between saying nothing and going to jail for murdering your friend or telling the world what really happened— even if no one would believe your story."

"How can he do that?" Lucas asked.

"He has his ways," Bill replied.

"What do you think he'll do?" Felix asked, looking away from the window.

"I'm not sure," Bill said. "But we'll find out shortly. In the mean-time, your stories must be aligned in case any questions are asked."

"Like what?" Felix asked.

"Did anybody see you leave campus with Harper last night?" Bill asked.

Felix shook his head. "No. We used the sidewalk on First to get to the parking lot. We didn't run into anybody."

"That was smart," Bill said. "Which one of you is Harper's roommate?"

"She doesn't have one," Allison replied. "Her roommate trans-ferred to another school."

"Excellent. If anyone asks, you all went to bed last night at around midnight, and that was the last time you saw her."

They stared back at Bill without speaking.

"Is everyone okay with that?" he asked. "Is it clear?"

They nodded in agreement.

"Good. Now, let's get you cleaned up. First, you need to shower. There's one down the hall and two upstairs. I'll give you plastic bags to put your clothes in. I'll put them in the washer. The family that used to live here left a few boxes of clothes in the attic. I'll find something for you. Look at yourselves in the shower and check for any lacerations or swelling. Allison, I noticed you were limping. Is it your ankle?"

She nodded. "I think it's just a sprain."

"Let me take a look at it. It's nearly five o'clock." Bill knelt down to examine Allison's ankle. "I need everyone cleaned up now. Go."

An hour later, they were showered and sitting in the living room, trying to avoid looking at one another, lost in their own thoughts. Bill had found clothes for them and tended to their injuries. Allison's ankle was badly sprained, but the worst injury was to Felix's back. He had an eight-inch gash that ran from just below his collar to the bottom of his shoulder blade. Bill wouldn't let him go to the hospital to get it sutured. He anesthetized the area and expertly stitched it up in just a few minutes. "I'm more than just a groundskeeper," Bill replied, when Felix asked him how he knew how to stitch up a wound.

As the sun began to rise, one by one, they started to doze off. Bill sipped his tea and watched over them.

Chapter 47

Felix was awakened by sirens. His head snapped to attention, and he was instantly alert. He scanned the living room. Only Bill was awake, silently sipping tea in a leather club chair next to the sofa where Caitlin and Lucas were curled up. Felix cocked his head toward the window and listened, but the sirens sounded like they were far away. He shifted in his chair and smelled the sleeve of the track suit Bill brought down from the attic. It was bright orange with white stripes on each leg and was probably last worn in 1979. It smelled like mildew and mothballs.

"You think that's the police?" he asked Bill.

Bill walked over to the window and looked outside. The sun had come up an hour earlier, but nobody was stirring in his idyllic neighborhood. Another siren blared, this one loud and high-pitched at first, and then softer as it receded into the distance.

"That sounded like it was close," Felix said.

"What's going on?" Allison asked groggily from her chair. "Are those sirens?"

Caitlin and Lucas stirred from their small couch.

"Something obviously has happened," Bill said over his shoulder as he continued looking out at the quiet street.

Lucas looked worried. "What? Do you think..."

"There's nothing to worry about yet," Bill said. "I'll call Professor Ishikawa. We went to college together. His brother's a detective with the Portland PD. He may know what's happened."

For several minutes they sat and listened to the sirens as Bill appeared to be deep in thought. Finally, he took out his cell phone and pushed a button. The call with Professor Ishikawa was brief. Bill apologized for calling at such an early hour, and then asked if he knew anything about the sirens. Bill listened for a few minutes, thanked Professor Ishikawa for his time, said goodbye, and ended the call.

"Professor Ishikawa and his family live just a few blocks from here," Bill said. "He also heard the sirens. He said his brother is working the graveyard shift and should be on duty. He's going to call me if he learns anything."

His phone rang before he had a chance to put it back in his pocket. He held it against his ear. "Hi, Ken. Thanks for calling back. I see. Okay. Of course. Thanks again. Goodbye." He slid the phone back into his pocket.

"Well?" Allison asked.

Bill sighed and rubbed the thick stubble on his face. "The police found a girl's body in the back of a van behind a bar on First Street. They think she's a Portland College student."

Chapter 48

The following afternoon, Felix took his Western Civ final. He walked into the classroom and went through the motions like an automaton. He sat at the first available desk. When the teaching assistant said, "Begin," he opened the packet and tried to read the questions. One confused him, but he didn't bother to re-read it. He started writing, not really thinking about whether he was answering the question, and not caring.

Felix wasn't the only one unable to focus on exams.

Reports about a student having been murdered just a block away from campus started to surface the previous morning. The news spread like an Arizona wildfire, and within hours, there wasn't a student on campus who didn't know about it. That afternoon, the police department confirmed that a Portland College student was murdered, and released the name of the victim: Harper Dupont.

That same day, rumors began circulating, first on the Internet and then by word of mouth, that young people all over the world were suddenly dropping dead from a mysterious disease. As evidence was gathered and some of the rumors were confirmed, the major news networks picked up the story. By noon, there were reports that as many as one thousand people, all between the ages of fourteen and twenty-four, had died of unknown causes in the early hours Sunday morning.

Government authorities across the globe mobilized their resources to investigate the cause of the disaster that was coined the "Sunday Incident." Victims were being reported in dozens of countries and on every continent. The number of confirmed deaths climbed by the hour, and as Portlanders sat down for dinner that evening, the death toll surpassed 1,400. In the late edition of the *Oregonian*, the headline story reported that eight people living in the state died in the early morning hours of unknown causes; all were between the ages of seventeen and twenty-two.

The BBC was the first to report that the victims appeared to have died at exactly the same time. News agencies around the world ran with the story. And in an unusual display of international cooperation, the United Nations established a central command center in Manhattan to assist the Centers for Disease Control and its foreign counterparts in collecting and analyzing data on all suspected victims of the Sunday Incident.

At eight o'clock, the Centers for Disease Control released a statement that preliminary autopsies of seventeen victims definitively ruled out a virus or any communicable agent as the cause of death. The agency confirmed that all victims did in fact die at the same time. The actual cause of death, however, was still officially "unknown." The French, German, Brazilian, British, Japanese, and South African agencies released similar statements within the hour.

Conspiracy theorists, both on the Internet and on the PC campus, were having a field day. Rumors spread that the Sunday Incident was the result of a massive government cloning experiment gone awry. Other theories involved the release of biological weapons, an alien invasion, toxic meteorites, water supply contamination, interplanetary radiation, and a terrorist attack.

But the theory gaining the most traction was that the First Seal of the Apocalypse had been opened, heralding the arrival of the Antichrist and the commencement of the great Tribulation. Christians around the world gathered in cathedrals, churches, and community centers awaiting the Rapture—the return of Christ as prophesied in the New Testament. Some gatherings were spontaneous. Like the faithful who began streaming into Saint Peter's Square in Vatican City as soon as the first reports about the Sunday Incident broke, seeking guidance from the Pope. Was the Antichrist actually revealed? When would Christ return? Was the Last Judgment imminent?

Other assemblages were frantically organized by Christian leaders taking advantage of social networking sites to stage massive demonstrations in cities and towns around the world. One prominent televangelist from Atlanta claimed that over two million members of his "flock" would soon be marching on Washington, DC to demand that the President confess his sins to Christ and acknowledge that the Antichrist was revealed—for if he didn't, who was to say that the President himself might not be the Antichrist?

Those leading the demonstrations preached a very simple message: repent now, or spend eternity in hell, for the End Times were upon us. The Final Battle for the future of humankind—the battle between Christ and the Antichrist—was about to begin. Ancient scriptures and sacrosanct belief systems that had survived for thousands of years were introduced to the reality-show-adoring masses by twenty-first century mass media. Much to the chagrin of priests, theologians, and scholars who preferred to exclude the less erudite from the serious discussion of such topics. TV networks were running everything in their archives featuring the Antichrist and the Apocalypse. Tens of millions of people feverishly debated the subjects on the Internet.

The discussions generally centered on two questions. First, if the Antichrist was in fact revealed, who was he? And second, when would Christ return to save humanity from the Tribulation and defeat the Antichrist? As for who was most likely to be the Antichrist, the early favorites were the Secretary General of the United Nations, the leader of the Church of Scientology and the quarterback of the New York Jets.

A prominent West Coast newspaper conducted a poll showing that more than eighty percent of the respondents believed that Christ would return before the New Year. The poll's results were borne out by the millions who walked along city streets, suburban neighborhoods, and farmlands looking up at the sky like children seeing an airplane for the first time—according to New Testament scripture, Christ was supposed to return on a cloud flanked by an army of trumpet-playing angels. No one wanted to miss that amazing sight. As for the "battle to end all battles," the *New York Post* was running a betting line—Christ was presently favored to knock out the Antichrist in the third round.

As the Sunday Incident death toll rose and panic swept through the PC campus, most students came to the conclusion that Harper Dupont must have been one of its victims. And despite what the CDC was claiming, rumors were rampant that anyone who had been in contact with her was in grave danger.

In response to the crisis, President Taylor's office, apparently in an attempt to assuage the growing anxiety among the student body, sent out a campus-wide email. It stated that no students, faculty, or employees of the university had died. And that the CDC was vigorously investigating the incident and already concluded, without a doubt, that the Sunday Incident deaths weren't caused by a communicable agent.

The email didn't have the intended effect. Parents began pulling their children out of school. Nearly two thousand students held a rally in the Courtyard demanding that the administration come clean with everything it knew about the Sunday Incident and Harper Dupont. With the fear of imminent death hanging over their heads, students were threatening to leave campus without sitting for exams.

The following morning, the Dean of Students, Dr. Borakslovic, sent a campus-wide email to debunk the rumors of any connection between Harper's death and the Sunday Incident. She reminded the students that the Portland College community was spared from the global calamity. She stated that Harper's death was in no way connected to the Sunday Incident. And that more information regarding the circumstances of her death would be released by the Portland police department later that day. Furthermore, the Sunday Incident, by all reliable accounts, was a single isolated event. There was no evidence that anyone else was in danger, including those within the "at risk" age group. Exams would be held as scheduled. Students who failed to sit for an exam would receive an F. No exceptions or waivers would be granted. The email concluded with an invitation to all students to attend a memorial service for Harper in the Courtyard at eleven o'clock the day after finals.

The media coverage of Harper's murder took a backseat to the Sunday Incident and the resulting worldwide panic as the death toll reached 1,700, but the local media still provided occasional updates.

Later that morning, just before Felix left Downey for his last final, the local CBS affiliate ran a "News Flash." The pretty newscaster with the unnaturally white teeth reported that the police department had issued a statement regarding Harper Dupont's murder. She reported that a prison escapee, Nick Blair, the notorious mass murderer known as the Mormon Mephistopheles, was responsible for the murder of Ms. Dupont. Early reports indicated that Blair stabbed to death a store clerk at the Capitol Deli, a 24-hour convenience store located just one block from the Portland College campus. After killing the clerk, Blair waited behind the register for his next victim. Ms. Dupont entered the store to purchase a bottle of water and a pack of gum, apparently believing that Blair was the clerk. The receipt for the purchase was found on her body with a time stamp of 4:16 AM. Blair then forced Ms. Dupont inside a van he stole from a used-car lot in southeast Portland. The van was parked in the alley behind the store. Ms. Dupont fought bravely to save herself but was overpowered by Blair. Before she succumbed to multiple knife wounds, she took Blair's life by turning his own weapon on him. The reporter called Ms. Dupont a heroine and an inspiration to all women.

Felix finished the English Lit exam and walked out of the building. He could barely remember sitting in the classroom for the previous two hours. He had no idea what he wrote. He felt numb. He walked back to Downey and climbed into bed.

Chapter 49

Bill looked out his office window at the gathering of somberly clad mourners mingling in small groups in the Courtyard below. He wore a black suit and tie with a crisply starched white shirt. His face was clean-shaven, and his hair was combed back from his forehead.

He took out his cell phone and hit the call button.

His father answered on the first ring. "So good of you to call," he said unctuously. "I haven't heard from you since you sent the boy into Ardsley Forest. It's not like anything has happened recently."

"I've been busy."

"And I've been watching the news. It seems such a terrible tragedy that so many young people have died so suddenly and without any apparent cause. The numbers are a little staggering, I must admit. Landry must still have thousands under his control. But don't you find it fascinating how the public has attributed the Sunday Incident to the Antichrist? And now the stupid sheep are loitering on street corners proclaiming the end of the world and awaiting the return of Christ. It's really rather amazing. I only wish Constantine were around to see it. He formed his Council at Nicea almost seventeen hundred years ago for this very moment. Of course, Constantine couldn't have predicted that his secret societies would one day evolve into the Templars. Or that the Templar leaders would forge the four Amulets. But Constantine knew that the Antichrist's arrival would be accompanied by a global calamity. What shape it would take, he couldn't have known. But if it wasn't the Sunday Incident it would have been something just as earth shattering. He truly was a man of unusual abilities to have known how it would all unfold so many centuries later. Instead of panicking, the masses have fallen back on the crutch of religion. As he knew they would."

"Constantine wouldn't have gone to the trouble of hijacking Christianity unless he understood how the people would react," Bill replied.

"Yes. Yes. Yes. That's it exactly. If not for the belief in the Antichrist and his imminent defeat at the hands of Christ upon his return, our entire society would unravel. There would be no explanation for the Sunday Incident. Utter chaos would surely ensue. Marx had it all wrong, you know. Religion is much more than just the opiate of the masses. It's the glue that holds the whole thing together. If not for Constantine's actions at Nicea, we would be reduced to a society of hunter-gatherers within a generation."

"And we may still be if Landry has his way," Bill said. "I didn't actually call to philosophize…"

"Of course not. I apologize for the digression, but it is rather amazing to witness the flowering of seeds sown so many centuries ago. In any event, you really should have called sooner, William. I wanted to congratulate you on your success. The boy obviously destroyed the First Templar Amulet. I've been anxiously waiting to hear the details. And by the way, I would have thought you'd be in a better mood. You sound rather forlorn."

"I'm relieved the Amulet was destroyed," Bill replied without any emotion.

"Relieved?" his father asked quizzically. "I see. Nearly twenty years of planning, and you're relieved. So tell me what it is that's dampening your enthusiasm after just experiencing the greatest success of our lives."

"Landry was at the facility. He wasn't in Egypt. I made a mistake."

"*Landry?*"

"Yes."

"Landry was there?"

"Yes."

"And the boy's still alive?"

"Yes. But one of his friends was killed."

"I see. That's unfortunate, of course. But a small price to pay for the destruction of the Amulet. But it's very curious, don't you think?"

Bill didn't respond. There was a long pause. He glanced outside. The crowd was growing larger.

"Do I really need to say it?" Bill's father asked.

"Say what?"

"Don't act naïve! You know exactly what it is. Why is the boy still alive? He's just learning to control his powers, and he survived an encounter with Landry? How is that possible?"

"Perhaps Felix is more powerful than you think."

"I don't doubt his power, William, but I do doubt his ability to defend himself against Landry. So I'll ask the question again. Why didn't Landry kill the boy?"

"I don't know. Maybe Felix was simply fortunate."

"Fortunate? Landry doesn't deal in chance. You know as well as I what happened—he must have allowed the boy to live! But why would he do that? Why?"

"I wouldn't be so sure," Bill replied. "Felix did some rather remarkable things in that forest to save himself."

"Is that so?" his father replied skeptically. "I still don't like it. I assume the boy encountered Landry after he destroyed the Amulet?"

"Yes."

"So once Landry saw that the First Templar Amulet was destroyed, he obviously would have concluded that the boy was a Holder, correct? He would have known that he's a Tinshire and therefore a threat. So why didn't he kill him?"

"I don't know. Maybe there's something we're not considering."

"Such as?"

"I don't know!" Bill shouted angrily.

"William, think for a moment, will you? Felix killed his parents. He not only controls matter, he creates it and converts it. He has created fire, of all things. And now we know that Landry let him live knowing that the boy's a Tinshire. If the boy was Myrddin, wouldn't Landry have killed him on the spot? Isn't it obvious to you by now that the boy is not Myrddin? He is the Antichrist. And now we have two abominations to contend with."

"But why would that matter?" Bill asked. "Why would Landry allow him to live even if Felix is the Antichrist? He's still a Tinshire, right?"

"Yes…yes…that is true. Perhaps there is something we're missing. If only we had the rest of that damn journal. Or the Dead Sea Scrolls. But even then, there are too many signs that point in the wrong direction. The boy is not Myrddin, so we…"

"So what do we do?" Bill shouted. "Haven't we discussed this a thousand times? If you're so certain he's the Antichrist, shouldn't we kill him now? Isn't that what you want me to do? Should I invite him to my office and shoot him?"

"Maybe you should," his father answered quickly. "That would be the right thing to do, but…"

"But we need him? Is that it? We still need him?"

"Landry is still alive. And he does possess the Second Amulet. We can be sure of that. We don't really have a choice, do we? Yes. We still need the boy."

"Then let's make sure we're in agreement on this." Bill enunciated every word with perfect clarity. "For now, we let Felix live. Do you agree?"

His father sighed. "If you believe you can still control the boy, then yes. For now, we let him live. May God forgive us."

"I wouldn't count on that."

"But can you control him?" his father asked.

"He's not the simple kid he once was."

"I see. I see. And what of the Draganaks, William? Seeing as how Felix is alive, he obviously didn't encounter those monsters in the forest. I find that surprising. Why would that be unless Landry deliberately held them back?"

"We're going in circles, you know."

"Fine, William. Fine. But now that the First Amulet is destroyed, the Draganaks and the Second Amulet are our biggest concern. You realize I'll need to speak to your grandfather now. He's the stubbornest man alive, but he'll have to bury this grudge he has against me. Nobody knows more about the Draganaks than him. He'll have to forgive me for selling the company and ensuring the financial welfare of our entire family for a hundred generations. He's so bloated on his pride that…"

"We can discuss that later," Bill interrupted listlessly.

"The Draganaks won't wait! And neither can we. They're our most imminent concern and…"

"No. Our most imminent concern is Felix. I have to go. He should be here any minute."

Chapter 50

The day of Harper's memorial, Felix arrived at Bill's office wearing the only suit he owned and a tie his mom gave him on his eighteenth birthday. He'd received a text from Bill earlier that day asking him to stop by his office before the service.

Felix knocked on the door and stepped in without waiting for an answer. Bill was packing up his office. Cardboard boxes were stacked up along a wall next to the desk, and the office wasn't as cluttered as it normally was.

"Books," Bill said simply as he placed a small stack into a box on his desk. "I'll be spending part of the summer in Massachusetts. I like to have my books with me. I've decided that it's about time my father and grandfather resume talking to each other."

Felix didn't understand what he was talking about, and didn't particularly care that Bill's father and grandfather apparently weren't on speaking terms.

"So what did you want to talk about?" Felix asked, listlessly.

"I thought you might want to discuss the events of the past three days?"

Felix didn't. He and his friends had barely spoken a word about what happened in Ardsley Forest. It was too painful.

"The number is over nineteen hundred now," Bill continued.

Felix knew he was referring to the number of dead Vessels—the number of victims of the Sunday Incident.

"What do you think about the millions of people who are expecting Christ to return at any minute?" Bill asked.

Felix looked around the office. He didn't trust Bill. Bill told him that curses die once broken. Landry told him just the opposite—that curses never die. Felix was well aware of what the distinction meant. If Landry was being truthful, then Felix was born in violation of the McGaughey curse. And if he wasn't the reincarnation of Myrddin, he'd be an abomination—an Antichrist, just like Landry.

Felix could understand why Bill would lie. If Felix was really the Antichrist, Bill was just trying to hide it from him. He wouldn't want him to know the truth about who he really was. That was pretty simple. But he still couldn't figure out why Landry would lie. Maybe Landry had some reason for wanting Felix to think he was the Antichrist— if he wasn't the Antichrist, that is. Or maybe he was just messing with his head. Felix wasn't sure about any of it, but he was certain about one thing. One of them was lying—one of them was trying to manipulate him. He just didn't know if it was Bill or Landry. And until he knew for sure, he wasn't going to trust Bill.

"Felix?" Bill asked, arching an eyebrow.

"I don't know. I guess the media kinda has it right, doesn't it? Although I think people might be disappointed if they knew I'm what they're waiting for. I mean, I don't exactly hang out with angels or ride clouds. And I'm not gonna save any souls or anything like that."

Felix stepped over to the window and looked out at the Courtyard. The organizers were finished setting up rows of white folding chairs on the lawn. Students wearing somber clothes were huddling together in small groups quietly talking among themselves.

"How many are out there?" Felix asked over his shoulder.

"Sorry?"

"How many Soulless Humans and Human Vessels? More than nineteen hundred Vessels just died, right? Isn't that what you just said?"

Bill rubbed his pointy chin. "There's no way of knowing the exact numbers. The large number of dead Vessels is obviously an indication that there could be many, probably thousands. But I suppose it's possible that Landry created more Vessels than he needed in order to offer more options to choose from—an extra incentive for people who are inclined to transfer their souls. Look at it like this: Would you rather be John Doe or a millionaire celebrity?"

"I bet he has thousands," Felix said. "So what am I supposed to do? Landry knows who I am. Those things could be anywhere, and anybody. They could be following me everywhere. How would I even know?"

"You wouldn't."

"That's really helpful. So if I think someone's following me, should I just grind them into the ground and ask questions later?"

"I don't have an answer," Bill replied. "I would hope that you wouldn't have to live your life in a state of constant paranoia, but I can understand why that might be difficult. I suggest you always be aware of your surroundings and keep your guard up."

"More helpful information. Thanks a lot. Oh! One other thing. You know back at your house when you told my friends they had nothing to worry about? That Landry wouldn't come after them? That was all bullshit, right?"

"I would never lie to you, Felix," Bill said, looking him in the eye. "But yes, I wasn't completely truthful with your friends."

"So you lied."

"Yes. What good would it do to tell them the truth? If Landry wanted to kill your friends, he'd simply do it and cover it up like he did with Harper. He does have thousands at his command. Just like that Nick Blair."

"The one who they're saying killed Harper? The Mormon Mephistopheles."

"Yes. He was obviously a Soulless Human—a convicted murderer and a fugitive from the law. Landry must have transferred Nick Blair's soul into a Vessel and then controlled Nick as a Soulless Human to stage the murder. And of course the Vessel that Nick's soul was transferred into would have eventually rejected Nick's soul. And Landry, the monster that he is, would have swallowed it up. Which means that one of the Lost Souls you encountered in Ardsley Forest was Nick's. Ironic when you think about it, don't you think? I'm sure that most Soulless Humans have similar backgrounds to Nick Blair's. When given the opportunity, why would an incorrigible piece of garbage like him refuse to transfer his soul to a Vessel? He wouldn't. The Vessel, after all, would presumably have money and everything else that goes with being a decent, law-abiding citizen. It would be quite an upgrade for a convicted murderer like Nick Blair."

Felix shrugged. He couldn't care less about Nick Blair.

Bill changed the subject. "What are your plans for the summer?" he asked, placing more books into a box.

"I'm heading to Cove Rock later today. I think I'll get a job there doing something—something outdoors, maybe. Keep myself busy. You?"

"I'll stay in Massachusetts for a while. Then I think I'll go to England."

"England? What for?"

"I think I might have a lead on finding the part of the journal we're missing."

"Really? After what—like eighteen years?"

"It's a long shot, but I'm going to have a look around. And I hope to speak with someone who used to work at Ardsley Castle."

Felix walked back to the window and looked out at the Courtyard. The seats were filling up, and a crowd was congregating on the grass behind the last row of chairs.

Bill scratched his chin for a few moments and appeared to be deep in thought. "Felix, there's something else I wanted to talk to you about. Knowing what kind of person you are, I'm sure you've spent the last few days blaming yourself for the death of your friend. But you shouldn't."

Felix turned to face Bill.

"I'm responsible for her death," Bill said.

"What? What are you talking about? "You weren't even there! I didn't protect her. It's my fault!"

Bill shook his head. "No, Felix. Harper should never have been there—none of you should have. You see, I...I misread the email from Mary—the woman who works indirectly for Landry."

Bill took a sheet of paper from the desk and handed it to Felix. He read it.

William, I'm so sorry about missing our last appointment. Devory had me working around the clock on Landry's travel plans and I completely forgot about our meeting. I'm so sorry!!! But now that he's in Egypt—he flew out this morning—hopefully he'll get off my back for a few days. Again, I'm so sorry. Making travel arrangements for Landry is such a nightmare—everything changes 100 times!!! You wouldn't believe everything that goes into it. I promise I won't skip my next appointment!

Mary

Felix read it again. His hand started to tremble, and he crumpled the piece of paper into a ball.

"You mean Landry didn't even go to Egypt?" he shouted angrily. "It was this other guy—this Devory?"

"Yes. I'm so sorry. Mary was the one making the plans for Landry's trip. So when she said *he's in Egypt,* I thought she was referring to Landry. It never crossed my mind that it might be Dev..."

"Are you fucking kidding me? You're telling me Harper's dead because you can't read?"

"I'm sorry. I'm just so..."

"Sorry's not gonna bring her back!" Felix screamed. "Look out the fucking window. Hundreds of people are out there for Harper's memorial service. Her memorial service! She's fucking dead!"

"I'm so..."

Felix snatched a teacup from the table and hurled it across the room. It missed Bill by mere inches and struck the wall behind the desk. It shattered. He grabbed the only other item on the table, a small porcelain teapot. He threw it as hard as he could. It hit the center of a glass-framed map of Lower Egypt that hung on the wall. The glass frame and kettle both exploded with a loud *bang*. Felix screamed, picked up the nearest chair, and heaved it with a loud grunt. Bill flattened himself against the wall as the chair sailed across the room and landed on the desk, knocking off a half-filled cardboard box, stacks of books, papers, and an assortment of personal items Bill was preparing to pack away. Felix reached under the antique walnut table and flipped it over like a Scotsman tossing a wooden pole at the Highland Games. It knocked over the remaining chair, hit the floor with a resounding thud, and rolled end over end with all the gracefulness of a flat tire before stopping against a wall. He looked around for something else to vent his anger at, but couldn't find anything.

"Because you can't fucking read!" Felix screamed at Bill, his face crimson.

"I'm sorry, Felix. From the bottom of my heart, I am truly sorry for my mistake. I don't know what else I can say. I realize how inadequate it sounds."

"It doesn't matter! None of it matters! It's all my fault! I couldn't save her!" Felix grabbed a handful of books from the nearest bookshelf and flung them across the room. Bill didn't attempt to avoid them. He just stood there, looking defeated and helpless.

"Felix, please listen to me. You did everything in your power to protect Harper. Sometimes our best isn't enough. That's one of the harsh realities of life. But don't let this destroy you. Don't let the pain control you! That's what happened to your mother. It ate through her like a cancer. Don't let that happen to you!"

Felix felt like a caged animal, pacing back and forth in the small room. He screamed and pointed at Bill. "You know what, Bill? Do you know how fucking tired I am of all your goddamn advice? I don't need it. I'm done with it. And you know what else? Fuck Landry! And fuck all this destiny bullshit! I don't give a fuck if he is the Antichrist! He can have the world! I don't fucking care! What's the point in saving it if everyone you care about is dead? What's the fucking point? And you wanna know something else? Fuck you!"

Felix stormed out of the room without looking back.

Chapter 51

Felix bolted out of the building and started down the footpath next to the Courtyard. He walked past the stage where the podium was set up. He was beyond furious. How the hell could Bill have screwed up so badly? How could he have misread a goddamn email? Harper should've never been in that forest.

He tried to compose himself. He focused on his breathing and willed himself to relax. He looked across the lawn at the sea of white folding chairs. Every chair was filled, and hundreds of mourners were standing in the grass. Slowly, his heart rate returned to something close to normal. By the time he walked past the last row of chairs, he no longer felt like his head was in danger of exploding. He saw Lucas, Allison, and Caitlin standing among a large crowd that gathered behind the last row of chairs. His friends were dressed in black like everyone else. The last time his friends all wore black, they were getting ready to go into Ardsley Forest. Harper was with them then. He exhaled slowly and tried to clear his head.

"Hey Felix," Lucas said. "You all right? You look pissed."

"I'm fine. Why aren't you sitting up front, Caitlin?"

Caitlin's eyes were bloodshot, and her nose was red and chafed. Harper's death was harder on her than anyone. She'd spent the past three days in her room crying. She couldn't sleep. She wouldn't eat. Lucas and Allison tried to cheer her up, but she was inconsolable.

"I think it's just for family members and faculty," Caitlin sniffled. "I saw Harper's mom a little while ago. She waved. The family's receiving visitors at the College Chapel after the service. Would you guys please go with me? I want to go, but I can't do it by myself."

"Of course," Felix said.

"I'm sorry," Caitlin said softly, wiping at her tears.

"There's nothing to apologize for," Allison said. "We're here for you, Caitlin."

Felix felt like someone was watching him. He turned his head slightly and saw that Dante Smithwick was glaring at him. *Just look away, Dante*, Felix thought. *Look away. You have no idea who you're fucking with*. Dante seemed to hesitate for a moment and then he turned away, facing the stage in front.

Somebody at the podium started talking. It was a woman Felix didn't recognize. It was hard to hear her remarks over the noise of the crowd. She said something Felix couldn't quite make out and then she introduced Jerry Taylor, the president of Portland College. The woman stepped off the stage, taking a seat in the front row.

President Taylor opened his address. He was talking about a remarkable young woman named Harper Dupont he recently learned about through conversations with her family and friends.

Felix half listened to what he was saying. He thought about the first time he saw Harper, the first time he saw her smile. He thought about her sitting across from him at the Caffeine Hut. How her hand felt when she put it on his for the first time. And their first kiss under the tree in front of Astoria Hall. The way she smelled that night with the branches hanging above, forming a canopy over them.

President Taylor was telling a story about Harper when she was a child—how she would never back down from a challenge or wither in the face of adversity. When Harper was four, she decided that her bicycle no longer needed training wheels. She took them off and got on her bike. She fell to the ground, but she got back on and tried again. Each time she fell, she got back on. Over and over she got back on that bike. She wouldn't give up. Both knees and both elbows bloodied and bruised, her parents were forced to take the bike away from her. They hid it. But the next morning when her parents came outside looking for Harper, they found her riding the bicycle in the driveway—without training wheels. She'd found their hiding spot and spent all night learning how to ride the bike.

Some in the crowd laughed at hearing the story.

Harper loved to laugh. And when she did, her bright blue eyes lit up like sparklers, and little dimples formed on her cheeks. He loved those dimples. There was just something so perfectly Harper about them. When they were together that night—the only night they'd ever be together, he touched them. He'd never be able to touch her face again. Or see her perfect smile. Or hear her laugh. She was gone. She was gone forever.

President Taylor was still talking. He was saying something about Harper refusing to live life in fear of the impossible—of boundaries that others would impose on her. Felix tried to clear his mind of the images of the girl with the beautiful blue eyes. They were too real. They were perfect—too perfect. Just like Harper.

Caitlin and Allison were sobbing loudly now as President Taylor continued. Tears were streaming down Lucas's face. Felix blinked his eyes. He wasn't going to cry. He shook his head and focused on what President Taylor was saying at the podium just as the sun hid behind a bank of clouds the color of ash.

"Harper was unique in every respect," he said in a clear voice. "She was stubborn and brave and full of life. A beautiful young woman with a beautiful soul who died just as she lived—undaunted by life's challenges and unwilling to be a victim. Her life may have been cut short. But because of the way she lived, her memory will live on forever in the hearts of those who knew her."

Chapter 52

The crowd eventually dispersed, and the students returned to their dorms to pack up their belongings. Felix and his friends mingled for a while. They talked with Larry, Jonas, Salty, Brant, and a few others who came over to pay their respects. When there was no one else to talk to, they started walking toward the College Chapel.

If not for the Old Campus buildings, the College Chapel would have been the oldest edifice on campus. It was a narrow brick building with a steeply pitched slate roof and beautiful stained-glass windows. Above the main entrance was a steeple topped by a large weathered cross made of copper, its aged patina dull and green under a graying sky.

When they reached the steps leading to the chapel's double entrance doors, Caitlin stopped and steadied herself against the wrought-iron railing. "I don't know if I can do this," she said, trying to fight back tears. "I can't stop crying. I don't want to upset Harper's family. It's already hard enough for them."

"I think this is one of those occasions when it's okay to cry," Lucas said, managing a small smile for her.

Caitlin returned a weak smile. "Thanks. I guess we should go in then."

She walked up the stairs with Lucas alongside helping to steady her and Felix and Allison following behind. The one-room chapel was filled with black-clad mourners. There were rows of pews on either side of a wide aisle that ran down the center of the room forming an axis between the main door and an altar in front. Behind the altar was a life-sized statue of Christ on the cross. On his head lay a crown of thorns, and blood flowed from his side. Felix stared at the statue and felt a chill. Was he looking at an image of himself? Or was he looking at his opposite? Was he the Antichrist? And if he was, should he really be inside a church? God must have a rule against Antichrists entering His house, right?

Christ's interlaced feet, bloody and nailed to the cross, became visible. They'd been blocked from Felix's view by something dark and black and...it was the bearded face of Professor Malone, his psychology professor. He was standing underneath the statue, staring up at the image of the crucifixion. He turned and looked directly at Felix. He smiled and straightened his tie. Then he took three giant steps and exited the chapel through a side entrance.

What was that all about? Felix wondered.

"There they are," Caitlin said, pointing in front of her.

Standing in the aisle near the center of the room was a stately-looking blond woman wearing a finely tailored black suit. Next to her was a tall, silver-haired man with a handsome tanned face. Harper's parents were exactly as he'd imagined. And standing next to them was *Harper.*

Felix did a double-take and gasped. How could that be Harper? He walked toward her without thinking, passing by Caitlin and Lucas. *She's alive! Oh my God! She's alive!* How could Harper be alive?

She looked up at Felix as he approached and then quickly looked away.

Why didn't she say anything? Wasn't she happy to see him? What the hell was going on?

Harper's mother turned toward him and looked over his shoulder. "Caitlin," she said in a sweet voice. "Hello, honey. Come here." She gave Caitlin a tight hug, which caused her to sob uncontrollably. Caitlin finally pulled away with a look of embarrassment and wiped the tears from her face.

Felix couldn't take his eyes off Harper. Why wasn't she talking to him? And why did she look so sad? Why was everyone even here when Harper was still alive? She was standing right in front of him.

He felt a sharp pain in his side. Allison dug a bony elbow into his ribcage, apparently in an attempt to get him to stop him staring.

He looked at Allison, trying to comprehend how she couldn't have noticed that Harper was alive.

"It's her twin sister," she whispered.

"Huh?" How come nobody had told him she had a twin? Shouldn't that have come up at some point during the year?

"I'm sorry, Mrs. Dupont," Caitlin sobbed. She tried to say something, but the lump in her throat wouldn't allow her to speak.

"It's okay, dear," Harper's mother said, rubbing Caitlin's arm.

Felix watched the scene in front of him. He could see the pain in their eyes. Mr. Dupont's face was expressionless. He stared blankly at the wall behind Felix. Harper's sister clung to her mother like a child, occasionally nodding when someone offered their condolences. Mrs. Dupont was obviously trying to hold the family together. She was the brave one, but Felix could almost feel her anguish.

And all of their pain was his fault. If not for him, Harper would still be alive. She'd be at the dorm with everyone else, packing her bags and getting ready to spend the summer at home with her family. The guilt felt like sticky molasses covering his skin. It was a black oozing tar that jealously clung to him. He knew he'd never be able to get rid of it. He wanted to scream. To hold his head back and scream up to the rafters that it was his fault—he killed Harper. It wasn't some guy named Nick Blair.

"And what is your name, dear?" a woman's voice asked. "Dear?"

"Felix," Allison hissed.

"Huh?"

"Your name, dear," Harper's mother asked gently.

"I'm Felix," he answered softly. "Felix August."

"Felix!" she exclaimed. "Of course. I've heard so much about you. And you two must be Lucas and Allison."

They nodded.

Mrs. Dupont gestured at her husband and the girl who looked so eerily like Harper. "This is Harper's father and her sister, Hannah."

Mr. Dupont didn't notice that he was introduced. He continued to stare at the wall.

Hannah said hello in a small voice.

She even sounded like Harper, Felix thought.

"I hope you know how much Harper loved all of you," Mrs. Dupont said, her voice beginning to waver for the first time. "She talked all the time about you—and how much fun she had here at school." She dabbed at her eyes before she continued. "I'm just glad you got to know a small piece of the Harper that we knew. She was a beautiful girl, and I...I can't believe that she's gone." She started to sob. Mr. Dupont snapped out of his trance and put his arm around his wife, trying to console her.

Tears began to roll down Hannah's face. She noticed Felix watching and returned his stare. And then she smiled at him. There was no joy in it, but as she smiled, small dimples formed on her cheeks.

Felix dropped his eyes to the floor, feeling embarrassed and guilty.

They left the chapel and walked toward the Courtyard.

"Somebody could've told me Harper had a twin," Felix said.

"Oh," Caitlin replied, dreamily. "I guess it never came up. Hannah looks just like Harper, but they're really completely different people."

"She looks exactly like Harper," Lucas said. "I thought I was seeing a ghost."

"Are you going straight home?" Caitlin asked Allison.

"Yeah. I'm starting work in a few days—waitressing at the *Crab Shack*. I did it a few summers in high school. It's not bad and some of the tourists give decent tips. Are you heading out soon?"

Caitlin nodded and then looked like she might burst into tears. "I can't believe I'll be driving back by myself this time. It was nice having Harper to...you know...we..."

"Look on the bright side," Lucas said. "The long drive will give you plenty of time to think of a way to break it to your parents that you totaled your new car."

"Oh, yeah," Caitlin said, sounding very tired. "I didn't think of that. What am I gonna tell them?"

"That you joined the off-road club?" Lucas offered.

"The what?" Caitlin replied. "We don't have a... Oh!" She forced a smile.

"Hey!" Lucas suddenly exclaimed. "I forgot to tell you guys with everything...you know...everything going on. Anyway, I'm not going home to Minnesota yet. I got a call from the producers of *Summer Slumming*. They're doing an all-star show in New York City. There's ten of us, and I guess I made the cut. I'll be living in a sweet Soho loft for the next six weeks."

"Try not to forget your mom will be watching," Caitlin said, scowling.

"Is that a good idea?" Felix asked.

"I don't know," Lucas replied, shrugging. "Probably not, but I got nothing better to do. Why?"

Landry already knew who Lucas was, Felix thought. Would it matter if he was on TV? What could he do about it? Lucas was going to New York. Caitlin was going to California. And Allison was staying in Oregon. How could he protect his friends when they were so spread out? There were thousands of Soulless Humans and Human Vessels out there doing whatever Landry wanted them to do. There was no way he could protect all of them. Or any of them.

"Felix?" Allison said, looking concerned. "Are you all right?"

"Huh? I don't know. I think I just need to be alone for a minute. I'll meet up with you guys back at the dorm." He turned and walked away.

He wasn't sure where he was going—he just needed to get far away from the chapel. It was just another place where people were mourning because of something he'd done. His legs carried him of their own accord until he found himself in a familiar spot. He was standing underneath the Douglas fir tree, looking out at the Courtyard between two big brick buildings. It was where he thought about giving up football and quitting school. Because he cheated on his SAT. Because he didn't think he was smart enough to be at Portland College. It was the place where he shared those things with Harper.

He sat on the ground and looked out at the Courtyard. A light rain started to fall. Workers were folding up the chairs used for Harper's memorial service. They were cleaning up his mess. His mess...

What if Landry was right? What if curses never die and he was the Antichrist? How would he even know? It wasn't the sort of thing he could look up on the Internet. And there was nobody he could trust—not even Bill. Were there signs he should be looking for?

He could control matter and create fire just by thinking about it. That wasn't normal. But did it prove he was the Antichrist? Or did it prove he was Myrddin? Did it prove anything? He killed his parents. He almost killed Allison in her dorm room. He also killed the two men in Ardsley Forest—completely obliterating them into nothing but two wet splotches on the floor.

He didn't mean to kill his parents. That was an accident. It didn't make him feel any better about it, but he knew it wasn't something he wanted to happen. With the two men at Landry's facility, it was differ- ent. He tried to kill them. And he was glad that he did. He was glad. How could he be happy about killing people? Surely that was a sign. What was happening to him? Maybe he was the Antichrist. If he was Myrddin, wouldn't he feel bad or guilty about taking another person's life?

And he let Harper die. There wouldn't be any white chairs out on the Courtyard if he'd kept his promise. He thought of the moment just before the man in the green tie impaled her with the steel bar. Harper had looked at him. She pleaded with her eyes. And his eyes met hers just as she felt the cold steel piercing her skin. In that instant, before she died, she knew that he hadn't kept his promise. She knew that he just stood there and watched her die. And in her last moments, she must have hated him for breaking his promise—for letting her die. He felt the tears forming in his eyes, but he fought them off. He wasn't going to cry. He looked away from the Courtyard, trying to think of something other than Harper's blue eyes filled with fear as she was about to die. He dug his palms into the sockets of his eyes—he dug them into his face until it hurt.

But in the end, there was nothing he could do to stop the tears.

CPSIA information can be obtained at www.ICGtesting.com
Printed in the USA
BVOW040431130112

280455BV00005B/5/P

9 781432 783181